From the reviews of *Scenes from Early Life*:

'Beautifully packed with detail . . . Hensher's novel is another chapter in British fiction's deep engagement with the subcontinent, and an important one . . . It does for Bangladesh what Salman Rushdie did for India with *Midnight's Children* . . . It is a remarkable re-creation of a land that most of us know little about.' PHIL BAKER, *Sunday Times*

'A deeply interesting book . . . The joins are seamless . . . It is inventive, clever and loving.' CHARLOTTE MOORE, *Spectator*

'One of the most delightful and engaging descriptions of family life to have been published for many years . . . from one of the best novelists of his generation . . . this delightful book shows for the first time what Hensher has largely concealed in the past: his heart.'

AMANDA CRAIG, *Independent on Sunday*

'Philip Hensher's new novel is a remarkable piece of ventriloquism . . . Hensher proves himself a literary god of small things.' ADRIAN TURPIN, *Financial Times*

'This is his most purely pleasurable novel to date.'

MICHAEL ARDITTI, *Daily Mail*

'He has an ear for the ways in which stories glue people together: legends, calcified old anecdotes, necessary falsifications. Hensher has created a greater thing than just a record of childhood, or war. It probably isn't Zaved's story any more, but it's great just the same.' BELLA BATHURST, *Observer*

'With this writer's work you take the rough with the slightly less rough and just feel a sense of gratitude that someone with such zeal, and such a gift, for entertaining has devoted his life to the novel.' LEO ROBSON, *New Statesman*

'Throughout all the political tumults the prose is lilting, soft: a calm antidote to the magic realism of Salman Rushdie or Gabriel Garcia Marquez. Wonderfully artful.' JEROME BOYD MAUNSELL, *Times Literary Supplement*

'Warm, poetic and precise . . . It is quite literally a labour of love.' HERMIONE EYRE, *Prospect*

'Hensher develops the narrative with fine artistry, offering a compelling picture of a society in turmoil . . . a book suffused with tenderness, yet altogether free from sentimentality. One feels the writing has been a labour of love.' ALLAN MASSIE, *Scotsman*

'Bold and startling' *Evening Standard*

'A life eventful enough to be only minimally garlanded with invention benefits from the novel's capacity to blend the absurd and heartbreaking so effectively.' *Guardian*

PHILIP HENSHER

Scenes from Early Life

FOURTH ESTATE • *London*

Fourth Estate
An imprint of HarperCollins*Publishers*
77–85 Fulham Palace Road
Hammersmith
London W6 8JB

This Fourth Estate paperback edition published 2013
1

First published in Great Britain by Fourth Estate in 2012

Copyright © Philip Hensher 2012

Philip Hensher asserts the moral right to be identified as the author of this work

A catalogue record for this book is available from the British Library

ISBN 978-0-00-745010-7

Printed and bound in Great Britain by Clays Ltd, St Ives plc

For Richard Heaton

Contents

1: At Nana's House

1.

Even the shit of a dog smells good to you, if it's English.

(*Ingrazi kuttar gu-o tomar khache bhalo.*)

My grandmother used to say this to my grandfather. He was very pro-Empire. That was my mother's father, who used to call me Churchill when I cried. At first I did not know who Churchill was, but my grandfather would explain to me, and after a while I knew who he meant when he said Churchill. He meant me, and often he would ask to have me sit next to him at the lunch table. 'I want Churchill here,' he said, and I would be led up by my ayah, not crying at all. I felt very proud. The theory was that when Churchill was a little boy, he used to cry very much. All the time. He was a great reader of biographies, my grandfather.

When he went out to a friend's house, we would drive there in a big red car – a Vauxhall, I think. He was an income-tax lawyer, the president of the East Pakistan Income Tax Lawyers' association. Later, the Bangla Desh Income Tax Lawyers' Association. There, at one old man's house or another, I would be allowed to stay in company for a while. He liked to show me off, and would call me Churchill in front of his friends. I don't believe that, as he said, he thought I would be the Churchill of Bangla Desh when I grew up. I think he mainly called me that because I cried.

My grandfather's great friend was called, by us, Mr Khandekar-nana. He had been a friend of my grandfather's from college, all the way back in the British time. They used to share a room when

1

they were at college, a long time ago in the 1930s, and ever afterwards, they were friends with each other. They had gone on being friends when they moved to Calcutta to be lawyers. (That was where they were in 1947.) And afterwards they had both moved to Dacca. My grandfather was Nana to us and his friend was Mr Khandekar-nana.

They both lived in the Dhanmondi area, very close to each other. It was the best place in Dacca to live. Nana's house was in road number six; Mr Khandekar-nana's was in road number forty. Both of them were two-storey houses with glass walls to the porch and flat roofs, both intricate and complex in their ground plan. It was only a ten-minute walk from Nana's house to Mr Khandekar-nana's, and it was a pleasant walk. The roads of Dhanmondi were quiet, and lined with trees, all painted white to four feet high, to discourage the ants. 'Ants can't walk on white,' my mother used to say. 'They are frightened of being seen. So that's why they paint the tree trunks white.' I still don't know how true that is. On the walk from Nana's house to Khandekar-nana's house, you would see only the occasional ayah, or mother, walking with her children, only the occasional houseboy loafing outside against the high, whitewashed walls of the houses, in those days. But my grandfather had a big red car, a Vauxhall, I think, and we drove the short distance to Mr Khandekar-nana's house.

Among the keen interests they shared were plants and flowers, and they kept their gardeners up to the mark. In front of their houses were roses, jasmine, dahlias, even sunflowers – English flowers, often. The two of them took pleasure in choosing flowers together, and their gardens were only different in small details. They were planted neatly, in rows, against the neat white Bauhaus style of their houses, and the mosaic in ash and white and green on the ground. The flowerbeds were in the sunniest part of the garden, away from the tamarind tree at the front of my grandfather's house, the mango tree at the front of Mr Khandekar-nana's.

The visits to Mr Khandekar-nana's followed the same sequence. My grandfather and Mr Khandekar-nana would go up to the balcony, shaded by the mango tree, and I would be allowed to go up with them. The tea would arrive and a plate of biscuits. My grandfather and Mr Khandekar-nana would take one biscuit each – one, one, judiciously, carefully, as lawyers do. Then I would be allowed to eat the rest. My grandfather would boast about how many books I had read, and as Khandekar-nana's wife arrived, to greet us and bring my grandfather up to date with her grandchildren, he would mention that he thought in the end I would be the Churchill of Bangla Desh.

A great friend of mine was the daughter of another friend of my grandfather, a child specialist who lived quite opposite Nana's house. She was ten years older than I was. When we visited them, she would take me to her living room and feed me biscuits from her own tin. It had English pictures on top of it, of a house with hair for a roof and a pony eating from a lawn. She had a lot of books and a phonogram; still, it is the biscuits that I remember. I wonder now whether I was notorious in the neighbourhood. But I will explain why I was allowed to eat whatever I wanted when I come to it.

2.

He had a driver, my grandfather, which always very much impressed me. The driver's name was Rustum. Rustum stayed in the family for fifteen years, living with his family just next to the garage, outside the courtyard of the house. He was always very friendly to us children. I got to know him not because of our Sunday trips to my grandfather's friends, but because of what happened during the week. My grandmother would often ask Rustum to go to market for her. Rustum, too, liked me, and he would ask me and sometimes my sister to go with him. We always went because he slipped us a lozenge or a jujube at the end of the trip.

It was important that we would slip off with Rustum without mentioning it to anyone – the trip, like the secret jujube, was no fun if the grown-ups knew about it. But when I and my sister Sunchita were missed, my mother would start to shout and panic. My second aunty, Mary-aunty, would start to shout and panic. I know this because when we returned home, they would go on shouting and panicking at us, and at Rustum. 'Why couldn't you tell anyone that you were taking the children?'

We were kept under close surveillance, Sunchita and I, because we could never stay still. We were always chasing the chickens, climbing the mango tree in the garden, sneaking off to the market with Rustum, who conspired with us against the grown-ups. In the end, Rustum was sacked by my grandfather and died of tuberculosis.

3.

My grandfather and my grandmother fought a war of attrition over the balcony on the first floor. My grandfather thought it his possession, the place he could retreat to from the noise and crowd elsewhere. He had an image of his balcony as being like Mr Khandekar-nana's balcony and, I believe, thought of himself sitting on the cool open space, a cup of tea and biscuits to one side while the grandchildren and children, cousins and nephews and visitors from his village on business rampaged through the rest of the house.

There was a wooden armchair on the balcony, an orange-brown plantation chair with extendable limbs on which you could rest your legs. But it was generally pushed to one side, because my grandmother had her own ideas for the balcony. She encouraged the cook to see it as a useful space where things could be stored or placed to dry. Almost always, jolpai and mango were laid out there for drying, covered with dry spice on banana leaves; against the wall, rows of bottled pickles in mustard oil. It drove my grandfather mad with irritation that the balcony was being used in this way. 'This house is like a pickle factory,' he would mutter as, once again, he retreated from his balcony and went back downstairs to his library.

My challenge was to get on to the balcony while my grandmother was busy with other things. The tamarind tree was old, and thick-leaved; its boughs thrust beneath the roof and into the balcony's space. If nobody was about, I climbed the tree and dropped softly on to the balcony. Or sometimes my sister Sunchita and I would conceal ourselves behind a curtain, or underneath a table, waiting for the servants to go by, and then we would run up to my grandfather's room, and afterwards on to the balcony.

There, we hid. I liked to taste the pickles that had been laid out; I liked the pucker they made on my tongue.

4.

We did not live at my grandfather's house, but we went there for the weekend, almost every weekend. We especially went there if there was a good movie on television. We knew that there was a movie on television every Sunday afternoon and Saturday evening. It was often a Calcutta movie, an old Satyajit Ray film or something of that sort. Still, my father refused to buy a television for us, and so we went eagerly to Nana's house.

The television was placed in the dining room, at the end of the polished mahogany table, which could seat, and often did seat, twelve people. Only Grandfather and Grandmother, Nana and Nani, had their own allotted places.

As well as having no television, my parents had, at that time, no car. We would arrive on a rickshaw at lunchtime on Friday – a cycle-rickshaw, with room for four. There was always a fight between me and the younger of my two sisters, Sunchita, over who would get to sit on my mother's lap. My elder sister was above such things, and my big brother, Zahid, too. He was aloof, and came when he chose.

At lunch on Friday there would be guests from my grandfather's village, his cousins or sisters, on a journey to Dacca for purposes of their own. The faces came and went. There would be hilsha fish, rice, some of the cook's pickles, such as a mango pickle from the mango tree at the back of the garden, or jolpai. Jolpai is a small sour berry, about the size of an olive. My grandmother, with her sharp tongue, ruled over the lunch table on Friday. It was a time for children and for the women, of whom there were many in our family.

After lunch, we children went to bed. At night we slept downstairs, but in the afternoon we were put to bed in an aunt's room, upstairs. It was Mary-aunty's job to get us to bed, and she shouted at us: 'Go to bed – take a book.' But we did not rest. My sister Sunchita and I would spend the time fighting. We always wanted to read the same book, though Sunchita was a better reader than I was. I liked books with pictures in them; Sunchita read a novel by Sharat Chandra Chattapadhaya when she was only eight, a novel for adults. ('Why are you reading this book? This book is not for you,' my grandfather said, surprised but not angry.) In the hour of rest, I would demand that Sunchita read her book out to me, or if I was crotchety, that she give it to me. And so we fought.

My grandfather came home from his lawyer's chambers at five, or half past five. The creak and gong-like echo of the opening gate; then his red car, a Vauxhall, driven by Rustum, with its engine noise unlike any other engine noise; and then my grandfather's voice downstairs. 'Is anyone here?' he said, his voice hardly above conversation pitch. But, of course, there was always somebody there. It was a game between him and me. Of all the people in the house, I called, 'Nana, I am here.'

Then he would say, 'Churchill! You are here. When did you arrive?' That was the signal to get up and go to greet my grandfather.

My grandfather was a very competitive person, and once he had changed out of his Western suit into what he liked to wear in the evening, a white Panjabi and white pyjamas, he might tease my mother with stories of what my father, his son-in-law, had got up to during the day. As my father and my grandfather were both lawyers in the same field of income-tax law, they sometimes found themselves on opposite sides of a case. My grandfather never let this opportunity fall.

'Mahmood tried to be very intelligent today,' he would say, waiting for the tea, biscuits and nuts – he was very fond of nuts – to arrive. 'But it all fell very flat.'

'Which case was that?' my mother asked. Before she married, she, too, had started to train as a lawyer; she still helped out with legal research. She liked to talk about the law with my father, and her father, too. My grandfather explained, going into detail. 'I'm sure he made a very good case,' my mother said loyally.

'Mahmood tried to be very intelligent today,' my grandfather said, laughing, 'but it didn't succeed at all.'

7

5.

These are the names of the aunts who came to dinner at Nana's house almost every Friday night.

Mira-aunty had moved to Canada, so she did not come.

Nadira-aunty was in England, in Sheffield, with her husband.

And Boro-mama, Big-uncle, the eldest of Nana's children, had his own house in Dacca and his own family, so he did not come, although he had left one of his sons behind with Nana and Nani, as if absent-mindedly.

Those aunts and that uncle did not come for dinner.

But Nana sat at the head of the table, and to his left sat Nani, my grandmother. She had a highly polished teak stool for her leg to rest on; it had a long hollow on it, which I used to imagine had been worn away by her leg, over hundreds, thousands, of family dinners. But I think it was really made that way. From time to time she would call for a servant to give her a massage in the middle of dinner.

My grandmother loved to talk about food, though for her the best food was always food she had eaten in the past, and not the food she had just eaten. She allowed a certain amount of time to pass – years, usually – before she would award a compliment. The only daughter who loved food as much as she did was Bubbly, and they could keep up conversations about individual long-ago dishes for hours. Bubbly could remember, in quite specific detail, the dishes her sisters had had at their weddings, and she and her mother would happily go over them, or food they had eaten at other times.

'Do you remember?' Nani would say, her leg resting on the teak footrest. 'Do you remember the steamed rui that Sharmin taught Ahmed how to make when everyone was living here? Do you remember, Bubbly? It was so good, that steamed rui with lemon and ginger. And she taught him, and he never got it right afterwards. I don't know why. But it was never so delicious ever

8

again. He didn't listen properly, or he made some changes of his own, wretched boy, and completely spoiled the dish. Oh, I loved to eat that steamed rui. I could have eaten it every day.'

'It was so clever of her,' Dahlia would say, calling from half a table away. 'It is so strange that it was her to be so clever with fish, being Bihari, and not liking fish as much as we do.'

'Well, Dahlia,' Nani said. 'She didn't like fish at the beginning. But she came to like it because your big brother likes it so much. And now she likes it as much as anyone, and she has such clever ways with it.'

'Because, of course,' Bubbly said, taking no notice of her mother, 'there was not always a great choice of things to eat, that year, but you could often get rui when there was no other fish to be had. I wish Sharmin would come back and teach Ahmed how to make it again, but she says she can't remember, and she says she doesn't know what's wrong with the way Ahmed cooks it, so that would really be a fool's errand.'

Nani and Nana had the best view of the television, which was at the far end of the table, on the sideboard next to a little fridge for all sorts of odds and ends. Dinner took place at eight, because that was when the television news was on.

Next to my grandmother sat Mary-aunty. She was the eldest of the sisters, after my mother. It was her job to keep the children under control, but she could often be tearful when faced with determined opposition, and I wonder if she was very good at her household task.

Next to her sat Shibli, who was Boro-mama's son. I was very jealous of Shibli. Whereas we only came to visit Nani and Nana at weekends, Shibli lived with them all the time, and visited Boro-mama, his father, only occasionally. This seemed to me the height of glamour, and it made me sick to see the ways in which Shibli was spoilt by my grandparents.

Choto-mama, Little-uncle, came next. His name was Pultoo. He was not much older than the bigger children, and was still at college. He was not a lawyer; he was an artist. In an odd way, my grandfather was rather proud of that: he used to say, 'If Pultoo wants to, he wants to.' Some people assumed that Choto-mama had to sit next to Shibli, with his spoilt ways, as a punishment from my grandfather. But that was not true: my grandfather had given Pultoo a large room with sunny windows on the ground floor of his house as a studio. He was rather proud of him, as I say.

Then his sister, Bubbly-aunty, the youngest of my aunts, and then Sunchita and Sushmita, my sisters. They sat at the end of the table, next to the television, which they could not see very well, and the fridge, which they often had to open and fetch something from for my grandfather.

The far end of the table was not a good place to sit, and there might be placed a village aunt or uncle, a cousin travelling to Dacca on business. And next to them, working back on the other side of the table, might be Dahlia-aunty, my favourite, and Era-aunty. And I was between them and my mother. My grandfather called me Churchill; the rest of the family called me Saadi. Dahlia would lean over and encourage me to eat, especially delicious little things; she would talk to me about pickles in her memory. Nadira I loved, because she was such a good singer, though, of course, not at the dinner table. And my mother sat by my grandfather, as the eldest daughter.

Two uncles, Boro-mama and Choto-mama, Big-uncle and Little-uncle; six aunts, Mary, Era, Mira, Nadira, Dahlia, Bubbly. Dahlia was my favourite and I was hers.

6.

Once, Pultoo-uncle was late for dinner. He was expected, but had gone out in the afternoon and had not returned by the time my grandfather came back. Pultoo had a wide circle of friends at the college of art, and occasionally he was seen in a café or ambling

10

through a park, gesticulating and talking in the middle of ten friends. He was the only one in the family to wear traditional dress all the time, a long shirt and pyjama trousers. The rest of the family were proud of him, and thought that he could dress as he chose. He was thin and dark, with hair that swept back like a film star's and big eyes set deep in his face. When he was excited, as, in conversation, he often was, his hands chopped the air, like a cook's at work.

It was understood that Pultoo-uncle had gone out to a class at the college of art that morning.. My sister Sunchita and I had been allowed to watch the television in the dining room. We had seen *Double Deckers*, and *Tom and Jerry*, and a new programme made in Bangladesh. My sister, who liked to lie on her stomach on the dining-table when she watched television, had been shooed off when the table was set; the children's programmes had come to an end, and the adults' programmes begun. Soon it would be the news and dinnertime. About the house there was the sense that the kitchen was ready and waiting, the dishes now being kept warm. My grandfather was not a stickler about mealtimes, but he liked to know if someone was going to be late.

'I hope nothing is wrong,' Mary-aunty said.

'Wrong?' Era said, alarmed.

'Nonsense, nothing could be wrong,' Dahlia-aunty said, although everyone remembered the time, not so long before, when young men had failed to come home and were never seen again. That possibility lingered for many years, and people did their families the kindness of being punctual, on the whole, to save their nerves.

But Pultoo-uncle came in, as the clock in the hall struck eight, brushing his hair back with his hand and depositing a table-top-sized folder by the front door, apologizing as he came. Warm, he smelt of geraniums, and his long shirt was dusty with the red dust of the street. He had two friends with him, two other artists. Their names were Kajol and Kanaq. Kanaq fascinated me and my sisters because she came from a tribe; her appearance was highly

11

exotic, with her slanted eyes and sleepy air. It was not unusual for Pultoo to bring friends for dinner, and these two often arrived at my grandfather's house in the late afternoon on a Friday, and stayed for dinner with only a little urging, only one diffident invitation. They lived in lodgings, and I believe they enjoyed the chance of a family dinner. My grandfather did not really care who came for dinner; my grandmother, on the other hand, liked to be given the chance to offer an invitation.

'Can we find space for these two?' Pultoo said, when he came back from washing, his face wet and glistening, his white teeth shining. 'I'm sure there is space.'

My grandmother muttered something, and went off to the kitchen with the bare appearance of graciousness.

'I do like them,' my sister Sunchita said, in her adult, mature, book-reading way about the guests, as we went back to the dining room to catch the rest of the television before the news started. 'But their painting is awful.'

7.

When the news was finished, my grandmother asked Pultoo what he had been doing at the art college that morning. He asked her permission to get out the drawings from his life class, which he had left in the folder. He passed them round the table; they were charcoal drawings of a naked man sitting on a box. 'I think this one is the best,' my grandfather said simply, when they got to him.

'And we were late because we were planning something,' Pultoo said.

'Yes,' Mary-aunty said. 'You certainly were late.'

'Late, yes,' Era said. She often agreed with her sisters, in an echo; she was shy and did not venture her own opinions easily. Even her echoes of opinions were often given first in the direction of her plate.

12

'We really got carried away,' Kanaq said, her slanting eyes looking at the biriani. 'It is such a good idea.'

'We are going to produce greetings cards,' Kajol said. 'People always like greetings cards – we are going to give them something special.'

My uncle went on to explain that their plan was for hand-made cards, sketches in pen and ink, in watercolours and in pencil, and to sell them on a stall in Ramana field in the first instance. 'After that, if it is successful, we can think about opening a shop,' Pultoo said. 'It is such a good idea, I don't know why no one has thought of it before.'

The cards would be for the new year. In Bangladesh, Choto-mama said, people were always sending cards for any reason; but they were mass-produced, the same cards that were sold anywhere, and did not speak to the sender or to the recipient. 'I saw a birthday card,' my uncle's friend Kajol said. 'It was a photograph of a mountainside in the Himalaya, I expect, and the message inside was "This is what I dream of . . ." It means nothing, that kind of thing. Produced in factories, designed by slaves.'

'Yes,' Pultoo said, in his excitable way. 'People would not buy that if they could buy the sort of thing we are going to make for them.'

'What sort of thing?' my grandmother said.

I wondered whether their idea was to make cards with pictures of naked people on them. I did not think people would want to buy those. But Pultoo-uncle explained that they would be drawing and painting famous views in Bangladesh, typical scenes of Bangladesh, such as a village house or a tea plantation, perhaps even well-known corners of Dacca. 'I would much prefer to see a hand-drawn picture like that,' Pultoo said.

'When are your teachers coming?' Shibli called to Dahlia-aunty. 'The musicians.'

'Quiet, Shibli,' Nani said, in her stagy way. 'Don't you have any respect? Your uncle is talking about your country.'

'Your country, yes,' Era said.

13

8.

The servants in my grandfather's house held a fascination for me. I never knew how many there were. After Mary-aunty had put my sister and me to bed in the afternoons, we would often start up a row, a pillow fight, a shouting match, and soon she would come to see what the noise was. But she was somebody who could not pass another human being known to her in any degree without greeting them. So we could hear the passage of Mary-aunty through the house from her slapping chappals, and from a constant stream of greetings, and expressions of concern and interest: 'Good afternoon, Rustum'; 'how are your children, Timur; is your daughter happy with Mr Khandekar . . .' That sort of thing. There were enough servants to slow her progress, to warn us and allow us to calm down and pretend to be asleep by the time she opened the door to shout at us.

My grandfather had a gardener called Atish. Over the years, he had become both an inside servant and an outside servant, according to need. I was not allowed to follow Atish about when he was inside, cleaning and polishing. When he was gardening, there were no objections to my walking about with him and asking him any number of questions. There was plenty to occupy him: the huge bougainvillaeas that poured out of pots and formed a blazing arch, the way that the terrace and entrance needed to be swept of dead leaves and flowers. He trimmed back the flowers in the flowerbeds; he carried out mysterious surgical operations with saw and secateurs on the fruit trees – the guava tree, the mango tree, the jackfruit tree, the banana tree, the tamarind tree, with its neatly diagrammatic leaves and its extravagant flower. There was plenty of digging and pruning and planting to do, with a small boy gazing and a chicken or two following round in the hope of an upturned worm.

Atish was a poor Hindu who was left behind in 1947. Grandfather and Grandmother had had to leave Calcutta in a great hurry and come to Dacca. Nana had bought a house in Rankin Street from a rich Hindu, who had had to leave Dacca in a great hurry and go to Calcutta. I wondered why they had not simply swapped their houses, but they had not. Atish had not gone like the rich Hindus to Calcutta: he had stayed where he was, and Grandfather had taken pity on him and employed him in the garden. It suited him.

Nana liked to employ poor and vulnerable people. All of them stayed for ever. And Nana's relations with them sometimes surprised his friends, since he encouraged the people he employed to speak their minds to him. Sometimes they developed independent habits, which could prove inconvenient to the rest of the household. Rustum, Nana's driver, was another of these vulnerable people, but after a while, he developed the habit of taking the car out on his own, or of ignoring instructions. Sometimes my grandmother would come out after lunch, expecting Rustum to be there to drive her to a friend's house, and would find that he had gone out with the car, and no one knew where he had gone. When he came back, I had heard him blame Dahlia-aunty, saying that she had told him to go and fetch something from a shop on the other side of Dacca. She had demanded, he would say, a particular sort of sandesh, one that could only be got in a confectioner's shop on Sadarghat. He knew the sort of blame that could be convincingly put on Dahlia. But if this got back to Dahlia-aunty, she would fly into a furious passion. It was the first thing that came into Rustum's mind, it seemed, and it did not occur to him that anyone might ask Dahlia whether there was any truth in his story.

'How could he? How could he? How could he?' Dahlia would shout, sometimes audibly from outside the gates of the house. To passers-by and neighbours, it did not seem obvious that these screams were caused only by a servant's unreliable events; surely, they must have thought, a husband or father must have threatened a beating to the victim, at the very least. But nobody beat anyone in Nana's house, and Dahlia screamed because Rustum had pretended she had ordered him about.

Finally there came the terrible day when Rustum had a fight with Nana himself. It occurred in the week. When we arrived that Friday, Rustum was not there. This was not unusual, but it was strange that the red Vauxhall was in the garage when both Nana and Rustum were out of the house. When Nana came home, he came home in a cycle-rickshaw, and I understood that something atrocious had happened. Rustum had been asked to leave. 'I could forgive him for taking the car without permission,' my grandfather said, a week or two later when he could bring himself to talk about it. 'But it was the lying afterwards I could not put up with.' My grandfather, however, immediately felt guilty about evicting Rustum and his family from the flat in the servants' block, and made it his business to find Rustum another place to live and even another job. When, five years later, Rustum was diagnosed with tuberculosis, my grandfather paid for his treatment.

Atish the gardener was not as popular with the children as Rustum. He did not have the glamour of a red Vauxhall car to carry out his trade, but only a spade, a hoe, a trowel and a fork; among his tools, only the secateurs, with their terrible grip and savage slice, had the power to fascinate. But I liked to follow him around the garden, and watch him at his tasks, and he did not object. Sometimes he let me undertake a small task to help him, such as filling his two watering-cans. If it was cold, Atish used to wear a shawl about his shoulders, a scarf wound right around his head, like a sufferer from the toothache; his set face emerged from a kind of red cotton nest on the coldest days of the year.

Atish would start work at the front of the house, where the tamarind tree shaded the entrance. There were always things to sweep up here. Then he would move on to the flowerbeds at the side of the house in the full sun, and then to the back of the house, with the other fruit trees, the lawn and, underneath the jackfruit tree, the chicken house. The chickens were allowed to wander the garden, eating whatever they could find. One of the days that Atish devoted to digging and turning over the earth in the flowerbeds was a festival day for the chickens, as they could eye and pounce on a worm or a beetle that Atish's spade had uncovered. They stood, beadily eyeing his work, like supervisors in a factory.

The chicken house had been made and painted, decorated, by Choto-mama Pultoo. He had started it when he was still at school and showing signs of artistic and practical talent. He had painted a frame, put a tidy little net in its front, and then, he said, he had wondered what he would like in his house, if he were a chicken. So the chicken house contained the dead branches of trees for the chickens to perch on, and the back wall had a landscape painted by Pultoo. 'So that they can think of the wide open spaces of the countryside, even when they are confined in a small garden in Dacca,' Pultoo poetically observed. The chickens seemed to take more pleasure in the dead tree, on which they happily roosted and slept, than in the landscape, which they ignored. Within a few months, the mountain view was dimmed and smeared by chicken feathers and chicken shit. Pultoo was not put off, and carried on adding ornament and furniture to the chicken house in the hope of broadening their mental horizons. The latest was a series of terracotta yogurt pots, which he had decorated with some folk-like paintings of milkmaids.

'Come on,' Dahlia-aunty, who was a good sort, would sometimes say to me when we arrived at my grandfather's house for the weekend. 'Let's go and see what Choto-mama has done to the chicken run this week.'

Atish never made any comment on Pultoo's chicken run, or on the chickens themselves for that matter. He stayed silent on the subject, even when the cat next door got into the garden and killed three chicks. He ignored the chickens standing by his side, watching him hoe and dig, though he would pause in his regular rhythm if they darted forward to grab a worm.

I could stand there all morning, watching Atish work and the chickens eat the grubs he found for them. The only things he said to me were odd horticultural pieces of advice: it was necessary to prune a mango tree in March; the first sprouts from seeds that would turn into sunflowers must be thinned out when they had reached an inch tall; you could not water a bougainvillaea enough. It was as if he thought I was going to become a gardener like him when I grew up. The way he gave horticultural maxims is clear in my head, but not what he said exactly. I may have got them quite wrong. But I stood or squatted there all morning, watching Atish at work, watching the white chickens dart to and fro.

9.

My father came before lunch on Saturday. He did not come with a dramatic flourish, like my grandfather; he did not come with excitement, like my mother and my sisters. He came under a pile of papers, tied up with red ribbon, and in a pernickety, unenthusiastic way. Sometimes he was carrying so much that it threatened to overbalance him. It is not easy to travel with a large bundle of papers in the back of a cycle-rickshaw, and he often turned up with his arms in a desperate position, clutching them like a large escaping fish. I liked to watch him arrive. The cycle-rickshaw he always used was glittering silver, polished, with the faces of film stars under a setting sun painted on the back of its canopy; like many of the other rickshaws of Dacca, its canopy was lined with tinsel, like a fur-lined hood. The rickshaw driver, however, was a taciturn, serious man, whom you could not imagine decorating his vehicle in this way, and so was my father, sitting in the square middle of the rickshaw with his papers on his lap, his lawyer's white bands around his throat.

Both I and my father were hypocrites – he, because he did not really want to come to my grandfather's house: he was a government lawyer, my grandfather was a lawyer for the people, so they were always on opposite sides, and my grandfather could never resist needling him about this argument or other that he had undertaken with less success than he had hoped for. He came because he felt he ought to, and because the Bar library in which he did so much of his work closed at weekends.

I was a hypocrite because, towards the end of Saturday morning, I made a habit of going up to Nana's balcony to watch out for Father's arrival. The balcony had by far the best view down the street, and it was where anyone sat to keep an eye out for an eagerly awaited visitor. From there, you could see the curious events of the street: a handcart laden with megaphones, like silver tropical flowers, heading to a rally, or a pitiful hawker, selling a single useless part of a household object, such as the handles of a pressure cooker, laid out on a cloth in the forlorn hope of a purchaser. I went up there, making sure that everyone knew I was going up there, to watch out for Father's arrival in a cycle-rickshaw. In fact, my father's arrival was nothing to look forward to. I disliked the way my mother and aunts had less time for me, busy with meeting his needs. He was much more remote than my aunts and my mother, and the idea of creating fun for his children would not have occurred to him. I made a great perform-ance out of my anticipation because I thought that was the right, or the dramatic, thing to do. But in fact I did not much care that I had not seen him since early breakfast on Friday, and would not have minded if I had not seen him until Monday morning. Like many little boys, I wanted to have my mother to myself, with her warm iron-scented flesh, her ripple of silk against my face when she embraced me.

The one thing that made the weekend visits to Nana endurable for my father was that Nana had an excellent law library of his own. Although the public law library was closed at weekends, my father could, once he had eaten lunch with the aunts, his parents-in-law and the children, retreat to Nana's library and carry on working in its rusty warm light. Sometimes he would call Sunchita and me in, and set us the task to find a particular book in Nana's library, or a particular case within a book. I believe he thought he was providing us with some fun, as well as with a little education.

The library had a double aspect: one barred window looked out to the tamarind tree at the front, the other at the flowerbed to the side. Out of the front window, I could see the watchman leaning on the bonnet of the red Vauxhall. The big front gate of the house was open, and he was talking to someone I could not see. From the side window, there was Atish, attending to the flowerbeds. There was no one to fill his watering-cans for him, and he was trudging backwards and forwards with an uncomplaining uneven gait, like a badly oiled clockwork toy that threatened to start walking in circles. 'Liberty Cinema versus CIT,' my father said, in his light-toned voice. 'Have you found that one for me?'

Elsewhere in the house the television was on, and Shibli was watching; Mary-aunty's slapping chappals were coming down the stairs, and she was greeting the cook by asking about her daughter. My grandfather was laughing somewhere. Behind everything, the quiet of the Dhanmondi street, and the peaceful burble of the chickens in the garden.

2: The Game of *Roots*

1.

The children all around watched American television shows with absorption, and would not be distracted. They watched *Knight Rider* and *Kojak*, *Dallas* and *Starsky and Hutch*, and other things still less suitable for small children. Afterwards, they rushed out into the street, into each other's gardens and homes, dizzy and full of games of re-enactment. For weeks after Starsky and Hutch had rescued a girl bound and imprisoned in a church crypt, nurses, ayahs, mothers and aunts kept discovering small girls in their charge tied up with washing line to jackfruit trees. They had been abandoned in the joy of the game and, unable to untie themselves, wailed until someone rescued them.

'Little brutes,' Dahlia-aunty would say, when Sunchita, Shibli and I roared in after a morning playing some delirious game, wild-haired and dirty. 'Go and wash yourselves immediately.'

'Immediately,' Era would add.

The games were played in the street, in gardens, on any spare plot of ground, with fervour and without planning. When we came across a neighbour's children or grandchildren, we would start a game of *Starsky and Hutch* without any discussion. We knew all the children for many houses around, all the short-cuts between gardens, and the houses we would be chased away from.

In the streets, we lost all our respectability, and became, as our aunts told us, little ragamuffins. Sometimes, in our racing about, we got as far as Mirpur Road, where we were forbidden to go

21

on our own. It was exciting there: the streets were suddenly full of trades. You could see the aubergine-seller, frying white discs in his yellow oil, the black iron cauldron precariously balanced on the gas stove; the cracker of nuts; a pavement cobbler; the barber with his cut-throat razor attending to a man leaning back in a chair under a tree, a broken scrap of mirror all he had to work with to perfect the moustache. There was the chai-wallah with his little terracotta cups, waiting to be filled with tea, and a hundred potsherds lying around him from the morning's custom. We raced around all of them, playing our TV games, further than we ever meant to go, ignoring their curses and delirious in our rule-breaking. We all knew that Mirpur Road was where a little boy had been kidnapped and eaten by starving people, and we ran through its chaos and indifference, yelling like urchins.

We played *Kojak* and *Knight Rider* and *Double Deckers* constantly, without much preference for one game over another. Perhaps there was not much difference between the games. *Dallas* was more of a girl's game. My sisters never got tired of parading up and down the garden and pointing a vengeful finger at the small girl from Mrs Rahman's house. 'Ten million dollars!' they would cry. The rest of us were happy pretending to be talking cars, being kidnappers, or trying to walk like Hungry Bear.

The hold these television programmes had over our imaginations was swept away in one moment by a new series. My aunts talked about it seriously some time before it even started. The whole world, they said, had watched this series, and now it was coming to us, to be shown on Bangladesh television. It was the first time I realized that the programmes we watched were not made especially for us, although most of the television we watched was about people who did not look at all like us.

The programme was called *Roots*, and was about a family of black people. They started by living in Africa, then were kidnapped and taken to America, where they were slaves. We were entranced. It did not seem to agree with our idea of America at all. The next day we lifted the bolt, pushed the iron gates open and ran out across the street, not troubling to close the gates behind us. For once, we did not mooch or loiter until we came across some children we knew. We banged on doors like drunkards, demanding that our playfellows came out. 'Did you see *Roots*?' we shouted, and everyone had. Finally, there were twenty children, all nearly overcome with excitement, spilling across the quiet street under the trees and shouting their heads off.

'I want to be Kunta Kinte,' one said.

'No, I want to be,' another said. And my sister said she would be Kunta Kinte's wife. Shibli was a brother who was to be killed. He liked to be killed in games, so long as he could stand up straight away and go to be killed all over again.

'So I'm walking down the riverbank with my wife,' Kunta Kinte said, balancing along the gutter. 'Oh, wife, wife, I love you so much.'

'Oh, husband,' Sunchita said. A fight was breaking out between the slave-traders and the Africans. 'Stop it, stop it, you've got to watch me. Look, watch me, I'm walking with my husband Kunta Kinte.'

Shibli got up from being killed. 'Who's the chief slave-owner? I want to be the chief slave-owner.'

'You can't be,' a boy called Assad shouted. 'You don't know how to kill anyone. I want to be the chief slave-owner. I want to come and put Kunta Kinte in chains and steal him to America.'

'You don't know how to kill anyone either,' Sunchita said to Assad. He was a boy we only sometimes saw. We had not called at his house, three houses away; he had heard the noise and the shouts of '*Roots*' and had come out of his own accord. 'You can't be the chief slave-owner.'

'I know how people are killed,' Assad said. 'It's not fair.'

I was clamouring like all the others to be allowed to be the chief slave-owner, the Englishman. That was the thing I wanted to be. And then a miracle happened. Kunta Kinte intervened and said, with calm authority, 'Saadi should be the slave-owner. After all, he's the palest among us. He can be the white man.' And that was that, and I was the slave-owner, because, after all, Kunta Kinte was the hero of the game and what he said went.

Assad rushed at me with both fists flying. I hated to fight – when I fought with my sisters, it was always in play. I had never done anything worse to anyone than throw an orange directly at Sunchita's head. I dodged behind my big sister Sushmita, who had no such reluctance. She pushed him, hard, and he fell over in the dust, wailing.

'I don't want to play this game,' Assad howled. But he did not run away. The game was too good for that. In ten minutes' time, he was lining up gleefully with all the other slaves behind Kunta Kinte and his wife, while I growled, 'This is my slave ship, and you are all under my power for ever and ever.' One of my two assistant slave-keeping Englishmen had got the plum role of the man with the whip – a torn-off vine – and he now dramatically brought it down on the backs of the ten slaves, hunched and moaning. Two small girls of the neighbourhood, the daughters of Mr Khandekar-nana's niece, were happily screaming for help. They were tied with washing line to the roadside trees. Over the road, a houseboy was watching with fascination, perhaps wanting to abandon his duties and come over to join in. It was the best game we ever played, and we played it every Sunday afternoon for many weeks.

2.

Whenever a chick emerged from Pultoo-uncle's chicken house, my sisters, Shibli and I would rush to see it. We would have warning. A mother hen would sit on her eggs inside the chicken house, blowing her feathers out into a big angry ball and clucking. And then one morning there would be some small puffs of yellowish feathers with the big feet of a toy, and eyes with a strange, tired, aged look. My sisters made small girlish piping noises to echo the little squeaks; Shibli would always pick one up, sometimes making the mother hen rush at him with her neck outstretched. The hens were so sharp and businesslike, getting on with their occupations, but their chicks were fluffy and yellow and not like animals at all, but like things run by inner machinery. I did not torment them, but liked to watch them, dipping their heads into the waterbowl left for them by Atish the gardener, running back to their mothers, making their small cries for attention. I could sit on my haunches, watching them, for hours.

Once, I was alone in the garden watching some day-old chicks in this way, quite silently. The others were inside – Sushmita was reading, Shibli was making a nuisance of himself in the kitchen, and Sunchita had been sent to bed in disgrace. I had seen chicks hatch from their eggs; the struggle inside the shell was hateful to me – I always feared that the effort would be too much for them. And when they emerged, they were so wet and slimy, so ugly, I could not help imagining how frightening they would be, with their sudden sharp gestures, if they were the same size as me.

But within hours they were small and round and fluffed quite yellow, and seemed nearly at home in the world. They stretched their plump little wings, like stubby fingers, and, not able to fly, fell from the chicken house on to the lawn under the jackfruit tree. Their movements were undecided and sudden, and you could not know what would cause them to take fright, or when they would move confidently.

'They're born standing,' Atish the gardener said. He had laid down his tools and was now standing behind me. I think he liked watching the newly hatched chicks as much as I did. 'Not like human beings. Human beings can't feed themselves, they can't walk, not for years. A chicken makes his own way out of the shell, punches his way out, and then he cleans himself off, and he stands on his two feet and off he goes like you or me. First thing he does is to find something to eat, and it's the same food he'll eat all his life.'

This was true. I watched the chicks pecking at the seeds on

the ground. It was exactly what the fully grown chickens ate. From the house came the sound of music: Dahlia-aunty was having a music lesson, with tabla and harmonium, and her lovely singing voice filled the garden.

'Can I have a chick of my own?' I asked Atish.

'It's not for me to say,' Atish said.

But he reached into the pocket of his grimy shirt and took out a chapatti. It might have been there for him to eat later, or it might have been in his shirt for some time. He tore off a corner and gave it to me. 'If you get a chick to come to you,' he said, 'it will be your friend.'

I took it, and held it out on the palm of my hand. I had the attention of the chicks. I lowered my hand almost to the ground. After a moment, a chick detached itself from the others, and came up, quite boldly, investigating. He pecked swiftly at the corner of the chapatti in the palm of my hand. He was not committing himself, staying in a place he could run from if I turned out to be an enemy, tempting him into a trap. I wondered at the cunning of a creature so small and so young in days. But then, as I did not move, but just let him go on pecking at the corner of Atish's chapatti, he made some kind of decision, and hopped up on to the palm of my hand, where he could get at the bread more comfortably. He was darker than the other chicks, almost brown in hue, with two parallel black squiggles along his back, running along where his wings were.

'You see?' Atish said. 'That one likes you. He'll always remember you, now.'

'How can he remember?' I said.

'I don't know,' Atish said. He threw his shawl over his shoulder, picked up his fork again. 'But he always will. Sometimes when they come up to you, they think that you're their mother, and then they never change their mind.'

The idea that my chick thought I was his mother was so funny that I trembled with laughter. The chick jumped off my hand, but did not run away; he went on pecking nonchalantly around my hand as if the movement of my laughter had been an inexplicable quake. And in a moment he returned to me, and hopped back on my palm.

When I went back into the house, I told everyone that I had a chicken all of my own and had decided to call him Piklu. My sisters, Mary-aunty and Bubbly-aunty, who had come from Srimongol to visit, all came out to see my chicken. 'Don't go too close,' Mary-aunty warned. 'You'll upset the mother and she might even eat her own chicks.' But I knew that would not happen, unless my sisters and aunts came running across and crowded them. I approached the mass of new chicks pecking at the ground before the chicken house, walking softly, and what happened did not surprise me at all. The chick with the two black squiggles down its back, the one a little darker than the others, detached itself quite easily from its brothers and sisters and came to say hello to me. I squatted down, and held out my hand, and the chick hopped happily on to my palm.

'This is Piklu,' I said. 'He's my chicken.'

And Bubbly-aunty was so impressed, she went to fetch Dahlia out of her music lesson to show her.

3.

Every aunt had her occupation – to paint, to cook, to help Nana with legal research, to attend to the chickens. Bubbly, who loved food, was forever in the kitchen, though her particular task was to supervise the making of the pickles. Mary's was to keep the children in order; Nadira's was to sing. Though she was in Sheffield now, the other aunts talked about her ceaselessly. I could remember her wedding, how beautiful it had been, how beautiful she had been. Her singing had been good enough for her to appear on Bangladeshi television, performing Tagore songs. 'Do you think she has her own programme, by now, on British television?' Mary asked guilelessly.

'I wouldn't be at all surprised,' Nani said.

At the time when Tagore was banned by the Pakistanis, before independence, Nadira had hidden her music with all the other Bengali music, poetry and books in the secret cellar at my grandfather's house. When it was safe to bring it out again, it was clear that she had not forgotten any of it. That was her occupation.

Dahlia was my favourite aunt. Nadira had been fascinating and dramatic, always ready to shout and stamp or even to cry for effect in public. But she could also say, 'Be off with you, wretched child.' Dahlia was as fragrant as Nadira had been, and as pretty as her name. She, too, had her music. It was understood that Nadira was a better singer, but Dahlia took lessons from the two musicians who came to the house. Her occupation, however, since Nadira had taken music as her first choice, was to sew: she embroidered very deft, very intricate scenes of country life, not using patterns, but quite out of her head. If you asked her, she would explain that this figure was a man she had seen working in the fields near my grandfather's village last summer, that this was his wife, waiting for him at home and cooking a delicious supper, that these were what she imagined his children looked like, and these were the mountains in the distance, with cows and goats on them. Pultoo was very scathing about Dahlia's sewing and her designs, but many people loved them, and she was always being asked for her next one by friends of the family. It often took her a year or more to finish one, however, and they tended to stay in the family, in the rooms of the children of this aunt or that. Sometimes Dahlia just placed them in a large biscuit box she had at home, and only took them out if you asked her.

Sunchita had once asked her if she could make a picture of something in particular, a picture of children she knew, queuing up and travelling on an aeroplane. Sunchita had asked for this very fervently, but Dahlia-aunty had laughed and said she would make that for her, one of these days. That day had not yet come. I had one of Dahlia's tapestries on my wall at home, and I had named every single figure in the image, and had a good idea of their relation to each other, the stories they were embarked upon.

Dahlia was busy in a corner of the salon, her head bent over her half-finished work. She heard me coming in, and called to me. There was no one else in the room, and I went to sit by her. She tutted, and smoothed my hair; she took a sweet-smelling folded handkerchief from the short sleeve of the dark blue blouse under her sari. She spat a little into it, and wiped my cheeks, one after the other. I must have been smudged from the street. 'Little urchin,' she said.

'Dahlia-aunty,' I said, and told her all about the *Roots* game we had been playing. I went into details. She listened patiently, laughing sometimes.

'I wondered what you were all doing,' she said. 'Nani came down from upstairs where she had been dressing the mango to dry, and said that she had never been so shocked. She saw a group of street-urchins tearing up and down the street, making a terrible din, and she thought that never had such a thing been heard of in Dhanmondi.'

'And it was us, wasn't it, Dahlia-aunty?' I said happily. I took her hand, and pulled the thimble off her forefinger; that silver top joint of the finger was fascinating to me, and I could only think of it as a sort of toy. I loved to put my finger into it, and twirl it about.

'She called down to me, and I went up, and then the whole gang of you rushed past, and I said to Nani, "I think I know one or two of those street-urchins."'

'Are we in trouble?' I asked.

Dahlia held up her needle to the light, licked the end of the blue thread, rethreaded the needle. She unsmilingly held out her hand, and I, smilingly, took the thimble off my too-thin finger. Instead of putting it on the palm of the hand she held out, I reached around and put it on the finger of her left hand; an intimate, professional thing to do, like a servant's task. She gave way: she smiled, and gave me a kiss.

'Who are those boys that you play with?' she said.

'I told you once,' I said, exasperated. I ran through the names, but she stopped me.

'Assad,' she said. 'Is that the little boy who lives three houses away?'

'I don't like him,' I said. 'I don't like him at all. He wanted to be the slave-owner, but everyone said I should do it, and he cried at first, but now he just wants to be another slave-owner. He doesn't play the game properly.'

'But he lives, doesn't he, three houses away? I mean, to the left, up the road, towards the main road?'

I thought, and then agreed.

'Saadi,' she said, 'I want you to promise me that you won't go to that boy's house, and you won't ask him here. You can play with him in the street, if there are lots of other children, like today, but don't go to his house, and don't have anything to do with his big brothers, or his father, or any of his family. Can you promise me that?'

I promised. 'I don't like him,' I said. 'I don't want to go to his old house, anyway.'

'Has he asked you?'

'No,' I had to admit.

'If he asks you, don't go,' Dahlia-aunty said. 'Your grandfather wouldn't like it. You know why. Now. I've been hard at work all afternoon – my fingers are red raw, look. Shall we have our tea, just you and I?'

I felt I had made a solemn and binding contract with my aunt, something which was beyond my sisters' capacity, and it was with an adult's serious walk that I went to the kitchen to call for tea and biscuits. If a guest had brought some or the kitchen had made some, there might be semai, chumchum, or rosogallai. These were the sweets that my aunt and I liked to eat together.

When my aunt said to me that I was not to play with Assad, and that I knew the reason why, she spoke the truth. At that time, there was only one reason why we did not associate with people of the neighbourhood, and that reason was known to everyone in the house, from the oldest visitors from the village down to the smallest child. It came to us as we woke, and was with us when we went to bed. We understood very well the reason why a child was forbidden our company. When Dahlia gave me this instruction I understood very well that it must have been his father who had sided with the Pakistanis.

4.

In Dhanmondi, where my grandfather lived, associations between neighbours were generally relaxed and easy. A gardener or a chauffeur would be lent without a thought; the women went between houses all day long. This was even true of the president of the country, Sheikh Mujib, whose house was four away from Khandekar-nana's house. My mother used to tell the story of going to visit Mujib's daughter, Sheikh Hasina, at her father's house, to find her in a terrible rage. She had been expecting a certain number of bags of chilli to be sent up from their estate in the country; the bags had arrived, but there were two short. 'There should be two more! Two more!' Sheikh Hasina had shouted, over and over. She barely paused in her rage to greet my mother.

'Imagine that,' my mother said. 'Her father is the president of the country, and she was angry for the lack of two bags of chilli, which she could well afford to buy from the market.'

But there were some families in the neighbourhood who walked out alone, with their heads held high; we did not know them, and we did not lend our servants to them; we did not greet them, and my grandfather said their names were unfamiliar to him. There were a number of families like this. If the children of such a family walked out with their ayah, they would walk in a regimented way, in their best clothes, looking neither to left nor to right. That expression, with a head held high, not scanning the horizon but directed forward, like a horse with blinkers, was characteristic of all of them. When the gate of their house was opened, and a car drove out, with some older members of the family in it, you saw it then, that upright, distant, ignoring expression. They would not catch the eyes of anyone in the street. You could recognize these families. They dressed beautifully, dustlessly, in conventional and traditional ways. My aunts mostly put their clothes together from this and that; Mary-aunty thought nothing of borrowing her brother Pultoo-uncle's stained painting jacket to wear on top, if she was cold.

'Why can't you dress like Nadira?' Nani would say to her daughters, if they seemed to be going too far – if, say, she recognized an old pinstriped jacket of Nana's on Era's back on a cold January morning.

'Like Nadira?' Era would say, astonished.

Unlike Nadira, whose passion for clothes and makeup was legendary, they all shuffled about in old pairs of chappals, or slippers trodden down at the heel. It was accepted that they did. But Nani would not ask why her daughters could not dress like those neighbours of theirs. Those other families were immaculate in appearance, and they dressed as if they were living in the year 1850. They were the only ones in the neighbourhood where the women wore veils before their faces, where the men wore a covering on their heads. That was why I had not recognized the boy Assad for the type that he was.

These families mixed with each other, but not with us. To see the men with their friends was always unexpected; then they were at ease, greeting, laughing, chatting quite easily, their wives and sisters to one side. For those moments, despite their immaculate clothes, they resembled our own families, but of course they were not like them at all. And then they would say goodbye, and without warning, the men would resume that remote gaze of theirs. They would not acknowledge their nearest neighbours, and their nearest neighbours would ignore them, too. It was as if there were two cities laid on top of one another, each quite invisible to the other, each engaging only with its own sort.

A child knew what these people had done. They had taken money from the Pakistanis; they had betrayed their own kind; they had worked on behalf of the foreigners. They had taken the wrong side in the war, and that would never be forgotten. They had fled, often, to Pakistan, and had returned with the amnesty, buying a big house in Dhanmondi with the money they had made out of threatening Hindus and denouncing intellectuals. That was what we all believed of them. 'If everyone had their just deserts,' my aunts would say, 'such a person would not be living opposite your grandfather. They would be in jail.' And yet explaining to Assad that he must leave us and must play with his own kind was beyond me. He came from a family we could not mix with, and I did not like him. But I could not banish him on my own.

5.

During the week we lived at home and I went to school. We had no car and no television, and there were only the six of us: my mother, my father, my two sisters, my brother and myself. It was quiet in our house, and my mother's attention was all on my father's needs. My brother Zahid was to become an engineer, and his serious spirit filled the house in the evenings. I was to become a lawyer, like my father and grandfather, but although my head was bent over my books, I was only pretending to get on with my work. At school, my teachers were always shouting at me and throwing pieces of chalk at my head when they saw that I was daydreaming. My sister Sunchita was eleven months older than I, and was in the same class. She was always being held up as an example to me, with her eagerness to read, her love of studying; in the bosoms of my teachers, the memory of my serious, intelligent, practical brother Zahid was just as warm, although he was ten years older than I was. My teachers could show me that

I was not as good a student as Sunchita, who basked in the praise, and they were certain that I would not grow up to match Zahid. I knuckled down – and pretended to concentrate on the picture book of geography. The boy I sat at a desk with tugged our shared copy back into his half, and I kicked him.

At school and at home, pretending to work, I was thinking only of one thing. I was thinking of my chicken, Piklu. Piklu had a carefree life compared to mine. He woke up and made a brave little leap from the brink of Choto-mama's chicken coop into the garden. There would be fresh seeds to peck at, fresh worms to eat. He would puff out his little feathers, and go to explore the new morning. And that was all he had to do all day long. I worried that he would miss me. He would look about to see if I was there, but there would be only Atish, to whom one chicken was much the same as another.

My weeks were filled with worry on Piklu's behalf. While I was not there, he might eat a poisonous berry by mistake, not knowing the difference. Or a cat might get into the garden and kill him. This had happened once before, and the neighbour whose cat it was had merely apologized and told my grandfather that these things would happen. The cat must have returned to its owner with a prowling, sated gait, blood around its mouth and its whiskers adorned with fluffy yellow feathers. They must have known what it had done, but they had not cared. I could not endure that such a thing might happen to Piklu.

There were other dangers that might fall on him while I was not there. But the first among these was that Piklu might forget me between Sunday night, when we left, and Friday, when we returned to my grandfather's house.

It is astonishing how fast a chicken grows. From one week to another, an almost globular chick turns into a grey bony thing, with a great beak and awkward corners, and then, no more than a week or two later, into something that resembles a chicken, its feathers puffing out. Piklu had changed every time we arrived at my grandfather's house, and I hardly recognized him. But he recognized me. When I came towards the chicken coop, Piklu separated himself from the rest of the flock and came to greet me. I recognized him from the two irregular lines down his back, and I bent down to give him some crumbs I had kept for him. He was my chicken and I was his boy. The bond between us made Shibli jealous, but it amused almost everyone else: I had said I wanted a chicken of my own, and I had bound a chicken to me by willpower.

The best *Roots* game remained the one of capture and imprisonment. That was because of what came at the end of it: the game of auctioning off the captured slaves. There was a dramatic poignancy to that, which Shibli, who played the auctioneer, never failed to exploit. First the Africans played house, quietly at home in Africa before the slave-drivers came. Then I arrived with my henchmen, cracking whips and making the Africans scream and run. Once you had touched an African on both shoulders simultaneously, they came on to your side and chased the remaining Africans until they were all transformed. Then Shibli played the auctioneer, and sold the slaves.

'What am I bid for this fine slave?' he called, as I growled and pranced. Half of the Africans had to take the role of the bidders at the auction, or it would not have worked out. 'Am I bid one thousand dollars? Two thousand? Three?' Or sometimes he would vary it by suggesting that nobody would bid more than one cent for this miserable slave, and give them away for nothing. Nobody knew what Shibli would do; the auction part of the game filled us with a terrible, inexpressible excitement. It was what we looked forward to most.

The game started almost immediately after lunch for most of us, and continued all afternoon. It began as soon as enough people were there to join in. Assad came later. His family were religious – his mother, big sisters and aunts covered their faces with a veil, and his father, uncles and brothers, like Assad, wore a cap, a tupi, on their heads. When the call to prayer was heard, five times a day, none of my family took the slightest notice, and most of my grandfather's neighbours were the same. But you could see the family of Assad hurrying home, and we knew that they all prayed constantly. For this reason Assad was never there at the start of the game. He appeared at five o'clock, between prayers; sometimes he would say that he had given his father the slip, that he had gone to the mosque but had left him behind. He seemed to have no sense of decorum; he did not know that it should have been embarrassing and shameful to him to admit to having parents at all.

Everyone in the game had seen my chicken Piklu. He was famous in the neighbourhood. Everyone – friends of my aunts, visiting cousins from the village, the children of the *Roots* game and their families – had come to see Piklu. The way he separated himself from the flock and came to greet me, but only me, was celebrated in Dhanmondi. 'Have you seen Saadi's chicken?' people would be saying, or so I imagined, all over Dhanmondi. 'You should visit. It is worth the visit.'

If the subject came up while Assad was there, he would squat on his haunches against a wall and say nothing; he would smile in a secretive, silly way, and wait for the conversation to turn to something else. He had nothing to say about my chicken. Because, of course, he could not come to see it; I was forbidden to ask him to my grandfather's garden, and I was not sure I was really allowed to include him in the game. His uncle and father had taken money from the Pakistanis, and had told them where they could find intellectuals – musicians, poets, scholars, professors, schoolteachers – to kill. Everyone knew that, and knew that they would never be prosecuted for it. So Assad, in his tupi, with his fact-hiding, knowing smile, would never be allowed to come into my grandfather's garden to see Piklu.

6.

It was easy to escape from my grandfather's house, and when Mary-aunty had put us to bed in the afternoon, I let her walk away, then started to plot my manoeuvres. The most exciting was to get out of the bedroom, cross the landing into my grandfather's room and go out on to his balcony. There might be drying pickles out there, or just my grandfather's chair. He did not rest in his room in the afternoon, but said he would work in his library, often going to sleep there in his armchair. Only once did I come into his room to find him, his legs stretched out, on the balcony. 'Churchill!' he said. But normally it was possible to leave the aunt's room, go into my grandfather's room and through on to his balcony without discovery.

I noticed, from the balcony, that the front gate had been left open when the car had been brought in. A thought came to me. In a moment I had gripped the branch of the tamarind tree, and in another I had shinned down it. The house and the garden were absolutely quiet. I sauntered out of the front gate gleefully.

A small figure in the street, a hundred or two hundred yards away, was disturbing the peace of the afternoon. A ball of red dust with arms and legs emerging, like a fight in a comic, stopped under a tree. The dust subsided, and it turned out to be Assad in white shirt and tupi, kicking up the dirt, his arms windmilling with aimless fury. I went towards him.

'I was supposed to go to the mosque,' he said. 'But I ran away and hid, and they went without me.'

'I was put to bed,' I explained. 'But I got out.'

'Where's everybody?' he said, sinking down and jogging up and down on his haunches. 'I thought everybody would be here.'

I shrugged. I thought it was possible that the others had seen Assad on his own, and decided not to come out. You could not play the *Roots* game of slave and slave-owner with only two: what role would I play, and what role would be Assad's? Other people in the game might have thought this, and remained inside their houses. My aunt had told me I was allowed to see Assad if there were plenty of other people around, but I knew she would not like it if he became a friend of mine.

Other families must have said the same thing. I was always

susceptible to pathos when I was a child. When Mary-aunty's cat gave birth to kittens, one of the kittens fell from the balcony in the night and was found dead in the morning. My sisters and I were inconsolable; we gave it a funeral and a little gravestone, and decorated the mound of the grave with flower petals. There was something noble to me about the state of being moved, and we tried to encourage Mary-aunty's cat to stand with us as we wept over the unnamed kitten; she would not, however. So, when I saw Assad in the street, kicking at the dust and trying to see if he could rotate his arms in opposite directions, I thought of everyone who had seen him alone and decided not to come out. It was a terrible but a sad business, being the son of an informer.

'Have you seen my chicken Piklu?' I said.

Assad brightened. 'No,' he said. I knew he had not.

'Do you want to see him now?' I said. Naughtiness came over me. But I felt it was in an admirable cause. I was following a higher duty than family commandments. I went behind my aunts' backs and offered friendship to Assad because he was separated from his family, and still nobody would greet him. In that moment, I assigned fine feelings to him, and a future in which we sloped off school and went fishing together.

'You're not allowed to invite me,' he said, his face falling.

'There's no one about,' I said. 'I don't care whether you come into the garden or not.'

'My father says I'm not supposed to play with you,' he said.

'Where's your father now?' I said, shocked; I had not thought that the prohibition went in both directions.

'I don't want to see your chicken, anyway,' Assad said.

'Yes, you do,' I said. 'I know you do.' I turned back to my grandfather's house, and Assad trotted beside me. 'He knows who I am,' I said. 'He comes to me whenever I go into the garden and I call his name. He'll take food from my palm. He's getting big now – he's almost a full-grown chicken.'

'Does he think you're his mother?' Assad said.

'No, he knows who I am,' I said.

'How big is he?' Assad said, as we went through the front gate of the house. 'Is he big enough to cook and eat yet?'

'No one's going to cook and eat him,' I said. 'He's not that sort of chicken. He's my chicken, my special chicken.'

'Just because he's got a name doesn't mean they won't come and get him for the pot,' Assad said. 'If they know his name and they recognize him, they might come and get him first.'

We came round the house into the garden. There was nobody there, not even Atish the gardener.

'No one would do that,' I said. Assad had let me down with his scepticism, and I was full of scorn for him now. He understood nothing; he did not understand Piklu's place in our household. He did not deserve to be introduced to Piklu. The chickens were scattered about, feeding from the ground, like walking clouds against a dark sky. They raised their heads and, just as I had promised, Piklu with the two scribbled brown lines down his back came straight to me with joy in his strut.

I had nothing to give Piklu. I felt in my pockets, but there was nothing there. He pecked enquiringly around me, walking backwards and forwards like a sentry before me. 'This is Piklu,' I said. 'Did you see how he came straight to me? That's because he recognizes me. He knows he's my chicken.'

'How do I know that's the chicken you said is yours?' Assad said. 'All I saw is a chicken that came over looking for food. It could be any chicken.'

Assad was horrible, I saw that now. But I knew that we were not horrible to horrible people. That was not the way we were. We understood that it was our responsibility to behave in civilized ways, even when we were confronted with uncivilized people. So I said, quite mildly, 'You can tell it's Piklu because he has those two lines down his back. He had those when he was a chick, straight from the egg.'

'You could just have said that,' Assad said. 'What else does your chicken do? It doesn't do anything interesting.'

'He doesn't have to do interesting things,' I said. 'He's not in

39

a circus. He's my chicken. Anyway, you don't do interesting things. I've never seen you do anything interesting. Piklu's much nicer and more interesting than you are.'

'I can do lots of interesting things. I know how to do all sorts of things you don't,' Assad said. His voice had coarsened and deepened. 'I know how . . .' He lowered himself by stages, gently, gently, towards the ground, and then, quite suddenly, his hand shot out and caught Piklu round the neck. 'I know how to kill a chicken.'

Piklu was trapped by the neck under Assad's hand; his feet were running frantically in the dust.

'The principle is the same,' Assad said. 'It's the same for anything that you want to kill. You slice through the neck –' for one moment I thought he had a knife in his pocket, that he was going to kill Piklu in front of me, but he was just slicing against Piklu's white throat with the edge of his hand '– and then it bleeds to death, quite quickly. It makes a terrible mess, my father said. Not with a small animal like a chicken. But with bigger animals, it makes a big mess.'

I knew this was true. I had seen the slaughter of a cow in the street at the festival of Eid, and walked afterwards through the slip of blood on stone, the gallons of blood churning the streets into mud, the stench filling the street, like the crowd, pressing up against you. And afterwards, the stink that came from the tanneries, down by the river. It was unavoidable if you had to take a boat from Sadarghat, and the smell of the black water was the smell of large animals being slaughtered. If you lived in Dacca, you knew the big mess that a bigger animal made when it was killed.

All at once I could move. I rushed at Assad, screaming, my fists held high, and he let Piklu go. My chicken jumped to its feet, shuffling its feathers, and ran away to the far corner of the garden. I hit Assad with both my fists in the certainty that Piklu would now never again come to me of his free will: he would remember the day that I had asked him to come to me and I had delivered him to Assad. He would remember being held down by his throat against the dirt, and the thought that he was about to die, and he would run from me. I pummelled Assad, and he hit me back, his tupi flying from his head.

Then Nani, my grandmother, was in the garden. 'Stop that at once,' she said. 'Brawling like street-urchins. Stop it. I'm ashamed of you, Saadi. What would Nana have to say? Do you think he would call you Churchill now?'

We stopped, our faces lowered towards the mud our fight had made. Grown-ups, when they interrupted our fights, had a way of insisting that we shook hands, apologized and made up with each other. It was their way. But Nani inspected Assad, his dirty shirt, his muddy hair, and the tupi lying on the leaves of a shrub, like washing laid out to dry, and made no such demand. 'I know who you are,' she said to Assad, taking his dirty head in her hands, turning it this way and that, like a shopkeeper with a fine vase. 'I want you to leave my garden now, and never come back. You should never have come into my garden. Go away.'

Assad went. Nani watched him go every step of the way; she followed him to the gate, and shut it behind him with her own hands. 'I don't know how that was left open,' she said. 'Saadi, go and have a bath. I'm ashamed of you.'

7.

It was our ayah's job to go and hail a cycle-rickshaw to take us, each Friday morning, from my parents' house to my grand-parents'. When she opened the gates, you could see the woman who always squatted there, under the tree, breaking bricks and stones into rubble all day long; her skin was dry and white with the dust, and we were forbidden to speak to her. While our ayah was finding the cycle-rickshaw, my mother lined us up and inspected us. My sisters were wearing their best frocks; I was in my newest and whitest shirt. My brother was coming with us, unusually. He was wearing his best shirt. We knew what this meant, and before we set off, my mother asked us to behave especially well. There were people coming to Nana's from the village. They were especially looking forward to seeing us, and we should not disappoint them by rolling in the mud, by saying that we were bored and could we watch the television, or by stuffing rice into our cheeks at the dinner table and pretending we were rats. That was always disgusting for other people, but it would be very disappointing for Nana's visitors to see us behaving in such a way. 'That was only Saadi,' my sister Sushmita said.

My sister Sunchita whispered into my ear, 'It's the witch who's coming,' when we were safely jammed into the cycle-rickshaw – our ayah had found a good one, polished silver with a big picture of a tiger on the back. 'It's her time of year to come.' The rickshaw driver fastened his blue cotton lungi between his hairy, bony knees, above the cycle crossbar, spat into the dry earth of the street, and we set off.

Our great-grandmother was called by Sunchita and me 'the witch' for no very good reason, except that she scared us. She was the last of the two widows of Nana's father. I could just about remember the other one, and what they had been like. They had lived together where they had always lived, in Nana's father's house in the village. Nana's father was the last person in the family who had married more than one woman; the question had never arisen afterwards, and now never would. The elder of the two had died when I was very small and, until then, they had come to see Nana once a year, around this time. The surviving one had carried on. Nana never travelled from Dacca to her village, although he sent small presents whenever any of his children went there in the summer. Nana always chose saris for her; he liked her to wear white saris with a thin band of colour, of blue or purple, at the edge, or sometimes a band of silver. (I could still remember her and the elderly senior wife, matching in their white and purple saris.) And the second one, the survivor, came to Dacca every year, in the summer, where she frightened, without knowing it, her great-grandchildren.

At Nana's house, everything was in a state of confusion. The gardener's boy was cleaning the car with a bucket of water; Atish was weeding the flowerbed. In the upper windows, great white birds appeared to be plunging in the half-light; beds were being changed and aired. My great-grandmother had arrived, and had found fault. The servants, who were used to their own ways, did not look forward to her visits any more than I did. Attention fell on her in unwelcome ways; attention was simultaneously taken from me, and neither of us enjoyed it.

We were led upstairs in our best clothes, and there in her room was my great-grandmother. The maid who always served her was already hard at work, brushing her hair; it was absolutely white – 'As white as snow,' I dreamily said to myself, a comparison from English books and not from experience. She could keep her maid hard at it all day long, going from one intimate task to another. While her hair was being brushed, she was at work preparing paan.

43

She had her own pestle and mortar for this, and would prepare paan to chew; sometimes Nani took some, out of politeness, to give her mother-in-law some company. She pounded away at the tiny red rubble in her wooden bowl, the wooden pestle long since stained as if with blood. Her task was like that of the woman stone-breaker outside her house, but fragrant, elegant, clean and beautiful. She did not trust or like preparations of paan that had been made by anyone else. She carried the ingredients round in small pouches, making it out of dried leaves, pebble-like substances, samples of mysterious red matter, all just as she liked it. Her pestle and mortar, as well as the wooden clogs she always wore that gave you warning of her approach, were somehow carried over from the senior wife. She seemed to be carrying out a dead woman's wishes, and she scared the life out of me.

We submitted to being kissed by a paan-smelling old mouth, and my mother reminded her who we were, and how old we were now. She seemed to take it all in, nodding over her stained moustaches. But then she immediately started explaining who had done what to whom in the village. She lived in a large property, given to both women by my grandfather, and she was the centre of village complaint and litigation. Everyone had always come to the pair of them with disputes, and nowadays she passed down the law without hesitation.

(Nana had a story about his mothers' intrusions. He told it endlessly. It seemed that a village couple had decided to give their new baby daughter a Western name, and had somehow heard of 'Irene'. Unexpectedly, the mother gave birth not to one daughter, but to a pair of twins, and the couple could not think of a suitable second name for some time. Then they were struck by inspiration, and decided to call the second daughter 'Urine'. This was one of the many occasions on which my great-grandmothers descended into the private lives of the villagers, and told them what they could not do, brooking no contradiction. Nana could never remember what the daughters were called in the end, with the agreement of his father's two wives.)

The stories of litigation and irritation reached their first pause, and the enquiries had run their course into how Zahid was growing up into a fine young man, and I would be a lawyer like my father and grandfather. My mother had gently reminded her that Sushmita and Sunchita would have their own professions, too. We were permitted to go downstairs, but only to sit quietly and to read a book, not to turn on the television, not to trouble the servants, and certainly not to go out and run in the garden, just underneath the window of Great-grandmother's room.

I wanted to see Piklu, my chicken, but I knew better than to disobey my mother when the witch was there. We filed downstairs and took up our books in the salon, sitting on two cream-and-brown sofas at right angles to each other, Sunchita reading a long sentimental novel, Sushmita a Feluda detective story, and my brother Zahid a physics textbook, which seemed to give him as much pleasure as anything. From time to time, Sunchita would sigh affectedly at some occurrence in her book, and even remark on an event that had moved her. I had my book, too, but I could not stay still. I thought of Piklu, out there; I did not know if he would come to greet me, or whether I would remain unforgiven for what Assad had done to him the previous weekend. Piklu changed from week to week, although now he was a proper, grown-up chicken, as big as his mother, and I did not want to be separated from him. From time to time I leapt up from the scratchy wool sofa, going to the window to see if I could see Piklu. But I could not. The other chickens were pottering about, pecking at the dirt as usual, but Piklu must have been inside the chicken coop, waiting for me to come.

8.

'Ah, children,' Mary-aunty said, coming into the salon. She, too, was wearing her best clothes, with a gold band down the edge of her sari. 'I hope you're all being good. Oh dear.' She fluttered, and left. In a moment Dahlia came in. She came straight to me, picked up the book I was reading from my lap and looked at the title. Ignoring the others, she gave me a kiss on my nose; she shook her head, and hurried out again.

The aunts came in, singly and in pairs, and found some reason to address me before leaving in an absent way. I could not account for it. My aunts had different favourites, and sometimes our own gestures of fondness were not returned; Sushmita had thought Nadira, with her dramatic entrances and her immaculate appearance, was marvellous, but Nadira, before she got married and went to Sheffield, was at best indifferent to the small, impressed offerings of gaze and giggle that Sushmita laid at her feet. Today every aunt came in and, one after another, stroked my head or called me a little sweetie. It was as if they wanted something from me. It was unusual in any circumstance: when Great-grandmother was there, making demands and criticizing the household, calling for people to brush her hair and listen to her stories, we children were used to being ushered into a quiet corner and expected to remain silent. The attention I was getting was pleasing, but unnerving. I wondered whether I was about to get a present.

'And he is studying at college now,' Great-grandmother said at table. She was talking about the son of a neighbour of theirs, a neighbour in the country. 'Studying to be an engineer. He has made a good success of his life. When you consider who his father is. There was constant trouble with his father. Running wild. And now he is going to Libya,' she finished, hunching over her plate.

'Fateh is going to Libya?' Nana said, puzzled. He remembered the farmer, his youth, running wild.

'Libya?' Era said.

'Not Fateh,' Great-grandmother said, her brilliant white hair combed back now. 'Fateh could never go to Libya. Fateh stays where he was born. His son, he is going to Libya. He is studying at college. Studying to be an engineer. And afterwards, he is going to Libya.'

46

There was a satisfied pause. The dining-room door swung open, and in came a succession of dishes, steaming hot. All at once, the table broke into conversation.

'Were you at your college today?' Dahlia called across to Pultoo-uncle.

'No, because—'

'And Mahmood had a great success today,' my mother called across to Nani, gesturing at my father who, in honour of a great-grandparent, had come, for once, to dinner on Friday.

'I'm so pleased for him,' Nani said. 'Era, did you hear what your sister was saying?'

'Yes, Mama,' Era said. 'A success, today . . . I was just about to say . . .'

It was mystifying. The lids of the dishes were taken off, in a shining line down the long table; the richest of the dishes before Nana. 'Good, good,' he said, poking in it with the serving spoon in his usual way; it was as if he suspected the most delicious parts to be always hidden deep in the dish. 'Good. Chicken.'

Around the table, there was a nervous little spasm of conversation, and I had the sense of aunt turning to aunt, and smiling shamefully at me. 'Do have some, Saadi,' Mary-aunty said. 'It's especially for your great-grandmother, since she has come all this way to see us.'

A horrible thought came to me. 'Where did the chicken come from?' I said to Nana. 'Nana, what is this chicken?'

But I had been shunted down a place by the arrival of my Great-grandmother, and he affected not to hear my shrill demand. 'Nana,' I said. 'Nana.'

'Quiet, Saadi,' Bubbly-aunty said, next to me. 'Don't scream in people's ears. It's a chicken from the garden, as usual.'

'Which one?' I said. 'Which chicken are we eating?'

'I really don't know,' Bubbly said. 'I really don't know the difference between one chicken and another. They'd be very happy, I'm sure, if they knew they were going to make such a lovely dinner for all of us. Now, I'm sure you're not going to be a bad little boy. I'm sure you're going to be a good little boy, and eat your dinner, aren't you?'

In my family, we did not leap up and push our chairs over; we did not scream and denounce our relations; we did not punch and pummel the servants, even the ones who had seized our pet chickens and put them in the pot without a second thought. We did not run howling out into the garden in search of our lost chickens. What we did was push the dish away when it came to us, and say, with murder in our voices, 'No, thank you. I don't care to eat a friend of mine.'

'What did he say?' Great-grandmother said.

'I didn't hear,' Nana said. 'Pay no attention, and everything will be quite all right.'

9.

I sat in mutinous silence all through dinner. I would not look at or answer my great-grandmother, for whose sake Piklu had been killed and eaten. I promised myself I would never speak to her again, not until she died like the other one, which would be soon. And when dinner was over, I gabbled out the formula asking for permission to get down from the table, and went swiftly out of the front door into the street. It was still light, and my shadow went before me as I walked, shivering and dancing like a puppet, making its own dance, as I tried to walk like a big man down the Dhanmondi street, trying my best to walk like a slave-owner, to walk as a talking car would walk, to walk down my grandfather's street like Hungry Bear.

3: Altaf and Amit

1.

The best place to watch what was happening in the street was from my grandfather's first-floor balcony. The houses in the street were fronted by high walls, dusted with green lichen, for security. But the balcony on the first floor was high enough to see over. From there, you could see visitors approaching. It might be a family member returning: Nana in his red Vauxhall, driven by Rustum, or my father in a cycle-rickshaw, laden with papers, or some aunts returning from a visit in the neighbourhood. As you negotiated your way between heavy jars of pickles, or slices of mango laid out on kula to dry, you could see if there was a war going on in the street between children of the neighbourhood. Sometimes, when I was very young I would see Sheikh Mujib sweep by in his big official car, with a policeman on a motorbike driving just before. And you knew that he was the prime minister of the country. I never forgot that sight.

Or there might be visitors. Mr Khandekar-nana came sometimes, simply, on foot, with his wife and a son or two. Pultoo-uncle's friends Kajol and Kanaq would arrive with their folders of art under their arms, sticking out from either side of a cycle-rickshaw. You could hear them arguing from a hundred yards away: they always turned up in a towering passion, appealing to anyone in the house to settle the dispute by taking one side or the other. From Nana's balcony, through the branches of the

49

tamarind tree, you could see all the way down the street to the left, and all the way down the street to the right. I spent hours up there, in the odour of spice and fruit drying in the open air, in the shade of the tamarind tree.

Some days, a sweet-seller would set up shop opposite Nana's house. He would make those yellow calligraphic sweets that look like a circular signature in Arabic; I loved to watch. First, he would take a bag of wet dough, then write quickly, a round and a squiggle and a zigzag, directly in the boiling yellow oil, then another one, then another. The sweets would coagulate, then bob to the surface. He would know exactly when to fish them out to drain on newspaper. And then he would start again. It was a little marvel of the street, across the wall at the front of Nana's house. I could have watched him all day.

I craned out, observing neighbours and guests and street-wallahs and unfamiliar figures; I got to know them from the way they walked, their usual belongings, the way they arrived in a rickshaw or a car or on foot. The most familiar of relatives looked unsure of themselves when surprised from up here, making their way down the public highway in Dhanmondi. Dahlia-aunty, for instance, so confident and cosy when going between Nana's salon and the kitchen, looked fretful, nervous, and unsure of herself when making her way out of the gate to walk a hundred yards to visit a neighbour. She revealed a different side of herself. Or perhaps that was just the way she looked from Nana's balcony.

On Saturday morning the cleaner came. You watched him approach from the far end of the street. He did not look at ease, or in the right street; he cringed as he walked even in the empty street, the walk of a man who had been hit too often. He came to do the heavy work that no one in the house would do, to clean the drains and the toilets. He was not Bengali, but Bihari; many of his type had left for Pakistan after 1971, but he was a poor Bihari, and had stayed to clean our drains. If you spoke to him, he answered in Urdu, the Pakistani language, cringing.

50

'Chota-sahib', he called me: little sir. It did not make me like him, though I understood that he wanted to make me his friend by abasing himself in that way. Years later I understood that I actually despised him. It was not a feeling I had had before, and I did not understand it when I was tiny. If you did not speak to him, he sang continuously: he always knew the latest Urdu pop song. As I say, I did not like him. On Saturdays, we got up early, before eight o'clock, because he was coming, and then there was nothing to do but go on to Nana's balcony and wait for his obsequious walk – he swayed from side to side, ready to bow to anyone.

But there were more welcome visitors, and ones I looked forward to. It was not always obvious why we would impatiently await their turn into the corner of road six, or what they had done to deserve our excitement. When we saw Nadira, after lunch, going to her room to fetch the harmonium, the tabla, and sometimes the sitar, we knew who was coming, and I went up to Nana's balcony to sit and stare at the corner of the road. Two figures turned the corner. One was very tall and thin, his head bald on top. Under his arm he carried two notebooks, and in the other hand, a black umbrella for when the sun grew too strong in the summer or against the rain in the wet season. The other was very short; he wore plenty of oil on his hair, and it would glint in the light. It was brushed close, immaculately.

These were Nadira's music teachers. They were not very well paid, and the trousers, long shirt and sandals that the shorter of the two wore were the only clothes I ever saw him in. They were soft and worn, and, if you looked closely, frayed at cuff and hem. All the same, they were both very clean – the short one very strikingly so, his white shirt brilliant in the sunlight from as far away as the corner of the street. I think he washed his shirt every night, pummelling away with soap and water and a stone, hanging it up to dry until the morning. He was the player of tabla. His colleague played the harmonium while Nadira sang. You could not help but think, as they hurried towards Nana's house, talking quietly and with a professorial air of respect to each other, that they were glad to be coming to teach her. And this was true. They were glad.

I was permitted to sit in on Nadira's lessons. She was a beautiful singer, and the two instrumentalists took more instruction from her than the other way round. She sang songs by Tagore, and more recent songs about the countryside in Bangladesh, too; they accompanied her on the fluting harmonium, the pattering little song of the tabla and if you looked out of the window, you could see that even the gardener was slowing his work and listening. The tabla player would often ask me to fetch him a glass of water before he began, and as a reward would let me try to play on his small tuned drums, to fetch a melody from them. But I never could, and quickly started to bang on them with my fists. Nadira would never put up with that. 'You're making a horrible noise. You can leave, or you can sit on the sofa and listen.' The harmonium player would never invite me to play on his instrument, with its odd flapping front; balding, tall and serious, he made no effort to befriend small boys. He would never say 'Chota-sahib' to a child, and I utterly respected him for it.

They would stay for two hours, accompanying Nadira. They would perform five or six songs. First they would play one through, then return and repeat a section. This was very dull. I would have preferred it if they had just performed their six songs, and then gone away, like a concert. But I understood that they had to practise. My aunt had the loveliest voice I ever heard, and she sang Bengali songs, by Nazrul as well as Tagore. She was quite a different person in these lessons, humble, respectful; she took comments and advice from the two musicians very easily. They seemed more like honoured guests in our house than people who were paid to teach my aunt. I always hoped that they would sing the song about the flower. It was my favourite.

The flower says,
'Blessed am I,
Blessed am I

52

On the earth . . .'
The flower says,
'I was born from the dust,
Kindly, kindly,
Let me forget it,
Let me forget it,
Let me forget.
There is nothing of dust inside me,
There is no dust inside me,'
So says the flower.

They would come to the end of their two hours. Once I had settled, I could listen very happily for all that time, so long as there was more playing than rehearsing, as I thought of it. Nadira would offer them a cup of tea, or a glass of water, and they would accept. If there were other people in the house, at this point they came to greet them. My family knew and respected both of the musicians, from many years back, and so did Khandekar-nana's family. The tall musician would give an imperceptible sign to the short tabla player. They would get up and go. That was the end of their lesson. The whole family came to the door to say goodbye to them.

2.

In 1965 Altaf Ali was twenty-nine years old, and Amit Mukhopadhyay was twenty-eight. They shared a flat in a block owned by Mrs Khandekar, the wife of my grandfather's best friend.

They had met in the following way. The radio station in Dacca held concerts of Bengali music every Saturday night. The programme was very popular, and had resisted all attempts so far to remove it from the air. A large roster of Dacca musicians supplied the regular basis of the listeners' pleasure. It was not always possible for musicians to play, however, in established pairings and groupings. Listeners would find their admired musicians combining in unfamiliar and unprecedented ways. This was one of the appealing things of the programme: the sense, like Bengali street life, that you never knew who you might hear talking together.

Sometimes a sitar player would arrive without his regular partner on tabla. Sometimes a tabla player would say he had no idea what had happened to a harmonium player. Musicians are not the most reliable class of people, and if at worst they could be drunkards and gamblers by inclination, at best they were always open to a better offer from others. When a musician failed to turn up at the recording studio, he had often been offered a well-paid job at the wedding of a rich man's daughter. The radio programme commanded a large audience. But it could not compete with the fees possible when accompanying a famous singer at a lavish Dacca wedding. The producers understood this. They were always ready to match up instrumentalists and singers who had only a small acquaintance. The musicians were ready, in their turn, not to make difficulties about this, although in practice the performances that were broadcast sometimes came close to catastrophe.

Altaf and Amit met each other in just such a way. Altaf was expecting to see the same tabla player he had been playing with for the previous three years. But the producer came into the musicians' room – a crowded, cramped room in the old British barracks that the radio station used. (The recording studio next door had its windows muffled with blankets and the door reinforced; still, some noises and voices of the city tended to seep into the programmes that were broadcast.) He hailed Altaf, and looked about the room. 'This is Amit Mukhopadhyay,' he said wildly. He was always in a hurry, referring frequently to the big black-bound book in which the logistical details of bookings and commitments were entered. 'He'll be playing with you today.' Then the producer disappeared, without once looking up from the bound volume, or even over the top of his half-moon glasses.

Altaf had not noticed the man. Now he looked at him: he was short but well turned out. His shirt and trousers were very clean, and his hair was neatly brushed, with a tidy parting that drew a white line on his scalp. His face gave the impression of liveliness, without actually engaging to the point of saying anything. Altaf greeted him; the short man greeted him back. They quickly discussed the music. Altaf explained the mode he would be using, and two or three other details about how he liked things to begin, and how to conclude. If the tabla player was good, that would be enough for him. It was all a matter of quick-wittedness, improvisation and response. A bad musician simply played. A good one listened as he played. A very good one would anticipate.

Sometimes a new friend slips into your life unobtrusively, as if you have been walking quietly along when out from a doorway steps a familiar easy presence. He makes a brief remark in greeting, and falls companionably into the rhythm of your stride, so that you hardly remember what it was like to walk alone. So it was with Altaf and Amit. Once they were in the studio, and they started to play the evening song, with Altaf leading, they were attuned to and easy in each other's musical company. There were none of those false starts and assertive blunders that unfamiliar pairings often made, and practised musicians knew how to conceal. Instead, there was a considerate listening presence. Amit's playing was, as it were, full of himself: not in a bumptious or assertive way, just as an egg holds meat. It was simply full of a strong flavour, which was Amit's personality. His playing was free and lucid, complicated, but easy and interesting to follow. There was now a little hesitation, like the lyric breath at the brink of a sneeze, as Amit hung fire before plunging into a decisive monsoon-patter; then there was a rapturous run between tones, without hesitation. All the time Amit's playing was full of pensive thought and possibility. Altaf felt that those pauses and falterings, like a bird cocking its head and waiting between flourishes of flight, came from Amit's listening to Altaf's harmonium. A musician as good as Amit would have been as good with most competent partners. But Altaf could not help taking their broadcast that afternoon as a compliment. And performing to the ear of so good and attentive a partner, Altaf could hear his own musical lines grow more flexible, inward and fantastic. He could not imagine, after ten minutes, how he had ever endured such a thudding banger as Mohammed, his usual partner, which, apparently, he had done week after week until now. After the recording, Amit was flushed and cheerful, although not much more talkative. They found themselves walking in the same direction.

3.

Altaf had five younger brothers still living at home. He had to share a bedroom with the thirteen-year-old and the seven-year-old. He could not remember ever having had a room of his own, although when he was born, for the three years when he was not just the eldest but the only one, he must have lived in such a way. Now, the bedroom had to serve for everything – not just for his brothers' homework, which they did kneeling on the floor before an old gateleg table intended to support a teacup or two, but his harmonium practice, too. He kept his instrument on a high shelf where his brothers could not get at it. His brothers regarded his harmonium as a toy, and not as the tool of his trade. He practised when they were at school, and put it away out of reach before their return. Every Saturday, he polished the rosewood case with beeswax. He believed it improved the tone.

There was no point in remonstrances with his mother and father. There was no more space in the house to be had. He supposed that he would find a place of his own when he married. But he was poor and did not have the means to marry, and wives expected children, so there would not be any time in which he could live and play in peace. Altaf accepted all of this.

Amit had come to Dacca from Chittagong to play the tabla. He had no other skills. He did not want to do anything else. He did not come from a rich family. (That was how he put it, walking along with Altaf, another recording session over.) But he was making some headway for himself and would progress in life, he believed. He taught, during the week, in a boys' school, an hour's bus ride away from where he lived in a quiet way with an old Dacca aunt of his father's, a widow. There was not enough work to allow him to teach the boys music only; he had to teach them the rudiments of Bengali poetry, too. That was no hardship. The boys were good, intelligent and lively. He sometimes found it hard to keep discipline. Once, an older master who was conducting a class next door had stepped in to ask what the meaning of the unholy bedlam could possibly be.

(Amit, without making any obvious effort, was a good mimic. Altaf laughed at the vividness of the impression, though he did not know the man.)

That had not been pleasant, Amit went on. And naturally, afterwards, the boys had been still harder to keep under control. But it was a good school, and Amit had been lucky to be taken on as a junior master, teaching the boys music and poetry. He taught them to sing Bengali songs, often famous songs by Atulprasad, Tagore and Nazrul, and talked to them about other poets and writers of Bengal. They read the work of these writers together. When the boys were interested and quietened down to listen, they were good students. Amit considered himself very lucky to be able to teach in such a good school, yes he did, and he did not think the daily journey too much. There were neighbours of his aunt who travelled two or three hours every day to go to their place of work. And the other masters were reasonable people.

They stopped at a pavement sandesh-seller; the sweets were all of the same stuff, but shaped in different ways. Some people had their favourite shapes. Altaf did not, but now, talking to Amit, he found himself hovering, unable to decide which shape of sandesh they would settle on and share.

Amit reached the end of his account of his circumstances, and ate a sweet. He had one of those faces which, in movement or in conversation – even when he was working up to saying something – looked open, innocent and trusting. When he sank deep into thought, it looked quite different; it could take on a furrowed, even rather angry appearance. Altaf had known him for almost a year before he realized that the positive way in which he spoke about his circumstances did not reflect an optimistic personality. Instead, Amit spoke well of his bestial pupils and insulting colleagues because he did not trust anyone. He believed that a bad word might get back, and he spoke guardedly, even to Altaf. When he stopped speaking, his face grew dark; he looked on the verge of shouting in rage. And then he ate his sweet with open, boyish enjoyment, and looked quite trusting again.

Altaf was from a Muslim family; Amit was a Hindu. His aunt had a small corner in her flat devoted to some of her gods. Altaf believed that this trait of Amit's – his inability to trust people, or think that anything was for the best in the end – came ultimately from his family's religion. He did not say so.

It was hard for Amit to be honest when things had gone wrong in his life. His problems with his flat had been going on for weeks, for instance, before he mentioned them to Altaf. He mentioned them in such a closed and quiet way that Altaf would hardly have realized at first that they were problems at all, if he had not known Amit quite well by then. They were walking along in Old Dacca on their way to meet a possible new singer.

'I may be moving into a new place,' Amit remarked out of the blue.

'Why? I thought you and your aunt were quite settled together.'

'I thought so too,' Amit said. 'But it appears I have been living in a fool's paradise, all things considered.'

'In what way?'

'My aunt has told me that she has had enough of living in Dacca,' Amit said. 'I can't blame her. It is no place for a widow to grow old. Only last month, a rude child called something out to her in the street. It upset her for days. And then there are the Pakistani soldiers. They searched her shopping sack once.'

Altaf believed that sort of thing happened to nearly everyone, and had heard, before, of these two incidents. Amit had mentioned them twice: his aunt, Altaf believed, talked of very little else. 'Still,' he said, 'she has you to look out for her, doesn't she? You wouldn't move out unless you had to.'

'She talks about when I get married, when I leave her alone – then how will she cope?' Amit said. 'I have told her many times that I am not in a position to get married, and if I ever do, I will make sure that a younger brother of mine would come from Chittagong to take my place. She is a wonderful woman. I wish you could meet her.'

Altaf had his own views on this matter. 'But what has changed?'

'Her son wrote to her from Cox's Bazar, and suggested that she come and live with him in her declining years,' Amit said. 'He has told her about the healthful sea air and his beautiful house, and the peace and quiet. He is a very generous man, I know.'

'He is worried that she is going to die and leave her money to you,' Altaf said. 'That is why he is making this invitation. I have heard about this man before.'

'Well, she ought to bequeath him her widow's mite,' Amit said. 'That would be the right thing to do. I really don't blame him, and I can see why she wants to go and live with him. But that is not the problem.'

'What is the problem?' Altaf said. 'Something is worrying you.'

'It seems very silly,' Amit said apologetically. 'But I don't know where I am going to live.'

'Why can't you take over the lease of the flat where you are living? Is it too expensive?'

'No, not at all,' Amit said. 'The landlord is really very reasonable. The rent is a good one, all things considered, and I think I could pay it. Unfortunately, my aunt never really got round to telling him that I was living there and paying rent for the spare room. So he never knew that anyone else was in the flat. How could he, if you think about it? I went to him, and explained the situation to him, and asked if he could consider me as the tenant after my aunt gave notice. I set out how very reasonable it would be for him – he would not have to struggle to find a new tenant, he would not have to ask people, or take anyone on trust. He would have the same tenant he had had for the last three years. I put it to him like that.'

'And what did he say?'

Amit looked up at the sky; he looked down at the road. A cart loaded with old books, pulled by a bent man crying out, 'Mind, mind,' separated the pair of them for a moment. When they came together again, Amit had failed to produce any kind of positive interpretation to put on his landlord's reply.

'I am sorry to say he told me to be out of the flat with the rest of my aunt's rubbish,' Amit said. 'Those were his words.'

'He can't do that,' Altaf said.

'He can do what he likes with his flat,' Amit said. 'I don't know where I am to live. I think I will have to go back to Chittagong.'

'No, no,' Altaf said. He looked at Amit. To his surprise, there were tears in his friend's eyes. No one, after all, likes to be removed from their house at a time not of their choosing. 'I know exactly who to speak to.'

4.

For eighteen years, Altaf and his family had lived in Dacca, and all his brothers, except two, had been born there. But his family had not always lived in Dacca. His mother and father had married in another part of Bengal, but one which was now part of India. They had made the decision, in 1947, to leave the settlement fifty miles outside Calcutta and go to the new country of Pakistan.

They went to the eastern division, where the largest city in the region was Dacca. Not all of their relations had done the same thing. Altaf still had cousins who lived in Calcutta, who had not been killed in the mob violence and rioting. They owned a tailor's shop around the corner from the American consulate, in a very respectable part of the city, or so Altaf believed.

Altaf had been ten. He remembered bundling under the seat in the train, that one time, clutching his six-year-old brother and holding his mouth shut. His mother and father remained in their seats, holding the baby his mother had not known how to surrender; she made little gulps and gasps as the train juddered to a halt. Who had stopped the train? Everyone knew what happened to the passengers in trains bound for Pakistan, in 1947: the trains were stopped by murderous gangs, and the gangs killed all those inside. That was why his mother had pushed him and his brother underneath the seats. The gang that had stopped this train might murder his mother and father, but they would not think to look under the seats, and Altaf and his brother, alone, could make a new life in Pakistan. She had not known how to surrender the baby she held. Altaf's blood ran cold to think of the sacrifice she would have made, and at the thought that it would not have worked. The Hindu gangs knew how to look under a train seat.

It had not been a Hindu gang of murderers, but a party of soldiers. They had actually stopped and boarded the train to protect the passengers from gangs further up the line. That terrible journey had finally come to an end, the five of them in a strange city with no possessions but alive. Much later, Altaf had realized that many people had not made the journey in the same way they had. He wondered what had happened to most of the boys he had known at the madrasa and the mosque in the small town outside Calcutta. They had been planning to leave with their families as well, and to make the journey to the new country. Some had arrived; some had stayed. But there were also some who had been killed, as everyone knew, and others whose end had not been discovered.

Altaf's father had made his way in Dacca: he was a small book-seller for college students. He spoke of himself as a Paragraph-wallah; most of his business was selling volumes of Paragraphs, small essays in the English language that every schoolchild had to write sooner or later. It was a good, steady business, down in Old Dacca, not far from the ferry terminal, a back-street business where no schoolmaster would find his way. When the wind blew in the wrong direction, the stink from the nearby tanneries made the atmosphere for learning in the back-street unendurable. Generations of schoolboys went there, and turned in the same Paragraphs, year after year, with the same mistakes. The family business gave Altaf a respect for Amit's profession; it also gave him some sense of connection with the sort of people who read and thought.

Among those who had, like Altaf and his family, reached Dacca alive was the son of the most important landowner in the village. He had sacrificed a great deal. He had been a lawyer in Calcutta, whose name was Mr Khandekar. Because of the position his father held in Murshidabad, Altaf's family were accustomed to approach Mr Khandekar on any question of law or of business. He had always helped them, and always would.

It was interesting and strange to Altaf that Amit did not have such a person in his life. He seemed entirely vulnerable and friendless. The only lawyers he seemed to know, or know of, were the broken-down ones who sat by the courthouse with ancient typewriters balanced on planks on their knees, saying, 'Affidavit, sir?' to anyone who passed by. Altaf's heart went out to him: he decided that he would take charge of Amit's problem. He was sure that the landlord could not, in fact, evict Amit from the flat he had lived in for three years without any problem, and that Mr Khandekar would bring about a happy conclusion. His only concern was whether Amit, as he said, could really afford the rent of the whole flat. It was possible that Amit would make this claim to Altaf, without it being true, to save face. If the flat were awarded to him, Amit might himself need to take in a lodger.

5.

Mr Khandekar lived in a wealthy part of Dacca, where Amit and Altaf had rarely, if ever, been. They had planned to get there early in the morning, so as not to intrude on Mr Khandekar's day, and so that it would be more likely that he would be at home. Altaf, in explaining about Mr Khandekar to Amit, had stressed how important and busy he was in his law practice. Perhaps he had overdone it. The night before, Amit had interrupted Altaf's explanation: 'Let's not bother him. I'm sure I will be perfectly all right. There are plenty of places to live. I don't think I have a leg to stand on.' But Altaf explained that Mr Khandekar would be very helpful, so long as they arrived at his house early enough and did not interrupt his working day. He was the most important person Altaf knew.

But they were not very familiar with Dhanmondi, where Mr Khandekar lived. They got off the bus on Mirpur Road, which circled the district, and it pulled away. The servants, drivers and other unimportant people who had got off the bus at the same time scattered swiftly in every direction. Altaf had been to Mr Khandekar's house before, and had thought he would be able to find it easily. But in fact they had got off the bus half a mile too soon, in their nervousness. It took half an hour of doubling backwards and forwards to discover the direction in which the wide, leafy avenues were numbered, and an hour beyond that to find road number twenty. That was the road in which Mr Khandekar's house lay. In this district, there were few people about, and none to ask for directions. In Altaf's part of Dacca, a request for help would pull a small crowd, eager to explain that the goal of the journey was beyond the mosque, down the small road behind Suleiman's hardware store and so on. Here, the only people to ask were scurrying ayahs or servants, late for their tasks, slipping behind high white walls. From time to time a large car murmured down the centre of the road, and behind a shining window, a small face inspected Altaf and Amit, unfamiliar figures in this rich and green-shaded neighbourhood.

It was quite late in the morning when they found Mr Khandekar's house. The gate was ajar, and they pushed it open nervously. From the white-painted square house, the noise of a discussion was going on and, somewhere deeper in the house, the clamour and clang of cooking pots. They stood under the dense shade of the large mango tree at the entrance. 'We should go in,' Amit said. 'Or knock on the door.'

'I can't remember,' Altaf said. 'There might be an entrance at the back. For clients.'

But Amit walked forward, quite boldly, and pushed a button to the side of the door. Inside the house, a bell rang – an electric two-note song. The door was opened almost immediately, and behind was Mr Khandekar – Altaf recognized him. He was obviously going out: he was wearing a black suit and a white shirt, and was struggling with a white cambric stock at his throat. His collar was detached, and flying away like the wing of a bird: it was clear that Mr Khandekar was trying to do everything in the wrong order. 'Salaam,' he said, fumbling with the stock. 'Good morning to you.'

'Sir,' Altaf said, 'if this is an inconvenient time—'

'Please, introduce yourselves,' Mr Khandekar said. Altaf did so, reminding Mr Khandekar of his family, and of his knowledge of his father's family, his respect for Mr Khandekar's father. 'Thank you, thank you,' Mr Khandekar said. 'I don't have the time to see you now. Come in, walk with me.'

They went into the dark wooden hallway of Mr Khandekar's house and followed him through the salon into a room lined with books. 'Explain, explain,' Mr Khandekar said, as he walked. He had given them each one assessing look, from top to bottom, at the front door. But then he had averted his eyes and talked to them without looking, rummaging about in the drawers of his desk, pulling out a paper from a pile, picking up a clever neat little stud to hold his white collar down and pushing it into a hole, somewhere at the back of his neck. 'Explain, explain,' Mr Khandekar said, picking up a second collar stud and getting to work with it.

Altaf stood in front of this furious activity, and started to explain about his friend, his friend's aunt, the nephew in Cox's Bazar, the will and the legacy, the spare room, the terms of the lease—

'Explain, explain,' Mr Khandekar said. 'I can't find the last collar stud. It must be here. Explain, explain.'

Altaf explained about Amit, how his aunt's landlord had known perfectly well that he was living there but now chose to say that he was flabbergasted to discover it, and that Amit wanted to stay on there, but the landlord's view was that—

'There it is,' Mr Khandekar said, with relief, pouncing on a small silver stud, like a chicken on a seed. 'Now I can go. Come with me.'

Altaf had feared they were about to be ejected – Mr Khandekar seemed so busy and unconcerned. But he knew that great men were not as you expected. He had expected that they would be asked to wait in an antechamber, rather than following Mr Khandekar about his house as he dressed. Mr Khandekar had his own ways, and he had been listening to them in his own fashion. He had been friendly, manly, and would now be helpful. Altaf had stumbled over the story, but Mr Khandekar had followed its disorganized path and had made sense of it, and now he would present them with a solution. Mr Khandekar led them out of his study. He paused at a looking glass in the salon, and with one hand smoothed down his greying hair; he licked the tips of the forefinger and thumb on his left hand and, in a gesture Altaf half knew, half remembered as being characteristic, wiped them across his eyebrows in a single opening gesture. 'Come with me,' he said again. They followed him across the crowded salon, stepping cautiously between little tables and low stools, and through the hallway. Mr Khandekar stopped at a closed door, knocked briefly and pushed it open.

65

'I don't have time for this,' he said. 'Two fellows from the village.' He turned to Altaf. 'What did you say your name was? A problem with accommodation. Talk to them. See if you can do anything. I have to be off. I'm fearfully late. How are you, Nadira? Always a pleasure.'

He turned swiftly, in his immaculate black-and-white dress, the white stock now quickly tied and beautifully neat at his throat. There was genuine warmth in the greeting or, Altaf supposed, the farewell to the girl. 'I always like to see old friends from the village,' he said. 'Always, always. Explain everything to my wife – she is the true power in this house. She can do so much more for you than I can, believe me.' The front door opened anonymously, smoothly, and in front of the house, under the mango tree, a car stood idling. A driver was waiting for Mr Khandekar.

'Goodbye, goodbye,' Mr Khandekar said. 'Always a pleasure.'

6.

Mrs Khandekar was a tiny woman, dressed enchantingly in a pink sari and a single simple necklace. The room she came to the door of was also pink, and lit by the light of the morning sun, coming through the leaves of the tree outside. It was a graceful, charming room, with two Chinese vases on either end of a teak sideboard, the sofa and armchairs upholstered in pale green silk. On the low teak and glass table was a tray with tea things on it, a blue-and-white Chinese set, and a plate of sweet biscuits arranged in a little fan. In the small brown vase on the table, a branch of fruit blossom.

Mrs Khandekar had a guest. She was a girl of perhaps fifteen, who craned her head at the visitors as Mrs Khandekar rose and went to speak to Amit and Altaf at the door. The girl sat very upright, and her hair was arranged in an upwards style. She sat as if aware of the way she would be looked at. Mr Khandekar had called her Nadira.

'I am so sorry about my husband,' Mrs Khandekar said, smiling. 'He is always in such a rush. But perhaps I can help you? You are an old friend of Mr Khandekar's father, I think?'

Altaf explained. Standing at the door to Mrs Khandekar's sitting room, he found it came out in a much more orderly way. Amit's problem seemed to unfold to an easy, elegant, listening audience. Amit stood, listening to Altaf's explanation with a furrowed brow.

When Altaf had finished, Mrs Khandekar said, 'I see. It happens to many people, that sort of thing. But do you think your friend's landlord is at all likely to change his mind? He sounds quite set in his decision.'

'He doesn't want me to stay in the flat,' Amit said, speaking for the first time. 'I'm sure he has his own good reasons.'

'I don't think anyone can force him to rent his flat to someone, once he has made his mind up,' Mrs Khandekar said. 'It is unfortunate, but there it is.'

She looked at them, levelly and not without kindness.

'I'm sorry to have troubled you in your home,' Altaf said after a moment, lowering his head.

'But what would you hope for, at the end of all this?' Mrs Khandekar said. 'Don't think about how you would achieve it but what you actually want.'

'Somewhere to live,' Altaf said. 'Merely somewhere to live.'

'Mrs Khandekar,' the girl in the pink sitting room said – her voice was low and melodious, and she had an air of adult confidence about her. 'Excuse me, Mrs Khandekar. What about—'

'This is Nadira,' Mrs Khandekar said. 'The daughter of a very old friend of my husband's, come to visit and take a cup of tea in the morning. It is so kind of her to drop in like this.'

Altaf and Amit bowed in her direction. 'And now,' Mrs Khandekar said, 'I wonder if the best thing for me to do is not to start telling you about lawyers and law courts and the laws relating to landlords and their tenants, but just to try to help you to find somewhere to live. After all, that is all you want, I believe?'

'That was just what I was going to say,' the girl said.

67

Mrs Khandekar, she said, owned a block of flats in Old Dacca. They had belonged to her father before her, and he had left them to her. They were nice flats – a little old-fashioned, perhaps, but in good order, well looked after and in a very respectable, quiet neighbourhood.

'What are your professions, gentlemen?' Mrs Khandekar said.

Altaf let Amit say, 'Schoolmaster,' which at least sounded regular and respectable.

Somehow, it seemed to be established in Mrs Khandekar's mind that the two of them were looking for a flat together, and he found himself saying, 'I am a musician,' adding for good measure, 'I play on the radio,' and going on to explain the Saturday-evening programme on which he was a regular.

'How delightful!' Mrs Khandekar said, with real warmth, clapping her hands together in pleasure. 'My husband and I never miss it. We must *listen out* for you.' She used an English expression.

There were some landlords who would be put off by the idea of musicians, but Mrs Khandekar was not one of them. In fact, once she had discovered that Amit was not just a schoolmaster but also a musician – 'A famous musician,' she flatteringly said – it appeared to act as a recommendation and a passport. She asked them into her sitting room, and offered them a seat and a cup of tea. Before long, it had emerged that Nadira, the assured and dignified girl on the sofa, liked to sing and, after a little more conversation, they had agreed to come to her house to teach her, the next free afternoon. In half an hour, everything seemed to have been arranged, and Mrs Khandekar had told them where to meet her the next morning to look at a flat in the block that had become vacant in recent weeks. 'It is rather small, I am afraid,' she said apologetically. 'You must say at once if it does not suit you.'

But of course it would suit them. Altaf thought of his bedroom at home, with the rosewood harmonium placed beyond his brothers' reach, the noise and the stolen half-hours between hours of chaos. He thought of a door that he could close and a life of his own. Amit's face showed that, from the beginning, he had considered Altaf a part of his plans for living. Altaf's heart swelled at the kindness of his friend, and at the degree of understanding between them that went without words.

7.

'I've been to see the hall at the university,' Altaf said.

It was a year later, and they had been very happily ensconced in Mrs Khandekar's apartment, just the two of them. It suited them perfectly. It was on the third floor of an old building, and the streets that ran in front of and to the side of it were quiet ones. This was in the furniture-makers' quarter, and all day long the streets were crowded with bed frames, like brown grazing cows. The smell of wood-shavings perfumed the air; the day was filled with the sounds of honest labour. In the corner of the sitting room, Amit's mattress was rolled up and tied: he unrolled it every night when Altaf went to the bedroom. The flat was quite dark, with its small windows, but it suited them both and they were happy there. The musical instruments and the copies of music, including 'Githo Bitan' by Tagore, were on a shelf in the bedroom. In the sitting room there was a radio they had bought together, which they referred to as 'our radio'. They had always battened on to the radios of others – an aunt's, a mother's – and it was a pleasure to share one instead. There was a portrait of Tagore tacked to the wall of the sitting room, and in each room, a kerosene lamp for when, as now, the electricity failed. Altaf and Amit were sitting by the light of the kerosene lamp on the floor of their small apartment. Mrs Khandekar's apartment had a table, but they often preferred to sit on the floor to eat. Before them, lay plates of rice, fish and dal, cooked by Amit on the kerosene stove. Altaf and Amit were steadily rolling up the food into balls with the fingers of one hand, and eating them in one gulp. Their dark fingers glistened in the warm light with grains of rice.

'What hall?' Amit said, after a pause.

'It will be for singers, for writers, for scholars like the professor, and for musicians. It can be a place for everyone to meet, and for people to share their knowledge of the Bengali traditions. It will be wonderful, Amit. There are so many people who are interested.'

Amit stopped. 'They won't permit it,' he said. 'The government.'

'They won't have any choice,' Altaf said.

'They tried to make everyone write in their script,' Amit said. 'They'll try again. They don't like us singing our own songs. They'll respond if Bengalis start gathering to sing their songs and read their poetry and show their paintings.'

'They needn't know anything about it,' Altaf said, with bravado.

'Oh, yes?' Amit said, quite mildly. 'Do you think there's nobody at the university in the pay of the police? They probably already know about the whole plan.'

'Well,' Altaf said, 'if they already know, we might as well continue with it.'

'Oh, yes,' Amit said. 'We might as well continue.'

This conversation took place just when memories of previous suppressions were fading, and people like Altaf and Amit were making their plans.

Nadira, who was my Nadira-aunty, had been taking music lessons from them for a year, ever since they had met her at Mrs Khandekar's house. There was even talk of Nadira going on the radio and singing with them, on a Saturday afternoon. They sang classic songs, and read Bengali poetry together, and loaned each other novels in Bengali. There were classics, and new novels: everyone adored *Sangshaptak* when it came out, and soon Shahidullah Kaiser was a regular presence at the little group. After a few weeks, Nadira had introduced the two musicians to her sisters and even to her smallest brother, the eight-year-old Pultoo; after a few weeks more, her father – my nana – came in and greeted them. There was always a great respect for culture in my family, and from the beginning, Nana and Nani treated Nadira's music teachers not as servants and lowly tutors, although of course they were paid to come, but as honoured guests.

In time, friends of Nadira asked if Altaf and Amit could come to teach them music, too. There was soon almost more teaching than they could cope with, and they grew to know the numbered streets of Dhanmondi very well, and wondered how they could ever have got so lost that first morning, when they had tried to find their way to Mr Khandekar's house. There was even talk, at one point, of them being introduced to the household of Sheikh Mujib himself: Sheikh Hasina, his daughter, was said to have enquired about them of a friend. Nothing came of that, though they did see Sheikh Mujib and his daughter occasionally at the sort of gatherings in Dhanmondi where they sometimes played to an audience. They did have half a dozen regular visits to pay, and that was more or less the limit of what they could achieve.

The respectable and quiet streets of Dhanmondi had become

fervently enthusiastic about the culture of the Bengalis. Behind the walls of many houses, conversations continued late into the night. Conversations about writers, artists, musicians, poets. Once the gates were shut against the outside world, against neighbours who could not be trusted, against the policemen in the streets and the laws of an alien people, households in Dhanmondi relaxed, and started to talk, and to listen to girls like Nadira-aunty singing a song as Altaf played the harmonium and sang too, and Amit's palms and fingers pattered like rain on the tabla next to them.

> The flower says,
> 'Blessed am I,
> Blessed am I
> On the earth . . .'

Institutions started to open up. A school might decide to hold an exhibition of paintings on Bengali themes by its pupils – Pultoo was, at ten, the star of one of these exhibitions. At parties, the girls of the family might dance to the sitar and the harmonium; in other households, a member of the family might recite their own poetry. In Dhanmondi, on summer afternoons, families went from household to household, taking their music with them. Fifteen years before, the occupying Pakistani forces had tried to suppress the language of Bengal, and to force all in the province to write in an unfamiliar and alien script. (My own parents had demonstrated against this, in 1952, and had been thrown together into police cells; it was a happy and a romantic memory for them.) Now, in the last years of the 1960s, the Pakistani policemen stood around menacingly, and everyone knew who, in the neighbourhood, had been an informer, and probably still was one. Nothing seemed to matter. The Bengalis went from house to house with joyous abandon.

Among them were Altaf and Amit, who were universally welcome, and Nadira and her sisters; there were Nana and Nani and Mr and Mrs Khandekar; there was, too, Sheikh Mujib, whom you could see everywhere, on his way to forging a new country in the fires of his soul. He was the leader of a political party; his daughter was the one who had fretted and raged to my mother about the two missing bags of chilli. He lived under the constant threat of imprisonment, and sometimes he was trailed for days by the police, who sat endlessly in a car outside his house, a hundred yards away from Mr Khandekar. Sheikh Mujib came to these parties when he could; he said it made him glad to hear the songs of the Bengali. He made no particular fuss when he entered a room as a guest; still, he was who he was, and the room was drawn towards his big glossy hair, his plump, humorous look. The room stood up at his entrance: he would force a friend, perhaps a distinguished poet, to sit down again, before him. A special place was made for him, and perhaps for his daughter, Hasina, too. He would accept the special place while, all the time, protesting mildly with his hands. You never knew who you would meet at one of these parties. The gates stood open, and almost everyone was welcome.

It was after one of these parties that the idea had been raised for a school that would teach the Bengali arts; not just gatherings, but an institution. Sheikh Mujib had heard, and said it was a wonderful idea, and so it had to be done. Khandekar, who could speak to Sheikh Mujib quite naturally, as an equal, volunteered to discover whether the university could find some place or other for it. Speaking, again quite naturally, as an equal, to Altaf, he asked him quietly if he could talk to a professor of Bengali he named to discuss the matter. 'Quite hush-hush for the moment,' he said. 'I know I can trust you, Altaf.'

Altaf did not feel he was in a position to refuse Khandekar anything. The parties they played at were so nice. You had a feeling of something quite new starting up in everyone's lives, as afternoon faded into evening and the tea-lights in the garden were lit, the manservants going silently with their tapers from lantern to lantern. Altaf made a small gesture with his head. He would go and ask the professor for the loan, once a week, of some rooms in the Curzon Hall at the university, and make himself useful to Khandekar.

In the early evening, in a crowded room, the song began. The room fell silent.

4: A Journey in the Dry Season

1.

My father lived where he worked. His chambers were attached to the flat where we – my parents, my sisters, my brother and I – lived. The flat was even more crowded than my grandfather's house. In both of them, transitory residents gave them the air of slight chaos, but at Nana's house, at least Nana always knew who they all were – cousins from the village, brothers of his driver or gardener, dependants of his two mothers – and could explain who any stranger was. My father had strangers of this sort and, like Nana, employed vulnerable people – my ayah and the boy who served his chambers. He put up with their dependants in turn. But most of the crowds in our flat were clients: belligerent, impatient, wronged and sometimes rather smelly.

The antechamber to my father's chambers was quite full. It was a dark room, with only one window looking out on to a blank wall where a building had been put up a year ago; it had been painted a light yellow colour in a not very successful attempt to lighten the mood. Outside office hours, it was not a place to linger: there were twenty mismatched chairs about a central table, a desk and a seat for the clerk, and nothing much else, except some files and a short bookcase, a black cashbox on the top shelf behind the clerk underneath the Supreme Court Calendar. In office hours, there was nothing to do but linger, and most of the time it was full. The first noise of the morning was the ring on the doorbell by the first client: it almost always woke us. Soon after that, the sick chatter of the clerk's typewriter would begin, and continue all day. My father worked hard, at any aspect of law he could think of – criminal law, property law, tax law, family law – and his clients kept him busy.

It was not always as full as it was that afternoon. The clients, as usual, would have been what I thought of as 'poor people' – people who came to a lawyer's office in long shirts and loose pyjama trousers, or with lungis wrapped about their middle and their legs. They were people who did not even think of putting on shoes other than sandals or chappals. Their disputes and feuds were endless, and a steady source of income for my father. They were not, in fact, as I thought of them, poor. When the time came to pay, they would delve meditatively into the depths of their lungis, brightly eyeing the clerk as he turned, with his invoice before him, for the cashbox; what they produced was a fist solid with banknotes, held by a rubber band or a bulldog clip, as thick as a cream roll. Somehow all this money had been concealed in their lungis' waistband, in some miracle of knotting known only to country landlords. They knew what they were about, those landlords and rentiers and farmers from the country, wearing their dusty sandals to their lawyer's chambers. They respected my father, who had no snobbery about the clients he would take. He respected them too, treating them with an honour that might have been due to zamindars, and not just for the thick roll of banknotes they brought out to pay his fees.

The waiting room was quite full, and three clients were standing in the doorway of the chambers. The boy had brought round cups of tea on a tray, several times. 'How long now?' one man with a huge dyed-red beard called out to the clerk, sitting behind his desk, cowering a little at his typewriter. By this time of the day, the room was dense with smoke – the waiting clients and, between invoices and briefs, the clerk smoked steadily through the day their strong-smelling K2 and Captain's cigarettes.

'Advocate-sahib is busy,' the clerk said. 'But he will see

everybody today. It may take a little longer than usual, gentlemen. But a little patience, a little patience.'

Somewhere outside the room, in the domestic parts of the flat, a noise: a door slamming, a child shouting, another child calling for its mother, quickly silenced.

'We have been waiting for over two hours,' a client said.

'Three hours, three and a half,' another put in.

'I would prefer to return tomorrow rather than wait a further two hours,' the first said. 'I could return tomorrow at first light.'

'I am sorry,' the clerk said. He was a small, slight man with uneven dark patches on his cheeks and neck, and broken stained teeth from his habit of smoking and of chewing paan. 'I am truly sorry. But Advocate-sahib leaves town very early tomorrow for a family holiday, for some weeks. He leaves Dacca for the country, and will not return soon. He undertakes to see every one of you today, however long it takes. You will not be turned away dissatisfied. All I ask in return is a little patience from you, gentlemen.'

In the corridor, somewhat closer, the same child's voice was raised in complaint. 'But he always—' the *always* in Bengali a sibilant, carrying objection. A low woman's voice, urgent and silencing; again the girl, louder now, saying, 'Always—' and then the noise of tears, a foot stamping, the girl's voice almost screaming with rage. The Advocate-sahib's door opened, and my father came out. With his glasses in hand, he walked straight through the waiting room and past the clients at the door; they shrank back respectfully.

'That's quite enough,' he could be heard saying. 'Go back to your room immediately, Sunchita. I don't expect to hear these noises during office hours. Go back straight away.'

'But, Daddy, he always—'

'That's quite enough,' my father said. 'I have very many important clients to see this afternoon. Tomorrow we go to the village, and everything can be play and noise in the fields, if you choose. Today has to be business, and I expect you to be quiet in the flat. Is that clear?'

My sister agreed. My father returned to his office; Sunchita, her eyes red with frustrated tears, came back to her room, where I was sitting on her bed, her possessions cast on to the floor. In the suitcase on the bed, there was one wooden pistol.

2.

It was always the same, the afternoon before we set off on our long journey to the village. My father had a lot of work, a lot of disgruntled clients to get through – his appointments system extended to asking people to come on a particular day, and if they asked to come on a day when we would be on holiday, he could not resist asking them to come on the last day before we left, rather than putting them off until we returned. The last day was always as overcrowded as this, and sometimes he did not finish with his clients until one in the morning.

My mother and the ayah, Majeda, would go to the kitchen and prepare the food we would be taking with us on the journey the next day – parathas, dry masala chicken, vegetable bhaji, aloo, papaya, potol, the Bengali pod-like vegetable that looks, when raw and piled, like a heap of big green eyes. My mother and father liked their own food, and took it with them when they travelled. While my mother and Majeda were preparing the food, my sisters and I were set a simple, useful task: packing our own suitcases.

Sunchita and I shared a large suitcase. We had already successfully laid out all the clothes we were to be taking – or, rather, Majeda had helped us to choose them, earlier, and we placed them in the suitcase, like a good little boy and girl, taking half the suitcase each. Sunchita's idea of a holiday in the country was to take as many books as she possibly could; she put in a thick, almost geological, layer of books she was now reading and others she hoped to get round to reading, as well as two or three favourites, which she thought she could do with in the country. This was a good number of books: Sunchita always had three or four on the go simultaneously. I insisted on having my own book, as well, pushing aside one of Sunchita's favourites.

'That's babyish,' she said. 'I finished reading Shukumur Roy years ago. That's a book for babies.'

'Look at what you are reading,' I said, picking up her book. It was an adult novel by Shahidullah Kaiser. I remembered the immensely cutting remark my grandfather had made about my sister's reading. It seemed the cruellest and most witty thing I could say. 'This book is not for you,' I said, with an echo of Nana's grand sweeping gesture. 'What are you doing, reading such a book?'

Sunchita grabbed it from me, and walked out of the room. I knew she was going to the kitchen to complain about the way I was treating her. I saw my chance. Not everything I had demanded be put in had been agreed to. One of these was my wooden pistol. It was a key part of the *Roots* game – I loved to stand, my legs apart, before the cowering slaves and wave my pistol menacingly about my head. I felt sure that I would find a use for it in the village, among the farmers' children. It would add greatly to my own prestige. Quickly, I removed the layer of books, throwing them on the floor, then pulled out my shirts, trousers, Sunchita's clothes. I got to the very bottom of the suitcase, and put the wooden pistol there, exactly where it would never be discovered.

'Saadi,' my ayah said. She was standing in the doorway. 'Saadi! What have you done? You have destroyed the packing. I'm very cross with you.'

My sister pushed past her; she had left her books and clothes neatly packed in her half of the suitcase, and now they were lying anyhow on the floor. She broke the rule about keeping her voice down during office hours. She ran at me, cuffing me about the head. 'But he always—' she shouted, then turned about, pushed past Majeda, and into the corridor. 'He always—' she went on.

We heard the professional click of Father's office door opening.

3.

A word about Majeda. She came to us in the following way.

She was from a family of six daughters and one son, in a village near Faridpur. She was the eldest, and beautiful from quite a young age. Her father was a farmer on a small scale. In the way of things, she attracted the attention of the son of the shopkeeper in the village. The shopkeepers made a good living. They could charge what they liked, and if a villager fell out with them for whatever reason, they could refuse to give him any service. Sometimes they would wilfully charge someone they disliked twice as much; if they thought they could get away with it, they would double the price of a bag of rice. In popular films of the time, the shopkeeper of the town is almost always villainous, and there was a good reason for that.

The shopkeeper's family was well off, by village standards. The eldest son would not normally have been allowed to marry the daughter of a small village farmer. But the son saw Majeda, scattering rice seed to the chickens, and fell in love with her. He insisted that he only wanted to marry Majeda, and finally his family agreed to it. They insisted that her family put up a substantial dowry, however. That was the way they could save face in the village, by demonstrating that the new bride's family had more substance than people knew. Or perhaps they were just keen on money, and believed in squeezing new wives. Majeda's father lost his head, and promised a much larger dowry than he could really afford. With six daughters to marry, he could spare only a small amount.

After the marriage, Majeda's father could not pay the dowry he had promised. Majeda's husband, who was a decent man, was prepared to forget all about it. Perhaps he looked at the situation and thought that his family had enough to support Majeda, whom he genuinely loved. But his parents did not see it in that light. They thought that Majeda and her father had defrauded them by pretending to be much richer than they were. They were furious, and after a time, they turned Majeda out of the house.

In later years, the demanding of a dowry became illegal because of cases like Majeda's. In some extreme cases, brides whose families defaulted on their dowries were actually murdered. But Majeda was merely forced to leave her husband. Instead of returning to her family, in the village where she would have had to face her in-laws every day, she came to Dacca. She had a connection of some sort who was a near neighbour of ours, and my mother came to hear about her situation. Zahid, my brother, was a toddler at the time, and my mother needed a nurse. She met Majeda, who was a nice, modest girl with a pleasant manner, and decided to employ her.

She was still there fifteen years later, and was still quite beautiful. My parents did not pay her well, I believe: she got fifty taka a month. But she had her room and board, and my parents paid for her to return home to see her family at least once a year. They also bought her good-quality and even elegant clothes to wear. I am sure they would have done just the same if Majeda had not been beautiful at all, but as it was, when she came to meet me from school, I always thought that my ayah was much more beautiful and well-dressed than anyone else's. It may have been, too, that my mother, with six sisters herself, felt the uncomfortable situation Majeda's father had been placed in with some sympathy. Of course, Nana would not have found himself obliged to provide large dowries, so the situation was not really very similar.

Majeda had an air of romantic sadness in her eyes – they were so black that there was no distinction between iris and pupil, just a deep circle of black. She had a quiet, musical voice. I never heard her regret her life, though my mother often told me that she greatly missed her husband. She believed that he had always loved her and never remarried, even though he had had some good opportunities. I do not know how my mother knew this. But that is the story of how Majeda, my ayah, came to live with our family.

4.

Our suitcase had been repacked, and we had been put to bed. At the far end of the flat, there was still the grumble of the waiting clients, and the smell of their cigarette smoke. Father would continue to see them until he was done. We were in our beds, side by side, and Sunchita and I were talking about all the things we were going to do when we got to the village.

'I want to go to the sugar-cane field,' I said.

'And cut down sugar cane, and eat it,' Sunchita said.

'I want to find that tree, the one with the seeds,' I said. 'The big red seeds, the hard ones.'

'I'm going to collect the seeds and make a necklace out of them, like I did last year,' Sunchita said.

'I'm going to bring back a big bag of seeds,' I said.

'I'll make two, three necklaces,' she said. 'So they'll last all the time until we get to go again.'

'I'm going to teach the cousins about *Roots*,' I said. 'They don't know about *Roots*. They haven't got a television. And I'm going to make a fishing rod, and go down to the river to climb into the tree, and sit, and wait until I catch a great big fish.'

'I'm going to go into the mango orchard,' Sunchita said, her voice growing heavy and slow, pausing between one word and the next, 'and I'm going to climb up into a mango tree, and I'm going to take a book, and I'll sit there, and I'll pick a mango, and I'll suck at a mango, and I'll read my book, and no one will find me . . .'

My sister was in my mind, in the low branches of a mango tree in the mango orchard, hidden behind leaves, her book resting on her knees. She turned a page, and her face was down and she was absorbed in her book. And I was lying underneath the tree, looking up into its dark and light, and losing my dappled sister the more I tried to find her.

5.

My father had a terrible fear of being late for the bus to the village. Even if he had not finished with his last client until after one in the morning, he would insist on everybody being woken at half past four for a bus that did not leave until after seven. My mother complained, every year, at this imposition. Father said that it was important to get there early, to get the best seats; my mother would point out that the seats had been reserved, weeks before. My father would then say that it was not a question of the seats on the bus, but of the best place to put our luggage, in the cage on the roof, so that it should not fall off and be lost. The conversation ran the same course every year, and my father always had his way.

The suitcases and the food for the journey were in a neat pile in the hallway. The boy who worked in the chambers was woken and sent out to the nearby main road to wake three cycle-rickshaw drivers in their turn, sleeping in their cabs. The rickshaws would be loaded up with our luggage, and Mother would inspect us all: father, Majeda, my brother Zahid, my sisters Sunchita and Sush-mita, and me. We were in our best travelling clothes; I wore a short-sleeved shirt and short trousers. The rickshaws took us in twos and threes through the streets of Dacca, rattling past whole families under temporary roadside shelter, and only the very occasional figure standing on an unknown, solitary task at a junc-tion. We travelled to the village at the same time each year, the mango season. It was quite dark when we got up; by the time we were in the rickshaws and on the way to the bus station, light was painting the sky in pale streaks.

Later, the bus station would be crowded and noisy, with passen-gers pushing and shoving, hawkers selling toys, labour-saving devices for the home as well as snacks and whole meals. Later still, the noise would be overwhelming, and the mass of humanity holding up the corner of a sari or a handkerchief to get through the black, belching smoke from the back of the hundreds of buses. But if you arrived, like us, before six, the crowds were on a smaller scale. There were still boys going from bus to bus, calling out, 'Chai, chai,' with their trays of glasses of milky tea; I admired their skill in balancing a tray on one hand and with the other scratching themselves under their lungi or under their grubby white singlets. I never knew anyone who bought a cup of tea from the bus-station boys. There were families like ours, sitting on piles of luggage, and there were buses being loaded up.

My father had no difficulty in identifying the bus that would take us across seven rivers to Jhenaidah sub-district, then to Shailkupa-thana, and to Mirzapur village. I could recite it. My father's skill in tracking down the bus in Komlapur bus station in Dacca, among the dozens of identical idling buses, all brick-red BRTC buses with the same open caged windows, was prodigious to me. It seemed on the same level of skill as the bus drivers' in tracing the route away from the knot of roads that wound up into Dacca. Anyone could find their way to Dacca, it seemed to me, but only a BRTC driver with his cigarette and his jaunty manner and, in later years, his cassette player firmly wedged under his seat, could find his way to a given place, starting from the capital.

Quickly and inexplicably, my father found our bus; the suitcases were loaded on to the roof, in a spot where they could not fall off, and we took our reserved seats. 'You can't sit there,' my father said to me. 'It isn't safe for little boys.' I was moved from the place next to the window, and we sat and waited for the station to wake up, for the bus to fill over the next hour, for it to depart.

We set off, and the streets of Dacca had come to life. Those sleeping families were awake, and washing underneath the street-corner taps; men rubbing their faces and glistening torsos, snorting in and spurting out water from their nostrils, women trudging along with their baskets, and people hurrying to their daily tasks. The sun was up, and the first wave of traffic in the city was immense. It took hours before we reached the first river to cross, and most of those hours were spent, it always seemed, getting through Dacca. The road was humped and rough; the bus banged and hurtled through the air as it hit each bump. 'Ai – ai – ai,' my sister Sushmita cried, on the other side of the aisle. She hated to travel; she grew pale, sweaty and sick in the heat and petrol-smell, and the hammering leaps of the bus over the humps in the road were painful to her.

'Slow down, slow down,' the passengers yodelled to the driver.

The conductor, an efficient man whose job was never clear to me, came to tell us that if the driver slowed down, he would never reach his destination in time. The families of doctors, lawyers, university professors about us remonstrated, and the conductor repeated what he had said.

I greatly enjoyed the cross exchanges between the passengers and the conductor. They got worse as the journey progressed. 'Ai, ai, ai, ai, ai,' a passenger shouted. 'Stop, stop, stop – my fruit, my fruit.' We had seen the whole drama. He must have arrived at the bus station long after us and placed a basket of oranges, packed in hay, on the very top, where the loading was unstable. With some pleasure and excitement, an hour on the road out of Dacca, we had seen the basket fall heavily behind the bus with a crash. Before anyone could do anything, the bus behind had driven right over it; behind us, the squashed oranges were a catastrophe of mud, juice and hay, and the passenger wailing his bad fortune and the carelessness of the BRTC. Once, the bus had a puncture six hours into the journey. 'Why didn't you check the tyres on the ferry?' my father shouted at the conductor. 'That's your job, to check that the tyres are in perfect condition before you set off, and again on the ferry.'

'There's nothing you can do against a nail on the road,' the conductor retorted, and my father made his own objection to this. The bus had juddered to a halt between paddy-fields, and in the midday heat, we all got off. 'Don't wander too far off, Saadi,' my mother said. She had a great fear of kidnappers, and felt that at any moment I might be grabbed by criminals, disguised perhaps as rice-farmers. So I had to stay close to Majeda.

We got off, and with great fascination watched the conductor and the driver prise the burst tyre off its axle, jacking the bus up off the ground. The conductor went to the back and fetched the spare tyre. 'What happens if there is another nail on the ground?' I said, but Majeda didn't know. She was the only woman in the small crowd of men and boys, standing about watching the interesting act of a wheel being changed. All about us, other men from the bus were taking an opportunity, and peeing in a ragged line into the ditch at the side of the road; the mothers and sisters were fanning themselves in the shade cast by the bus, taking no interest in the mechanical doings.

6.

The first river was crossed by means of a bridge, but the second was the Padma river. That was what we in Bangladesh called the Ganges as it came towards the Bay of Bengal, the open sea. My father, who admired the British almost as much as Nana did, always said, as we approached the Padma on our summer journey, 'I will never understand why the British did not build a bridge over the Padma, and save us from all this kerfuffle.'

My brother, who was literal-minded and interested in engineering, explained at this point that it was not possible to build a bridge over the Padma, because the river constantly washed away the mud of the bank. The ground was too soft and sifting to support the huge piles that a bridge over the Padma would require.

The Padma was an enormous river, and coming to it impressed us with the scale and drama of our nation. From one bank, it was impossible to see the far bank; it was like a great sea. The banks were uneven cliffs of clay and, as Zahid said, the river constantly tore away at it. You could see great bites of clay and grass collapsing into the flood.

There was no bridge: you crossed on a ferry. However big the ferries were, they could not meet demand. There were always at least two hundred buses waiting at the ferry ghat to embark, and it could be a long wait. It was my favourite part of the whole journey. I got off the bus with my sisters, Zahid and Majeda, and Majeda took me to a place where I could pee into the river. She turned her head decorously, as I could not go while anyone was watching me, but she stood not far off. A temporary encampment, a middle-sized town, had sprung up. Like the mud banks, it slid from time to time into the river and was carried off; constantly, from the back, it was renewed with more buses, more people, more hawkers, more of everything.

The food my mother and my ayah had prepared was brought

out. They had made all sorts of dry cooked food, nothing that would add to the pungent smell of the hot bus, and nothing that could not be eaten with a napkin and fingers. We knew a place nearby, in the shade, away from the worst of the noise and the confusion. We referred to it as 'our place', a little hollow underneath a tree, and resented it if, when we got there, another family had set up their picnic. We never considered that they, too, might think of it as 'their place'. I grew tense as the time of the picnic approached. The riverbank was lined with men selling freshly cooked hilsha fish; the smell was almost unendurably delicious. More than anything, I longed for my mother to augment her already lavish picnic with a pair of hot bought hilsha fish. My mother and father did not like to buy and eat other people's cooked food. They hardly ever went to a restaurant if they could help it, and certainly never bought food from a stall in the street. For my father, to do such things was the habit of a poor law student without his own cooking facilities, wife, servants or children. He thought it a waste of money, and he did not believe it was safe to eat from the stove of a stranger. Certainly, we children were expressly forbidden ever to buy anything from the street, except an unpeeled banana or the water of a green coconut, freshly opened. The sweet stalls that had sprung up on the bank of the Padma were not, we understood, for us, and the children who were permitted to buy a bag of lozenges from them would, we knew priggishly, be in agonizing pain and perhaps even dead before the end of their journey today.

The sweet stalls were one matter, and we filed past them with our eyes decorously low. But the piles of hilsha fish smelt so good that we could not help looking longingly at them, and then at Mother. In the past, she had spontaneously pulled at Father's shirt-sleeves, and once or twice before on this journey, we had found that she, too, could not resist the sweet nutty smell of freshly fried hilsha fish. It would do no good to beg; my sisters and I simply tried to catch my mother's eye. But this year, it did not work. She continued on past the fish stalls, carrying, with

88

Majeda, the cold picnic. She was following my father and my serious, ungreedy brother, as the two of them went on discussing the many difficulties that would have to be resolved, if Bangladesh were ever to construct a bridge across the great span of the Padma river. Into the huge flood of the river, the ferry boats continued to launch themselves, like floating seed-pods, heavy with their burdens.

7.

It took two or three hours to cross the Padma on the ferry. The river was thick with mud at its edges, and as the ferry slipped its bonds and set off into the flood, it churned behind grey and brown. We were on the deck of the boat. Behind us, the land sank back, with its load of trucks and coaches, and the stevedores preparing for the next ferry.

There was so much to watch out for in the river: the storks picking elegantly, like rich ladies in white draped saris, through the mud, and the river dolphins. Long-nosed, they threw themselves out of the flood in gangs, their wet flanks flashing in the sun. They seemed to have no reason to do it but their own pleasure. We lost count of the river dolphins, there were so many. River birds followed, shrieking, in the wake of the boat, hoping for waste food to be tossed overboard. Life on the river had its own rhythm, and the men who crewed the ferry from one bank of the Padma to the other, four times a day, were practical, hard-faced, but somehow light in spirit. They did not give the impression of being proper sailors, but to have settled for this particular rank in life as they strolled the decks and talked out of the corners of their mouths. They had their own ways of speaking. And by the time we reached the middle of the Padma, busy and torn by dolphins, the muddy water of the banks had clarified. The river, just there in the middle of the

89

stream before it started to thicken and obscure again, was a translucent, veiled blue, like the sky.

8.

There were seven rivers to cross. The Padma was the biggest. It was only the second we came to. After that, there were rivers with bridges, and then ones with ferries. After the Padma, the buses went off in different directions, like rolling coconuts. When our bus reached the next ferry-crossing, there were many fewer buses waiting. The ferries were much smaller, however, and could only take four or five buses at a time. These smaller ferry ghats still had life, and boys went between the waiting buses with fruit and sweets and tea.

After the Padma, it was easy to fall asleep. I would wake up and ask how many rivers we had now crossed. It would outrage me that nobody woke me up at each river bridge; I liked to count the rivers out. My sister Sushmita never slept: she could not. During the long journey, as she followed us on or off of the bus, she complained ceaselessly about the discomfort and the unpleasantness. My mother said, quite mildly, that she was not very good to complain so much about a journey. She should remember the journey that Nana and Nani took, when they were thrown out of Calcutta in 1947 and had to go to Dacca without any idea of what they would find there. There were no bandits on the road today, waiting to kill Sushmita and the rest of us. There was only a lovely journey, with some exciting rides on ferries, and at the end of it, everyone in the village would be excited to see Sushmita, and disappointed to see such a grumpy face.

My sister Sushmita's stomach felt as if it was going to explode when it travelled over bumps in the road. She hated the strong smell of the river. She longed for her own chair, her own bed, her own things. It was no consolation to her to remember that the older members of her family had undergone a much worse journey thirty years before. When she reached the village – she could be heard to mumble under the noise of the bus's engine – she would go straight to bed and stay there all night and all day the next day. That was what she was looking forward to doing.

After seven rivers, three ferries and four bridges, the bus pulled into the station at the main town of Jhenaidah. Here we got off. The station was the centre of the town. Baggage bobbed about on the heads of porters above the crowd, like flotsam after a shipwreck, and all the time the hawkers were crying out their offers of tea, hot food and sweets. A chain of porters swiftly assembled to take the luggage down from the roof. I held tight to my mother's hand, and she pulled me after her down the bus's rotting tin steps; Sushmita and Sunchita were trusted to stay and look after each other, hand in hand. Behind all of us, Majeda hovered, making vague shepherding gestures with both hands. 'That's ours – that's ours – that's ours – four – five,' my mother called, as the porters handed down our suitcases. The country porters were in awe of women like my mother, capable city women used to organizing others and raising their voices when it was absolutely required. She got her way.

My father was already elsewhere. He relished the moment of arrival in the main town of Jhenaidah. It was here that he would start to be recognized. In the mass of Dacca, he was not known by more than one person in a thousand, and he passed through the crowded streets with his head borne down by anonymity. As soon as he returned to the district where he had grown up, he knew he became an object of pride. He was a popular man in his profession and society; it was only the numbers of Dacca that concealed this from him. Here, his popularity was made apparent to everyone by the way he could simply stand there and wait for people in the main square of the town to greet him. This they did by hailing his name in a familiar way, by saying, 'Advocate-sahib,' or by abasing themselves. My father's head was high in the crowd; he was talking with confidence and fluency to a small circle, already in place. He was making an effort not to look too overcome with joy; his expression was even a little irritable. But he loved being greeted and surrounded. For once, it corresponded with the valuation he held of himself in the world.

'There is the bus,' my mother said, referring to the bus that we were to transfer everything on to, the small country bus that would take us all the way to the village. 'It is waiting. We should get on to it.'

'There is no hurry,' my father said, from the middle of his crowd of acquaintances, friends, acolytes and cronies. 'There will be another bus along in fifteen minutes. They go constantly.'

After some time, Zahid and I would be called over and exhibited to the friends of his youth. After hours of travelling, we did not look as fine and elegant as we had at the beginning of the journey. But we were conscious that we still looked like the children of a Dacca advocate. The children of the small town gazed at us from behind a thicket of adult legs, clutching to what they knew. We talked to each other loudly, making sure our voices could be heard. All about, the tones and music of the town's speech were strange and even comical to us; the country accent was not the same as ours. My father's courtroom voice, his lecturing voice, carried on, explaining that Zahid was to become an engineer, and had done very well in all his exams this year, and was top of his class, and that I was to become a lawyer, 'like his father and like his grandfather'; explaining all of this to people he was friends with, people whom he just about knew, people whom he did not know at all.

It could take an hour before we finally detached ourselves from the group, assembled our luggage again and got on to the small, local bus that would take us the remaining part of the journey. It was much less comfortable than the big bus: its seats were wooden slats, and the people on it were local people, going back to their small villages from the large market town. They held wicker baskets of mangoes and oranges in hay, chickens, eggs in straw, sleeping or crying babies; they looked at us with curiosity, and sometimes with recognition. To either side of the narrow road, the fields were green with growing rice, with sugar cane, wet fields of grass, with jute, or with the brilliant yellow of the mustard plant. Orchards of mango trees, of jackfruit, tamarind, palms bearing bananas and dates rippled off into the middle distance. Every five minutes the bus stopped, and a passenger or two got off, heaving their burden from underneath the seat, walking off across the field towards a cracked mud house.

9.

My father had grown up in these fields, in this village. His father was a teacher at the village mosque, and many of his brothers and sisters were much more religious than my Dacca relations. Some of my father's sisters wore the veil, and his brothers went to the mosque at least once a day. My father had escaped from all that. He had come to Dacca to study law, and had stayed with my mother's father, Nana, who had married an aunt of my father's. So my mother and father were first cousins. When he was a child, he had run in these fields with his brothers and sisters and the boys from the village. He had studied hard, and was the pride of the place. Even some of our relations called him 'Advocate-sahib' now, though not the close ones. Some of them remembered the boy who, as I did now on our visits, took a long twig, a piece of string, a hook and a worm from the earth, and then sat over the river, waiting for the fish to bite. But they did not mention it until my father did – he liked to share these memories with me, and a trip to the village meant a relaxation of his stern ways.

When the bus stopped for us, there were three relations waiting; a brother of Father's, and two of his sons, between Zahid's age and mine. Behind them was a cart, pulled by a waiting cow. The heat of the late afternoon was still high, making the surface of the farm's ponds a beaten bronze. We dismounted, the driver helping us to unload our suitcases and parcels from the roof of the bus. We stood, and the uncle and his two sons respectfully went down, and touched my father's feet, my mother's, my brother's, my two sisters', and even mine, in greeting. The bus pulled away, leaving us with a pile of luggage in the dusty road. Behind the roadside ditch, a wall of jute, twice a man's height, fine and green. There was a path cut in the jute, and from this, a small man emerged in a lungi, carrying an immense machete. 'Who is this? Who's arrived?' he called, in his yawning, singing country accent.

'It's Mahmood and his family, come from Dacca,' my father's brother called back, and the farmer made a great certain wave in the air, a greeting with his machete, before going back into the dark sylvan depths of the crop, its top stretching wildly above the farmer's head. My father had remembered him.

From the back of the cart, behind the cow's backside lumbering to left and right, like a piece of furniture being laboriously moved, we saw farmers raising themselves from their crop, ambling along the road, smallholders and rice-growers. They saw the familiar cow, lumbering from side to side, pulling a cart with unfamiliar children, and they called out exactly the same thing: 'Who is that? Who is arriving?' We felt like royalty. We imitated our father and waved back, and then he would tell us who they were, and my father's brother would explain what had happened to them in the last year; who had married, who had died, who had had children, whose crops and chickens had done well and whose had failed, leading them into debt. And then there was the family house, and Grandfather in his beard coming out to meet us. Now the day was beginning to fade; soon it would be night; soon we would be fed, and put to bed.

But tomorrow I would run out into the fields, to the brook, with a rod I had made myself from a thin branch, a string, a hook and with a worm I had found myself. There would be the friends from last summer, the boys from the village and the cousins in the country. We would fish, and get into the sugar-cane field and eat as much as we could. My sister Sushmita would stay inside, not getting up the whole day, complaining about her headache and her exhaustion, lying in the dark as awed country aunts brought her tea and soft, white, affectionate things on small plates to tempt her appetite.

And Sunchita would pick her moment. She would run out into the mango orchard, a book and a stolen red silk pillow from the dusty salon under her arm. She would find a tree with low-lying branches, and jump on to the lowest, gripping the trunk of the tree. She would climb up into the dark foliage where the red mangoes hung like Chinese lanterns. She would find a place to rest her back, and then reach forward from time to time in the dappled interior light, plucking a ripe mango from its long stalk. She would pummel the fruit, and pinch a hole at the bottom, and suck the flesh out whole. All the time, in this light-and-dark-strewn hiding place, her concentration would be on the book she held. Wedged into a tree in a mango orchard, the red silk cushion behind her back, she could read for hours, the distant shouts of farmers and cousins not disturbing her, hardly noticing the song of the birds sitting at rest, like her, in the trees.

5: A Party at Sufiya's

1.

First, some history.

In 1947, the British left India, and it was split in two: India and Pakistan.

Pakistan was to be for the Muslims, and India for the rest. Many people died making their way to their new homeland, killed by gangs on the railways or on the roads.

Pakistan was a single nation, but anyone could see that it was split in two. To the left was West Pakistan, where they ruled, and spoke Urdu, and wrote in an alphabet that flowed like water under wind.

To the right was East Pakistan, where the Bengalis lived. They spoke Bengali, which chatters like a falling xylophone, and is written in an alphabet that looks like a madman trying to remember a table's shape.

The two new countries – India and Pakistan, East and West – they looked on the map like a broad-shouldered ape with two coconuts, one on its right shoulder, one under its left armpit.

The new government wanted to make Bengal speak and write in its language, Urdu. They also wanted to change Bengali so that it would, in future, be written in the flowing script of Urdu.

There were riots in Bengal, and in 1952 some students from the Bengal Language Movement were killed in Dacca. My parents were among those protesting, and were placed in jail overnight, to their subsequent great happiness.

In the years afterwards, the Bengali language, Bengali poetry, music and culture became important for those who wanted independence for the Bengali nation. It also became a point of honour for the government in Pakistan to observe and suppress the Bengali language wherever possible. Governments went on trying to persuade Bengalis to write their language in the Urdu script.

The situation could not continue, for one reason. There were very many more speakers of Bengali in the whole nation of Pakistan than there were speakers of Urdu. And yet Bengali culture was suppressed and its language occupied an insecure position. In the 1960s Mujibur Rahman, who was the head of a political party, the Awami League, looked forward to a day when the Bengali majority might vote for a Bengali leader of Pakistan as a whole. There seemed no reason why this should not happen. It would be interesting to see what would happen in the Pakistani capital when this came about.

In the meantime, in the respectable houses of Dhanmondi and elsewhere in Dacca, it was considered patriotic and, indeed, very enjoyable to hold parties in which Bengali music was played and Bengali poetry recited. The daughters of the houses walked openly past policemen in their Pakistani uniforms, holding sheaves of music, chattering boldly like singing birds. Sometimes Sheikh Mujib came, too, when he was not being sent to prison.

2.

This afternoon, for instance, there is to be a party at Sufiya's house. Sufiya is a good-hearted woman, and very popular in Dacca. She is friends with everyone, from Syed Hosain, the advocate, and Khandekar, the lawyer, to Sheikh Mujib himself, poets and painters and folklore specialists; she has a word to say to the musicians, always knows a kind word to settle the children and stop them running around too violently. Her daughters, Sultana and Saeeda, do much of the hard work of hospitality, welcoming people, arranging the food, making sure everyone is seated with someone they will have something to say to. At every party of Sufiya's, everyone must meet somebody new to them, as well as greet their old friends. The hard work is her daughters', because Sufiya's role at the party is to read her poetry. She is a famous poet, and people labour to secure invitations to her open house. They do not have to labour hard. Sufiya likes to meet new people, of every sort.

It is four o'clock. The weather is oppressive and steamy, the air thick and still. In the salon, Sultana and Saeeda sit, fanning themselves with broad leaves from the garden. The plain terracotta pots about the sitting room are filled with simple white flowers. Sultana, at eighteen, has just started her English degree; her younger sister is a gifted artist. They will welcome the artists and the musicians, the politicians, too, between them. Sufiya does not like to be found waiting for the first of her guests: she thinks it makes a better party if she descends when a few guests have already gathered. At the moment she is in the kitchen, checking the Bengali cakes the cooks have made: pati shaptha, pancake roll stuffed with coconut halwa, the fudge-like borfi, puli pitha, the dumplings. She likes to be sure of everything in advance, and is going over everything at the last moment. If she leaves it any longer, Sultana remarks to her sister, she is going to be caught out by the first guests, and will be deprived of her entrance. But there are still the bought sweets to go over and count, the things the confectioner supplies: chumchum dusted with icing sugar, black gulab-jamun with a secret interior of brilliant pink, the rolled yellow balls of laddu, sandesh like toy bricks, some with a coat of silver. 'Is there enough chanachur?' Sufiya's voice can be heard from the kitchen. She has, surely, asked after this before, and is now going over old ground. Now there is the sound of a cycle-rickshaw outside the gates: the first guest is here, and Sufiya must hurry herself upstairs to hide for the first half-hour. She hurries through the house in her simple white cotton sari. The

98

house has french windows to the front. The terrace at the front has two sofas, and a bookcase. More bookcases in the hall can be seen from the path through the front garden, and even, through the openwork iron gates, from the road, as the french windows are open. Sufiya's disappearance upstairs must be noticed.

In the hallway, the maid is occupied dusting the shelves as the first guests come up the stone path, between flowerbeds, under the coconut palms and lychee trees to either side. They come in through the half-open door. It is Salim, his wife and his three children. He is a schoolmaster. His daughters are pretty little things, in white party dresses puffed out with ribbons, but very noisy. Salim's wife is a nice woman, though she is Bihari; born speaking Urdu, she prides herself – prides herself perhaps too much – on the way she has transformed herself into a Bengali. 'You are quite one of us,' Sufiya had once said generously, and something in the way Mona has dressed herself today makes Sultana say the same thing now. Still, she hopes that Mona will not try to emphasize her acquired Bengali-ness by offering to sing a Nazrul song later in the party. She has never lost her foreign accent, and the last time she did it, the audience giggled until Mona could no longer pretend not to hear, her hands clenched to the grim end of the song. 'Would the girls like to play in the garden?' Sultana asks. 'My mother will be down soon.' And there is the young doctor, a new friend of Sufiya's – she collects young doctors; he is with his new wife, only six months married. Salim and his wife Mona stand with the doctor and his wife. They do not know each other, but they talk very easily, and in a moment, one of them suggests sitting down. Salim hands his wife to a chair, and Sultana sees from his solicitude that Mona, again, is pregnant. She wonders whether to say anything.

The guests come promptly. Sultana does not immediately recognize the two young men who arrive next, both very clean and innocent-looking, but they announce themselves as the musicians, and then of course she remembers. 'Is Nadira here yet?' the tall one asks. 'She asked us to come at the same time as her, but I am not sure we know what time she was planning to arrive.' Saeeda assures them that they are very welcome, whether Nadira has arrived yet or not, and makes a special point of calling for tea for the pair of them – they seem to have walked to the party. And then there is Khandekar and his wife; they greet Sultana and Saeeda quickly, circumspectly, before going over to make a point of greeting the two musicians. Everyone knows that the musicians are tenants of Mrs Khandekar. In Dacca in 1968, that is of not much concern.

Now there are enough guests here, there is a commotion at the top of the stairs, and Sufiya, smiling in her owl-like glasses, gathering her simple white sari to her throat, is coming down. The guests gather at the entrance to the salon to greet her. 'You have seen the paintings?' she says, but nobody has: they did not know that there were to be paintings today. The art has been laid out in the courtyard of the house, on tables arranged into an L-shape. Sufiya leads the way through the back windows. There are views of Old Dacca by, she explains, a promising young artist from the university. They are done in charcoal and pencil. 'I hope that Zainul is coming,' Sufiya says; Zainul Abedin is her great friend from Calcutta days, a great painter. Everyone knows his ink drawings of the Calcutta famine; all Dacca, and all India, too. 'I do so want to hear his opinion.' These are pinned against board and, in the humid afternoon, are starting to curl up at the edges. Interspersed with the drawings, Sufiya has placed some folk art – pottery and small tapestry work. They are simple things, bearing images of farmers and milkmaids, but interesting. She gathered them on a trip last month into Jessore. The guests admire them, picking them up and turning them over. The peasant art is having more success than the skilful, elaborate drawings of corners of Old Dacca. Sufiya's poetry, too, is simple and unadorned. She likes the simple statement, and the line that anyone can understand. Her poetry is like these white pottery jugs, simple, useful, but pleasant to handle.

Now there are more guests: Sufiya goes back into the salon to greet them with tea and cakes and lemon water. It would not do if she were in the back room, fussing over cakes, when Sheikh Mujib arrived, or even Zainul Abedin. She keeps an eye on the degree of disruption at the gates, signalling an important guest, as one waiting for the monsoon to break.

'Sufiya,' a new guest says, after she has been welcomed – she is the wife of an architect, recently returned from Europe, 'do you know those men?'

'Everyone is welcome,' Sufiya says. 'The gates are open, you know.'

'The men standing outside,' the architect's wife says, 'I thought they must be . . .' She gathers her shawl to her throat. She is not quite clear what she thought they were.

Sufiya goes into the hallway, and out through the front door. There are, as the architect's wife said, two men standing there. Their clothes distinguish them from Sufiya's guests. They are standing there as people dismount from their rickshaw and come in. The guests lower their heads as they pass: the men stare insolently into the faces of the guests. She keeps open house, and sometimes people she does not know arrive, and are very welcome if they are interested in Bengali culture, take an interest in the pottery, sit quietly and appreciatively during poetry and music. These are not people of that sort. They are wearing salwaar kameez, the Bihari shirt with a collar and buttons; her other guests, if they are wearing traditional dress, are wearing the Bengali shirt without collar. Some, like the architect, are wearing quite glamorously embroidered shirts, but the people outside are wearing everyday, even rather dusty clothes. They are standing on either side of the gate without looking in at the party or at each other. They do not seem to have come to a party at all.

'Karim,' Sufiya says, not raising her voice, and her darowan, the gatekeeper, is next to her, 'have you seen those men?' She does not need to say who they are. Karim has been with her for twenty years, and he knows what to do. He walks out, just as three of Hosain's daughters are piling out of a rickshaw, Nadira in the front. They know better than to linger, though the scene is interesting.

'What are you doing?' Karim is saying. 'Why are you loitering here? You have no right to be threatening Madam's guests like this. Be off with you.'

'We're not threatening anyone,' one of the men says. 'Got a perfect right to stand where we like.'

'Go and stand somewhere else,' the darowan says. 'You're not welcome here.'

'If you don't like it,' the other says – he has broken teeth, stained from paan, and now cleans his mouth, spits on the ground, 'if you don't like it, you can complain. To the relevant authorities.'

No one doubts that the relevant authorities are precisely the people who have sent these two men to stand outside Sufiya's house. Mona, Salim's Bihari wife, has turned decorously away; she has let herself be absorbed in greeting Nadira and her sisters, Dahlia and Mary. Salim has seen that the familiar debate is happening at Sufiya's gates, and has come forward to add his weight of persuasion to Sufiya's steward's. When Sufiya next looks, the men have been talked into leaving. They had carried out their task, after all.

As if waiting for the departure of the goons, the gates open, and in steps Sheikh Mujib, followed by one of his daughters. His famous simplicity is evident here: there is no car outside, and he has, as usual, walked the five hundred yards from his house to Sufiya's. He smiles to right and left, and comes through the gate as Karim, the darowan, lowers his head and says, 'Salaam.' Sufiya comes forward to greet this most important of her guests. Behind her, on the veranda, the guests have risen from their seats, and inside, the chatter is ceasing as people come to the window. 'Now the party can commence,' she says. 'I am so happy that you have come.'

'I would not dream of missing it,' he says. 'Some wretched people tried to inconvenience me, to prevent my attendance. But

I would not let them stand in the way of my old friend's party.' He presents his daughter.

Everyone has stood up, and Sufiya takes Sheikh Mujib around the party, first to the veranda, then inside to the salon, presenting him to everyone – to her daughters, to Salim and his wife, who lowers her eyes, to Nadira and her sisters, to doctors and architects and poets and painters, even to the musicians. The Friend of Bengal is easy and approachable, and greets the musicians with particular kindness. 'Now sit, sit,' he says to Sufiya, almost forcing her into her chair; it is his usual gesture, to insist that Sufiya should sit before him and, after demurral, she does so. The other guests, however, wait for Sheikh Mujib and his daughter to sit before taking their seats again. On cue, Sufiya's servants start to circulate with plates of sweets and cake, and cups of tea. Nadira, Altaf and Amit gather, and in a moment they start on a song, its long sweet lines over the tabla like rain on a river. In five minutes, Sheikh Mujib rises again, goes outside, and admires the pottery, taking a small crowd of guests with him, each with a cup in hand.

The doctor greets Hosain, the lawyer. They live close to each other, and regularly take an afternoon walk around the lake in Dhanmondi. The doctor – capable, brief in conversation and intelligent – is in fact the man Hosain goes to for advice and help, even on family matters. He stands loose-limbed, his face defined by his small round glasses; he gleams like a health-conscious revolutionary.

'I am glad to see you,' Hosain says.

'I thought I would see you here,' the doctor says.

Then Hosain plunges straight in. 'I am concerned about Pultoo,' he says. 'My youngest boy. He shows no aptitude for anything. He does not do well at his classes. All he does is draw, all day long. His teacher says he sits and dreams during mathematics, he gazes ahead without concentrating in all his other lessons, and if he seems to be working, he is really sketching something. He draws all the time. I do not know what to do with him.'

'You say he has no aptitude for anything,' the doctor says.

'Yes, that's right,' the lawyer says.

'But he draws all the time.'

'Yes, he can't be stopped – he draws in the notebook he is supposed to be working out sums in, during mathematics.'

'Is he good at drawing?' the doctor says.

'Yes, I think so. He makes his classmates laugh by drawing them, and his teachers, and sometimes he draws the view from his classroom window. And he made a very good drawing of the gardener at home. Yes, I think he can draw.'

'I don't understand why you say he has no aptitude for anything,' the doctor says. 'It sounds as if he has an aptitude for art.'

'Oh, for art,' the lawyer says. 'That is not a very useful aptitude.'

'The world needs a good artist more than it needs an incompetent engineer,' the doctor says.

'I so agree,' says Sufiya, passing. 'Now, have you seen the art in the garden? I was so hoping that Zainul would come. He promised he would come early. I so wanted to show him some drawings of a young friend of mine, and Saeeda, my daughter, you know, she is painting so beautifully nowadays. I particularly wanted him to come early. It is really too bad.'

'But there he is,' the doctor says. He looks surprised. 'There he is, talking to my brother's daughter.'

'Oh, that is too bad,' Sufiya says again, but affectionately. 'He always does that. He always sneaks in quietly, with no word of hello, and then finds a quiet corner. He really is too bad.'

You would never know that Zainul Abedin is who he is, if you saw him at a party. He arrives quietly, with nobody knowing; he finds a quiet corner, with nobody much in it, just an old friend. He would spend any gathering perfectly happily talking to small children or to somebody's aunt, visiting from the country, talking about their concerns and small worries, listening about the failure of the crops or a pet chicken or a girl's best friend, now her worst enemy. He listens with his full attention; sometimes only much later, years sometimes, does his new friend discover that this kindly gentleman, his fingers stained with paint and nicotine, was the great painter. Sometimes never; and once or twice Sufiya has found that her oldest friend Zainul Abedin has been to a party of hers, never said hello, sat on a stool in a dark corner, chatted to hardly anyone, and departed quietly, having had, he would tell her later, a very nice time.

He is sitting with a small girl, the niece of the doctor, in a party dress. Their full attention is on something Zainul Abedin is holding on his knee.

'You see,' he is saying, 'I came on a bus today.'

She looks.

'And this was my ticket,' he says.

She looks at the small piece of paper he is holding on his knee.

'And it has print on one side, but not so much on the other side,' he says. 'So here's a pen, and here's some paper' – it is only one inch by two, the bus ticket, hardly that, even – 'and the pen wants to draw something, but it doesn't know what it wants to draw. What is it going to draw?'

The small girl looks at the pen, poised above the bus ticket resting on this gentleman's knee, and says something into her fist, very shyly.

'Is it going to draw Papa?' the painter says. The girl nods, and quickly, with six, seven strokes, a scribble and some dabs, like the nib pecking at the paper, there he is; her father, a thin, serious fellow, leaning over to catch what his brother-in-law is saying, not at all aware that he has been caught for ever in this attitude on the back of a Dacca bus-ticket; his portrait, by Zainul Abedin, given to his daughter. The girl's eyes grow wide – she reaches out with both hands. She recognizes her father in those few strokes. For a moment it had been just strokes of the pen, and then it was her father, all at once. 'Do you want it?' Zainul Abedin says. 'You're very welcome, but, just one moment.' He waves the bus ticket around in the air, three times, to dry the ink. 'And here you are.'

'My dear old friend,' Sufiya says. 'Up to your old tricks again. Now,' turning to the small girl, 'let me get a little envelope for that. You must always keep that safe, you know. Have you been to see the drawings yet? And Saeeda would never ask herself, but she is painting so very interestingly these days, she would love to hear what you have to say.'

'I was just about to get up to find her,' Zainul Abedin says. 'But she must be busy with your guests. I can come back tomorrow.'

Elsewhere in the party, Sultana has been waylaid by Mary, her friend.

'So what happened?' she says.

'What do you mean?' Sultana says.

'You arrived at the university the other day in a large black car,' Mary says. 'I know it was Sheikh Mujib's. How is it that he is turned into your chauffeur these days?'

'He was not in the car,' Sultana says. 'He had got out earlier. All right, I'll tell you. What happened was that I was late getting up, and it was almost a quarter to nine when I left the house. I had a class on Wordsworth at nine at the university, and you know what a stickler old Das is for punctuality. So I was really thinking about whether it would not be best to go back home and tell Professor Das that I had been ill when I next saw him – but then I thought about Ma, and how I could tell her that I had missed Das on poetry just because I slept late, and I saw that would not do either. So I was really on the horns of a dilemma when a car drew up alongside me, standing on the road like a hopeless case, and the window wound down, and it was Sheikh Mujib. He said, "You look a little late to me," and I confessed that I was late, and that I had a class at the university. So he said, "I can easily give you a lift," and I was so grateful, and I saw that it was really my only chance to get to university on time, that I accepted straight away. Never mind what Ma would say, I thought, when she heard that I was inconveniencing the Friend of Bengal. But it was much, much worse than I thought, because after five minutes of chatting about what I was up to, and whether I preferred Wordsworth to Keats, because Sheikh Mujib had read Keats when he was young, in Calcutta, and he was saying that, really, he thought there was no poetry in the world to touch the "Ode to the Nightingale", and I was sticking up for the "Ode to a Grecian Urn", because in my view—'

'Yes, yes,' Mary says. 'But what was the inconvenience to the Friend of Bengal – the more than usual one?'

'Well, after five minutes he said, "I am so sorry but I am going to have to leave you here – my driver will take you on to Curzon Hall, but you know, I must be punctual when I need to come here." And it was at the courthouse he was being left. I felt such a fool because, of course, Pa and Ma were talking about Sheikh Mujib being prosecuted again, and having to go to the courthouse to answer an invented case the very next day. "They may send me to jail again, or they may not send me to jail," he said to me, "but I know they will definitely send me to jail today if I don't arrive on time, and call it contempt of court. I am so sorry, my young friend, to be so discourteous as to leave you here, but the driver will take you anywhere you want to go. Don't be in a hurry, I may be here for some time." And then he got out and there was a huge crowd to meet him, and I went on. All the faces were pressed up against the glass – they wanted to see who I was, and all of that. I don't know what they thought.'

'But they didn't send him to jail,' Mary said. 'Pa was talking about it this morning, but Nadira and Dahlia were arguing about something else, and I don't think I heard properly.'

'No, he's out on bail,' Sultana said. 'I am glad to see him here. He is so nice, really. And now Ma is going to read.'

Silence falls, and Sufiya stands, a piece of paper in her hand. She begins to speak.

'"This is no time to be braiding your hair . . ."'

3.

Two days after her party, Sufiya receives some uninvited guests. They are two men. Not the two men who were seen loitering at her gates, staring insolently at her guests. But they may be assumed to have some connection with those men – perhaps their supervisors, their superiors. And these visitors have superiors, too. They come from a world where everyone has underlings and everyone has superiors, and they cannot conceive of any other existence.

Sufiya asks them in, perhaps unnecessarily. They refuse tea, and any other offering, and it is true that by the end of their conversation Sufiya would happily have slipped poison into any cup of tea she would offer them. Is it the case that she organized a gathering of individuals opposed to the government two days ago? No, it was a small meeting of friends, come together to drink tea and to listen to a little music. Nevertheless, among those attending were – one of the men, a moustachioed person with an unnerving, practised, direct gaze, extracts a clean typed sheet of names from his black leather briefcase – were well-known leaders of opposition and dissent. Who did they have in mind? The man begins to read out the names: he concludes with Sheikh Mujib's. An old friend, Sufiya says. She is aware that her daughter Sultana has come downstairs and is standing discreetly in the door of the salon, listening. She wishes she would go away: she does not want these men from the security service to recognize either of her daughters at any point in the future.

Is it the case, the other man says, clipped and neat-looking in his blue blazer and English tie, that among the topics discussed at this gathering was the founding of a dissident cultural institute? Sufiya cannot think what they are talking about, and says so. The man goes into more detail, and soon she realizes that they are referring to the room that the university is making available to any practitioners of Bengali arts. She sets her face. The men at the gate did not hear that conversation. She wonders who it was who overheard it and, for a shameful moment, her mind settles on Mona, Salim's Bihari wife. She dismisses the thought.

'Do you know it is forbidden to hold gatherings of more than twelve people without permission?' one of the men says. This may or may not be true, but is certainly one of the laws that would be applied only if the authorities wanted to stop a gathering taking place for other reasons. She does not believe that when the daughters of government ministers get married, official permission for the reception is applied for, or would ever be withheld. All the same, she acknowledges the statement, and after a few minutes, the two men run out of things to threaten her with. They stand to go. Sultana whisks herself off, out of the doorway and into the kitchen, where she cannot be seen. 'I am sorry I cannot be of more help to you,' Sufiya says sweetly, as she shows them to the door. She invited them in, after all, and they are, in some sense, guests of hers. They have the grace to look a little embarrassed at that. She shuts the door behind them, wanting to break a vase over their silly heads, and breathes deeply. Sultana comes out from the kitchen and, behind her, Hamida, the cook, both with deeply concerned expressions. No one says anything.

That was the sort of encounter which happened, with increasing frequency, in Dacca during this time, when Sheikh Mujib, the Friend of Bengal, was either writing impassioned articles and giving speeches to huge crowds, or was in jail on trumped-up charges, or in front of a court or, sometimes, was visiting his old friends, and drinking tea, and laughing as if nothing was happening to him, nothing at all.

6: How Big-uncle Left Home

1.

My father never got on with Laddu, my big-uncle, Boro-mama.
And Boro-mama never liked my father. It was a difference of
temperament, first, but their temperaments had led them to lead
their lives in quite different ways. They were always going to fall
out in a terrible way.

Of course, they were cousins before they were brothers-in-law.
My father's mother was Nana's sister.

Boro-mama was not the eldest son. The eldest son had been
killed in the Japanese air-raids during the war. Laddu was not
used to the new burden of being eldest son when he and his sisters
set off with Nana and Nani from Calcutta to Dacca, in 1947, and
he probably never got used to it. His clever sister married their
cousin, my father. But what was Boro-mama to do?

Boro-mama did not go on demonstrations in favour of the
Bengali language. He did not end up in prison cells with intellectuals. When Dacca was burning with intellectual fervour and
Tagore, Boro-mama was a plump boy of twenty, living at home
with his mother and father without any occupation or interests.

Nana conspired to conceal this fact, and to keep his son Laddu
busy with household tasks. Boro-mama was quite good with his
hands, and it was surprising how many small jobs needed doing
about the house. 'I noticed that the bath tap upstairs was dripping
yesterday,' Nana said, over breakfast. 'If you have nothing else
to do, you could see if it can be fixed.'

111

'It's probably the washer,' Boro-mama said knowledgeably.

'Well, perhaps you could mend it,' Nana said. 'If you have nothing else to do today.'

Round the breakfast table, Mary, Era, Nadira and Mira giggled at the thought that elder-brother might have anything else to do. Without a task, he would lie on the sofa from breakfast to dinner with his sandals off, listening to the radio or reading the newspaper. The nearest thing he had to action was to go out to the general store, where his neighbourhood cronies would sit all day long, deciding how they would improve the world over endless cups of tea. It was hilarious to his sisters that Laddu might have anything else to do. His youngest sister did not giggle: Dahlia sat in her high chair, looking from face to face with a cloth napkin about her chin, as her ayah spooned pap into her mouth. And his eldest sister did not giggle; my mother looked at her stern cousin, my father with a tie around his neck and a notebook and a frayed textbook by his plate, ready to go to his economics lectures at Dacca University. Neither of them saw this as very funny.

'No,' Boro-mama said slowly. 'I can do that this morning.'

So Nana set off to his chambers. Boro-mama's sisters, and his cousin, my father, went to university or to their different schools; Dahlia was carried off to her nursery. Boro-mama cut his newspaper-reading down to an hour or an hour and a quarter. He asked Nani for money for a cycle-rickshaw, and came back at the end of the morning with a small paper bag. After a cup of tea and some buns, he went in search of my grandfather's driver to borrow a small spanner from him; he returned in twenty minutes or slightly more. Finally, Boro-mama went upstairs and replaced the washer on the tap.

'There,' he said, coming down, glowing. 'That tap won't drip for years to come.'

Nani did not share Nana's view that it was better for Boro-mama to be doing small jobs around the house than nothing at all. She would have preferred it if Boro-mama had stayed at school until matriculation, and left with at least one or two qualifications. She also did not agree that Boro-mama's small occupations around the house would amount, in the end, to a life's work. She wondered who would ask Boro-mama to mend a tap if his father did not. So when Boro-mama announced, with an air of pride, that the tap he had fixed would not drip for years to come, she gave a small, tap-like sniff, and passed on.

When Nana came home from his chambers, Boro-mama announced the same thing.

'Excellent, excellent,' Nana said, rubbing his hands together. My father, coming in with Nana, with his notebook and textbook, made no comment. He went past to greet his cousin, my mother. They were in different faculties – my father in the economics faculty, and my mother in the political-science faculty. They often did not see each other all day between breakfast and their return.

'So that was one taka for the cycle-rickshaw to the ironmonger's,' Boro-mama said. 'And one for the washer – and I had to buy a new spanner, that was three more – and for the labour as well . . .' He totted it up in his head, his eyes going to the ceiling, then to the floor, then all around the hallway. 'That makes seven taka,' he said eventually.

'That sounds about right,' Nana said, and took out three notes, which he handed to Boro-mama. Behind him, Nani, my father and my mother, who had been listening to this, walked away in silent indignation. As Nani was accustomed to say, Lord Curzon himself would come back to mend your tap, in person, if you paid him that much.

2.

Nana and Nani lived, in the 1950s, in a house in Rankin Street. It was a handsome, two-storey house, with plenty of room for them, their son and their four daughters. There was space, too, for other relations to come and live from time to time, for months or even years. The longest-term resident was, of course, my father.

My father had come to Dacca to study economics, and it was sensible for him to stay with his uncle, my Nana. Nana took it for granted that my father would live in a bedroom-cum-study for the whole of his course; he also took it for granted that one of his daughters would marry my father. Both these things happened. I doubt, however, that my father had any notion that he was fulfilling Nana's will by doing either of them, and if he had suspected it, he would have withdrawn immediately. As it happened, my mother and my father were great friends, and went together to a demonstration against the suppression of the Bengali language by the government. They were thrown into a prison cell together, with dozens of other protesters, and spent the night singing Bengali songs and shouting slogans. My father had grown up in a small village where his father was the teacher at the small mosque. The most exciting thing that had happened to him all his youth was catching a larger-than-usual fish out of a ditch with a twig, a string and a worm on a hook. Being thrown into jail was the most enjoyable night of my father's young life. In the morning, when he and my mother had been released, he went home with her, still singing Bengali songs about national rivers being dammed by the Pakistani yoke. He took a bath and put on a clean white shirt. He oiled and combed his hair. He grew sober. Then he went downstairs and asked my grandfather if he could marry my mother when he had graduated and had found a job in the government service. That would be some years in the future. My grandfather approved in general terms of a respectable young man who worked hard and could think of his life five years in the future, even of one who had spent the previous night in a prison cell.

Then he sent for my mother. He called her to his chambers in the court building, to make the matter as serious as he knew how. My mother walked nervously through the building's white Saracenic arches framing the arcades, each of the arches spattered at ground level with fans of red spit where paan-chewers had cleaned their mouths. Through the open doors, under slowly moving fans, men with great beards and sorrowful expressions draped themselves over ribbon-tied piles of paper in the dusty sunlight, like old bearded mothers in the nurseries where lawsuits are bred and weaned. My mother came finally to her father's chambers, and her father's boy asked her to wait, then showed her in, as if she were a client. My grandfather's methods worked almost too well. He said that her cousin Mahmood was a rascal who had no business taking her to demonstrations, and confined her to the house for the next ten days, sending her home in a rickshaw. My mother wept all through the rickshaw ride, not realizing that her future had been decided in accordance with her wishes.

The future of the household seemed obvious. The daughters, one by one, would grow up, take some education, marry and move out. There would be more sons-in-law like Mahmood, though probably not all of them cousins. There might even, in time, be more children for Nana and Nani. And Laddu would stay at home, taking care of the house, organizing repairs, rebuilding and repainting, perhaps some day taking responsibility for paying bills and supervising the gardeners, the driver, the household staff. Nana supported any number of dependants, hardly any of whom were related to him. There was no reason to suppose that Boro-mama would ever have a reason to leave the house.

3.

One day in the monsoon season, Nana came home from his chambers, and slipped on the wet leaves on the path in the front garden of Rankin Street. There was nothing remarkable about this, apart from the fact that Nana had also slipped on the wet leaves on his way out of the house in the morning. He came into the house with his hands smeared and muddy where he had fallen, calling out for a towel.

'I thought I asked somebody to clear the path,' he said, as he wiped his hands and threw the towel at Mary, who had brought it to him. That was his way: never to refer to demands made of Boro-mama, but just to say, 'I asked somebody'. 'Has the path been cleared?'

'The path?' Era said, coming out of the kitchen.

'No, Papa,' Mary said. 'I don't think it has.'

'That's really too much,' Nana said. 'Where is Laddu?'

There was a certain amount of household bustling in response. Era picked up Dahlia, who had toddled into the hallway to greet her father, and cluckingly carried her off. Mary suddenly found it very urgent to take the towel her father had used upstairs to the laundry basket. My mother and father were bewildered.

'Mira,' Nana said. 'Go and find your brother.'

'Your brother,' Era said. She looked immediately guilty, and walked quickly away upstairs.

116

Mira, only seven, watched her go with a puzzled expression. She did not know how to conceal a fact convincingly. 'I don't think elder-brother is here, Father,' she said.

'What is this?' Nana said, as my grandmother appeared. 'Where is he? He was supposed to carry out one small household chore – I simply asked him to sweep the garden path – and he hasn't done it. That really isn't like him at all.'

'No,' my grandmother said, though she certainly thought that failure to carry out a task to the end was very much like Boro-mama. 'I don't know where he is. I haven't seen him all day. Mira – where is Laddu?'

'I don't know,' Mira said, and then she burst into tears.

'What is this?' Nana said. 'Is this some kind of madhouse? Why won't anybody answer my question?'

'Ask – ask – ask –' Mira said, through her tears '– ask Era. She knows.'

'Era!' Nana shouted. 'Come back here!' My grandfather never shouted. It was one of the things his family admired about him. He never had to raise his voice to get his way. For years afterwards, the time when he shouted for Era-aunty was a favourite family story. The disappearance of Boro-mama was the only occasion when he really yelled. The family would recount this story, with amusement, and if anyone was there who did not know my grandfather, they would pause and look in puzzlement, wondering why it was a story that somebody should shout a name. 'Era!' my grandfather shouted. About him, everyone looked in wonderment, and Era came slowly out of the salon with the burden of what she knew.

'Me?' she said.

Of course it was Era who had been entrusted with the story. Era was a great reader of romantic fiction, and had cast her elder brother in the role of a Heathcliff, the man whom all the world is against, who has every disadvantage but who wins the beautiful heroine at last. Alone among her sisters, she actually looked up to Boro-mama. Even little Dahlia took him for granted,

117

pummelling him and tugging her possessions rudely away from him, as if he were a nursery servant. Those long walks, those lengthy afternoons when Era and her brother were sequestered away, deep in conversation, they had discussed, it turned out, only one topic. Boro-mama loved to talk about himself; Era-aunty loved to listen and, no doubt, to echo the last thing he had said. He was wrong to think that she was a safe repository of secrets – as it turned out, she had been dropping hints to all of her sisters, apart from my mother, for weeks. They all knew where to point the finger on the day that my grandfather shouted. But she was the only one who had kept the entire story secret loyally.

'I think he has run off to marry Sharmin,' Era said, when they were all seated in the salon and some tea had been brought.

Nana looked at Nani, bewildered.

'You should never – never – have asked him to sweep the garden path,' she went on. 'That's why he's run away. You treat him like a servant. You would never ask Mahmood to sweep the garden path.' Era pointed dramatically at my father, punctilious in his white shirt and tie. 'You ask elder-brother to do all these things, and he does them without complaint. Just because he didn't go to university, like Mahmood.'

'But who is Sharmin?' Nana said.

Now it was Nani's turn to look shifty. 'I had no idea he was serious,' she said. And then the whole story came out.

Among Boro-mama's neighbourhood cronies was a man he had been to school with, Nawshad. Nawshad's family was not Bengali but Urdu-speaking: they came from Bihar. Nawshad was very much the same sort of wastrel as Boro-mama. He had grand schemes for making money – to open a cinema, to start importing American cigarettes into Dacca, to open a smart restaurant. None of these ever came to anything, because Nawshad had no money to invest, and none of the gang who spent their days smoking in the neighbourhood store had any money either.

Nawshad had a sister, however, called Sharmin. Sharmin was hard-working and academic, and was now studying at Mitford

118

Medical College. She would be a doctor in a year or two. No, she was not beautiful, but she was clever and interesting, and would get on in life.

She worked too hard, Nawshad said, and it was difficult to persuade her to go out, even to the cinema, once a month. But he did persuade her to come out to the cinema that Friday. It was a hot night, and wet; the cinema smelt of mould and bodies, and the film was an old one that broke down for ten minutes after the first reel. Sharmin had come out with her brother, and his friend Laddu had joined them. They had found plenty to talk about. He had made her laugh.

'Am I the only person in this family who didn't know about any of this?' Nana said.

It seemed that he was. Boro-mama had kept Era up to date with the details of their meetings, and their plans. Sharmin's family lived near Rankin Street, and were in fact known to Nana in general terms. Boro-mama had found opportunities to sneak out of the house and to meet Sharmin in quiet corners, underneath umbrellas, shaded by trees in the street, in the back corners of shops. It all sounded – to Era, and even retold bluntly when the story was over – terribly romantic. In time, Boro-mama had told Era that he wanted to marry Sharmin. He had asked her to explain the whole matter to their father.

'To Papa? I don't think I can, elder brother,' Era said, alarmed. She had enjoyed the stories, and relished the monsoon-kisses, hopeless-doomed-passion aspect of her brother's life. But it had not occurred to her that the story might have possibilities for development. She had had noble renunciation in mind. It was not really credible to her that her brother would want to marry this Bihari girl, rather than take her tear-stained photograph from a secret drawer once a year, and kiss it.

'Well, I certainly can't,' Boro-mama said. 'He would throw me out of the house.'

'Why don't you ask Mahmood?' Era said. 'Papa likes him. He would make him listen.'

A dark expression passed over Boro-mama's features. 'I could never do that,' he said. 'I don't want to be in Mahmood's debt for anything.'

'In Mahmood's debt? Well,' Era said, quite briskly, 'I don't see anything else for it. You will just have to go and talk to Ma. If she can't explain it to Pa, then I don't think anyone will be able to.'

No one knew what the outcome was of the conversation between Boro-mama and his mother, the day when he told her that he wanted to marry an Urdu-speaking Bihari girl called Sharmin. Nobody even knew when or where it took place, this conversation. They were both at home in Rankin Street all day long, with nothing very much to occupy them. It was to be supposed that Boro-mama wandered into his mother's sitting room one morning and stayed there until the outcome was clear. Neither of them shared the details of the conversation with anyone else afterwards. Boro-mama told his sister Era about every detail of his courtship of Sharmin – the meetings under trees, the snatched five minutes, the outings to the park or the walks along the muddy Buriganga river with Nawshad, who knew to remove himself to a distance of fifteen yards. But when the conversation with Nani took place, nobody knew, nor what had been exchanged during it. Only when it was too late for anyone to do anything did it become clear that the conversation had taken place: that both of them had agreed never to mention anything about Sharmin, ever again; that Nani believed that whatever she had said had put an end to the whole business. She had seen no reason to mention any of it to my grandfather.

'Era,' my grandfather said, quite calmly, 'I am not going to punish you. Do you know when it was that Laddu decided to run away and marry this woman?'

Era looked about her helplessly; she gripped her pink scarf to her neck. 'I don't know when he decided,' she said.

'What I mean,' my grandfather said, in his most dispassionate and lawyerly way, 'is when was it that you knew for certain that he was going to run away?'

'To run away? Last night,' Era said. 'He told me last night that he was going to do it today. I should have told everyone. I could have stopped it altogether.'

'Very well,' my grandfather said. 'So I think we can all stop saying that Laddu ran away because I happened to ask him if he would see that the paths were cleared this morning. Clearly, he had made his decision before I mentioned that. Are we all agreed on that point?'

'Yes, Pa,' Mira, Mary, my mother and Era said, and Nana left the room.

'Am I in trouble?' Era said. 'I'm not going to be punished, Ma, am I?'

'Yes,' Nani said. 'You are in serious trouble. I am sure that when your father comes out of his chambers, he will tell me what your punishment is going to be.'

4.

For the next two years, nobody saw or heard of Boro-mama. The only fact that filtered back to Grandfather's house in Rankin Street was that he had, indeed, married a Bihari woman named Sharmin. Incomprehensibly, her family were as deeply opposed to her marriage as our family was. They did not see the apparent honour involved in her marrying Boro-mama, a man without profession, character or education, whose entire prospects had been torn away by the severing of relations with his father. 'I hope his father-in-law finds small jobs for him to do about the house,' my father said caustically. He had endured enough insults from Laddu about cuckoos in the nest, over-educated clowns worming their way into the bosoms of other people's fathers, and other mixed metaphors. He saw no reason to hold back when there was nobody but his cousins about.

Curiously, once Laddu had left the house, my father did not

find it a more comfortable berth. It might have been thought that, with the departure of his only male cousin, my father would find life in Rankin Street very easy. My aunts were fond of their cousin, in general terms, although they did not pretend to understand the esteem in which my mother held him; my grandfather greatly respected him, and was forever holding him up as an example of hard work, discipline and moral rectitude to anyone who would listen and to a few who would not. But perhaps my grandfather needed to berate somebody; perhaps my father feared that he would soon find himself being given the sorts of household tasks that Boro-mama had found so profitable. I don't know this for sure, but perhaps once – just once – Nana asked my father if he could possibly spare the time from his economics studies to have a look at the tap that seemed to be dripping in the downstairs bathroom.

My father was an independent-minded sort of person. Two months after Boro-mama's sudden departure, and a couple of weeks after news had reached Rankin Street that he was irrevocably married to a woman who barely spoke Bengali, my father had moved out too, to a university hall. The gossips exaggerated: Sharmin, even then, spoke perfectly serviceable Bengali, though it was not her first language.

In the next two years, my father finished his economics degree, and then his MA in the same subject. He applied for the government service, and finished almost at the top of his cohort. He was appointed to a job as assistant district commissioner in Barisal, a middle-sized town twelve hours' journey by rocket launch from Dacca. It was decided between him and my mother that they could get married in the middle of 1959. My grandfather and grandmother were very pleased. There seemed no reason to think that Mahmood would disappear from their lives in the way that Boro-mama had done.

During the British time, a space had been cleared in Dacca for a park. It was not made by the British, but it nevertheless had the air of pallid pleasure of the sort that the British enjoyed so much. It was called Balda Garden. As often with the British, it had an educational, almost museum quality. There were collections of botanical specimens from all over the world, some in the open air and some in a few rather crumbling hothouses. There were lawns and flowerbeds, and to that the British had added their own rather limp notions of enjoyment – a lake that had perhaps once been intended for boating parties, but was now just a kidney-shaped lake, and a picturesque Joy House, a combination of Swiss rest-house and Greek amphitheatre to one side. These joyless festival sites had now been taken over and colonized by my nation and its sense of fun. Constant supervision could keep Bengalis on their best behaviour for only so long. There were vendors of sweets and of tea; there were large families spread out comfortably on the lawns; there were picnics that took an entire afternoon to reach the end of; there were balloon-sellers and even, once, an acrobat. Under the trees, where it was quiet and shady, couples sat in peace and quiet, feeding each other from their picnic boxes, blushing, and laughing under their breath. It was a favourite place to visit on a Sunday, which was then the day of rest and pleasure in Dacca, as Friday is now.

My mother and father, before their marriage, regularly met at the Joy House on a Sunday evening. They would walk around the park, talking in the sort of privacy you can only have on the street or in crowds in Dacca.

Both of them were highly punctual people, and when they agreed to meet at the Joy House at six, both of them would be there at six. My father, however, was still more punctual than my mother – in fact, he often regarded her as a poor time-keeper. This was unfair, since she generally arrived at the time specified; my father would arrive a good fifteen or twenty minutes in advance, and pace up and down, inspecting his watch.

At twenty to six, my father was already standing at the Joy House, waiting impatiently. It was a favourite place for meetings, and he stood among people who had made arrangements to meet at half past five as well as a few early arrivals for six, like himself. Along the path came couples, families and small groups of young men, out for a Sunday-afternoon walk. The sun was in my father's eyes, and the groups approaching from his left were mere silhouettes. When a figure greeted him, hesitantly, my father did not know immediately who it was, and greeted him back without hesitation. When he realized that it was Laddu, who would not have realized that my father was standing in a blinding light, it was too late to withdraw the greeting.

'We often come here,' Laddu said. 'It is so pleasant. I wonder – could I introduce my wife to you?'

Boro-mama's wife was, it appeared, the small, sweet, round person by his side. She was not a beauty, but had a pleasant, open face and pale, rather yellowish colouring. Her name was Sharmin, and my father greeted her politely. In the heat, the pre-monsoon congestion in the air, she fanned herself with curt and efficient gestures. Boro-mama asked after everyone, and was surprised to learn that my father no longer lived at the house in Rankin Street. My father thought that Laddu gave him a look of near-respect on hearing this. Like many habitual dependants, Boro-mama made a point of denouncing and disapproving of other people's sponging, as he often called it.

They talked, quite cheerfully, for ten minutes, until my father mentioned that he was waiting for my mother. A look of doubt crossed Boro-mama's face, and he seemed almost on the verge of running away. 'Oh, Laddu,' Sharmin said, taking hold of his arm. To my father's surprise, Laddu suggested that they meet later in the week, perhaps to see a film. My father said – I am sure he said – that he was very busy with work, and with preparations to go to Barisal to take up his post as assistant district commissioner. But Boro-mama pressed him, and eventually he agreed. It was five to six: Boro-mama and Sharmin said their goodbyes and left. It was obvious that they would not risk an encounter with my mother, or with any of the rest of Laddu's family, just yet.

124

5.

The night after my father and Laddu went to the cinema
together, my father was invited round to Nana's house to have
dinner. He had a regular weekly evening there as the guest of
my mother. While he was waiting to take up his appointment
in Barisal, my father had continued living in the university
residence. It had its disadvantages. The price he paid for the
independence of living there was perpetual hunger. In the residence, food was provided as part of the living expenses. But
there were hundreds of other hungry young economists living
in the same place, and the food was basic, dull and prepared in
great vats. Like all male students, at any time, at any place, my
father was appallingly hungry from one end of the week to the
other. His evening at Nana's would set him up for the barren
remainder of the week, eking out the institution's thin dal and
rice, the meagre pickings of its birianis with memories of Nana's
dinner and the occasional bought treat. He was punctilious
about waiting for an invitation, and would not have come if he
were not asked; fortunately, my mother was just as punctilious
about asking him, once a week.

The monsoon rains had broken that week. My father, the aunts
and Nani sat inside the house, looking out on the veranda. The
garden was already soaked with mud; the rains made a deep,
resonant trill on the flat surfaces of the house, made the trees
spatter and slap. Because of the sound of the rain, nobody heard
Nana's car approaching, and the first anyone knew of him was
his voice in the hall. 'Is nobody here?' he called, and then they
heard his umbrella being rapidly opened and shut, two or three
times. His daughters came out to the hall to meet him behind
Nani; my father following somewhere in the back.

'What is that sound?' Nana said, after he had greeted them all
and handed his raincoat and umbrella to the boy.

'What sound?' Nani said.

'That sound of dripping,' he said. 'It kept me awake all last night. Can you hear?'

The aunts compared notes, discovered that they could not hear any particular dripping. Mira asked if he meant the sound of the rain on the terrace, and was asked if she thought he was a fool, and not to be so pert, child.

'I asked for something to be done about it,' Nana said. 'I distinctly asked for something to be done.'

Nani asked, and it became clear that my grandfather was talking about the tap in the upstairs bathroom. It had started dripping the day before. My grandfather could not endure the sound of a dripping tap in the house, and in the end, he said, he had got up in the middle of the night and placed a towel in the hand-basin to mute the sound. As was his way, he must have said, as he left the house in the morning, 'Somebody ought to do something about that dripping tap.' What had happened was that the towel had been removed from the basin, and nothing else had been attempted. My grandfather gave my father, as the only other man in the house, a long, assessing, unfair look, as if he had been there to overhear the suggestion in the morning, and should have done something about the dripping tap. My father looked back.

Once they were seated at table, and my father's first brutish hunger had been satisfied – my mother's sisters used to watch him, stifling giggles, as he laid into the mutton curry – he sat back in his chair and began a conversation.

'It is interesting, this new film,' he said.

'What film are you talking about, Mahmood?' my mother said. He was not a great cinema-goer. Normally he barely listened when my mother's sisters talked about a film they had seen, or some other entertainment.

'There is a film in the cinemas that was shot near Dacca, on the delta,' he said, in a measured way. He stretched his neck, rotated his shoulders, took another mouthful of curry.

It was like my father to assume that nobody else could have known about this film. It had been discussed during its filming

126

by the intelligentsia. A film-maker had gone into the delta and shot the ordinary people at their tasks of fishing and working. It had been said in advance that this would herald a new age of film-making in the region. But *Jago Hua Savera* had come out and nobody had gone to see it at all. Apart from my grandfather, who referred to the cinema scornfully as 'the flicks', everyone in the family was a keen film-goer. But in this case, Era and Mira had gone to see it and returned with big yawns, saying that they had never suffered so much in their lives as at the hands of *Jago Hua Savera* and its fisherfolk.

'Yes,' my father said. 'It is an interesting film.'

'Did you stay to the end, Mahmood?' Era said.

'Yes,' my father said. 'I stayed to the end.' My mother took a large spoonful of rice, poised it above his plate, gave it a good shake, and then offered him a bowl of dal. 'It is only playing in one cinema, I believe.'

'Which cinema is that, Mahmood?' my grandfather said.

'The Shabistan,' my father said. 'It is a very old cinema.'

'I never saw a film as wonderful as *Pyaasa*,' my grandmother said. 'Did you see *Pyaasa*, Mahmood?'

'Oh, yes, *Pyaasa*, that was a film,' Era said. She started singing at the dinner table, a thing my grandfather utterly detested. 'And so sad! One could have cried.'

My grandmother and aunts started comparing their favourite scenes in *Pyaasa*, a film that had taken Dacca by storm two years ago, and was still being talked about. Probably there were cinemas, even then, which were still playing it to faithful audiences. When they had finished, my father said, 'That sounds quite different from *Jago Hua Savera*. I liked it, but Laddu found it dull, just as you did, Era.'

'Who found it dull, Mahmood?' my grandfather said.

'Laddu,' my father said.

'Laddu, did you say?' my grandmother said.

My father went on to explain – he had the attention of the table now. There was no question that not all his sisters-in-law-to-be

127

held him in the great esteem that my mother did, and my grandfather did. For some of them, he was a not very exciting country cousin who, by means of hard work and honesty, had made his way in the world, and was to be the man their eldest sister would marry. They were not rude to him, but they were not accustomed to give him their full attention at the dinner table. They had never spent a night with him in the police cells, singing songs of resistance and independence, and had always found it tricky to visualize the story when my mother told it to them, as she quite frequently did. But once or twice in his life, my father successfully dropped a bombshell, and made people listen to what he had to say. This was one of those times. The whole family listened to him, explaining that he had met not just Laddu, but Laddu's wife Sharmin. At first by chance, in the Balda Gardens, by the Joy House, but afterwards by arrangement: the three of them had gone to see *Jago Hua Savera* only the day before.

'You met her, Mahmood?' Mira said. 'What is she like?'

'Laddu was full of plans,' my father said. 'He kept talking about the cinema, all through the film – he kept saying that nobody had done anything to this cinema for years except change its name. He kept saying that if he had some money, he could run the cinema, transform it into a wonderful place, that it could hardly fail. I don't think the film really held his attention. But I enjoyed it.'

'But what is she like?' Mary said. 'Is she tall or short, fat, thin, is she pretty?'

'I wouldn't say she was pretty,' my father said. 'Not pretty, exactly. But there is something quite agreeable about her face.'

There was a long pause; the whole table sat waiting for my father to continue, but he just went on eating. That seemed to be all he had observed about Laddu's wife.

'And is she sensible, or is she a fool?' Nani said finally. 'How could she marry Laddu in such a hole-and-corner way?'

'I don't know,' my father said. 'We didn't go into all that.'

'I suppose we could ask Laddu and his wife to come here for

dinner,' my grandfather said. 'It seems ridiculous never to see him. And I should meet his wife, before she decides to give us grandchildren. Yes, on the whole, I think Mahmood is right. We should ask Laddu and his wife round here for dinner next week. Not next week – ask them to come as soon as they may. Tomorrow. Push the boat out.'

My father had not, in fact, suggested asking Laddu and Sharmin round for dinner at all. But my grandfather was thinking about the dripping tap in the bathroom next to his bedroom.

7: Nana's Faith in Rustum

1.

In the autumn of 1959, my father and mother married in Dacca. Immediately after their marriage, they went to Barisal, where my father took up his government post as an assistant district commissioner.

There is a large album of photographs of their wedding; formal, well mounted, in a solid volume. Nana used to collect the albums of all his children's weddings, a long line of them in the sitting room; nowadays, I believe my sister has them. In one of the photographs, my mother sits among her sisters. They are solemn-faced: being photographed was still a novelty in the 1950s. The photographs, now, do not seem very festive to us. People lined up and faced the camera. Still, in their lovely pale saris and their wide eyes against the dark wall, my mother and her sisters look like a floating grove of water-lilies. Nani, to one side, still looks young; interested; responsible. I never thought of her as beautiful in her old age, when I knew her, or as one of those women of whom one says, 'How beautiful she must have been when she was young.' But here, just short of fifty, surrounded by her daughters and one son, with one white streak in her hair, just that, she seems at the confident peak of her looks and health. The bright-eyed boy at her feet, her competent hand resting on his head, is Pultoo; the baby in her arms must be Bubbly-aunty. And my mother? Well, that is just my mother. My aunts and the rest of the family may have called her Shiri, but to me she will always be just my mother. The photographs of my father, with his father, his father-in-law, and other male relations seem by comparison tense and wary; my father has somehow been pushed unwillingly to the front of the picture, where he would rather not be. Both sets of photographs seem posed, but only my aunts give the impression that they have been looking forward to posing for the photographer.

They are very different from the photographs of my wedding, as I suppose my wedding was very different from my parents'. Among my wedding photographs, there are images of my new husband feeding me cake; of some rather drunk guests dancing in globes of disco-lighting; of serried ranks of canapés waiting for the party to begin; of many other things that did not happen at my parents' wedding, exactly fifty years before mine, and many things, including the fact of my wedding itself, which were not thought of in 1959, in a country that did not yet exist. But my parents' wedding was a happy day.

Somewhere in the picture of my father with his male relations there is the dark face of Boro-mama, Big-uncle. My grandfather had sent Laddu and his new wife Sharmin an invitation. It had been discovered, after my father had made an approach to them, that the two were living with Sharmin's sister while Sharmin completed her medical degree. Nani was indignant that her eldest son had, apparently, absconded from her house, not to make his own way in life but to go to live off somebody else; not even his wife, since she was studying, but his wife's sister, of whom nothing was known. She kept her comments to herself, and to her daughters, her women friends and neighbours; Nana, who may have thought some of the same things, said nothing whatever against Laddu's domestic circumstances. My parents' wedding would be the perfect opportunity for Laddu to introduce his new wife into the family circle, and to allow himself to be forgiven.

Laddu apologized, but his wife Sharmin was expecting a child, and would not be able to come. However, he was happy to come.

Looking at the photograph, in which Boro-mama stands in a charcoal suit between grandfathers, I try to distinguish some awkwardness, resentment or embarrassment in his face. But he has exactly the same formal, sober, puzzled expression that every Bengali seems to have assumed whenever he was faced with a camera in the 1950s.

2.

After the wedding, my mother and father travelled to Barisal, and my father began his professional life.

The experience was harder for my mother than for my father. My father had grown up in the country. He was used to a quiet existence, and an unsophisticated one. He did not mind a small circle of acquaintances, and did not long for novelty or excitement. He had, too, while studying in Dacca, learnt about self-reliance. These were the characteristics that my mother had admired in her cousin when she agreed to marry him. She was the least extrovert of her sisters, and had never thought of herself as the product of a big city, fashionable or forward in any way. But when she found herself living in a district like Barisal, she discovered that she had, after all, the imprint of some metropolitan habits.

Barisal was a port town, sleepy and remote. Much of it was built of red brick, flushed and rather angry-looking; the largest building in the city was the post office, a palace of almost military grandeur, which in more important towns the British would have faced with marble. The estuary front was busy with rusting launches and fishing boats, coming to and fro, puffing black smoke into the air, the water made slick by their discharges of oil. The ferry port was a constant host to those families, their luggage piled up like great clusters of grapes on the quayside, who are always and will always be transporting themselves from one side of Bengal to the other, as long as Bengal exists. There was something greasy and rusting about the whole town.

In those days, you travelled by rocket launch from Dacca. The government accommodation provided for assistant district commissioners was furnished, so my mother and father travelled with only a few things to begin their married life. A case, between a suitcase and a trunk in size, took my mother's clothing – she knew she would never be able to buy good-quality silk in a place like Barisal – with a box of jewellery buried deep inside. Another case held their books – they had packed separately, but Mahmood had left his books at Nana's house when he moved out, so it seemed sensible to combine his small professional library with my mother's books, a few novels and anthologies of poetry, and pack them all together. My father's clothes and possessions filled a single brown suitcase, and on top of the pile on the back of the porter's wagon, lumbering towards the port and the rocket launch that would take them to their new home in Barisal, was my grandparents' wedding gift: a fine pier-glass in a gold frame, wrapped in layers of cardboard to survive the journey. Other gifts, such as the dining table and chairs, which the uncles had clubbed together to provide, had stayed in Dacca for the time being. Nobody thought that my mother and father would remain in a place like Barisal for very long.

The area was remote and rudimentary. There were, it was said, tigers still roaming the countryside, and one nearby had taken a villager only months before. My mother had only ever seen a tiger in the Calcutta zoo. Many towns in the district were cut off by road from civilization for weeks on end during the rainy season. As the roads that ran along ridges between paddy-fields could be washed away, even when the waters receded there could remain weeks more of isolation while they were rebuilt. Of course, as my father said, during the rainy season, Dacca was often cut off as well. My mother wondered what Dacca was cut off from. It seemed quite sufficient in itself. Whether it was raining or not, Barisal seemed far away and strange, connected only by the water that, for much of the year, isolated other settlements. Shiri regularly thought, during the three years she and my father spent in Barisal, of the heroines of Chekhov, longing for Moscow: he was a writer she had often read without ever quite understanding before.

My mother had expected to live more simply in Barisal than she had in her father's house in Rankin Street. When the porters drew up in front of the ill-kept red-brick bungalow in a line of similar bungalows, however, she realized she had made a mistake in her mind. Her notion of simplicity was of a quality opposed to ornateness or, she realized, the processes of accretion, which had happened in her father's house. Despite moves, war and forced emigration, her father's house had comfortably acquired possessions, furniture, adornments in large numbers. But so, too, it seemed, had the furnished semi-detached bungalow. The caretaker, once found and hailed by the carter, let them in, and the pair of them carried in their three cases.

Once the cases had been deposited in the hallway, and the brownish, flickering electric light had been turned on, it was clear that no preparations had been made for a newly-wed couple. The house was filled with furniture – the rejected, colossal mahogany sideboards, caryatid-supported sofas and tallboys, polished brown and malevolent as giant horrid beetles – that had been out of fashion for forty years at least. Every piece would, on its own, have been too large for the modest rooms; three or four of the hardwood behemoths made an impassable labyrinth. The sad, unchosen selection was very different from her father's warm, mismatched rooms. In the weeks to come, they would discover that the bungalow had been left uninhabited for a year and a half. It had slowly become the repository, among all their neighbours, of any inherited furniture, perfectly good in itself but no longer needed, especially those pieces of giant furniture, which had an aura of evil, rendered in mahogany. Mahmood had lived very simply, with no real attention to comfort or elegance, all his life. But even he seemed dismayed by the bungalow; even he could tell the difference between the warm, damp garden smell of his father-in-law's house, with its easy comfort and soothing lights, and this low, dank place, green mould covering half the back wall and sharp carved mahogany ornamentation, deliberately barking your shins at every turn.

The next morning Shiri woke, and went in the early-morning light through her overcrowded rooms. Outside, in what she thought was her garden, a man was squatting, folded up like a fan, gazing down the muddy road as if at the dawn, waiting for something to happen.

The neighbours soon made themselves known. Like Mahmood, they all worked for the government in Islamabad, filing reports in Urdu and supplying information at their remote superiors' requests. There was little variety. Shiri had never had much of a taste for society; her social life was led among her sisters, a few friends and the daughters of neighbours. In her family, she was a byword for her reluctance to leave home and pay a call. She had never loved the passing of compliments over the tea table and, before her marriage, had never felt concern that Mahmood might deprive her of her very ordinary social life.

But, very soon, she felt first a vague dissatisfaction and then a positive dismay at the limits of the world in which she found herself. Around her was no social variety but the families of her husband's new colleagues. They had come to Barisal from all parts of Pakistan – not just from the Bengali-speaking side, from Dacca and the surrounding provinces, but some, too, from the Urdu-speaking part of the country, the western segment. The men had been posted here, and brought their families. Those families, living for the most part in the bungalows around, were the only society to be had. It did not seem possible to gain access to people who had been born, had grown up and remained in Barisal. And so my mother, who had never felt addicted to social variety, found herself in a world too restricted even for her.

At tea parties, among the mothers and wives of Mahmood's

colleagues, Shiri sat quietly. 'We have had to let our girl go,' one woman said. 'When I counted the sacks of rice, she had been feeding her whole family on our supplies for months.'

'They are so dishonest,' another woman, a Pakistani, said, 'these people. One took an entire bag of chillies – he thought I would not notice. It is really extraordinary.'

Shiri thought she would contribute. 'At home,' she said, 'my friend is great friends with Sheikh Mujib's daughter, Hasina, and she tells a story about a tremendous fuss Hasina made once about the very same thing. She was expecting fifteen sacks of chilli from their estate, and what arrived were only thirteen. She made such a fuss – as if she did not have other things to interest herself in than two missing sacks of chilli.'

But there was a shuffling, an inspection, and a moving on. What was it? Did they not know who Sheikh Mujib was? Did they think there was nothing so very funny in a complaint about servants' honesty? Shiri looked about her, at the young mothers and wives, three of them pregnant; she heard herself beginning to tell the story again, but this time as a story of motherhood, disloyal servants, and the difficulties of living in Barisal. She had not married Mahmood for this.

My father had got to know his colleagues first and, when he returned home at night, he was able to tell her the names and habits of those colleagues. It was like an interesting story to his new wife. And as the weeks passed, she found herself meeting the families of the people that Mahmood had talked about and, in the end, meeting them at home, or in their homes. But now she had got there, everything seemed so hierarchical, and she had to learn who could invite whom first. But in time she got the hang of it, just as the walls were scrubbed and repainted, and most of the furniture cleared out. She and my father made a go of it. It would not be for ever. Four months after they had moved to Barisal, my mother was pregnant. It would be with my elder brother, Zahid.

3.

Even in 1960 it was possible to write a letter from Barisal to Dacca. It was not a swift process. To travel there oneself meant a long journey in rusty old ferries. Even with the best organization and a purposeful will, it would take days rather than hours. And the same was true of a letter, which in any case had to travel in precisely the same way.

When the letter from my mother to Nani turned up in Rankin Street, probably nobody considered how it had had to travel. If they had thought of the ferry, and the heavy plummeting and plunging of its journey, the request would not have been made; the answer would have been different. There was, too, the question of travelling along the roads of the town, in vehicles that probably had iron-rimmed wheels. It was reckless of my mother to think of travelling over such roads in such a way while pregnant. But in the end all was well: my brother Zahid was born at the normal time. Life is full of such decisions, and turns that come to no harm; moments of normality, where no story springs and nothing goes wrong.

The letters were laid out on my grandfather's desk each morning. My grandmother liked to go through them, and separate them into correspondence from clients, and personal family letters. The letters came in one bundle, and Grandmother had to pick out her private correspondence from the general pile. That morning's pile included my mother's weekly letter: she was a punctual correspondent.

My grandmother opened the letter at the desk with the creamy old ivory paperknife, and stood in the study, reading in the slatted light. Alone, she smiled, smoothed out the page on the green leather surface of the desk; she let herself be alone with the knowledge for just one moment. Her other daughters were downstairs: Mary was minding little Bubbly; Era and Mira could be heard talking quietly, intermittently – they were both reading and passing comments as they went.

My grandmother opened the study door carefully. Her chappals clapped against her feet as she carefully went downstairs. She measured her tread. There was no reason to hurry with her news. In the salon, playing with little Bubbly, along with Mary, was Laddu's wife Sharmin. When she did not have classes, she quite often came round to her mother-in-law's house, these days. She made herself useful, and welcome.

'There is a letter from Shiri, from Barisal,' Nani said, to the room in general. 'She says she is having a baby.'

'Shiri, a mother,' Mira said, jumping up and dropping her work on the floor. 'She was only married six months ago. How can someone have a baby when she is only just married?'

'Just married! Don't be such a baby yourself,' Era said, setting her book down. 'Such exciting news. Is Mahmood excited too?'

'It is so strange to think of them being mother and father,' Nadira said. She had been upstairs, and had followed her mother down; she stood, posing, at the foot of the stairs, her arm outstretched along the banister. 'They will be so strict. What clever, dark little babies they are going to have. Sharmin, you have never met my sister Shiri. You don't know what they are like. I can't imagine her having a baby.'

'No,' Sharmin said. She had a charming, unusual accent; it had made her sisters-in-law smile at first, and then, of course, it was just Sharmin's way of talking. 'No, I have never met her. But of course I have heard you all talk about her, and I have met Mahmood. I know what he is like. I would have thought that he would make a very good father, Nadira. Do you think that you are going to make a good aunt?' She heaved herself upwards; she herself was heavily pregnant, and her own confinement could only be days or weeks away.

Nadira's eyes grew big. Taking small, graceful, half-running steps, she went to the mirror in the hallway to inspect herself. 'I had not thought of that,' she said. 'Me an aunt.'

'But you will be an aunt,' my grandmother said. 'And so will Mira, and so will Dahlia, and even baby Bubbly will be an aunt.'

'How can Bubbly be anyone's aunt?' Nadira said. 'She is only just born herself. She can hardly walk. She is no use to anyone. How can she possibly be allowed to be an aunt?'

'Nevertheless,' Nani said, 'she is going to be the baby's aunt. Now, are you going to sit quietly and listen to what else your sister has to say in her letter?'

It may seem strange that my aunts grew excited at the news that they were about to become aunts at the birth of my brother when, by their side, their sister-in-law was also heavily pregnant. They were not being rude. The reason for this was that in Bengali, there is one word for an aunt of a brother's child – the aunt of Laddu's son, who when he was born was called Ejaj – and there is another word for the aunt of your sister's child, such as my brother Zahid, whose impending birth was causing so much excitement (khala and fupu). And, of course, to be the aunt of Sharmin's child was quite a different excitement and a different name altogether, which had been got over with and forgotten about. We like to have as many family excitements as possible, we Bengalis.

My grandmother read the letter out loud. In it, my mother complained rather about Barisal; she said that she did not much like the house they were in, which she had said before, and that Mahmood was getting on well at work with his colleagues, where he was much respected, but that it was difficult to find good servants and that the arguments with the cook had continued, and they had had to find a new maid-of-all-work when the old one had proved dirty. (The cook had turned out to be the master of only three dishes, which came about with terrible monotony, and resisted any suggestion from my mother about a fourth dish – her eventual departure in a rage, an hour before my father's superior and his wife arrived for dinner, was another of my mother's few stories of their life in Barisal. Not that the cook's three dishes were very delicious – the food, my mother said, in Barisal, was simply inedible.) None of these complaints was new. Still, she went on, with all these difficulties, they did have some good news, which she would not hold back from them further: she and Mahmood were to have a baby, in six months' time. And this was fresh to my mother's sisters.

('You see?' Era said to Mira. 'She is not having her baby now. It is coming in six months' time. Now do you understand?'

'Yes, I think I understand,' Mira said.)

They were very happy at this news, my mother wrote, but it was impossible to imagine having the baby in Barisal. The facilities were so wretched, the local doctor old and ignorant and set in his ways. And my mother could not imagine having her first baby without her mother and father and sisters around.

'Sharmin, do you think . . . ?' my grandmother said.

'I think,' Sharmin said slowly, 'I think she might not exaggerate. Some of these country doctors! And perhaps the hospital in Barisal has not been renovated since the British time – since it was built, even. I am afraid that the government in Karachi does not always think of hospitals in East Pakistan when they have money to

140

spend on improving matters. Sometimes mothers-to-be worry needlessly. There is no doubt about that. For myself' – she gestured downwards generally – 'I would not want to have my baby in Barisal.'

'Well, that is just what Shiri says,' my grandmother said.

'I could very easily look up the mother-and-child mortality rates in Barisal,' Sharmin said.

There was a general sucking of teeth, and Mary even made a warding-off sign. Sharmin was a practical, intelligent scientist: she sometimes forgot that she was not talking to other practical, intelligent scientists, but to my aunts.

'Shiri is in no doubt,' my grandmother said. 'She is going to come back and live here before the baby is born. So that is settled. She says that Mahmood will come when the baby is born, and then go back to Barisal, and she and the baby will go back and join them later. I wonder what they will call the dear dark little thing? I am sure it is going to be terribly clever. It will be doing sums in its crib.'

And that was insightful and prophetic of my grandmother, because, indeed, my brother Zahid was to grow up to be a scientist, and to be famous in the family for being able to do very complicated long division in his head before he was ten, and for asking his teachers if they could give him some more sums and equations to do, and sucking his pencil sagely, and for explaining to Nani how she should find out the height of the tamarind tree in front of her house with a protractor and a piece of weighted string, and so on and so forth in the way of very clever children of clever parents, which my parents certainly were.

'A very clever baby, however dark it is going to be. Once Shiri comes back to Dacca,' Era said, 'she is never going to go back to Barisal. She will make Mahmood come and work in Dacca, too. She loves the bright lights too much.'

At this absurdity of Era's, all her sisters giggled behind their hands until Sharmin, who had never met my mother, had to ask what was so amusing. My mother was certainly a modern, capable person, who took charge of business. In that sense she was the product of a city. But she was not someone who could be thought of as loving the bright lights, as Era put it. However, Era was right in her diagnosis, and after the birth of my brother, Ma only briefly went back to Barisal, and for ever afterwards talked about it with a shudder. At six months pregnant, she endured the rattle and shake of the journey back home on those terrible rust-and-steel launches, banging along the rivers like empty biscuit tins, the stench of their black smoke and the foul stink of the water as the boat ran by the tanneries turning her green and making her puke discreetly into a bucket constantly for twenty hours. But, in the event, no harm came to her or to my brother Zahid.

4.

I know what the wooing-and-courtship-and-engagement of my mother and father was like: it must have been very much like the way they behaved to each other when they had been married for decades. They never lost the air of formal respect for each other. My mother had respect for my father because he was so hard-working and ambitious a man. When he attained his ambitions, it did not increase her respect, since she had always had trust in him. My father had respect for my mother because of whose daughter she was: he always felt himself, to some degree, the poor cousin. To the end of their lives, they never used affectionate names for each other. They always addressed each other with the word 'you'.

But I do not know what the wooing-and-courtship-and engage-ment of Boro-mama and Sharmin was like. It was carried on away from the eyes of his family, and of hers; under umbrellas, in the rain, during walks in the public gardens and in cinemas, where they would arrive separately and then sit together. They married in secret, and went to live with Sharmin's sister, whom none of us ever really knew, while Sharmin was finishing her medical degree. So I do not know what they were like at the beginning of their marriage either. All I know is what they were like when my mother returned from Barisal.

'Sometimes a baby is born with two heads,' Nadira said, in the salon at Rankin Street.

'That must be useful,' Dahlia said.

'Useful, how?' Sharmin said. She hooked her fingers underneath the blouse of her sari, tugged and straightened, pulled a swatch of loose sari material, the anchal, as we call it, across her belly. All her sisters-in-law were there, apart from Bubbly, who was having her afternoon nap upstairs. 'How can it be useful to have two heads?'

'You could use one to look forward, and the other to look back,' Nadira said. 'Or you could talk with one head and read with the other one. Or, in the train, you could look out of the window and read the map at the same time. It would be wonderful to have two heads.'

'Your baby is going to be so lucky,' Era said.

'Lucky, how?' Sharmin said.

'Why, if it is born with two heads,' Nadira said, straightfacedly, 'it would really be a gift, if you think about it.'

'We saw a calf born with two heads,' Dahlia said, meaning herself and Nadira. 'It was in the village. Nobody thought that was very useful. They killed it.'

'Pay attention, now,' Mira said to Dahlia seriously. They were both sitting on the sofa, Mira showing Dahlia a stitching trick in needlework. 'Look – you see, I make a kind of loop here, and leave it, not too tight-tight, not too slack, and then – ah – yes. That's it. You see? Now you try.'

'That's right,' Nadira said. 'They did kill it, didn't they? But nobody would kill a dear little baby just because it had two heads.'

'My baby isn't going to have two heads,' Sharmin said composedly. 'Of that I can be sure.'

'Stranger things have happened,' Mary said. 'There is a picture in the encyclopedia of the famous Siamese twins. They were born linked together, at the chest, and they married a pair of sisters and died within three hours of each other at the end of a long life.'

'The end of two long lives, you mean,' Nadira said.

'The end of two long lives, I suppose,' Mary said. 'Well, they had two heads.'

'Two heads? But that is not the same, Mary,' Dahlia said. 'I don't think you quite understand. Those were twins who were joined together. They had two bodies as well as two heads. That is not the same thing at all as Sharmin's baby, if it is born with two heads. That is more like the calf in the village that had to be killed.'

'Babies are never born with two heads,' Sharmin said, without raising her voice. 'Or hardly ever. And I am sure that my baby is not going to be born with two heads.'

'Well,' Nadira said, 'it would be awfully sad if that happened.' And she cast a dramatic sigh. She got up, a graceful, glowing twelve-year-old in a floral, aquamarine cotton frock with puffed sleeves, and went over to the harmonium. She doodled a few notes, then sang a few more. She had a sweet, tuneful voice: her father, in company, would often ask her to perform, her sisters more rarely.

'Sing the song about the flower,' Era said. Nadira ignored her, doodling on the keyboard and singing in a half-voice, as if thinking through the music.

'The thing about a baby – an *unusual* baby –' Nadira said.

'Stop teasing poor Sharmin,' Mira said. She had been occupied, her head down over the embroidery, letting Dahlia follow the sequence of steps with the needle and the bobbin, wrapped tightly with pale blue thread. 'Really, Nadira – stop it. There will be no baby with two heads. Sharmin's baby will be simply perfect, you wait and see.'

'Simply perfect,' Dahlia echoed.

Nadira turned round from the harmonium, breaking off her song. 'But very pale. Look how pale Sharmin is, even sitting next to Era.'

'Yes, she's sitting next to me, and still looks pale, it's true,' Era said complacently. 'Until Sharmin came, I really was the palest of everyone. It must be so strange, everyone in West Pakistan being so pale, even paler than I am.'

'And Laddu has always been dark,' Mary said. 'Mama thought he was a monster when he was born, she told me once.'

'But he's very handsome now,' Mira said.

Era patted Sharmin's arm encouragingly. 'Even if he is dark. No one thought he was a monster.'

'But, Mira,' Dahlia said, 'you weren't there at the time. How could you possibly know?'

'Yes, they will have such dark little babies,' Nadira said. 'They will take after Laddu, I am sure of it. Such dear, dear, black little babies.'

'That's enough,' Mary said, looking up; she pulled the thread tight, held it up to her teeth, and bit to sever it. 'Sharmin, don't listen to them. They are all very silly and rude.'

'Oh, I don't mind,' Sharmin said. 'And it may well be true – Laddu is dark, and we say, you know, that the first baby takes after its father, and if it is a boy, it takes still more after its father. So the baby is bound to be dark, poor little thing. Dark babies are always full of energy, and I know this one will be – I can feel him kicking me all the time.'

'Doesn't that feel strange?' Dahlia said. 'A little stranger kicking you from the inside?'

'We can kick you from the outside, if you want to know what it feels like,' Nadira said. 'There is no problem whatsoever about that.'

5.

My father stayed in Rankin Street until my brother Zahid was born. He was born upstairs, in my grandparents' bedroom. My aunts sat downstairs in a line, handing cups of tea and biscuits to my father, who was quite calm. He was always quite calm. My mother's sisters reacted in different ways to the noises coming from upstairs, the hurrying up and down of the midwife and the house servants.

'I remember when you were born, Dahlia,' Era said. 'You were so quick arriving, the doctors had hardly got here when there you were, crying.'

'But Pultoo – what an age he took!' Mary said. Pultoo, who was five, had been hustled away for the day with his father, taken to the law chambers to sit in a corner and play quietly with pen nibs and paper. He could always be distracted in this way: and it was thought it was not good for small boys to overhear the noises of childbirth. Whether because it would distress and frighten them, or because they would prove themselves nuisances, I do not know. But Pultoo reached his teenage years, as I did and my brother too, believing that babies were what happened after you were taken as a great treat to Nani's law chambers, playing all afternoon with stationery, inkwells and the junior clerks. With five married sisters and a sister-in-law by the time Pultoo was in his teenage years, the day-at-Papa's followed by a return home to find a new tight-swaddled and squashed-face niece-or-nephew became a regular, sometimes twice-annual event, like a festival.

'Pultoo surprised Mama, even,' Era said. 'She said she grew bored with waiting for him.'

'But it was so cold,' Nadira said. 'It was December, and we were all sitting over the fire in sweaters and coats, remember? Papa said he had never known it so cold. Pultoo was nice and warm, and he didn't want to come out.'

All her sisters hid their laughter behind their hands. 'Don't talk such nonsense,' Mary said, on account of my father. But my father paid no attention to anything his sisters-in-law said on any occasion, and he just passed his cup to Mary, who poured him another cup of tea.

'What are you going to do, Mahmood, after the baby is born?' Nadira said.

'Well, I shall be the baby's father, I suppose,' my father said. 'But that is not a full-time occupation. I expect I shall go on doing just what I have been doing, but with the addition of a small extra person.'

'What did you mean?' Mira asked Nadira.

'I meant whether he and Shiri and the dear little baby are going to stay in Dacca,' Nadira said. 'I so want to see the dear little baby every day.'

'You can see dear little baby Bubbly every day,' Mira said. 'And you never seem all that interested in her.'

'Oh, baby Bubbly,' Nadira said. 'Bubbly is getting old and fat and argumentative. One of these days, she is going to go to school, you mark my words. She's no fun at all.'

'Well, there's Sharmin's baby,' Mira said. 'We go to see pretty little Ejaj once a week. Won't he do?'

'Laddu's child,' Nadira said, superfluously. 'I don't count that the same at all.'

'Can I help you to anything, Mahmood?' Mary said.

'I would like some rosogollai, please,' my father said, and my aunt passed him the plate.

'Did Shiri ever succeed in finding a replacement cook, after you had to get rid of the old one?' Mary said. She set the plate down on the yellow teak table and, with a symmetrical gesture of her two forefingers, smoothed the two black wings of her hair behind her large, pointed, elfin ears.

'Well, she was obliged to take on a boy as a temporary replacement,' my father said, continuing very equably with social conversation while his younger sisters-in-law tried to settle his future. 'You see, when they heard that we were returning to Dacca for four months shortly—'

'But I just don't see,' Nadira said, 'why Shiri and Mahmood can't return to Dacca, now that they are going to have a baby.'

'Well, people don't stop having babies simply because they have to live in Barisal,' Era said. 'And that is where Mahmood's job is. He has to be there.'

'But I want them to come back,' Nadira said. 'I want to see the dear little baby every day. Mahmood, can't you leave Shiri here? I'm sure it's bad for her to travel with a baby.'

'Travel with a baby?' Era said, alarmed.

'What is that noise?' Mary said, and it was true: the quality of the noise from upstairs had changed. At the foot of the stairs, a woman stood, smiling: it was the midwife, and though she saw this every day, hundreds of times a year, she had not forgotten that this might be the most important day of the family's lives. And my father's composure now proved itself as thin as a wafer, because he rose with a look of transcendence and anxiety on his face. The midwife said that he had a son: she asked him to come upstairs to his wife and child.

'Is that the baby?' Nadira said. 'Has he really come? Am I an aunt now?'

6.

A week after my brother Zahid was born, my father went back to Barisal. My grandfather in person went down with him to the Dacca port at Sadarghat, where the tottering white four-storeyed launches to Barisal and other river towns departed. This was not a common thing to happen. My grandfather left his daughter and baby grandson at home and ceremonially escorted Mahmood to the port. There was something in his behaviour that expressed some retrospective dissatisfaction with his first grandson, Laddu's child. But my grandfather was always the sort of person who would enjoy the children of his daughters more. And Laddu had married a woman from West Pakistan in secret, even though the child was born when they had been admitted once more to the family. In time my grandfather would be reconciled to Laddu and Sharmin and their children, and would actually take their youngest son, Shibli, into his house to be raised entirely by himself and

Nani. But for the moment, Nana would not have walked Laddu to the end of the road to get a rickshaw. There was a grand and beneficent quality about his taking my father to the Barisal launch on this occasion. It was something to do with the new baby Zahid, sucking contentedly in the warmth of his grandfather's house in Rankin Street, turning his face with interest to the light falling through the mango leaves, or just idly basking with cross-faced assurance in the constant love, curiosity and excitement of his six aunts. The six aunts, particularly the smaller ones, were constantly waking him up from sleep to try to make him give them a smile and a kiss at this time of his life. They wanted him to confirm their belief that he was very dark and very clever, which Zahid did by blowing a bubble on his own and giving them a stern look at being woken up.

The aunts and my grandmother and mother assumed that Nana's surprising offer meant that he had something he needed to say to my father, perhaps shortly before saying goodbye to him. This was my grandfather's way on occasion: to give out a firm instruction to someone when he knew they would not have time to think anything over and respond to it. If this was so, no one knew what Nana said to Mahmood, in the cool high back of the Morris Oxford he drove at the time. I can see my father's face between the arches on the ferry's upper deck, thoughtful to the point of puzzlement; I can see Nana, the best-dressed man on the quay in his white shirt and charcoal-grey suit, giving a single confident wave upwards and turning back between earth-scented bales of jute and tea, walking through the noise of the crowd. There he goes; stepping among the squashed fruit of the market at the gates of the old pink waterfront palace, past the line of hole-in-the-wall barbers' shops, the paper-bag manufacturers with their antique scales, the small engine shops that so frightened me as a child with their glimpse into a world of black oil and obscured metal intricacies. He walks among noise and filth, ignoring the blandishments of the rickshaw-wallahs with the unimpeded step of someone who knows he has given clear and easy instructions.

If there were, in fact, any instructions, nobody knew. But in three months, when Zahid was smiling, my mother broke her sisters' hearts by following her husband back to Barisal. There was no unwillingness in her departure, though everyone had heard her complaints about the place. It became clear that my grandfather had extracted a promise from Mahmood to come back to Dacca within the year, with their baby.

That is what happened, but when they came back, the excitement of my aunts over Zahid had subsided. And soon they themselves began to marry; and Boro-mama's wife Sharmin had another child; and the children of aunts began to be born; and sons-in-law started to move in, because Nani liked to have her daughters about her, and even the daughters who had their own houses tended to come back for dinner and weekends; and soon Nana began to complain that the house in Rankin Street was no longer big enough.

By that time my mother and father had returned to Dacca; my mother was pregnant again with my elder sister. Perhaps under instruction from my grandfather, my father had given up working for the government service. He had, instead, started to study to be a lawyer, which was the profession he held for the rest of his life. My grandfather took him under his wing, as the saying goes. He introduced him to his colleagues and friends, to people like Mr Khandekar-nana and the rest; he found him a set of chambers and passed on clients to my father, shaking his head when Father took on pro bono work; he gave him useful professional advice, which my father took with a good grace. And soon my father's name began to be known, and my mother no longer had to live in Barisal, but lived among the people she had always known and within walking distance of her sisters. My mother was very happy about this.

About one thing my father was absolutely firm. He would not live at my grandfather's house in Rankin Street, but would live in his own house.

'Mahmood is so stubborn,' Nana would say. 'Here is this great house, with plenty of room for everyone.'

There was a shuffling around the room, because quite often, Nana would comment in exactly the opposite way, on how crowded the house was, how impossible it was to live or do any work in it. My mother and father had heard him say this many times, and for this reason my father had insisted on finding a house of his own, in Elephant Road.

The house in Elephant Road counted for my mother as her first proper home. It was the house in which both her daughters were born. It was a two-storey house of the British time, brick-built and with a small garden in front, a larger garden to the back. My parents lived on the upper floor. The house belonged to a friend of my father, who lived with his family on the ground floor. When the upper floor of the house was offered to my parents, they were very happy to take the opportunity. My father's friend was, like him, a lawyer, from quite a distinguished family. His brother, for instance, was a senior officer in the Pakistan Air Force, one of a surprising number of Bengalis who at that time served in the forces, run from Karachi. Afterwards, his loyalty came to be tested.

The services were inconveniently separate from the rest of the house, so that food was always arriving cold or sometimes rained-on. Nobody had replaced the windows since the British had built it, and the small opaque window in the bathroom was stuck in a half-open position. Somebody had opened it and left it in a half-open position all through the monsoon so the wood had swollen and it could not be forced back into a closed position. There was a terrible problem with bedbugs, and only the neighbours on one side could be spoken to at all. Still, my mother and my father loved the house, because it was theirs. Only years later, when they had moved out, did they ever speak about it in a critical way.

Almost immediately after my mother and father moved to Elephant Road, Nana and Nani moved, as if to prove a point, to the house in Dhanmondi where they lived for the rest of their lives. That was the house I remembered them in; the house close to Nana's friend Khandekar-nana, the house with the tamarind tree at the front and the mango tree at the back. It was a much larger house than Rankin Street, and I think Nana could not believe that my parents would go on living in their single-storey house in Elephant Road when they could have a couple of rooms in his courtyard house. But he was mistaken. They went on living in Elephant Road. Nana and Nani, and most of the aunts and Pultoo-mama moved to Dhanmondi, where they were all extremely happy, but my mother and father were much happier to be allowed to go on living in the house in Elephant Road, with bedbugs and the bathroom window that would never close properly.

Nani came to see their house, with Pultoo and Bubbly in their best clothes, and Era and her new husband, living in Dhanmondi with the rest of the family, and Mary and Nadira, Mira and Dahlia. In the end, even Nana came, though his visiting was usually confined to those he had been visiting for years, and he generally expected his family to come to him. Nana enjoyed going round the house and pointing out problems. 'That tree is too close to the house,' he said. 'The roots are growing under the foundation. You will have problems with that.' Shiri shook her head, thanked Grandfather and afterwards, alone, said to Mahmood that the old man worried about everything, even things that were not his to worry about. And it was a pretty tree, which did no one any harm.

They all came, but Boro-mama and his wife did not come. They were asked, and said they would come; but they did not come. A year went by; a year and six months. They did not come. And finally somebody must have had a word because they agreed to come. It may have been Nana, who had grown rather fond of Sharmin, and would often exchange a word or two with her in private when he wanted to get things achieved. The day they were supposed to come, my father came home early from his new offices, and put on a new shirt and tie; my mother had put the children in new clothes and forbidden them to eat the cakes she

152

had brought from the confectioner's; the house had been cleaned from top to bottom, because still they did not really know Sharmin, and were a little in awe of her. The ride from Boro-mama's house to Elephant Road should not have taken more than twenty minutes. (Back then, you did not worry about traffic in Dacca.) But they waited, on the covered sofas, on their best behaviour, with the houseboy in a new white Panjabi waiting for the rattle of a rickshaw outside, and nothing came.

In time nervousness gave way to slight crossness. They wondered what could have happened to them. My father said something rather dismissive about Boro-mama; my mother said that he had never been the same since he had married that woman from West Pakistan. My father said, on the contrary, he had always been exactly the same, had always taken advantage of people and never tried to fulfil his obligations. My mother said that it was only an invitation to tea, and it hardly mattered whether he came or not. He could always come another day, if something important had occurred to prevent them coming. My father said, sharply, that he could not conceive of anything of any importance ever occurring in the life of Laddu.

And so my parents had one of their very rare arguments, although there was nothing in what either of them thought that would bring them to disagreement. Laddu and his wife never came, that afternoon. They were prevented.

7.

In Boro-mama's house, everything was in a state of chaos. Sharmin had discovered that Laddu had been paying attention to a widow of the neighbourhood, a woman of only twenty-eight whose husband had been shot in the street. Laddu had been seen coming out of the block of flats where she lived when he was supposed to be on a domestic errand. For this, she had told him to sleep elsewhere. 'Where should I sleep?' Laddu said. The house had only three bedrooms, one Laddu and Sharmin's, one each for their (now) two children. Downstairs, two rooms were Sharmin's consulting room and a small waiting room for her patients, and there was only a small sitting room and dining room. 'Where should I sleep?' Laddu said again. 'Should I ask Ahmed to move over and make room for me?' He was referring to their cook. But in the end Sharmin made him sleep on the sofa in the sitting room, which was now filled with Laddu's clothes and bedclothes, his film magazines and projects. A small lawnmower sat in the sitting room before the french windows. Laddu had thought he would repair it soon, and it was dripping oil on to the parquet.

Because Laddu could not sleep on the thin upholstery and rigid slats of the sofas in the sitting room, he was in a constant bad mood; because the sitting room was uninhabitable, and all family life was happening in the dining room or Sharmin's bedroom, Sharmin was in no less of a bad mood. The subject of the widow had not been raised since that first terrible argument.

'Don't forget,' Sharmin said, coming into the sitting room, 'we are going to visit Mahmood and Shiri in their new house this afternoon.'

'I remembered,' Laddu said, sitting up, tousling his hair and yawning. 'When are we leaving?'

'My surgery finishes at half past three,' Sharmin said, 'so we leave at four. Make sure the children are ready. Their clothes are in the press. Have you a clean shirt? Good. Tell Ahmed to go to the confectioner's for a box of something to take to Mahmood's new house. Good. What else? What are you planning to do today? Try to – it doesn't matter, Laddu.'

Laddu had met the widow when she was outside her apartment block, struggling with an umbrella that the wind had turned inside out. For a moment, he had thought she was the sister of one of his friends, or had thought, with a scarf blown over her face, that she actually was one of his own sisters – his story varied. He was good with his hands, and had quickly turned the umbrella the right way round, fitting the spines back into their sockets, testing their firm hold in the shelter of the widow's apartment block until the umbrella was as good as new and would be of use for years. It was shocking, Laddu said, how people could question the motives and behaviour of a respectable widowed woman and, in any case, he had thought he knew her, or she was his sister – his story varied. But two weeks ago, Laddu had been seen coming out of the widow's apartment block by his wife. She had been in a rickshaw, returning home. The thin scream of her displeasure had been carried past him, emerging from the caged and painted back of the rickshaw. He had wondered what that sound could be.

'Are the children ready?' Sharmin said, when she emerged from her consulting room, the last of her patients despatched with a prescription or a kindly word.

The children were neatly dressed, or placed in a basket for carrying.

'And the sweets?'

'And the rickshaw?'

Laddu had done everything, the motor-rickshaw and the driver already waiting outside. Between Laddu and Sharmin's house in Rankin Street and my parents' house in Elephant Road, it was not possible to walk. It was too far; there was a busy market area. These days, too, it was not always wise to walk in the streets of Dacca.

With parcels and children, they piled into the back of the rickshaw. The elder child sat on his father's lap, to the right; the younger, packed into a basket and firmly asleep, rested on his mother's knees. A white cardboard box of sweets, leaking sugar syrup that turned the corners translucent, sat squarely between them. The two-stroke engine started up, and they began the short journey.

On every street corner, there was a pair of soldiers, gripping their guns, staring contemptuously into car and rickshaw. Along

155

Dalhousie Street, the soldiers were waving down traffic, or waving it past. On the side of the road, one small platoon had stopped an old woman on her way to market, and made her unload her baskets of vegetables; they were going through her brinjal, dropping them on the road as they went, paying no attention to her screams of protest. 'Don't stare,' Sharmin said to her elder child. 'Look – there' – pointing at the other side of the road – 'is that Mary-aunty? There, I'm sure that's Mary-aunty, in the pretty pink frock.'

'I don't think it is,' Laddu said. He was slow to catch on sometimes. 'No, that definitely isn't.'

Sharmin paid no attention to him. But her attempt at distraction would have been unsuccessful in any case, because in another minute there was the sight of another pair of soldiers at work. They had stopped four country boys – probably brothers, and one of them could not have been more than eight years old – and had put them against the wall, their hands stretched out. The rickshaw was past before they could see what was going to happen to the brothers. Sharmin wondered whether something had happened; whether the army was responding to something. But she knew that this sort of thing had been happening for months. It was not safe to walk in the streets of Dacca, and the threats did not come from badmashes, thugs, mastans, but from the people in uniform. When anything happened in the streets, ever, a small crowd of onlookers with nothing better to do normally gathered, and stood, and stared. It was the natural order of things. Nowadays, when an old woman's basket of brinjal was turned out on the street, when boys were forced to stand against a wall with their legs spread and wait for humiliation, these were not sights that Dacca wished to stand and stare at. News had reached the people in the streets that they were not safe; they had not, like Sharmin and Laddu, been able to travel in a rickshaw. The best they could do was to hurry past these interesting sights.

'What is this?' Laddu said, as the rickshaw turned off Elephant

Road. There, at the end, was a group of six soldiers in uniform, standing across the road with their arms folded. 'What is this?'

'Roadblock, sahib,' the rickshaw driver said. 'Stay calm, please. Will all be fine.'

Laddu tightened his grip on the child as the rickshaw driver pulled to one side. Roadblocks were appearing in unexpected places in Dacca. They were searching for weapons, propaganda, anti-state activism. Since the ban on Bengali poetry and music a few months earlier, the definition of these things had expanded. Nobody would leave the house carrying a volume of Tagore, or even the children's magazine that bore the latest exciting adventures of Feluda the detective. Feluda the detective, who was just then taking all of Bengal by storm, was supposed to be all right to carry about, but you really never knew. Most people would not take written material of any sort in Bengali out of the house. My grandfather had gone as far as to seal up his library and hide it in the cellar of the house in Dhanmondi.

The soldiers at the roadblock came over and peered into the back; one, two children, two adults, and a box. 'Get out,' he said. He had a broad, dark face, his expression betraying nothing. He was Bengali, in another's uniform.

Laddu and the elder child got out of the rickshaw one side; Sharmin, carrying her baby, placed her box of sweets on the seat of the rickshaw, and got out on the other side. A wave of the rifle, and the rickshaw driver, too, got out. He leant against his cab, fumbling for cheroots. His bored expression suggested this was not the first time this had happened to him today.

'You – stay here,' the man who seemed to be the commanding officer said, taking over from the soldier who had ordered them out. Bengali was not the first language of this officer, and it took Laddu a moment to understand that he was telling him to come over to the side of the road. 'Here! Stay here!' Laddu and Sharmin walked over. The elder child was holding tightly to his father's hand. 'What are you doing with this woman – you? Speak!'

157

'This is my wife,' Laddu said. He had said that with pride many times before. He was proud to be married to a beautiful and clever woman, and had often enjoyed introducing her to his friends, family, to his acquaintances when he met them in the park or the street. Now he said it not with pride but with amazement. Of course Sharmin was his wife.

The commanding officer looked from Laddu, dark in the face, to pale Sharmin. 'Wife?' he said, with a jeer, and then broke into Urdu. Laddu spoke his wife's language only a little – it was typical of him not to have paid attention in school, and not to have acquired much skill in it afterwards. Sharmin intervened. 'Yes,' she repeated, in her pretty Bengali, 'this man is my husband. We are visiting his sister, who lives in this road.'

Before Laddu could understand, a soldier had taken his small son away from him, leading him back to the rickshaw, bending down to say something kindly and reassuring to the little boy. The commanding officer said something in Urdu again; it sounded not like a question, but like a sardonic comment. Sharmin said nothing. Laddu looked at her, but she sternly shook her head, growing pink. Whatever the comment had been, she would not translate it for her husband.

'Why do you marry this woman?' the commanding officer said, in his learnt Bengali. 'Tell me. Why do you not marry someone from your own sort?'

'That is not your business,' Laddu said.

'You must stay with your own sort,' the officer said. He smiled with bright, wet teeth. Laddu looked at his soldiers: they were all, like him, Bengali, and none made any sign of disapproval or shame.

'My wife is a doctor,' he said. 'You are insulting her now.'

'Laddu,' Sharmin said in warning.

'You must not speak to people like this with no reason,' Laddu said, his voice growing in heat. His sense of his own worth was being jeered at by a stranger, a Lahore thug in uniform who could hardly understand what was said to him. 'I will make a complaint about this treatment.'

'A complaint,' the commanding officer said wonderingly. Perhaps the word was unfamiliar to him. In a leisurely way, he walked over to the rickshaw. He reached into the back, ignoring the driver, and fetched the box of sweets. 'What's that?' he said, presenting the box of sweets to Sharmin. She opened the ten-inch-square white box: Bengali sweets, twelve by twelve, alternating like a chessboard. 'Give it to me,' he said, and she handed it over. He took out one, two, three; he dropped them back into the box carelessly, having seen there was nothing beneath them, not even a confectioner's invoice. He took a fourth, from the middle of the box, and bit into it. He grimaced, and spat the sweet out on to the road. Sharmin and Laddu said nothing, in indignation. The commanding officer handed the open box to his second in command. Not understanding, the soldier moved as if to hand it back to her, carelessly. But the officer in charge made an impatient move, and deliberately knocked the box and its contents to the street. The bright and glistening sweets scattered across the mud, and he stamped on them, three times.

'How dare you?' Laddu began, taking a step forward, but at the same time, the commanding officer gave a brief, certain nod. His second in command raised his rifle butt, and hit Laddu very hard on the side of his head. Laddu fell to his knees with a roar of pain, and the soldier, once more, hit him between the shoulder blades with the rifle butt. Laddu's face was in the dirt of the street, pressed into the mud and the scattering of fine, delicious sweets, and he saw a boot descending as he shut his eyes.

'That is not your wife,' the officer in charge said in a level voice. 'That must not be your wife.' He looked at Sharmin, screaming, and, with a thoughtful air, called her a terrible name. The small platoon stood back from the scene, and shortly Laddu, with Sharmin's help, stood up shakily and went back to the rickshaw. His beautiful, clean white shirt was smeared with mud and sugar and blood. Their small son had watched everything, and was burying his wailing head in a soldier's thigh-muscle.

All the time the rickshaw driver had not altered his position, and had continued to smoke his cheroot without comment or protest.

8.

My grandfather, about this time, believing that the ban on Bengali poetry and music would soon allow the soldiers of the Pakistani state to force their way into private homes and destroy private possessions had given orders for the library to be parcelled up, along with the best of the pictures, Nadira's harmonium, the collection of music and even four or five bowls. Nana had a beautiful library; much of it went back to his student days in Calcutta when, he said, he would always prefer to buy a book he really wanted to read rather than eat dinner. (Mr Khandekar-nana said that he usually insisted on eating dinner anyway, sometimes at the expense of Mr Khandekar-nana, who was not so much of a bibliophile in youth.) Nana made sure the parcels were well sealed against damp and insects; he had them placed in wool-lined tea chests, and sealed again; he had them taken down to the cellar of the house in Dhanmondi, and when his books, and pictures, and bowls, and music, and his daughter's instrument were safely stowed, he decided to have the door to the cellar plastered over, so that it would simply look like a single-roomed cellar beneath the house, with a few odds and ends that had been discarded, and a few broken chairs piled up against the false plaster wall. Rustum did all of this at my grandfather's command. My grandfather did not carry out any of these precautions in secret, but asked the servants of the house to pack and parcel and plaster. When the task was done, the house looked bare and dull, with nothing but law books on the shelves of my grandfather's study.

'It's just until things improve,' my grandfather said, and it was very unlike him to plead or cajole, in any circumstances. 'Think of it as packing for a long sea voyage. Imagine we're travelling to England, and won't be able to unpack any books for months, or even years.'

'You will never be able to remember, never, never, never,' my grandmother said. 'You have forgotten already what the wall was that you put everything behind. You will try to knock down the wrong wall and the house will collapse.'

'Rustum remembers,' Nana said. 'I have faith in Rustum. He remembers where the door used to be.'

8: How Amit Went to Calcutta

1.

At the school where Amit taught, there was a new teacher. He was a man in early middle age called Khadim Hussain. He was said to be an English master although, as far as Amit knew, no English master had left and none needed replacing.

The headmaster, Mr D. B. Chakravarty, introduced Khadim Hussain at a short meeting of all the staff. Mr D. B. Chakravarty usually did this but always before, when introducing a new member of staff, he had taken the opportunity to talk about the ethos of the school, the high standards it had maintained, and his hopes for its future. The school had been set up in the British time, and Mr D. B. Chakravarty was very keen on the idea that it had managed to maintain the best standards of the past to build a better nation for the future.

Amit had heard this speech several times before. It had been made when he himself had been introduced to the rest of the staff. He had wondered at the time what application it had to him personally, but had been flattered by such fine-sounding phrases. On subsequent occasions, Mr D. B. Chakravarty had made very much the same speech over the head of a series of different new teachers. Mr D. B. Chakravarty's speeches at Founder's Day, when the boys placed a garland of orange blossom around the marble neck of the bust in the great hall, were not intended for the boys whom they seemed to address. They were intended for the parents of the boys, who would understand what a good-quality education their sons were receiving. In the same way, when Mr D. B. Chakravarty made these speeches on the arrival of a new member of staff, they were intended to remind the rest of the staff of how they should behave, and the standards they were expected to keep up. The school was a good one, and the headmaster had succeeded, during his twenty years in post, in maintaining the standards he regularly proclaimed.

Khadim Hussain entered the staff quarters with Mr D. B. Chakravarty. They made a small kind of pantomime of politeness at the door: Mr D. B. Chakravarty offered to give way to this unfamiliar face. The unfamiliar face, a thin, alert face with hair divided down the middle, a large nose, thin eyebrows and not very good, rather broken teeth as he smiled, gave a generally not very trustworthy impression. The person insisted, as Mr D. B. Chakravarty offered to follow him into the room, on giving way to the headmaster. But he did so in a smiling, insincerely respectful way. It was not the way of a junior teacher. Amit had the impression, watching this performance, that this person was a government inspector of some sort.

And Mr D. B. Chakravarty did not make his normal speech of welcome and exhortation, but merely said, in a brief way, that this was Mr Khadim Hussain; that he was joining the school from a post in a different part of the country; that his particular area of expertise was poetry and drama, especially in English. He would also be moving about the school in the weeks to come, discovering 'how things are done here,' Mr D. B. Chakravarty said. But he turned to the assured man seated by his side, whose eyes were roaming brightly round the room, smiling with his bad teeth as he fixed on any member of the staff. It was as if Mr D. B. Chakravarty was enquiring of the newcomer how things were done here. 'I appeal to every member of staff to give Mr Khadim Hussain every aid and assistance in their power,' the headmaster finished. Without waiting to introduce himself to the other members of staff assembled, Mr Khadim Hussain nodded generally around the room. Without speaking, he left the room before the headmaster, holding the door open for him. The headmaster followed.

2.

For six years now, Amit had been teaching at the high school. He taught the boys the Bengali language, poetry and music. At first, he had found them a challenge to teach. Their liveliness had, in Amit's first year or two, spilled over into chaos. Once, an older master had stepped in from the next room to enquire what this unholy bedlam could be. Amit had believed, after his first year, that Mr D. B. Chakravarty would call him in and ask him to find another position in different circumstances.

But that had not happened and, in time, these matters had improved. In teaching these subjects, he had eventually discovered within himself an authority he had not suspected. He looked with interest, these days, at those of his colleagues who had difficulty maintaining discipline in their classes; he even gave advice to them from time to time. It was not a matter of shouting, he believed, but of a sort of strength within – a sort of stillness or perhaps attentiveness or . . . It had to be said that when you tried to express that sort of thing in words, it always sounded remarkably silly. But Amit, now, had no difficulty keeping the boys' attention. A firm look would quell the beginnings of rebellion. In reality, he believed that his classes were orderly and he was successful with the boys because the subject was beautiful and they could understand that. Of course they would pay attention, and Amit believed that his contribution to the school's reputation was generally respected and valued. When he went home to the flat belonging to Mrs Khandekar, which he shared with his friend Altaf, he was cheerful at the end of the day's work, even exhilarated, and had funny stories to tell his friend about the day's events.

It was two weeks before Amit came across Mr Khadim Hussain again. The boys were studying a poem by Jibananda Das. It was an advanced class, full of clever boys, and one of them, as Mr Khadim Hussain came into the room without knocking, was

164

standing at the blackboard and reading the difficult but interesting poem:

> Nevertheless, the owl stays wide awake;
> The rotten still frog begs two more moments
> in the hope of another dawn in conceivable warmth.
> We feel in the deep tracelessness of flocking darkness
> the unforgiving enmity of the mosquito-net all around . . .

The boys looked round as the door opened and Mr Khadim Hussain came in. The boys, surprisingly, stood up in an almost military way. Amit had, from the beginning, excused this class from standing up when he entered. They were nearly adults, and, besides, most of them were taller than him. But they stood up for Mr Khadim Hussain, who came into the room without saying anything. A boy at the back offered Mr Khadim Hussain his chair, and he took it. 'Sit down, boys,' Amit said. It occurred to him that the class were more likely to have come across Mr Khadim Hussain in the course of their day than he was. They knew what he expected. In the staff quarters, no one had discussed the newcomer, even when everyone knew that he had inspected a colleague's classes.

The class went on, in a more awkward way. 'What does this line mean?' Amit said, and the boys inspected their textbooks closely, not catching anyone's eye. 'Does the poet literally mean an owl when he speaks of an owl? Is there an owl before the poet's eye?' Amit was aware that he was rambling and blustering, and the boys had no response to make to him.

'Does the owl symbolize the world of nature?' a boy finally suggested.

Amit continued. Mr Khadim Hussain's piercing eye, at the back of the class, was on him. From time to time, he wrote something in his notebook. His pen jabbed and stabbed at the page.

At the end of the class, Mr Khadim Hussain closed his notebook and placed his pen carefully in the upper pocket of his white shirt. He smiled with his broken teeth at Amit. 'I believe we must vacate this room,' he said. Amit had seen his shape going to and fro in the school, and had grown to recognize his sharp, fussy, haste-filled walk in the corridors. He had never before heard his voice, which was deep and slightly lisping. 'We will talk while we walk.'

Amit put his books together in a pile, and together they left the classroom, leaving the boys to await their next teacher.

'That was an interesting poem you were teaching,' Hussain said. 'What was it?'

Amit explained.

'You did not ask the boys to explain the moral and religious aspects of the poem,' Hussain said. 'Or had you discussed that first of all, before I arrived?'

'I do not think the poem has a religious aspect,' Amit said. 'It did not occur to me to ask the boys to find a religious meaning in the poem.'

They were walking side by side as they talked; they might have been taken for two colleagues undertaking a serious, good-natured, scholarly conversation. Hussain gave a small, disappointed hiss. 'Have you not thought of teaching poetry first of all if it refers to the Prophet, peace be upon him? Surely that must be the best poetry to teach to our pupils.'

Amit thought that if Hussain taught English literature, he would find it hard to base his teaching exclusively upon writing of that description, but did not say so. 'Jibananda Das is a very beautiful poet,' he said. 'He is one of the best poets in Bengali.'

'There are other very beautiful poets who write on more elevated themes,' Hussain said. 'Owls and frogs, making their noises in the swamp. It does not seem a very elevated subject for poetry.' He pushed open the double doors that led to the staff quarters. By the headmaster's study, four boys were waiting on cane chairs to receive punishment for that morning's misdemeanours. 'And poetry on religious themes should take first place in education, do you not agree?'

166

'Jibananda Das may have written poetry with a religious aspect,' Amit said, aware that he was treading on dangerous ground here. 'But he was not a Muslim, so it would not have been the sort of religious poetry you have in mind.'

Mr Khadim Hussain turned and looked at Amit. Amit knew what he meant to convey: that in this school, Hindu poetry was being taught by Hindu schoolmasters, and this was going to come to an end. 'I think you teach music, too,' he said.

'Yes, I do,' Amit said.

'And the literature you teach, it seems to be the sort of literature, poetry, that men and women sing in whorehouses,' Mr Khadim Hussain said. There was no rage in his voice; he seemed perfectly calm, as if establishing a point. Amit could not respond to this. 'That is what I understood from this morning's – ah – display. Well, let us see how things develop in the next few weeks and months. We are shaping a new generation here, I believe. It would be a pity if their knowledge was made up exclusively of the ditties sung in the foulest back-streets of Gulistan. I'm sure you agree.'

He opened the door to the staff quarters, indicating that Amit should go in before him. But when Amit was through the door, it swung to behind him. Mr Khadim Hussain had gone on, without saying goodbye, to his next task.

At the end of that week, a typed notice, signed by Mr D. B. Chakravarty, Headmaster, went up on the notice board in the staff quarters, to the effect that Mr Khadim Hussain, BA (Hons) had been appointed deputy headmaster with responsibility for curriculum, with immediate effect.

3.

'The exhibition has been cancelled,' Amit said, at home, to Altaf.

'What exhibition is that?' Altaf said.

Amit poured out water from the jug into the blue china bowl; he splashed water on his face, then, cupping water in his hands, snorted it up his nose and spurted it out again. Once more, he took a handful of water and splashed it all over his face. When he was done and the dust of the street washed clean, he reached out for his towel. Altaf passed it to him before returning to his cooking.

'What exhibition were you talking about?' Altaf said.

'The boys' painting exhibition,' Amit said. 'It has been going on every year since anyone can remember, even the headmaster. Every January, there is keen competition to be included in the exhibition. There is no prize, but there is a plaque in the art room listing the people who have been declared the best three painters of the year, and the boys like it. "Mother Padma".'

'Yes?' Altaf said.

'That was the theme set for the exhibition this year. Mr D. B. Chakravarty likes to set the topic himself. He says it enables the visitor to the exhibition to compare like with like, and not have to worry about whether a drawing of tomatoes is better than a painting of the Maidan at Calcutta. And this year he set the topic of Mother Padma. It was a popular topic, I understand. The boys like to paint the river. They find it a challenge, and it requires a trip away from the art room, which of course they enjoy.'

'But the exhibition has been cancelled.'

'Mr D. B. Chakravarty set the topic six months ago. And that was really a long while back. It was certainly before the advent of Mr Khadim Hussain.'

'I take it that Mr Khadim Hussain does not approve.'

'He discovered about the art prize and the exhibition when he paid a visit to the art room last week, and found it filled with paintings of the Padma river. He does not believe that the school should be teaching art at all, of course.'

'Of course. Does he aim to turn the school into a madrasa?'

'And that afternoon, a letter appeared on the notice board saying that the annual art competition and exhibition would not now take place. It was signed by Mr D. B. Chakravarty himself but, then, all the letters that appear in this way are signed by him. I believe that they are written by Mr Khadim Hussain. His power waxes terrible within the school.'

'Who is he?' Altaf asked, at length.

Amit considered. 'He is the new deputy headmaster,' he said.

'I understand that,' Altaf said.

'But when he arrived, two weeks ago, he was introduced as a new teacher of English. That I do not understand. I would be very surprised to discover that he has taught a single class in English since he arrived, and there are other aspects of his conversation which lead me to think that he does not have a great deal of interest in English as a subject. I cannot understand why Mr D. B. Chakravarty would mislead us in such a way.'

Altaf placed the bowls of dal, fish and rice on the floor between them, and sat down, crossing his legs. 'I understand that,' he said. 'I understand how this man was introduced. But do you think that is who he really is?'

'No,' Amit said. 'I am sorry to say so. But I do not think he is a teacher at all.'

It was six months now since Altaf and Amit had last been to the school of the Bengali arts they had helped to start up. For three years it had been a success. The hall which the university had made available had become a public meeting place, and readings of poetry, exhibitions of art, tapestry and pottery, as well as musical performances and other matters, had taken place there with some popularity. If nothing else, people came there to talk. There was a sense of defiance. Sometimes when the people attending the school of the Bengali arts left the university, they found that there were police officers at the gate, or sometimes merely a group of badmashes lounging in a threatening way. But that had not discouraged the many people who came – the weekly attenders, the occasional regulars, and those who were just drawn in by an interesting subject, or out of a mild, unfocused curiosity. Only a year ago did the numbers begin to fall, until nobody was left but the founders and a pair of undissuadables. Something had changed. No longer did people leaving the Bengali academy sing as they left, as they walked past the police officers at the gate. They hurried out as if they might have been attending anything at the university. And then one day Altaf said to Amit that there was no point in attending the academy any longer; that they could achieve as much by performing at home, at Sufiya's, at Mr Khandekar's, at one of a dozen houses in Dhanmondi where they were welcome guests. But those evenings were happening less and less frequently, too.

'My days are numbered,' Amit said. 'I have to face it. This is no country for me any longer.'

Altaf froze. 'What do you mean?'

'Altaf, consider,' Amit said. 'I believe that Mr Khadim Hussain has been sent into the school to purge it of undesirable elements. Who has sent him? I do not know, but I think he acts in accordance with official instructions. What future is there in this school for someone of my sort, teaching music and poetry? They don't want a Hindu in front of a class. Mr Khadim Hussain more or less told me that I should stop teaching poetry by Hindus.'

'It is only one man,' Altaf said. 'You can get another job. Dacca is a big city. We can easily manage.'

'No, it is not only one man,' Amit said. 'For the moment it is only one man. But soon it will be everyone. They have put an end to the Bengali academy without having to pass any laws. If they want to stop anything further – the singing of poetry, painting, even those thousands of books they don't like – they will have to pass laws against them.'

'We can still sing at home – quietly, with the windows closed,' Altaf said. 'And there is your aunt's money, which you could live on.'

Amit's aunt, the year before, had died in Cox's Bazaar, leaving half her little all to Amit. Some division had come between her and her son, darkly hinted at in letters from Cox's Bazaar, and the legacy, Amit and Altaf had concluded, was by way of a posthumous point-scoring. The money had not been touched: Amit believed that his cousin would come demanding its restitution.

'No,' Amit said. 'Singing at home quietly with the windows closed, that is no good. That is *shameful*, Altaf.'

'What shall we do?' Altaf said.

'I can travel to Calcutta,' Amit said. 'I can take my things and go to India. I still have relations there. They will find a corner of a room for me, and I can make a living of some sort. And there is my aunt's money, as you say. It is safer for people of my sort there.'

'It may not get any worse,' Altaf said. 'It may not get any worse at the school. This man may have achieved everything he set out to achieve, and now things will start to improve. Please, Amit, don't do anything just yet. In six months things may be completely different.'

'Yes,' Amit said, in his lucid way. 'That is what I am afraid of. And if I leave now, it will be possible to make my way to Calcutta. But in six months' time, who knows? And who knows what the mob and their rulers will be doing to a poor Hindu musician? What they will be *allowed*, permitted by law, to be doing to a poor Hindu musician? Altaf, it is best if I leave now.'

'Let me come with you,' Altaf said. He was close to tears. He knew what Amit was like when he had decided something. At these moments, Amit's practicality came to the surface. He saw things clearly. But for Altaf, being with his friend Amit would always come first. It hurt him that, for the reasons of Amit's practicality, and not for the first time, it would be best if his own interests and wishes were neglected. Amit never had any suspicion, Altaf believed, that Altaf thought in any other way. Altaf had always hidden his vulnerability.

But Amit now surprised Altaf. 'Don't say something which will pain both of us,' he said. 'I would rather stay with you. But it is dangerous, you understand. And it would be dangerous for you to come to Calcutta with me. What would you do?'

'What will you do?'

'I will manage. And this is not going to last for ever. Perhaps only a few years. And then I can come back, and everything will be exactly as it was before, but Mr Khadim Hussain will be gone and never heard of. You will see.'

'Only a few years,' Altaf said. He really thought he would cry now.

'I will come back, and you will have a beautiful wife, and as I come through the door with a box of sandesh, there will be small children butting their heads at my knees. And you will hardly remember your old friend, returning from Calcutta. You will see how it will be. Altaf, this must be.'

'Don't go—' Altaf said, but his voice was choking. 'Don't go tomorrow, at least.'

Amit stared at him. 'But, Altaf – of course I am not talking about leaving tomorrow. Not this week, or next week.'

'When?'

'Soon. But not so very soon.'

4.

The next day, when Amit went into the staff quarters, he found his colleagues clustered around the notice board, peering through glass. He looked, too, and found that Mr D. B. Chakravarty, Headmaster, was taking indefinite leave, due to ill health. In his absence, which was expected to be lengthy, Mr Khadim Hussain, BA (Hons), had been appointed by the school governors and the Ministry of Education to take his place as Acting Headmaster.

A separate notice to the side of this one indicated that a meeting would be held of all staff at the close of the school day in the staff quarters. It was signed Khadim Hussain, BA (Hons), Headmaster (Acting).

Amit, with all his colleagues, attended that meeting and listened to what Mr Khadim Hussain had to say about the new laws emanating from the government about the public status of cultural products, and also about the lines along which this school must now be run. At the end of the meeting he concluded, without mentioning it to anyone at all, that he must leave for Calcutta without any further delay.

5.

When Amit left the apartment in the morning, one week later, it was still dark. Altaf must be still asleep. He would wake in two or three hours to discover that Amit had gone. Perhaps he would understand where Amit had gone. It had been made clear between them. It had proved necessary to leave earlier than he had promised, that was all. But in himself Amit knew what a betrayal this was.

And Altaf would not notice at once that Amit had left. In his hand he had only a very small grip. He understood from the start that it was not going to be easy to cross the border at Jessore. There had been no train from Dacca to Calcutta for years, since the beginning of the war with India. The border was guarded by the East Pakistan Rifles. There was no possibility that they would let anyone through with a large suitcase. In his grip, Amit had placed a clean shirt and change of underwear, for the journey; there were two leaves of soap, for the journey; and for the journey, however long it would be, an envelope of photographs; photographs of Amit's father, a photograph of Altaf and Amit performing together, caught unaware at a party. Was it at Begum Sufiya's? Amit was not sure. He placed the photograph with the other important ones, in the envelope, in the grip. In five separate places about his person and in the bag Amit had placed sums of money. The smaller sums he had left conspicuous, in the hope that the border guards and the roaming soldiery would be satisfied with that; the larger he had sewn into the lining of the grip. And, impossible to leave behind, there was a single book: it was a collection of poetry in Bengali. Amit knew most of it by heart, and he took it with him. He did not know what else he could do.

The rest of Amit's poor possessions he had had to leave behind him. It must be thought that Altaf would only slowly realize that Amit had gone. Amit had thought of writing a letter to leave on the table, but that was impossible. He would write, at length, when he was safe in Calcutta. And behind him he left his shirts and trousers, neatly folded in the cupboard; his own kitchen possessions, his knives and two plates; his rough towels and bed linen; his thirty or forty books, some of which he had had for ever. Most painful was the leaving behind of his tabla. There were so many reasons for taking that – it would be the means of earning a new living in Calcutta. But he left it where it was, on the trunk at the end of his narrow bed, like a gift. It would attract attention to him at the borders and beyond. But more than that, Amit was leaving behind him something that would anchor him to the place he had been happiest. He was a citizen of this apartment, and here was his surety of return. At first Altaf would think he had not left. But then, seeing the tabla at the foot of his bed, Altaf would understand that Amit meant to return.

Amit made his way through the before-dawn streets; the sleepers, shrunken bundles of humanity, buried in layers of blanket, paper, were wrapped in what they could gather from the street's detritus against the cold of the night; lying like giant seedpods for the day to waken them. One against the other they slept, the prime places against a building's wall where the warmth resided all through the night. The rest tucked up against each other, backs against each other, separated and sharing their night-coverings. Amit picked his way through their heavy tessellations. As he walked, he remained in the shadows under the trees where they slept. Once, at the T-junction of the main road, he saw, gathered together against the cold, a group of soldiers, manning a roadblock, stamping in the early-morning chill and yawning. They were on the other side of the road. Amit remained in the shadows under the trees, and walked confidently in the dark, knowing that he would not be seen if he did not want to be seen.

The people began to rise, and thicken.

The quiet air was disturbed with the honk and call of humanity waking, and moving, and, soon, beginning to pray. That would send him on his way. He was nearing the bus station. Perhaps in normal times, there would be silence here, in the late small hours of the morning. But yesterday, a hundred Mr Khadim Hussains had gone into a hundred schools, and offices, and businesses, and explained how things were to be from now on. Amit was not the only person who had thought on going to bed that he would rise early, and go to see if he could find a life somewhere else. Tomorrow there would be hundreds more, and the day after that, still more. One day – Amit did not know when that day would be – many hundreds of people more than this would arrive at the bus station, and would discover, at some point in their journey, that they were too late. Weeks or months too late.

Altaf, at ten, had left Calcutta with his family. He had fled from the city because of his religion and his family's religion. He had told the story of how the train had stopped, and people bearing arms had entered, while he had been stuffed in hiding under the seat of the carriage. In fact, it had not been partisans seeking someone to murder, but soldiers. Amit had heard this exciting story many times from Altaf. Now he was making the opposite journey, for the same reason. Or perhaps an opposite reason. At some point in the journey, people bearing arms might again enter the bus, and this time they might not be soldiers trying to protect them. That was how history worked: a good thing balanced by a bad thing. Altaf still had relations living in Calcutta. If Amit ever reached Calcutta, he would visit them and make an offering afterwards, to his gods, that the day he had chosen to travel was not the day that had proved too late, just as they had stayed where they were, and been saved.

6.

In the dark of the night, Amit fought his way towards the small beacon of the ticket window; the struggle through the crowd in silence. It was like the dim-lit struggles in dreams, through dense and limb-clogging stuff. Those around him were heavy, heaving, weighted, mud-like, and through the dark of the night they pushed against each other in silence or with muffled groans. There were so many of Amit's type, fighting to leave Dacca. At one point, the hips of two women closed on either side of his wrist, the hand holding the grip and all his money inside. The movement seemed choreographed, and he feared he was being expertly robbed. From somewhere, he found his foot, and went down heavily on a woman's foot – he had no idea whether he had hit his target, but the women moved, so slightly, and his hand and the grip slipped back to his side of the wall of flesh. It took forty minutes to fight to the front and provide himself with a ticket for the first leg of the journey. Although it was possible to buy a single ticket for the whole journey, it would be much more expensive than getting a bus to the Padma ferry, and on the other side getting a local bus to his destination. He was heading to Jessore. That was where you could cross.

And all the seats in the bus were taken when he reached it. He had no idea how long the journey to the ferry would take – sixteen, twenty hours – and it was with some relief that he saw that a seat by the window was not, after all, taken; a woman had placed a parcel in it, and as Amit forced his way past her, she was shrieking that it was her sister's place, that her sister was coming, she had sworn she was coming. Amit was firm and, as the first light of day fell and the driver took his place, he shut out the woman's shrieks and complaints into his right ear by closing his eyes and resting his head against the bars. He could have waited for the next bus to the Padma ferry. But he did not know if there would be a next bus to the Padma ferry, or Jessore, or anywhere.

Later – he did not know how much later – the bus stopped by the side of a river, and all the passengers disembarked. It was the Padma. He had somehow slept most of the journey. The men went to piss in a ditch. The sky was hot and blunt with light. The riverbanks were wet clay cliffs, rawly torn off by the flood, and the same grey colour as the river's turbulence. The women wandered off with their children to try to find some food, some sweets; one confided in another that she knew a perfect place for hilsha fish, the man who sold the best hilsha fish on the banks by the ferry wharf. But there was nobody. There was only a great queue of buses, waiting for the ferry to take them across. And there were no boats. Only one was now making its slow way from the wharf, for the long hours of the hot crossing. There was none at the wharf, and though the river was so wide the other bank could not be seen, there was no sign of another boat returning. That might be the only boat in service, making its laden way across the river as the hours came and went. And Amit could see that the bus he had travelled in would not be in the next boatload, or perhaps the one after that.

He rested under the shadow of a tree all day long; the boat came, took on one load, and departed. Night fell, and a hundred small camps made themselves apparent as cooking broke out. A constellation of modest fires spread across the riverbank. Amit had no food with him. He had not planned for a journey of this length, and had thought that the vendors he remembered from previous journeys would supply his needs. But perhaps the vendors were fleeing, like everyone else. As there seemed to be no chance of leaving on a boat soon, he lay on the grass under the tree, his grip under his head.

It was nearly dawn before a place was found for Amit's bus on a ferry. Red-eyed and frail, his bones aching but his grip still in his fist, undisturbed, he leant out from the upper deck of the ferry as it pulled into the river. The sky was lightening from the east and, in an hour, the river's midstream clarities of blue and silver were all that mattered. All at once, by the side of the ferry, a school of bottleneck river dolphins broke the surface, grey and plump and glistening. Mother Padma: Amit could have won a competition with his painting of it.

A fog of suspicion and fear seemed to lift with the river crossing, and by the end of it, Amit was sharing rice and fish with a family of seven, sitting companionably on the upper deck in the brisk warm breeze. The father was a professor of physics at the college in Jessore, and knew Amit's school. Indeed, they had acquaintances in common. That seemed to be a necessary condition before they – a Hindu and a Muslim family – could sit down together and share food. They were returning to Jessore from visiting relations in Dacca, and Amit? Oh, Amit was paying a short visit to an aunt in Calcutta, just for a very few days. Amit by now had the second-youngest child on his lap while the mother dealt with the baby; they were friends already. They laughed together about Amit's neighbour on the bus. Her shrieks and complaints had spread through the bus, and this family had pitied Amit when they realized he had nothing to do with her. When, towards the end of the morning, they saw the far side of the river approached, the family invited Amit to join with them in finding the small local bus that would take them on their onwards journey. 'After all,' the professor of physics said, 'we are colleagues in the same business, the trade of education, after all.' Amit gratefully accepted, and, once on the bus, they made themselves a small encampment, the eight of them.

'I do not know how the situation is at the border crossing,' Amit said to the father of the family. 'At Jessore.'

'I heard it is very bad,' the father said, his voice jolting. The road on this side of the Padma was terrible, unrepaired for years and perhaps decades. The bus banged and rattled into potholes, throwing the passengers about; cries of distress were coming from the front half of the seating. 'It is hopeless to arrive there after the very early morning. The lines are enormous, and if you arrive at midday, you may queue all day and half the night.'

'We have been travelling so long,' Amit said. 'I do not know when we are to reach Jessore.'

'I think it is two hours from here,' the father said. 'Or a little more. And everything is so much slower these days.' He joggled the child on his lap, who was sucking his thumb in his sleep, and smoothed the boy's hair. 'I do not think we will reach Jessore much before the sun sets.'

'And then to wait at the border crossing. How long?'

'I don't know,' the father said. 'Well, it is much easier for us than for you. Our journey ends in Jessore, but you have about as far again to go. Why not come and stay with us? There is no problem. With eight or nine in the house, one more will make not much difference. We will be glad to have you, if you don't mind resting on a sofa. A tight squeeze, but it will be perfectly all right. Your best plan is to get up very early, to get to the border crossing before first light. Perhaps then we will not have so long to wait.'

Amit was in no condition to refuse: he was dusty, dirty and sore after his night under the tree, and would welcome an opportunity to wash and change his shirt, at the very least. The second youngest child had taken a fancy to him, and Amit carried him on his shoulders from the bus station to the little house, twenty minutes' walk away, feeling the child's weight of tiredness fall from one side to the other, feeling that he, too, could welcome a shoulder to sit on, a great pair of arms to lift him into bed. Afterwards, he remembered nothing of this house in Jessore, or of washing or laying himself down or, like the others, of falling into sleep at once, even on this narrow and hard sofa.

In the dark, he was being shaken awake, and all about him were children, like a nightmare of misplaced responsibility and duty. He had no idea where he was, or what had happened to him. He could not understand why Altaf's apartment was filled with children in the dark. Then he understood where he was and what was happening. He was grateful for tea, but the owner of the house – who was he? – was waving him off, yawning, hiding his small-hours face. A professor of physics, Amit remembered too late, as he sat in the rickshaw. The border approached. For a moment he misconstrued the scene, and it seemed quiet, deserted. But then he understood what he was looking at. It was humanity, unmoving. At the front sauntered a pack of the East Pakistan Rifles, turning from side to side, assessing and ignoring the people before them.

7.

As he saw the posture and stance of the East Pakistan Rifles before the people they had subjected, were subjecting, were about to subject, Amit saw all at once his future. He saw himself manhandled and ordered about by the authorities; he saw the struggle to pass through the smallest of gates with a crowd pressing down upon him. He saw his bag being searched, its lining slit. He saw his money being docketed and counted and taken away from him, with nothing but a few rupees left to his name. He saw his life in India, arriving at his cousin's house with nothing but a small grip with a slashed lining and an apologetic face. He saw himself working at what he could get, sleeping in the corners of rooms, negotiating and explaining with Indian officials, getting nowhere in the course of weeks. He thought of Altaf, and what lay ahead of him, too. He saw no end to the war that was coming. He saw old women thrown to the street, and a boot crushing the face of a boy as he lay prone in a concrete-floored prison cell.

Amit stepped down from the rickshaw. He said to himself that what must be done must not be shrunk from. He took his place at the back of the gigantic crowd, fighting for admission to India. On the other side of the border, he knew, the train for Calcutta was standing.

8.

It would be five years before Amit returned to Dacca. Before anything else at all, he went back to Altaf's apartment, the one they had rented from Mrs Khandekar. He still thought of it as his apartment. He had not said goodbye, after all.

Amit seemed to be banging hard at the door of the apartment for minutes. He had concluded that Altaf must have gone out; he made this conclusion to ward off the worse conclusion that Altaf had moved away or, worse, was no longer of the world. He dismissed those from his mind. He would have heard. But how would he have heard? Who would have told him? Nobody knew where he had been living. The chain of acquaintance between him and his family, and his family and his life with Altaf, had been separated, long before the war. He would have heard, nevertheless. Some wound would have opened in the depths of him, and he would have felt that Altaf had given up on him.

There was no response to his knocking. He knew that when he had left, years ago, he would not have left without taking the keys to the apartment. But somewhere in the intervening five years of moving about and asking friends for space for a week or two, of living out of bags, the keys had been mislaid and lost. Amit felt this betrayal, but it was right that, having left Altaf in such a way, he could not in any case have reached for his keys and let himself in. Amit bent to his bag, to find a piece of paper to leave some sort of note for Altaf – he could say that he would return at the same time the next day. But then the door to the apartment opened. It was Altaf. In the five years since Amit had left the apartment without saying goodbye, Altaf had changed. He was thinner; older; his face was lined. Some pleasure lit up in his face on seeing Amit, but it was veiled, confused. Altaf's eyes were red-rimmed and exhausted. It was almost with a gesture of falling that he put his arms around Amit, and almost with a need for support that he stayed there, leaning on his short friend.

'Come in, come in,' he said.

'So, you see,' Amit said. 'I returned. I did return. I promised you I should. But there does not seem to be a wife in our flat. I thought I would return to find a wife and children, Altaf. I think I said I would. But there is no wife, and no children, unless they are out for the afternoon.'

Amit was aware he was babbling, and Altaf was calm and undisturbed by his arrival. It was not the way things had been before, he was sure.

'No,' Altaf said. 'There is no wife.'

'I was sure you would marry, once I had gone,' Amit said, sitting down in exactly his old space. Nothing at all seemed to have changed. It was with a small shock that he saw that the teak box was still in the place he had left it. He had brought it from his aunt's house, the box she had given him and which had been too large for him to carry away with him in his precipitate flight. He had given it not one thought in the previous five years, and Altaf had not moved it; had seen it every day.

'No, I did not marry,' Altaf said. 'There didn't seem to be a wife to be had. I looked for one, after you went. But there wasn't one to be had. Perhaps it was the war, and women having to stay inside. They did not want to meet a husband, and I am not much of a prospect as a husband, even if all the women of Bangladesh now decide to marry at once and have to find husbands. Yes, it must have been the war – the war that you ran away to avoid, before it started, remember, Amit? And of course I was doing work for Mrs Khandekar.'

'How is Mrs Khandekar?' Amit said. He wanted to ask how Altaf was. He wanted to ask how Altaf's war had been, and how he had been left at the end of it. But Altaf had made that impossible, and he said, 'And Mr Khandekar, how is he?'

'They are still fine, very well,' Altaf said. 'One of their sons is no longer with us, however. He was shot by the Pakistanis, retreating.'

'We Bengalis,' Amit said, experimenting with the sound of it.

He hardly ever said that, nowadays. There was only Altaf he had ever wanted to say it to. As for Amit, he had perhaps saved the word up for his friend to hear first. He did not know whether Altaf had done the same.

'We Bengalis,' Altaf said, and smiled. He raised his glass of water from the table where it had been sitting. Amit recognized the glass – a dark blue glass, bubbles blown in the side. Altaf took a deep drink from it, and set it back down. Amit, without asking, took it in turn. Altaf watched him raise it to his mouth without saying anything; a moment later Amit was spluttering. It was not water that Altaf had in his glass, but some sort of back-street firewater. Amit went to the kitchen, and spat out what he had in his mouth. The kitchen was unchanged, mostly, but bleak. When Amit had lived here, there had always been an onion and an aubergine in the vegetable basket, a small sack of rice and a tin of oil to hand. But there was nothing of that here. The basket was empty. There was only an unlabelled dark green bottle in the open cupboard. Amit believed that that was what Altaf had been drinking. When he had rinsed out the taste from his mouth, he came back in, slowly. Altaf already had the glass again in his hand, and did not look up.

'Is this how it has been?' Amit said.

'It was mostly like this,' Altaf said.

'I wish . . .' Amit said. But there was nothing to wish for.

'How did you think it would be?' Altaf said. 'How did you think it would be, when you returned? Do you know how life has been for us, since you went without saying goodbye? I don't believe you can know.'

'No,' Amit said. 'But I had to leave. You know that.'

It was at some point in the next few days that Amit reached up and, from the top shelf, brought down his tabla. That he had left here. Altaf had wrapped it in oilcloth, and the creases were thick with dust. The tabla was quite all right, however, and Amit next brought down what was in its place next to it, Altaf's harmonium. He had expected that the harmonium would be dusty, the wood of the case cracked, the instrument's tone gone through neglect and abandon. But it had been cared for, and regularly handled. Amit still had to master his understanding of the parts of Altaf's life that had been abandoned, fallen into disuse, and the parts, such as breathing, that had continued nevertheless. When Altaf came back in from his short walk – it was something Amit had told him to start doing – he saw the harmonium, out of its place, and the tabla, too, by it, and he understood. He smiled at Amit, and shook his head slightly before going back to his room to lie down and rest. The gesture was theatrical, kindly, and unconvincing; it meant to convey to Amit that music was over for Altaf, and he would never be able to explain quite why.

Amit smiled too, however, alone in the room; smiled to himself. Altaf did not fool him as easily as all that.

9: How I Was Allowed to Eat As Much As I Liked

1.

'What is all of this?' Nana was saying. He was upstairs in his house. He had come home a half-hour before; had greeted Nani, his daughters, his two mothers, his younger son, the elder son and his wife and children, another husband or two and a few more children of his daughters, such as Zahid, my brother, and my sisters Sushmita and Sunchita and his grandson, or adopted child Shibli, who appeared to be wailing for some reason. He had given a more distant greeting to the cousins from the village who had arrived the week before, asking for accommodation. All this greeting and enquiries after people's health had taken some time. When it was done, and Nana saw that the boy was preparing his tray of tea, he went upstairs. The cook, Ahmed, came to the kitchen door, and a veiled, warning expression passed between him and Nani, sitting on the couch reading the newspaper to my mother. Dahlia and Nadira exchanged a questioning glance; Nadira tightly shook her head to discourage comment. The cook went back into the kitchen. A question came from upstairs. My grandfather never needed to raise his voice. In that house, he was listened to.

'What is all this?' Nana said, coming downstairs with his barrister's stock in his hand.

'What is all what?' Nani said. 'You know quite well what everything is. Your question makes no sense to me whatsoever. You must speak more clearly.'

'On my balcony,' Nana said. 'My balcony is full of rubbish and detritus. What is all of that?'

'That is not rubbish and detritus,' Nani said, quite calmly. 'The chillis and tomatoes and mangoes and all of that are being dried, and will be preserved and pickled. It will be out of your way in a day or two.' Nana made a gesture of impatience, and retreated back up to his bedroom. 'Your father is quite right,' Nani said to her daughters. 'We should not simply have occupied his balcony without asking for permission first. But where else are Ahmed and I supposed to lay fruit out for pickling where no one will walk over it and the animals won't steal it? I don't think he has considered that. And if there is no pickling and preserving, what does he think we are all going to eat the next time we can't leave the house? We have no idea how long it will go on for, next time.'

When Nana moved from the house in Rankin Street to the larger house in Dhanmondi, the courtyard house that I remembered from my own childhood, he must have anticipated having more space at his disposal. Most of all, he wanted to have a balcony on which to rest at the end of his day's labours, where the servants would bring him tea and biscuits, and he could call, perhaps, for one clean and well-behaved grandchild to pay their dutiful respects. He had envied his friend Khandekar, who had exactly this arrangement, and a civilized habit of receiving guests in his private space. Within months of the move, however, the balcony in Dhanmondi was claimed by the alliance of Nani and Ahmed, the cook. They had discovered that it was the perfect space for drying chillis and tamarind and other things, for pickles. It faced the right way; it was secluded from the raids of children and animals; it had just the right extent for the load of pickles that could be dealt with in an afternoon, which is about as much time as anyone wants to devote to pickling.

In the same way, Nana had believed that his larger, more orderly house would only gain in gracious space in time. Boro-mama had left home, and had set up his own household with his wife and, now, three children. My mother and father had insisted on doing the same, and had been living in Elephant Road. Era-aunty had followed suit, and though Mary-aunty had so far not married, most of the younger aunts and, in time, Pultoo-mama as well would make homes of their own.

The normal process began to be reversed with Boro-mama's fourth child. Sharmin had been determined that she would have only two children, one to replace her in the world, the other to replace her husband. She firmly believed that it was wrong to go on populating the world in this way. But her husband, Laddu, held no such conviction. He hardly thought about his relations with his wife in terms even of whether they could afford to raise another child, let alone in terms of their responsibility to mankind. Sharmin believed that he had taken personal responsibility for not giving her a third child, who came as a surprise. When she found that she was pregnant with a fourth, she blamed Laddu entirely.

'Well,' Mira said at the time, 'I don't think it could have been completely big-brother's doing.'

'Sharmin must have played a necessary role,' Nadira said. 'Big-brother didn't bring it about all on his own.'

But that seemed to be Sharmin's belief, and she went about saying quite openly to Laddu's sisters that the only possible action for her to take was to abort the baby. Soft-hearted Dahlia overheard this – at thirteen, she would weep over the death of a baby bird or the fate of an old beggar, bent double over a stick in the street. She reported it, in tears, to Nani, who talked it over with Nana. So Shibli was born, and not aborted for the sake of his mother's principles. But almost as soon as he was born, he came to live in my grandfather's house, and was brought up by them as their own youngest son. At first a wet-nurse came in, and then Shibli provided employment for the same ayah who had brought up most of his aunts and his uncle. After all, my grandmother used to say, Shibli was only eight years younger than her own youngest child, Bubbly. It was a pleasure to have a baby in the house again after a short break. 'Come and see what little Shibli is doing!' Nani would call from her room, hanging entranced over his cradle. It was as if she had never had children of her own; or as if Shibli and the condition of grandmotherhood had returned her to her first moment of motherhood, looking after that son whom only she really remembered, killed in Calcutta during the war by Japanese bombs. There was something new and girlish about this stately, sharp woman in the company of Sharmin's baby.

(When we were children, this history of Shibli's was well known to us and, in particular, how Shibli should have been aborted. I do not know who told us the story in the first place, and it seems a harsh, ruthless fact to share with children. But for the most part it only confirmed my opinion that Shibli had been horribly spoilt and indulged by everyone, not just since the moment of his birth but well before that. His characteristic simper was that of someone who knew he had survived against terrible odds.)

Shibli, however, was just one small child. Shortly afterwards, Nana's two mothers arrived for a stay of three weeks. They were the two wives of Nana's father, the last man in my family to marry polygamously, and though only one of them was his real mother, he treated them both in exactly the same way, with an ostentatious courtesy of the door-opening, standing-up, rice-serving, deferential kind. He would perform these conspicuous gestures individually, and not to them as a pair; when he did so, the mother who had his attention would beam, her old face screwing up into a smiling pucker, as if she had never been so well treated.

The stay of three weeks was supposed to be a short visit, but they arrived with a substantial volume of luggage following behind in a cart. It was clear that they were unhappy about living in the country apart from the rest of the family. Things, they said, were not as easy as they had once been. So Nana invited them to stay as long as they liked. Perhaps that was what they had been hoping for. They made themselves useful about the house, minding

Bubbly, mending socks, fetching clean jars of water for Pultoo when he was at the easel painting, or even cleaning his brushes for him – they were great admirers of Pultoo's early work. Their limit came only with baby Shibli, whom they were prepared to coo over but not to bear responsibility for. Most of all, they made themselves useful by being pleasant and humble about the house, never intruding or making noise. The room they shared made no extra work for the servants. Nani might have disliked their constant grinding of paan with a pestle, the two of them sitting quietly in a corner muttering trivialities. They were keen observers, from their window, of the comings and goings of the neighbourhood, and always wanted to know when they glimpsed a child who he or she could possibly be. But, on the whole, nobody minded them being there, and it was with some surprise that Pultoo remarked one day that it must be a year since his two grandmothers had come to stay in Dhanmondi.

2.

The house of Khandekar, Nana's great friend, was quite different. When the roadblocks allowed, and there were fewer soldiers on the streets making a nuisance of themselves, Nana often went round there for some civilized company. There were only two sons, both students at the university, both clever, respectful, well-read boys, who would be a credit to their parents and to the legal profession. Khandekar and his wife had their home to themselves. There were never great crowds of daughters, sons-in-law and grandchildren demanding attention; never a party of cousins from the village muttering among themselves and asking to help with the preparation of food. Nobody threatened to dry mangoes on Khandekar's balcony. It was pleasant to visit for an hour or two, take a cup of tea; to continue the argument about a law suit, to chat quietly about the state of affairs, to drift back under the portico, with the rich, jam-like scent of mimosa and jasmine, to the pleasant subject of their student days in Calcutta. It was good to laugh and banter and forget the world altogether, as much as they could.

Nana would have gone to Khandekar's house every day if he could. But all too often, however, it proved impossible to get from one house to another, even though they were separated by only a ten-minute journey. Roadblocks sprang up overnight; bands of soldiers loitered at corners; men who in other times would have been the refuse of the street appeared out of nowhere, demanding papers with threats and refusing to state the source of their authority. There were many such people, these days, and they were especially evident about Khandekar's house. Many of them were Bihari, who had never felt at home, had always been dissatisfied among the Bengalis. It was impossible to know in advance whether one would get to the end of one's journey unmolested. My grandfather was not accustomed to put up with the impudence of soldiers and badmashes demanding papers. But he saw that there was no point in fighting it. He gloomily observed over the dinner table that, like an old-fashioned Munshi, he would soon have to forbid the women of his family to leave the house. The women of his family objected. But he laid down the law, and none of them, not even Nani, was ever allowed to go on a visit, or to the market, without taking Rustum to sit by them and stare down the soldiery. To Khandekar's house, they could not go at all, not unless they went with him. Just by there the roadblocks shifted, repositioned, multiplied. Across the road, from side to side, mysterious and unproductive workmen spread, making the way impassable. Once, a huge demonstration appeared from nowhere, blocking the roads in that quarter for hours. It turned out to be a demonstration of loyalty to the government in West Pakistan, and therefore hired for this specific occasion. Sometimes it was possible to reach Khandekar's house, so very few streets away, by ingenious means. But often those ingenious means failed; no resourceful improvisation on Rustum's part could circumvent

190

protesters, roadblocks, security checks, puffed-up and paid-for Biharis, or ersatz roadworks. The authorities were bending all their ingenuity on blocking these streets, because a few houses away from Khandekar lived Sheikh Mujib.

These days, Sheikh Mujib's face was everywhere in Dacca. His candidacy to become prime minister had spread and spread, and his face was on every wall. His thick glasses, his open, trustworthy, intelligent face promised that things would change. He was no longer seen at Sufiya's, and his usual enjoyment of walking in the street had come to an end. Occasionally there was a genuine demonstration outside Sheikh Mujib's house in support of him. Several times, Sheikh Mujib had made an appearance before bigger crowds, calling for some measure of independence. It was two years since the government had clamped down on statements of Bengal nationhood – meaning poetry, music, images. What would happen, people started to ask, if a Bengali were elected president of the whole country – if the capital of Pakistan were moved to Dacca, the first language of the nation became Bengali, and the national anthem became a song of Tagore's? It was unthinkable. But there was no obvious reason why it should not happen – Nana and Khandekar agreed on this. There were more voters in East Pakistan than in West Pakistan, and they were less divided. There might be no democratic reason why Sheikh Mujib should not be elected president of the divided country, and make his first presidential speech in the language of Dacca, to an immense crowd of Bengalis, on the banks of the Padma. Was there any reason why not? What would happen if it came to pass? The authorities did not propose to find out. Hence the fake roadworks and the hired demonstrators and the security checks, blocking in Sheikh Mujib's house. They often prevented visitors to his near neighbours, too, such as Khandekar, to my grandfather's immense irritation, as I said.

'I am astonished you reached us,' Khandekar said, coming to the door himself as my grandfather came in. 'Astonished. We were waiting yesterday all day for my wife's brother to visit, and the day before that, and the day before that, but nothing. He was turned back three, four times. What is your secret, my dear fellow?'

'I have no idea,' Nana said. 'I have not the foggiest idea. This is a very strange situation. Some days you cannot leave your house before being harassed; others you sail through without the smallest disturbance. I did see that the goons were drawn up the road somewhat, besieging your distinguished neighbour. Rustum said, "If I drive this way and that way, and double back, and then through and across and in between – then we shall reach our destination without the smallest trouble." And so it proved.'

'Ah, Rustum, resourceful fellow,' Khandekar said. 'Ask him to take his tea in the kitchen – we are lucky to have such people by us. My wife is joining us.'

My grandfather greeted Mrs Khandekar, neat and shining, something like excitement in her face.

'I was just saying,' Khandekar said to her, in a loud voice, 'how lucky it is to have a driver like Rustum, a clever, resourceful fellow like that. We will have tea in the study today. There. The truth is –' Mr Khandekar said, in a lower voice, having shut the door to his study and invited my grandfather to sit on the beige sofa underneath the bookcase '– the truth is that last week, my wife and I were talking on the upper veranda, quite innocuously, when I observed, over the wall, a pair of official goons standing in the street. They were evidently listening to what we were saying. Here, we will not be listened to.'

'If it were just the goons in the street!' Mrs Khandekar burst out. 'But when the listeners are within one's own house . . .'

'Surely –'

'I am afraid so,' Khandekar said. 'We strongly suspect that one or more of the servants are listening to our conversations. We could hardly believe it at first.'

'They have been with us for decades,' Mrs Khandekar said, 'every one of them. But I see that money and threats are greater things than loyalty in this world.'

'We cannot trust anyone,' Khandekar said. 'Do not trust anyone, my dear friend – not Rustum, not the gardener. Perhaps especially not Laddu's wife.'

'Oh, surely not Sharmin,' my grandfather said. 'She is quite one of the family now. I cannot believe—'

'Perhaps she is to be trusted,' Khandekar said. 'But what about her family? Are you sure that no cousin of hers, no uncle in Lahore ever asks her friendly questions about her husband's family? How could she not answer such questions, and how could she know what use the answers would be put to?'

'My dear Khandekar,' my grandfather said, 'if there were anything whatsoever that would interest the authorities in my family's—' He stopped. Evidently he thought at this moment about his beautiful library, concealed behind a plaster wall in the cellar. He had heard his daughters speak about it as a great joke among themselves. It had never occurred to him that Sharmin should be excluded from such conversations, and it would never have occurred to his daughters. But how simple for a cousin or uncle of Sharmin to ask a question or two, to discover so interesting and comment-worthy a fact! 'My dear Khandekar,' he began again, in a lower voice, 'surely you don't have anything to conceal. You lead so blameless a life. No authority could concoct a case against you on any grounds. It would be making bricks without straw.'

Khandekar and his wife exchanged looks. They were unread-able looks. My grandfather, horrified, came to an easy conclusion. His oldest friend was consulting his wife to discover whether he could be trusted. For a moment, he thought of getting up and leaving. But then he observed to himself that the situation would pass. The suspicion shadowing Khandekar's mind was unworthy, but perhaps nothing could be ruled out, with the soldiery rampaging through the street, unchecked. What pressures had been brought to bear, and what obligations called in – one never knew that about the oldest of old friends. So my grandfather forgave Khandekar, and Khandekar never knew that he had been forgiven for anything in particular.

And then the look between Khandekar and his wife proved a responsible one, because Khandekar's wife gave a small, tight, satisfied smile. 'The boys,' Khandekar said in a low voice. 'They have gone. No one knows. The servants all believe that they have gone to stay with their uncle, my wife's brother the civil engineer, in Chittagong.'

'But they have not,' my grandfather said.

'No,' Mrs Khandekar said. 'No, they have not.'

The tea was brought, and for some moments they talked of trivialities. There were few trivialities to be had in those days. Future plans, current activities, social life, mutual friends – all seemed to be tinged with disaster. We Bengalis, we love to talk, on any subject and on none, but the men in the street, the stench of their breath had entered Khandekar's study, and silence fell, unaccountably, between the three of them. The boy who brought the tea was familiar to my grandfather, his face politely lowered behind the tea tray. He had been with Khandekar's family for ten years, at the very least. How could such a man be suspected of anything, of deserving silence?

At length, the boy withdrew, leaving the tea things. Mrs Khandekar poured it out herself, as she liked to. After a decent pause, listening to the boy's noisy retreat in the hallway, she said, 'The boys have gone, you see.'

'Next week,' Khandekar said, 'Mujib will win this election. No one can doubt it. He will win it fair and square.'

'There is no doubt about that,' my grandfather said.

'And then what happens?' Khandekar said, his voice lowered. 'Of course, it is clear what will not happen. Mujib will not become Prime Minister of this country. He will not be invited to take up his position. How could that happen? Those people over there, they have gone to the effort of suppressing songs – *songs*, my dear old friend. What efforts do you suppose they will go to to suppress the result of something important, like an election, to make sure that the result is to their taste?'

194

'I have seen the soldiers outside,' my grandfather said. 'I know what you say is right.'

'The boys have gone,' Mrs Khandekar said again. 'It is best if they leave now, not after the election. We do not know what will happen once the election takes place. They have gone somewhere in readiness for any eventuality. I do not know where. It was best not to know.'

My grandfather nodded. He understood. They were good, brave boys, the Khandekar sons. One of them would be killed in due course, fighting against the Pakistanis for the independence of Bangla Desh. Vulgar people afterwards tried to describe that son as a martyr, but in later years, Khandekar and Mrs Khandekar would have no truck with such comments. They kept his photograph on the sideboard in their house, the one that I came to be familiar with when I made a visit with my grandfather in later years. The other, the younger of the two, returned after the war and continued with his studies, becoming, in the end, a very senior public administrator whom I always found cold and frightening to deal with. But all that lay far in the future. For the moment, the two boys had gone, and were preparing to fight for the freedom of their country in the struggle to come, though the expression 'freedom-fighter' was not yet coined. Where they were, the Khandekars did not know, or were not saying.

'If I may give my old friend some firm advice,' Khandekar said.

My grandfather nodded.

'Have your family around you. Ask them to come and stay in your house. Nobody knows how bad things may get. You will want to have them around you, to know that they are safe.'

At that moment, outside, as if to confirm Khandekar's advice, there was a shriek of brakes and a short burst of gunfire. There had been gunfire in the streets before, but remote, and possible to mistake for fireworks. This was close. There was no possibility of thinking that it was anything else. 'Rustum!' my grandfather called. 'Rustum!'

It was difficult to express what my grandfather might have been fearing, but he got up and opened the door into the hallway, and Rustum was emerging from the kitchen, wiping his mouth, with a puzzled expression. Behind him was a tall, thin man with neatly combed hair and a very clean white shirt.

'We are nearly finished in here,' said Mrs Khandekar, to this second man. 'Thank you for your patience.'

My grandfather did not know it – he did not recognize this man, though he had been in the same room as him a dozen times and he must have been faintly familiar. He did not recognize him, even though he was carrying his well-polished harmonium. It was Altaf, visiting at the suggestion of Mrs Khandekar, who had a particular task she wanted him to carry out.

3.

Nana wasted no time. As soon as he got home, again succeeding in avoiding the roadblocks, he went upstairs to his office and wrote three well-argued letters. He sealed them, addressed them, and sent Rustum out to deliver them to Laddu; to Mahmood and Shiri; and to Era, newly married and living twenty minutes' drive away. Rustum told them that Advocate-sahib had told him to wait for a response, so he sat in the kitchen of each house, and waited for the discussion to finish, and a reply to be written. Finally, he returned home. It was very late at night by the time his task was done. And it was a good day that my grandfather chose to send these messages round by hand. It would not be long before a curfew was imposed by the military authorities, and Rustum, driving about Dacca after dark, would have been shot on sight.

In my grandfather's house, there were already living Nana and Nani, of course. The unmarried daughters were there, Mary, Mira, Nadira, Dahlia, and ten-year-old Bubbly, in that house without

196

books, without the harmonium, where the possessions were spaced out in ways that had grown familiar in the last year or so. Pultoo was also still there, a thoughtful, quiet boy, good at occupying himself, and Boro-mama's son Shibli, who was a sturdy child, walking and talking now. There were also the two great-grandmothers, Nana's two mothers, and some cousins who had come in the last month from the village, and were remaining there. Now the other children, the ones married and away from home, read Nana's letters. They all decided that they must follow his instructions, and come back home for the sake of safety.

Era and her new husband were the first to arrive, the very next morning; they came with suitcases, as if for a very few days. And then Boro-mama and Sharmin came the next day with their other three children, wan and puzzled. Their possessions were innumerable and small, and several journeys back and forth were needed before all of them were piled up in the hallway of Grandfather's house. 'Look, it's daddy,' Dahlia said to Shibli, but he clung to her legs. For him, his mother and father were glamorous visitors, seen at weekends, and though he would play with his brothers and sister when asked to, he always gave the impression of playing alongside them, rather than with, always happier to retreat into his world of wooden blocks, singing a small song to himself. His father came to him and lifted him up into the air, making a puffing noise. Boro-mama's sisters could have told him that, of all things, Shibli hated being lifted from the ground. His cries filled the house, and eventually, when his father set him back down again and let him run back to his aunt Dahlia, they coagulated into words. 'Do not do that!' he cried. 'Do not do that! I am absolutely frightened when you do that to me!'

'Oh dear,' Nani said.

But in an hour Shibli, comforted with a sweet, was sitting quite contentedly by the side of his sister – his brothers, five and seven years older than him, considered themselves men like their father, and Shibli was unmistakably a child happiest when surrounded and pampered by ladies. His sister, resigned to her task, was nearer his age, and imbued with the duty of being a good little girl – her aunts privately thought her dull. She had recently learnt to read, and was turning the pages of her picture book for Shibli's benefit. His eyes, however, went round the crowded room.

'I don't see how we are to manage,' Boro-mama said.

'It is better that you are here,' Nani said briskly. These arrangements would not be for so very long, she assured him, wondering whether this was, in fact, the case. She looked about the room. Not everyone staying, or living in the house was there. Some of the girls were in their rooms, occupying themselves in privacy. But even so, it seemed very crowded already. Outside, in the street, there was a shout, followed by another shout, further away. Men's voices in this quiet street were not that common. It could not be understood what the voices had called. But the tone of command and acknowledgement was unmistakable; the tone of military command. Nana, retreating from the sitting room to go and sit in quiet upstairs, paused and gave a questioning look to Nani.

'Are the gates shut and bolted?' she said, to nobody in particular.

'Bolted?' said one of the great-grandmothers – they were both sitting on the two-seater sofa, upright and occupied with darning. 'Bolted?'

'What did she say?' the other great-grandmother said, the bigger, more assertive one. 'Bolted? What for? It's the middle of the afternoon.'

'Rustum shut the gates,' Boro-mama said. 'I don't know if he bolted them.'

'He bolted them,' Era said. 'Did he bolt them?'

'And Shiri has not yet come,' Nana said. 'She must not arrive to find herself bolted out.'

'Those were soldiers,' Mary said, in a low voice to Era. 'Those were soldiers, in the street. They were right outside the gate, just in the street, just there.'

'I wish Shiri would come,' Era said. 'And then we could bolt the gates and feel safe.'

4.

Sheikh Mujib won the election. For the first time since the founding of the two-part country, the leader of the country would represent the eastern half. But nothing happened; he was arrested; he was released; and then he made a speech announcing the independence of the Bengalis, and was arrested again. For many days, the sounds from the streets were of student protests, of shouting and chanting and the noise of official warnings, made over the loudspeakers. Finally, the Pakistanis came over, and began to have discussions with Mujib about his demands. But nobody believed in any of these discussions, and the protests continued and grew. People said – Khandekar, for instance, told my grandfather – that the commercial flights from West Pakistan to Dacca were full these days. Full of young, fit men with short hair, moving with purpose. Many people believed that these men were Pakistani soldiers in mufti, coming in large numbers to prepare for a crackdown.

My father, in the sitting room in Elephant Road, read his father-in-law's letter, requesting that they up sticks and go to stay with him for the time being, and his brow furrowed.

'How many are they, living there?' he asked my mother. She did not know.

'A lot,' he said. 'We are better off here.' It was true that the six of us had our own space, there in Elephant Road. The house was as secure as my grandfather's, which was only a short distance away, and even if the storm broke, they could stay where they were, communicating with my mother's family by telephone. So, for the moment, my mother and father decided that we would not move, and my mother tried to calm Nana down in a telephone call. My brother had his own room; my sisters shared a room; and the baby slept at the foot of my parents' bed. That baby was me: I had been born only a very few months before, and everybody called me Saadi. In any case, my father went on to say, there was the family downstairs, who were well connected and would see to our safety, whatever happened.

The next morning they awoke to the sound of an air-raid siren. In front of the house, there were two tanks of the Pakistani Army, pointing the barrels of their guns over the wall and directly at the front bedrooms of the house.

My mother hurried downstairs to try to understand what had happened. There, she learnt that the brother of their landlord, who had been serving in the Pakistani Air Force in a very senior capacity, had deserted on hearing that Sheikh Mujib had been arrested and the results of the election declared null and void. Where he was, nobody knew. He was what my father referred to when he said that the family downstairs had very good connections. It had turned out that they had very bad connections, or so it seemed, in those days. The military authorities had decided that the house in Elephant Road bore some sort of responsibility for the desertion, and the guns were pointed directly at them and, of course, at us.

My mother screamed and fainted and revived herself. She accused my father of leaving them in terrible danger, when they could have left the day before, or the day before that; they could have been secure in her father's house, where nobody could seriously discover a danger or a threat. Nobody would point a tank at her father's house; nobody in their family was in a position to desert. In a spirit of pure terror, she picked up the telephone and tried to dial. But that was too late, also. There was no dialling tone. Looking out of the window, she saw that the telephone wires to the house had been cut. They hung like a mop from the telegraph pole.

There was no means of getting out of the house, and soon a van with a loudspeaker went by, announcing a general curfew with immediate effect. That had been what the air-raid siren had warned of. When my parents listened to the radio, they discovered the detail of the general curfew called by the Pakistani Army. Not everyone was prevented from leaving their houses by the presence of a tank against the front wall. But everyone in Dacca was barred inside, on pain of death. It was 25 March. As that long day went on, the children bored and fractious and not understanding, the vengeance of the army on the rest of Dacca intruded on the street. Somewhere in the middle distance, a great plume of smoke was rising. Something was burning, or being burnt: something substantial, and rather nearer, from time to time, screams and shouts and the rattle of gunfire; very near, the metallic, clipped announcements through loud-hailers, announcing the penalty of death.

The radio had nothing to say about any of that. It was only much later that people learnt the army had gone into the poor parts of Dacca and burnt them to the ground; that the university had been entered and set to the torch. Afterwards, the dead came to be reckoned, but at the time, there was only black smoke and, too near, fire and shots. My mother and father, my brothers and sisters and I went to the back room of the house and passed the time as best we could. From time to time the neighbours downstairs came up to see how we were. But they knew no more than anyone else, and they could not comfort or explain the situation.

'They are going to blow up the house,' my mother said, and, without meaning to, she started screaming. 'If only we had gone to Papa's – they are going to break in and kill us, they will, they will kill us all.'

'We have done nothing wrong,' my father said.

'They are going to kill us,' my mother said. 'They will.' My brother, eleven years old, understood, and looked at her with solemn, frightened eyes. He was not familiar with the display of fear by the adults of his family. Quietly, I slept on.

The next day, the cook came into the salon early. 'There are people on the streets,' he said. It was around eight thirty. 'On bicycles and in cars, moving around normally.' The radio, when switched on, announced that the curfew would be lifted for a short time that day to allow people to fetch supplies and food. It would be reimposed, however, at one, and anyone found wandering the streets would be shot on sight. My father went into the front room of the house. Even after a day, it had the musty, miserable air of an uncared-for house returned to after a long holiday. Cautiously, he went to the windows. The street was empty; there was no one moving. More remarkably, the two tanks were gone. He tried not to look at what he saw at the end of the road, lying in the dirt.

'Where are you going?' my mother said, coming out of the back room with the baby in her arms. My father was going downstairs. 'We have to get to Father's house. We cannot stay here. They are going to kill us.'

'No, you and the children mustn't stay,' my father said, carrying on his way downstairs, quite calmly. 'You must go while you can.'

'But how?' my mother said. 'How are we to get a message to them? There is no telephone.'

From downstairs, my father's voice drifted up. 'You must pack a bag for you and the children,' he called. 'Do it quickly. Only what you need.'

Nothing seemed clear to my mother, but she did what she was told. She quietened the children, pretending as best she could that this was all some great adventure, and told Zahid that he must make sure the others made no noise, and stayed exactly where they were, in the back rooms of the house. Her main terror was that a child of hers, standing at the front window of the upper storey, would be seen by a passing soldier and shot for no reason. And then a miracle happened: a familiar engine noise in the street outside. She hesitatingly went herself to the front window. There, below, in the street, was the red Vauxhall car. Rustum, my grandfather's driver, got out hurriedly, looking quickly to left and right. He left the car's engine running, and the driver's door open. He banged on the gate of the house, but my mother was already taking her half-packed bags, one in each hand, and calling for the children. Behind her, Zahid and the girls were following, their faces pale. 'Where is Saadi?' my mother said. I had been left sleeping peacefully in the back bedroom. 'Go, go, go,' she said to Sushmita. 'Go and pick up your little brother. Do you think you can carry him?' Sushmita thought she could, and the five of us went swiftly downstairs. From the other flat, my father emerged and, sweeping us along, brought up the rear. My mother dropped the suitcase on the ground, and fumblingly opened the bolt of the front gate. 'I never said goodbye,' she said to my father, meaning to the neighbours downstairs.

'Go on, go on,' my father said impatiently, and between them, he and Rustum bundled my mother and the four children into the back of the red Vauxhall. Quite suddenly, the back door of the car was shut; Rustum got into the driver's seat. 'You go on,' my father said. 'I shall come along later today.' From the outside, he banged on the roof to tell Rustum to go.

'What is it? What are you doing?' my mother mouthed from the back of the car, but it was too late. My father had turned and gone back inside the house in Elephant Road, shutting and bolting the gate behind him, and again my mother, secure in the back of the red Vauxhall, began to scream. This time I awoke and, responding to my mother's screams, began to wail myself. She had had no idea my father would not come with us until he had shut the door of the car and banged a practical, necessary farewell on the roof.

It had been only fifteen minutes since the lifting of the curfew for five hours was announced on the radio. At one o'clock it would fall again. Nana must have ordered Rustum to go straight out and fetch us.

5.

Elephant Road was only a ten-minute drive from my grandfather's house. It was quite a different sort of place. There were small shops, selling groceries and household necessities; it was, in normal times, a pleasant, busy thoroughfare. There was a large Bata store, which acted as a landmark in Dacca, and other shoe shops, carpet sellers, hardware emporia, with rows of plastic bowls and aluminium pans hanging outside, tea stalls, confectioners, copper show-pieces, barbers, chemists and sherwani-merchants.

I slept peacefully through the short journey from Elephant Road to Nana's house in Dhanmondi. My mother, brother and sisters would never forget what they saw. The windows of Sushmita's favourite confectioner, the one with the best jelapi, the one where she loved to hang around and watch the expert confectioner piping a map of the world, a round Arabic signature, a piece of magical writing in the seething oil and let it rise; the windows of that shop were smashed. Inside, there was broken glass and spattered confectionery, milk and flour and sugar thrown like abstract fantasies across the oil-soaked floor. A house was on fire, its gates hanging from their hinges. The hardware shops had given up their contents, like great vomiting beasts. Across the street, pans and tools and plastic goods were strewn and crushed. And there was a rickshaw, turned over, lying in the street abandoned. 'There's blood on it – there's blood on it!' Sushmita screamed. There was; and underneath it was lying some kind of large packet, slumped and crushed.

'Don't look,' Rustum said. 'We'll soon be nice and safe.' But they had to look. Down a side-street, there was a platoon of the military, lounging against the cab of a lorry and paying no attention to the shop further down that was on fire, the gusts of flame and black smoke pouring into the street like great foul-fragrant blooms. It must have been one of the shops that made a good living renting out splendid garments in silver and thread-of-gold to guests at weddings; all that glitter and light, consumed in a moment. And one of the shop's mannequins – no, more than one had been dragged out of the shop and thrown into the road, lying there in an awkward position. Perhaps the person who had done it had wanted to steal the outfits from the mannequins, because they were quite bare, the arms raised, waxlike in the mud of the street, and more blood covering one mannequin's chest and running into a black stain on the road. But it was no mannequin. 'Don't look,' Rustum said again. Sushmita would never forget that sight: a man lying in the road, his throat cut, his fat little legs raised as if in an attempt to run. And then she was sick.

'Please, Rustum,' my mother said, when they were drawing up outside Nana's house. 'Please, just leave us here and go back for my husband.'

'It is too dangerous,' Rustum said. 'He would not come. He will come later. I can't go and make him get in the car. If he didn't come, it's because he has important things that he has to do.'

'He has to come,' my mother said, but now Rustum was out of the car and opening the gate. There were no soldiers to be seen. 'If you won't go, I shall go myself.'

Rustum ignored this, and between him, Nana, Nani and Boro-mama, who had all come out of the house, my mother and all of us were bundled together into safety. The children, Shiri and the baby came through the glass-framed porch at the side of the house, and were propelled by the servants and others along the passageway and into the large salon at the back of the house. My mother was screaming in terror, screaming for her husband, and Rustum explained how it was that my father had been left behind. Nana's face seemed to age in a moment 'Have mercy,' my grandmother said, and led my mother away.

My sisters were handed over to Shibli's ayah who took them upstairs to clean them up and make them respectable again. My brother Zahid, who had observed everything in silence, went over to his aunts, who greeted him politely, as if he were a grown-up and paying a visit. In twenty minutes, the noises of grief from Nani's room had subsided a little; and Zahid had found an interesting book to occupy himself with in a corner. For the moment, I was sleeping peacefully, swaddled in my blanket, guarded by Dahlia-aunty. The gates were shut and bolted. Outside, in the Dhanmondi street, the noises of battle, the crackle that a house on fire makes began to return.

6.

Many people had taken the same decision that my family had, and gone to wherever they could be together. They felt that they could best sit out the curfew if they knew where everyone was, and could feel reassured. One of these families was in a house only two streets away from my grandfather's. It was also a white courtyard house, very much in the same Bauhaus style, and there was, too, a large coconut palm at the front and a pair of green-painted gates against the street. In this house, which belonged to an important businessman, were living their children, two sons and two daughters, the eldest thirty-three, the youngest only nineteen. The two eldest were sons, and married, and their young wives were with them. There were also two grandchildren: a boy of four and a baby, which had been born only weeks before, to the younger son's wife. All these people had moved to the same house by the first day of the curfew, the day that we had been in Elephant Road with the guns of the tanks pointing directly at us.

All that day, the soldiery had roamed the street. They had not hesitated to shoot at anyone, even rickshaw drivers, who had been seen out, breaking the law. When they saw a shop with a Hindu proprietor, or one where they knew a grudge could be borne, they broke in. They threw the stock, whether sweets, or meat, or cloth, or paper, or books, or shirts, into the road. They poured petrol on to whatever they could find and set a match to it. Then they sat back and watched it burn. They drove to the university, and set fire to one of the main buildings. 'Intellectuals,' the soldiers said to each other. Another troop drove into the shanty town, where the buildings were made of wood and hardboard. There was no curfew observance here: the inhabitants lived half outside, and had no gates to close. The settlement burnt at the touch of a match.

The soldiery had been given orders, but there were just too

many of them. They kept meeting up with the same patrols, bellowing curfew orders into loudspeakers. And at some point, one tank patrol found its way into Dhanmondi, and outside the house with the green gates.

Afterwards, my family always believed that these soldiers had not found their way by chance to this house. We believed that there were families living in Dhanmondi who believed in the unity of the state; who did not speak Bengali much, and thought of those who did as traitors. Some of those families were happy to tell the roaming soldiery the houses from which rebel songs could be heard; where the flag of an independent Bangla Home had been raised from the roof. Perhaps, too, houses where they might find traitors who could easily be punished in an immediate way; even young women.

Some of these families who gave out such information, who directed the forces to particular houses during the war, went on living where they did after the war. Everyone knew who they were. They kept to themselves, and in after years, we children were not permitted to play with the children of such families.

In any case, perhaps the soldiers found their way to this house by chance. Perhaps they just heard something within, without paying for advice. A sound was coming from the house, a thin, high crying. It was a hungry baby. The soldiers knew that where there was a baby crying, there were young women. This was a rich area, but that meant nothing any more. The patrol hammered on the green gates of the house, and, when no response came, they got in their tank and drove directly at it. The white walls of the house fell inwards, into the garden.

'What is it?' the businessman was shouting, as he came out of his house – even then, he continued believing that he was living in the world he knew from a week ago. He did not see how things had changed, or he would not have come out shouting in outrage. The commander pushed him aside and went into the house. Five women – four young, one middle-aged, one nursing the baby that had been making the noise – were in what seemed to be the salon.

They stood up as eight of the soldiers stamped into the house; the mother made a gesture as if to draw her daughters to her. But one daughter – a plump-faced, pretty girl in a silver-edged sari – broke away and ran out of the french windows into the garden. Where was she thinking of going? There was no escape there. And if there had been an escape, that would have been breaking the curfew, and they could have shot her. Three soldiers followed her out, easily overtaking her and throwing her down on the ground. There was no difficulty in holding her shoulders to the earth while another soldier forced her legs apart, raising her sari. A fist went over her mouth, and a terrible stifled yell was all the protest she could make.

In the house, there was a single shot. The women screamed, and went on screaming. In a few moments, the soldiers killed the other brother, too, with two shots, then a third, and then the father, in the same way. But they did not kill the women until they had raped all of them. One of them, as she was borne down by the terrible weight of the men, tried to grasp and steal the pistol in the captain's holster. But her arms were held down, and she could not reach. The captain took out the pistol and waved it in her face, before hitting her hard on one side, then on the other, then again; there was the sound and the strange sensation, like wooden bricks moving about in a soft bag, of her jaw breaking under the blow. Then they raped her again.

They did not waste a bullet on the baby, but killed it with a knife they took from the kitchen. The howling child went the same way. Under the table, two manservants cowered, their hands over their heads, shaking, backwards and forwards, clutching at each other. What were the soldiery going to do with them? Nothing. They could spread the word. That was what would happen.

For ever afterwards, my family wondered how it was that Nana knew what the soldiers had done, and what they were capable of. From the start of the curfew, he was determined that not only should nobody step outside the house but that the house should seem to be empty. Nadira-aunty believed and said that there was no need for such precautions. She did not believe that the Pakistani Army would enter any house if there was no threat and the inhabitants were obeying the curfew faithfully.

'That is how it is to be,' Nana said quietly. 'Nobody is to make any noise, or light a lamp. This house is to seem empty, without interest, vacated. You are not to draw attention to this house. When night falls, we sit in the dark or we go to bed.'

My grandfather would not share what he knew about what had happened in the businessman's house, two streets away. There were many such stories in Dacca that day, and for weeks into the future. The rapes and murders of the businessman's family was the one my grandfather knew about. The two man-servants whom the soldiery had left cowering under the kitchen table had waited there, expecting their deaths, until the point where the platoon had driven away. They had emerged from their inadequate hiding place, slowly taking their hands off their heads. The curfew was still in force, and if they left the house and walked on the street, they would be shot. There was, however, a back way through the gardens of the houses that could take them to somewhere safe. They were, as it happens, friends or perhaps even relations of Rustum, my grandfather's chauffeur, and they thought of going to him. They knew my grandfather was a powerful man; they might have known that he had had some dealings with the authorities, and they might have believed that he and his household were in some way protected from the worst of the events. They decided to make their way to my grandfather's house. It would mean crossing two streets, out in the open. But only two. They could risk that. And there was no question of remaining in this house. The worst of the events lay, defiled, in the sitting room and the garden. There was only one way they could take, and they were obliged to start by going into the garden next door. For the two man-servants, passing through those scenes was the worst thing either of them ever had to do.

7.

When my father had waved goodbye to his wife and children, he went back inside the house. The neighbours downstairs were waiting for him. He had discussed the situation with them, and had agreed that he could help them to leave the city as quickly as possible. So when he went inside their house, he found them sitting in their chairs with fraught expressions, three suitcases in front of them. They had not managed to pack very much.

The wife was crying, quite helplessly, and the children – two young men, thirteen and sixteen years old – were trying to comfort her. My father had already established, in conversations with their father, that nobody knew what had happened to their uncle, the distinguished air-force officer who had abruptly deserted three days before. It was clear that they would have to leave the house as quickly as possible. The house was being watched, and there was no possibility of them leaving on foot with suitcases without being arrested immediately. My father had agreed to help them to safety, before going to his father-in-law's house in Dhanmondi.

My father left the house, walking two hundred yards to the busy intersection where the cycle-rickshaws normally sat. He tried not to see what was to the left and to the right of him. Despite everything, there were two cycle-rickshaws sitting at their normal place, and he summoned both of them. Ignoring the four men on the opposite side of the road, hunched up and observant, he went back into the house. The younger child and the mother, veiling her face, came out and got into one rickshaw, which drove off northwards, towards Gulistan. Twenty minutes later, the father, alone, came out and took the second rickshaw in the opposite direction. Neither party had any luggage, and they were informally dressed. It was important to give the impression that they had gone out only for half an hour or an hour, perhaps to buy food, perhaps to ensure the safety of others. The second boy and my father stayed behind; the watchers would know something was happening if all the family left the house at the same time.

In an hour, an unfamiliar car drew up outside, and my father, in the most casual way imaginable, came out to hail the driver. With the telephone wires cut, how had my father got a message to his old college friend, living half a mile away? Nobody knew – it must have been a note, delivered by a servant of ours or of the family downstairs. The watchers opposite did not move, even when my father came out with three suitcases, one, two, three, helped by the gardener's boy in a grubby shirt and gloves, and loaded them into the boot of the car. My father was not their concern. They did not register when the gardener's boy, having loaded the three suitcases into the boot and shut the door on my father's side, went back to the gate of the house and shut it from the street side. The boy stepped into the car in the most natural way possible, and it drove off. It was only much later in the day, when the army officers came to discover what had been happening to the house of the traitor's brother, that they reflected that the gardener in the house was, after all, a much older man who had not been seen for some time, and he had never had a boy to help him out at all. But by that time the family who lived downstairs had disappeared, and could not be traced.

Their destination was a house in the quieter north of Dacca, away from the fighting and protests and the bodies in the streets, in Mohakhali. The three parties – the mother and younger son, the father, both in rickshaws, and my father and the elder son, looking like the gardener's boy, in a car with the family's luggage – reached the house in Mohakhali by different routes, some quite complicated. Everywhere, the streets were filled with rickshaws heavily laden with luggage; at the sides of the road, families were trying to hail private cars, begging to be taken away. In the course of their journey, my father heard about what had been done in the previous twenty-four hours – the monuments desecrated, the university buildings destroyed, the people shot. Anyone who had raised a flag of the Bengali Home above their house had been targeted. About him, sitting incongruously in the back of the car with a dirty and shivering teenage boy, my father could see the abandoned and charred results of a day of violence.

My father's first idea had been to go, in pretence, to my grandfather's house in Dhanmondi, as if the suitcases really were his. But he saw how impossible that would be. He could trick my mother once, but not twice, and she would not let him go. So the car drove in a large circuit through Dacca, stopping once or twice as if on urgent errands. My father's resourcefulness ran out: he found himself going into paper-merchants and butchers and a hardware store when he saw a rare one that was not looted or destroyed, and had opened today. The mother's journey was similar: she left the cycle-rickshaw where it was, and went into shops and immediately out again; once she made a pretence of paying off the cycle-rickshaw and went into a large shoe emporium; the rickshaw cycled off, but in reality made a large circle through the streets and picked her and her son up at the shop's other entrance, seven minutes later. From there, she made her way to the safe-house in Mohakhali. There were other tricks and dodges, though none of them knew if they were really being followed, many entrances into houses and shops and swift exits at other points, much bold innocent play-acting among the wreckage and bodies of Dacca on the morning of 26 March 1971.

By twelve o'clock, the family from downstairs in Elephant Road were safe for the moment in their friend's house in Mohakhali. My father had an hour to reach Dhanmondi, in a city where everyone was trying to flee in different directions for safety. After that, the curfew would begin and, promptly, the shooting.

8.

In my grandfather's house, there had been some trouble in finding space for everyone. Most of the household had gathered and discussed, and proposed different arrangements. The servants had almost all been sent out to buy as much food as they possibly could. The curfew had been lifted for a few hours today, but might be reimposed for the whole day tomorrow; and shortly there might be no food left in the shops. The servants were despatched to different markets and shopping streets in different parts of Dacca to buy food to see the large household through a week or two.

In making practical arrangements such as these, my mother, Shiri, generally took the lead. She was a well-organized and sensible person, who could be relied upon to give her sisters and the servants a task each that would contribute to a smooth-running machine. Her sisters were accustomed to ask her what they should do next and, despite his bluster and complaint, so was her elder brother Laddu. But today they were obliged to make the arrangements themselves, under the impatient direction of my grandmother. My mother had come into the house and collapsed on a sofa in the corner of the room, drawing her shawl about her head. There was nothing else she could do.

In her lap was a baby wrapped in blankets. For the moment I was sleeping. There were plenty of children in the house now – Boro-mama's children, my brother and sisters, and at least one aunt's children, too. I was the youngest, and the only one who had no understanding at all of what was happening. The other children, even the quite young ones, were old enough to understand that they must be quiet, and stay in their room without making any disturbance. Mary-aunty was supervising them, from the eleven-year-olds, like my brother Zahid, down to the little but sensible ones, like my sister Sunchita. They were playing some very quiet game, like Dead Crocodiles, in which the player who can stay absolutely still for the longest time wins the game; or perhaps Mary-aunty was reading all the children a long, quiet fairy story. Downstairs, my mother sobbed into her shawl as quietly as she knew how.

There was no word from my father. He had disappeared back

inside the house in Elephant Road without any explanation, without even waving goodbye. Nobody could understand it. He had to be following shortly – there was nothing to keep him in the house, and he must understand how dangerous it would be to remain in the same place as the family of a deserting senior officer. His cousins, however, knew that Mahmood was stubborn, and that he would not be ordered around or threatened. 'He must be helping them to safety,' Nadira said to Dahlia, when she was sure my mother could not hear. 'How like Mahmood.' And it was like my father. But the morning turned into afternoon, and there was still no word. My mother continued to weep. She could not know that her husband had, three times, passed within two hundred yards of Nana's house in his doubling-back attempts to confuse any informers and stool-pigeons who might be trailing him. If she had, she would have run out on to the streets, hurling herself on the bonnet of the car.

Towards the middle of the afternoon, just as the family from downstairs was finally assembling at the safe-house in Mohakhali, the silent baby in its swaddling began to stir and warble, and to screw its ugly face up into a ball. My mother made no response, and soon I began to cry properly. It had been some hours since I was fed, and I probably needed to be changed as well. My mother, so sunk in herself, still made no response.

'Shiri!' my grandmother called. 'Shiri, wake up and pay attention. Your baby is crying.'

'Shall I take him?' Mira said. 'Shall I take dear little Saadi? He is only a little bit cross, and perhaps he could be hungry, too. He has been so good.'

'No,' my grandmother said. 'Shiri, you must take care of him. Get up and make an effort, now – this is not like you at all.'

'She thinks Mahmood will be caught out in the streets when the curfew falls,' Era said, in a low voice.

'How could he?' Sharmin said. 'Causing everyone such worry like this.'

'Causing everyone such worry – oh, that is so much like

214

Mahmood,' Era said. 'He would never consider what other people are thinking about, or worrying over. He just does what he thinks is the right thing to do.'

'A very annoying trait in a person,' Sharmin said, keeping her voice down.

'What is that noise?' said one of the great-grandmothers, awakening like me from her sleep.

'Poor little Saadi,' my grandmother said. She got up from her chair, shuffled and cast her shawl over her shoulder, and went over to my basket. She picked me up; with a baby's instinct for the unexpected, I began to cry with new force. Finally, my mother roused herself; she sat up, uncovered her face, and took me from her mother. Soon, as if through the repetition of routine alone, I had quietened down, and was feeding contentedly.

'What was that noise?' Nana said. He had come through from his study at the front of the house. Even in the current state of overcrowding, it was understood that he must have his own undisturbed space. His daughters and grandchildren and mothers and cousins might colonize the rest of the house, invading even the servants' annexe, resting the whole day in the salon, finding corners in which to pass the time with small-scale near-silent activities like paan-grinding, embroidery, sock-darning, pickle-bottling and the like. But Nana must have his retreat in his depleted library, and when he came out, the daughters and the little awestruck cousins busied themselves, knowing that something must have disturbed him.

'It is dear little Saadi,' Nani said. 'He was just hungry and woke up. Poor little thing, he can't tell us that he wants something other than by crying. But he's quite all right now.'

'Can't he be kept quiet with the other children?' Nana said.

'Mary can't keep him quiet with *The Snow Queen*,' Shiri said. Her face was red with weeping; she did not turn to her father when she spoke, but kept herself hunched over the baby. 'The other children will listen to stories or play games, but he's too little to understand any of that. Poor little mite.'

215

'Poor little mite,' said Era.

'He must keep quiet,' Nana said. 'We mustn't be heard from the street by anyone who passes.' His eyes went round the room, to his seven daughters, one upstairs, to his daughter-in-law and three female cousins; perhaps he thought, too, a dreadful thought, of a tableau; his wife and mothers and perhaps even the grand-daughters, too. The mind shrank from it. I was the youngest child in the house, and the only child of an age to cry incontinently, who could not understand what the situation was. My wails could be heard in the street, when I cried, and to the passing soldiery, it would be like the display of a rebel flag, a reason for forcing an entry.

'Poor little Saadi,' Mira said. 'He can't be expected to under-stand what's happening. We can't tell him not to cry, he wouldn't listen.'

'That's so,' my grandfather said, considering. His lawyer's logical brain went through various considerations. 'He must never be left alone, that's all. Carry him about with you – not just his mother, but the rest of you girls, too, take turns. If he wants to sleep, put him down but don't leave him. And have cake to hand at all times. If it begins to look as if he might be thinking of crying – beginning to look like that, no more – then distract him, feed him, interest him, jiggle him. He mustn't cry. Give him cake and mishti doi. Babies like that. He must be allowed to eat what-ever he likes.'

And that is how I was allowed to eat whatever I liked, without any restraint at all. There was no shortage of mishti doi, it being made in the kitchen rather than bought in from confectioners. From that moment onwards, my aunts took turns looking after me. I grew popular with them because a baby cared for at every minute, whose every need is anticipated and fulfilled before he has even begun to express it, is a placid and cheerful baby, as well as a very fat one. My aunts said they loved my chubby face; they loved my cheerful demeanour. They passed me from one to another with some regret, looking forward to their next turn looking after

216

Saadi. Anyone who came into the house would have seen me being cradled in an aunt's elbow as she crooned to me – Era, Sharmin, Mary, Nadira, Mira, Dahlia, even Bubbly, though she was no more than thirteen and, I was told in later years, not very good at it.

On the table or the armrest of a chair by them was a terracotta pot of mishti doi, a teaspoon stuck in it, and from time to time, not interrupting her burble of conversation or under-the-breath song, the aunt of the moment would lean forward, dig into the pot and bring another half-teaspoon to my little wrinkled mouth. In the whole of that time, I hardly had the opportunity to cry. No sooner, day or night, had my face begun to move inwards and my brow to furrow than an aunt moved in and embarked on a well-established routine of Saadi-distracting, involving the pulling of funny faces, jogging up and down, a favourite knitted rabbit, tickling on the tummy (mine) and the regular administration of half-teaspoons of mishti doi.

It is a sign of how desperate and serious those months of 1971 were that the other children in the house had no resentment or complaint against this exceptional treatment of a baby. They never produced, as far as I can discover, that universal childhood complaint, 'It isn't fair,' when they saw the constant watching and concern that I was attracting. They knew that it wasn't fair, none of it, even the very smallest of them. I slept contentedly, in an atmosphere of love, from the March curfew until the day in December that Bangla Desh was liberated, and I did not cry. The house in Dhanmondi was as quiet as a tomb, and no soldier was drawn by his curiosity in a baby crying to force the gates and enter.

But this is to move ahead in the story.

9.

'What is that?' my mother said.

'What is what?' Nadira said.

'That sound,' my mother said. They all listened. In the city, far away, a noise like a howl was rising. It was what they had all been dreading. Two days before, nobody had known what the sound had meant. It was a siren, driven about the streets of the old city, of Sadarghat, Gulistan, Dhanmondi, Mohakhali and the other parts of the city, in warning; it signified, a radio announcement had made clear, the beginning of a curfew. Now it was one o'clock, and the sirens were sounding. There had still been no word from my father. He was out there in the city somewhere. Nobody had the heart to tell my mother that he must have returned, in safety, to the house in Elephant Road – that her husband was a sensible man who would not risk his life in this way.

'Put the radio on,' Era said, and Nadira hastened to do so. The new audio cabinet, a stylish model in teak, included a radio. These days, it was kept permanently tuned to Radio Calcutta, which could be trusted.

The news ran through the events in Dacca and in the rest of the country. Universities had been burnt; intellectuals rounded up. There was no news of Sheikh Mujib. There were international condemnations. The curfew had been imposed and had been lifted for five hours during the day before being put in place again. Finally, the radio news regretted to announce the death of Begum Sufiya Kemal, in unknown circumstances—

'Oh,' Nani said.

'How could they?' Nadira said; her eyes began to fill with tears. Sufiya lived so close; the whole family knew her; they had been to her house many times. How could they?

'But all she did was to write some poems,' Mira said. 'How can they shoot women for writing poems?'

And Begum Sufiya would be remembered, above all, the radio continued, for poems that encouraged her countrymen and -women in the struggle for freedom. There was a brief pause, and another voice began to read a poem. It was Sufiya's voice; the poem must have been recorded at some time, and the recording

218

obtained somehow by Radio Calcutta. '"This is no time to be braiding your hair,"' the poem began.

'My friend's poem,' Nana said. 'I am glad they are letting her read this.' He had been called through from his study by the sound of poetry, or by the sound of his friend's voice on the radio. But he had not heard the news.

'She has been killed, Papa,' Nadira said.

'How has she been killed?' Nana said.

'They didn't say,' Nani said. 'Only that she has died. How could they?'

'They wouldn't,' Nana said. 'They wouldn't dare. We would have heard if she had been killed. This is a mistake, I know. She could not be dead.'

'The radio said that she is dead,' Nani said, with surprise.

'The radio is mistaken,' Nana said. 'Where is Mahmood? The curfew has begun now.'

And the strange thing was that Nana was right. Sufiya was not dead at all. The announcement on Radio Calcutta of her passing was mistaken, and taken from unreliable information. A street or two away, Sufiya and her daughters were sitting, just as my family was, inside, waiting for news, and she had the shock of hearing her own death announced, and then of listening to her own voice reading her famous poem. Three days later, my grandfather had the pleasure of reading an advertisement in the newspaper, placed there by Sufiya herself, in which she announced to all her friends that, contrary to reports, she was alive and well, and hoping to be listened to for many years to come. There was something steely and full of reprimand about the tone of the advert. Nobody could doubt that it was Sufiya herself who had written it, and there were no rumours about her having met her death from that point onwards.

In the street, the sirens howled like cats. Beyond that, there was no sound. 'Mahmood must be safely inside,' Era said. 'He has taken shelter. He will come tomorrow. Shiri, he is sensible, your husband.'

'I know he is dead,' my mother said. She gulped and clutched the gold hem of her sari. 'How could he – how could he go to the help of those people downstairs? We hardly know them.'

'He did what he had to do,' my grandfather said. It was so conclusive, the tone in which he said it, that the music of its serious finality drew the children from upstairs; they stood, lined up along the banisters, and gazed, shocked, at the adults giving way.

My sisters were the last to take their positions: they had been concealing themselves on the front balcony of the house, watching from behind a chair the distant fires of the city and the silent, empty street. They wondered, as they stood, why the aunts and cousins and the rest of the grown-ups were crying and silent. Surely their father would put things to rights when he came, as he would come. As he was coming, in fact. They had seen him hurrying along from a hundred yards away, hunched under the trees, swift and surreptitious, but, to his children, an unmistakable walk and silhouette. It was strange that he had not made an effort to arrive before the sirens started sounding but, after all, he was not so very late. In the past, he had often arrived twenty or thirty minutes late for dinner at Nana's house, kept behind at the office. It was ridiculous to make such a fuss when he was only five or ten minutes late for lunch. And before Sushmita, in her practical way, could say something to point this out, the gates at the front of the house were clanging open and shut; the grown-ups were rising to their feet; the light footfalls of Pa were heard in the glass-fronted side porch of the house, and there he was.

He looked tired and untidy; his jacket was over the crook of his arm. He was a little late, but he had had things to do all day, and sometimes things take longer to achieve than people anticipate and, after all, he was only six or seven minutes late. Sushmita and Sunchita were glad to see their father, but not excessively so. After all, everyone had been expecting his arrival, all morning, and here he was.

It was a surprise to them when Nana strode forward out of his chair, took their father by his thin shoulders and shook him hard. There were not many occasions on which Grandfather raised his voice; perhaps this one was the first one they would remember. He shouted into my father's face: 'Do not do that! Never again do that to my daughter! Never, ever, do that to my wife, or to me, or to my daughters! Never, ever, do that to my grandchildren!' My grandfather went on through the table of affinities. It was as if he were attempting to run through all the possibilities of insult and offence and the vulnerable. His rage took three or four sentences to lower from its highest pitch, as he remembered the need to remain quiet; after twenty seconds, the rage continued at a lower volume. Into my father's face my grandfather shouted, a mute in his throat but no restraint on his rage.

Sunchita and Sushmita watched, horrified and appalled, at the unknown sight of their grandfather shouting; the still less imaginable sight of their father taking the abuse. From any unjustified display of power their father, they knew, would walk away. Now he had arrived ten minutes later than he should have, and not only was Grandfather shouting at him, but Father was standing there accepting the abuse, as long as it seemed to go on.

My aunts and my mother, drying her tears and coming to her husband, found this a less unfamiliar sight than the children. They remembered the last time Nana had burst out shouting. It had been thirteen years before. It had been the day that Boro-mama had run away, leaving the garden path unswept; the day he had run away to marry Sharmin, who was now sitting in a placid way in a corner of the salon, keeping an eye on their four children. (She was glad to see her brother-in-law Mahmood: she had never really doubted that he would get here safely, and she went on knitting.) That was the last time Nana had shouted, when he had raised his voice and demanded the immediate attendance of Era, who had known all about it. My grandfather never lost his temper, and never raised his voice. He must have shouted as a boy, though it was hard to imagine. But in family stories, these were the two occasions when he raised his voice: to Era, when she knew all about Laddu's elopement; and to Mahmood, the day he came in after the curfew had been declared, making his wife cry. For the rest of his life, my grandfather never saw anything to make him shout. But that day, he did shout, and my father knew he was right to.

10: The Song the Flower Sang

1.

Between March and December 1971, the war of independence continued. The course of that war has been told by other people, many times, and so has the story of the hundreds of thousands of people who were killed. In December, the Indian government came in on the side of Sheikh Mujib's liberation fighters, and within a few days, an independent Bangla Desh was declared.

For those eight months, all Nana's family lived in the house in Dhanmondi. The domestic arrangements were complex, but they worked quite efficiently. Boro-mama and his family had a room to themselves, as did we; the great-grandmothers shared with two aunts, and the doubling-up went on in quite a sensible way. There had been talk of abandoning Dacca to go into the country but, in fact, that proved much more dangerous for many people. Millions of people, especially Hindus, had fled to India at the outbreak of trouble. But we did not do that. My grandfather had great faith in the idea that the worst trouble would not happen if he was certain enough that it would not happen. He faced down catastrophe. And perhaps he felt that he and Nani had suffered enough when they were young, living in Calcutta, and their eldest boy had been killed at fifteen by a Japanese bomb in the air-raids. Nothing afterwards could ever be as bad as that. And, strangely enough, nothing afterwards ever was as bad. They came through that terrible time, when the violence and terror washed up against the gate of the house, but no further. They survived, and were still there at the other end.

Nani had a strong emotion afterwards about this time. She was not exactly nostalgic about it, but in later years, when I was old enough to be placed next to Nana at dinner and be called Churchill, she would often mention this time. 'Do you remember,' she would say, her leg resting on the teak footrest, 'do you remember the steamed rui that Sharmin taught Ahmed how to make when everyone was living here, all through 'seventy-one? Do you remember, Bubbly? It was so good, that steamed rui, with lemon and ginger. And she taught him, and he never got it right afterwards. I don't know why. But it was never so delicious ever again. He didn't listen properly, or he made some changes of his own, wretched boy, and completely spoilt the dish. Oh, I loved to eat that steamed rui. I could have eaten it every day.'

'It was so clever of her,' Bubbly would say. She loved the details of food as much as Nani did – she could remember, years later, the exact sequence of dishes she had eaten at her sisters' weddings, recalling them in loving detail. 'Because of course there was not always a great choice of things to eat, that year, but you could often get rui when there was no other fish to be had. And we all simply loved it. I could eat it now, in fact.' She turned to a brother-in-law and began to explain the details of the steamed fish. He was a journalist; he often expressed surprise when, unlike most families, his wife's family's memories of the 1971 war of independence revolved around the dishes they had eaten, all summer long. 'I wish Sharmin would come back and teach Ahmed how to make it again, but she says she can't remember, and she says she doesn't know what's wrong with the way Ahmed cooks it, so that would really be a fool's errand.'

It was not a happy time, of course not. But it was the time when all Nana's family were about him, and nobody in his family circle met their end that summer, through some miracle.

At the very end of the year, when Bangla Desh was declared, Nana gathered his family around him. Rustum came in from the garden, and he had been asked to bring a sledgehammer with him. Preceding my grandfather and grandmother and everyone, Rustum opened the cellar door – the one anyone would have thought was a cupboard in the hallway, no more than that, and went downstairs to the oddly small cellar. The whole family could not fit in the cellar as it had been reconstructed, and the aunts and some of the children crowded up the wooden staircase. Outside, the two great-grandmothers, Nana's mothers, were asking each other what it was that could be going on, what he was up to now. At the top of the stairs, underneath the single lightbulb that illuminated the space, was my elder sister Sushmita, holding me up to watch Rustum's dramatic gesture. I gazed, bewildered, not knowing what Sushmita was pointing at.

But Rustum raised his sledgehammer, and struck at exactly the right point in the wall. He knew exactly where he should strike. There was a crack; he raised the hammer again, and struck again, and the thin plaster gave way. Behind the half-inch-thick layer, crates of books, of paintings, a harmonium could be seen. It was three years since the library and other treasures had been sealed up. Nadira came forward and pulled at the plaster; now the wall had been broached, it could just be pulled apart with bare hands. And then Boro-mama joined in, and Pultoo; in no time the secret library was there, and everyone was choking in a cloud of plaster dust. There was a cry at the top of the stairs. It was my sister, Sushmita. 'I couldn't help it,' she said. 'I dropped Saadi.' It was true. She had dropped me on my bottom, and I sat at the top of the stairs, wailing. It was a novel experience. For the first time, nobody rushed to stop me making that awful noise. 'I just couldn't help it,' she said. 'He's just – he's just so *fat*.' Everyone looked at me, and saw that she was quite right; Mary and Dahlia, at the bottom of the stairs, began to giggle helplessly. Months of feeding, of keeping me quiet with mishti doi, had produced a gargantuan infant. My eyes were deeply buried in fat rolls of cheek, like currants in a bun.

'Something must be done about that,' Nana said, quite seriously.

And then Nadira played a song.

2.

But other people had a different sort of time, during those months.

Mrs Khandekar's sons were constant attenders at the student rallies, the protest meetings that were an almost daily occurrence in the first months of 1971. They came home only to eat, bringing friends and fellow revolutionaries. Mrs Khandekar took to ordering large quantities of food for dinner, knowing that twelve very hungry people might arrive without warning. They sat about the dinner table with their wild hair, bringing a new atmosphere into the house, having the kind of argument that consists of everyone agreeing very energetically. They would sleep – the boys in their old rooms, the others in spare rooms, or, if there were too many, on sofas, however they could manage themselves. And then, in the morning, they would be gone, off to make their feelings felt at another rally.

The younger of the sons of Mrs Khandekar had begun to smoke in this wild-eyed, impassioned company. She had once made him promise that he would never smoke. But there were other reasons for her to worry about him, these days.

The two boys came to her, and said that they were leaving Dacca to prepare for the struggle to come. She muted her feelings. She understood why she could not know where they were. But it was hard for her.

When my grandfather came to see the Khandekars, to ask their advice, he did not know that in the kitchen, waiting to see Mrs Khandekar, was a man called Altaf. Altaf sat with the Khandekar servants and Rustum, my grandfather's driver, listening to their conversation but not contributing much. My grandfather left, and actually saw Altaf. But he did not recognize him as a musician who had played at many parties in the past, and he did not wonder what Altaf might be doing there.

When my grandfather had left, Mr Khandekar went to his study, and Altaf followed Mrs Khandekar into the pink sitting room with the chairs of green silk. It was the place he had first met Mrs Khandekar and talked to her about his problems, before she had solved them.

'Thank you for coming,' Mrs Khandekar said. 'I do hope there were no difficulties reaching us. Do put that down – I'm not expecting you to play today.'

Altaf put his harmonium in its case down. He wondered why Mrs Khandekar had asked him to bring it, if it were not to be played. And it could be the cause of suspicion, to carry a musical instrument through the streets, these days.

'Mrs Khandekar-aunty,' Altaf said boldly. 'I thank you for your every kindness to me.'

'We all live in hard times,' Mrs Khandekar said. 'I know that there was nothing you could have done about the change in circumstances. I could not take advantage of you because of something that you did not foresee.'

Since Amit's departure, Mrs Khandekar had agreed to let Altaf stay in the apartment in Old Dacca on his own, only asking him to go on paying the half of the rent that he had been paying. She understood, she had said, the situation. She had suggested at first that Altaf would not need to pay the full amount until he had found somebody else to share the flat with. But – with a shrug – there was no particular hurry for that. 'We are not,' Mrs Khandekar had said, 'living in normal times.'

Altaf was grateful for this. When Mrs Khandekar, a week later, sent him a note asking him to meet her in the English cemetery at a certain time, he did so. She had handed him a letter – a thick envelope, containing a long letter, and perhaps, Altaf thought, some wedges of banknotes, too. As they walked from one end of the cemetery to the other, they could have been a son and his mother. The decaying tombs, overgrown with creepers and grass, were little visited, and kept only by a sad old custodian at the gate, who did not care who they were. Most people were kept away by the fear of snakes breeding in the thick, undisturbed growth; a fear Altaf rather shared as Mrs Khandekar strode through the knee-deep vegetation. She had given him the address of a house in Azimpur. Altaf agreed to take the package there that afternoon.

He understood very well what Mrs Khandekar was asking of him, and he understood why it was him that she had asked. These days, Mrs Khandekar was followed when she left the house; if she had something to take to another address, that house would be watched, too. Altaf was not important enough to be watched. He was not an obvious part of Mrs Khandekar's life. So she passed him an envelope containing hundreds of rupees, and asked him to deliver it to a house in Azimpur. He had no idea who the people in the house in Azimpur could be.

Since then, he had done the same thing twice more for Mrs Khandekar. Once she had asked him to bring a tiffin-pail – the ordinary steel three-tiered sort that everyone had – and on a bench in Baldha Gardens in the shade of a red-flowering tree, they had unobtrusively swapped. She walked off with his, and he took hers to another house, behind a wall in Minto Street. She had given him the address. It was strangely heavy, that tiffin pail. Something thudded about inside it, something weighty. It seemed to be padded with cotton wool, or wrapped in muslin, or something of that sort. Mrs Khandekar on the next occasion had been meticulous about giving him back his own pail, the one she had taken away with her, washed. But that had been two weeks afterwards, and Altaf had by then bought a replacement tiffin pail. They were not expensive items, and he was grateful to Mrs Khandekar for other things.

He was not a fool. He understood that the Khandekar boys had gone away, like many students of that age. He himself had been to a meeting of tens, perhaps hundreds of thousands, at the racecourse where Sheikh Mujib had read a speech, and Sufiya Kamal had recited a poem. He had felt pride that in the past he had played at her house, and had been listened to by him. Many people who had attended such meetings were preparing to fight. It was to those people that he was conveying Mrs Khandekar's packages. Or, rather, it was to people who knew those people that his deliveries were being made. These houses were the first of a chain, in a sequence, and at the end of it, perhaps, were the Khandekar boys, who had responded to the times by retreating, and preparing to fight. Others, like Amit, were preparing for the war to come in their own way, by running away to India. He pushed the thought down as unworthy of himself. He had heard from Amit only once, in a letter that was not long, from Calcutta, where he was safe. There had been no return address: perhaps Amit had overlooked it, or perhaps he thought there was no point in giving one. He said he was moving from address to address at the moment, living on the kindness of friends.

In the pink-and-green sitting room, Mrs Khandekar made tense conversation of a neutral sort. Was it true that the Hindu family in the courtyard house across the road from Altaf's had moved away? How sad. And the children who lived opposite, they must be quite large now – ten, the girl must be? Time went so quickly, it was as if it were yesterday that she was born. Time was not going quickly in Mrs Khandekar's sitting room. She did not call for tea, perhaps because Altaf had already had his tea in the kitchen. Finally she stood up and went to the sideboard, bent down and pulled out a rosewood case from underneath. Altaf recognized it, in general terms: it was the case of a harmonium, another one. But it obviously contained much more than a harmonium, from the way Mrs Khandekar was struggling to lift it. She put it by his chair and sat down again on her sofa.

'It would be so kind of you to take this to a dear friend of mine,' she said. 'He lent it to me, and I think I need to take it back to him. I would ask the servants, but . . .'

No reason seemed to come to Mrs Khandekar's mind for not asking the servants to deliver it. But Altaf understood perfectly well.

'Take a motor-rickshaw,' Mrs Khandekar said. 'Take two, one after the other. You know what I mean. You can leave your instrument here. It will be quite safe, and I will ask someone to bring it back to you this afternoon – no, tomorrow, if that isn't an inconvenience. Here is some money – I do hope it isn't inconvenient.'

She gave him the address – a place deep in Armanitola, not far from where Altaf lived – and she stood up to say goodbye. He lifted the case: it was heavy. There was no harmonium inside it, he believed. He left the house, trying to carry the harmonium as if it were of normal weight; as if it were the case he had arrived with. He did not see anyone observing him, and certainly it would be hard for them to be sure whether Altaf had entered the house with a harmonium or not. He wondered if Mrs Khandekar had decided on a harmonium because she thought Altaf would carry it naturally, being accustomed to it; or perhaps she had not given the matter that degree of thought, and it was simply something conveniently to hand, very much like an object that she could ask him to bring, like the tiffin-pails they had swapped on a previous meeting. In any case, he walked down the leafy Dhanmondi street in a brisk way. The pavement cobbler with his last and his tools, settled in the shade of a tree, looked up as he passed; the security guard outside another house, sitting on a chipped wooden chair, fanning himself with a newspaper, greeted him in a bored manner, saying, 'Good morning, brother.' It was hard to know whether anyone else was observing or following him, but Altaf thought not. For some years, it had been deemed suspicious to walk the streets of Dacca with a musical instrument. Mrs Khandekar had overlooked that, and the harmonium case must have been exactly the right size for whatever it now contained.

At the corner of the street, he hailed a green motor-rickshaw. He told the driver to go to Armanitola, and the driver unhooked the cage that closed in the passenger seat. Altaf would not haggle over the fare today. 'Musician, are you?' the driver said, as they set off, and Altaf agreed that he was. 'You know my favourite song?' the driver said, and began to hum 'Amar Shonar Bangla', the Tagore song. You could be arrested for that, but neither of them seemed to care, and in a moment Altaf joined in. Around them the sound of the traffic rose, and the leaden scents of the busy street. Through the noise of hooting and the grinding sound of gear changes, none of the patriotic song could be heard. 'My golden Bengal,' Altaf and the driver sang quietly, and they could have been holding a conversation about anything, there in the motor-rickshaw.

The rickshaw dropped him two streets away from the address Mrs Khandekar had given him – in the end, the driver abandoned his brotherly gesture and, since Altaf had not named his price at the beginning, charged him twice over. Altaf walked in the opposite direction to the address he was seeking; dived inside a shop and then immediately out again; cut down an alley, and another, emerging in the main street; crossed the road and back again; and finally, through making reversals and cut-throughs, delaying and hurrying, he found himself at the blue-painted, rusty gate of the house. He banged on the gate, and quickly it was opened by a young man, his hair wild, his chin stubbled with a dusting of white; he wore round, wire-framed spectacles. To Altaf's surprise, the stranger embraced him before pulling him inside and closing the gate. 'We are old friends, you see, brother,' the man said. 'Now come inside. You need to wait for an hour before leaving.'

That was the fourth time Altaf had taken something at Mrs Khandekar's request to another part of the city. There were half a dozen addresses he made these deliveries to. He never knew where these packages went after he had passed them on, or who had given Mrs Khandekar six hand-guns and boxes of ammunition in a harmonium case – for example – to pass on to the freedom fighters who were already taking their positions by the beginning of March 1971.

3.

The rains were heavy that year. Mrs Khandekar's younger son was in the country in August, with a small group of commandos. He did not know exactly where – it was somewhere near Tangail. The country was quiet, undeveloped, and very wet. It came to them as grey, through a dense veil of monsoon.

Somewhere about there were Pakistani troops. A week before, and forty miles away, the commandos had had a success. Word had reached them that a Pakistani convoy would arrive in the district on a certain day. They had taken up positions in a ditch by the side of the road. They had endured three hours of rain and knee-high water, but then the convoy had come. They had hurled grenades into the lorries, and fired on the fleeing Pakistani soldiers. It was a successful operation. The commandos had swiftly moved south.

None of the commandos knew whether there were any Pakistani troops in the district. The villagers said there were. But they had rarely met anyone in their lives who did not come from the vicinity of Tangail. That might just have meant that they had met friendly commandos who talked Bengali with a Dacca accent. But the order had come to move southwards after the successful assault on the Pakistani convoy, and to reconnoitre the situation there.

So they stayed where they were, in the country east of Tangail, until further orders.

The elder son of Mrs Khandekar had known of better platoons. Manju, who had joined them three weeks before to direct the operation, had made it clear. His previous body of men had had enough tents, straw mattresses, plates to eat off, and even, he said, pillows. They had erected bamboo cottages to sleep in, with dry floors even in the monsoon. This platoon had only three tents for ten men, slept on the ground and ate off leaves or even fragments of artillery shells. Added to that was the discomfort of the monsoon. The elder son of Mrs Khandekar had not worn dry clothes for weeks. His skin itched constantly, all over. On his forearms, the sparks from the sten gun had raised blisters, which had become infected. Manju pointed out that they were Bengalis. They knew about the monsoon. They could live in rain for weeks on end, and it would be helping troops elsewhere to travel by boat and to swim. The Pakistani soldiers came from a dry country, and would be suffering far more than they were. They did not know what to do with water.

The elder son of Mrs Khandekar was the platoon's quartermaster. He obtained food for the men. For weeks now, they had eaten nothing but vegetables, lentils and rice. It was what villagers lived on, and what they could supply. Sometimes, for breakfast, there was nothing to be had but jackfruit. The elder son of Mrs Khandekar had half a dozen farmers and merchants in the district from whom he bought food; he circulated around them irregularly, coming at different times of day. He did not believe that his contacts would have informed on him to the Pakistanis, if there were any in the district. But there was no point in taking risks. Like all the others, he ate the vegetables, rice and lentils. They drank water from the ponds when they could find no well, and cooked the food in old, battered pots which made everything taste of mud. Once, he had eaten chicken from clean white plates, inside, in a warm room.

One of the farmers had told him that there was a big old house a mile or so beyond the ponds. He had never gone so far, but in the interests of making his movements unpredictable, had set off there one day, shortly before dawn. Those old houses where the zamindars had lived often had substantial stores of food. If the owner was sympathetic, they might even be able to move into a room or two. He trudged along the roads, the water coming down hard. It muted everything but the smells of the country, rich and earthy; the colours of the early morning dulled in the downpour, and there was no sound but the steady hiss of rain. Underfoot, the roads were brown and soft. The stream of water down the back of his neck was constant, as it had been for weeks.

The zamindar's house loomed up like a mirage in the rain. 'The first thing you'll see,' the farmer had said, 'is the mosque on the zamindar's land.' It was an old pink-and-white building, on the far side of a fishing lake. It was small, even for a village mosque, no more than twenty feet long, set against the walls of the zamindar's land. The elder son of Mrs Khandekar walked round the lake. In the gardens of the house, he could see an enormous rain tree – it must have been hundreds of years old. In the branches, the shrieks of parakeets were audible over the sound of the rain, and there was the nest of some huge bird, perhaps a fish eagle. There seemed to be nobody about. The gate to the property was hanging open, as if the house had been abandoned. He went inside the grounds. By the mosque was a walled grave-yard – the final resting places of the zamindar's family. He knew these places: it was where the family came home to, in the end.

The house was a single long building, painted red, and had not been lived in for some time. The windows were hanging open, and the curtains soaked with the rain. The front entrance had no door. But there were signs of habitation – a window frame at the left side of the house was blackened, suggesting that a fire had been lit within without care, probably just on the floor of the house. The elder son of Mrs Khandekar decided not to approach the house from the front. He scuttled along the inside of the garden wall, underneath the great tree, and quickly he was behind the house. He could see now that it had once been larger: the stone flags running at a right angle from the main body of the house suggested it had once had two wings. Behind the house there was a pretty old gazebo. It was properly roofed, and its pillars were covered with blue-and-white porcelain mosaics. The elder son of Mrs Khandekar looked at the solid brick flooring with envy. After weeks of sleeping in a tent in the mud, he had not yet allowed himself to consider a bed with soft, clean white sheets. But the idea of sleeping on solid, clean dry bricks filled him with longing. Beyond the gazebo, there was an orchard; two lines of old fruit trees. They were huge old mango trees, guava trees and, the elder son of Mrs Khandekar could see, a lychee tree. That last one was covered with a net against bats – he knew that the bats always get to lychees first, unless you shield them. But the net was ripped and full of holes: it must have been abandoned for two, perhaps three years.

In the rain, the orchard seemed enchanted, hanging weightlessly behind a veil. The elder son of Mrs Khandekar forgot his errand; he did not care that there was no food to be had in an abandoned palace. He gave himself up to the rapture of the monsoon, and to the perfumes of the fruit grove.

In the obscurity of the heavy rain, he was not alone in the mango orchard. Not thirty yards away, against the outer wall, a soldier was folded up, hip to ankle, shoulder to knee, compressed and, like the elder son of Mrs Khandekar, contemplating the orchard. He, too, had escaped from his platoon, because the zamindar's house was filled with soldiers. They had commandeered it, and most of them were sleeping inside still. The soldier had not seen the approach of the Bengali guerrilla in the heavy rain. Some sound of metal on brick must have penetrated, and he saw the guerrilla in the gazebo laying his rifle on the ground.

The soldier against the wall knew exactly what he had to do. He raised his rifle and shot, once, and then again. The noise of gunfire fetched the platoon of Pakistani soldiers running from inside the house.

4.

Mrs Khandekar did not know for years how her son had met his end. When she discovered, it came as a great relief to her. Her great terror was that he had been tortured to death over the course of weeks and months.

And at the end of it, there was a girl with a lovely voice, playing a harmonium by herself. The harmonium still had plaster dust on it; her long fingers cleaned the keys as they played in their languid way. The room was full of her family, and she sang:

The flower says,
'Blessed am I,
Blessed am I
On the earth . . .'
The flower says,

'I was born from the dust.
Kindly, kindly,
Let me forget it,
Let me forget it,
Let me forget.
There is nothing of dust inside me,
There is no dust inside me,'
So says the flower.

11: Structural Repairs

1.

Nana's two mothers returned to where they had come from, in time. They often liked to come to visit in later years. We called them 'the witches', which was unfair of us – they were only old and white-haired, and not very good with children. But by now they were very old, and each winter Nana wondered if they would come through the season of colds and flu and other infections. The end came for the elder one in a tranquil way. She caught a cold, which turned into pneumonia; she took to her bed, and never got up again. My mother nursed her with beef tea until her appetite left her; Nana's other mother, his father's second wife, sat with her, talking softly, as did Nani, her daughter-in-law. It was strange to think of Nani, by now nearly sixty, coming to her new mother's house in Calcutta as a young bride, so many years ago. The old woman dozed, and woke, and asked for small things, and dozed again. Once she said, 'Is he all right? Has he eaten?' But it was difficult to know whether she was asking the other mother or her daughter-in-law; it was impossible to know whether she was talking of her husband, dead these thirty years, or of her son, my grandfather, who came up to see her every evening. And one day she dozed, and slept, and did not wake up. It was an ending without disturbance, just as she would have wanted to go.

The funeral was a large one. By the time you worked it out, there were many daughters and sons, and their many children;

and the children of cousins, and nephews and nieces and their children, many from the country, whom we had never seen before. That was only the family. Because of who my grandfather was, many people wanted to come to pay their respects to his mother. There were so many people who wanted to come to my great-grandmother's funeral that many mourners had to be told they could not come to the house.

It was not the saddest funeral. Even for Nana's other mother, who had spent more of her life with the dead woman than she had with her husband, it was only a parting and the end of a long friendship. The hearse came – a shiny black vehicle, quite magical to a small boy – and the little shroud was lifted inside while the small crowd of select, intimate mourners stood behind Nana. Nani had placed her arm around the shoulders of the surviving great-grandmother. The mourners were silent as the back of the hearse was closed. All at once, Nadira-aunty broke out from the crowd, howling. She hurled herself at the back of the hearse, banging on it with her fists. 'No!' she shouted. 'No! No!'

'Nadira, stop that at once,' Nana said. My father came forward and pulled Nadira away from the car. She stood, tottered for a moment, then fainted, clinging on to the trunk of the mango tree as she fell to the ground. It was a highly impressive sight. I enjoyed it greatly, for one. Not many of the family would have thought that Nadira was so close to her grandmother that she would give way to hysterical grief in this way.

'The fact of the matter is,' my mother said afterwards, 'that no one asked Nadira to sing. And you know how she is. She does like to have an audience.'

But my father thought that was unfair: that Nadira, after all, had not had funerals in her life as often as many people. She would naturally be shocked and appalled by the first death of someone close to her.

'I still think she wanted to sing,' my mother said.

2.

Downstairs, in Rankin Street, the argument was reaching a furious pitch.

'And you have done nothing – nothing – about that tree in the backyard,' Sharmin was shouting. 'I told you to uproot it three weeks ago. And what have you done? Nothing. There are bats roosting in that tree. They will get in my hair, I know they will. You don't care about that. All you do is lie about all day long making plans. You Bengalis!'

We could not help listening to these arguments between Sharmin and her husband, Boro-mama, though naturally we never commented on them. My mother's only response to them, when Sharmin got to the point of making generalizations about the Bengali race, as she did, was to suck her teeth. My father would observe mildly, to his children, that he wished Sharmin-aunty would not say these things in places where anyone could hear her.

After the end of the war, some of the family found it difficult to see how they would make money. Many Pakistanis returned to their place of birth. Both Nana and my father discovered that their law practices had had many pale Bihari clients; many of those had now disappeared. It was more troublesome for Boro-mama, who did no work, and who relied on the medical practice of Sharmin. But Sharmin's professional future looked insecure. In the years after independence, not every sick person wished to be treated by a doctor from Pakistan.

Nana's solution to this was, as often, tied up with his property. When he had moved from the house in Rankin Street to the one in Dhanmondi, he had not sold the old one, but kept it as an investment. Now he told my father that we should move into the courtyard house in Rankin Street, living on the first floor, and that Boro-mama and his family should live on the ground floor. My father offered to pay Nana rent, but Nana said that we should pay Boro-mama directly. In return he would look after all the household tasks, pay the bills, and so on.

My father was not very pleased with this. He did not particularly want to divide a house with Boro-mama. He particularly did not want to live with him in the position of landlord and tenant. But the house just off Elephant Road, in which we had been living, had been destroyed by the military during the war. He agreed to move into Rankin Street as a temporary measure. But soon he found it was easier to have his chambers on the first floor of Rankin Street, just as Sharmin found there was plenty of space to have her clinic downstairs.

'I wish she would not shout like that,' my father was saying. 'It is quite wrong. My clients can hear her insulting Bengalis, and the children – I don't want the children to hear that sort of sentiment. And I expect her children hear it all the time. What must they think? And her patients, too. She seems to have no restraint whatsoever.'

'The strange thing is,' my mother said, 'that every Friday she takes a great pan of biriani down to Sadarghat, and hands it out to the poor. They could not think her more saintly.'

'That is just because she likes to get praise for her cooking,' my father said. They were talking in low voices. The conversation downstairs carried, though it seemed to have stopped for the moment. There was no reason to suppose that Laddu and Sharmin could not hear their upstairs neighbours. 'It is excellent biriani. I don't suppose Laddu ever tells her so, when she cooks it for him.'

'No,' my mother said. She laid down her book, placing a marker between the pages, on the arm of the sofa. 'They think of her as a saint. She is a good woman. I cannot understand why she says these things in front of her children, and where we can hear it – where any passer-by could hear it. It beggars belief.'

'If you want to know what I think . . .' my father said. He was about to say that living with Laddu would certainly put a strain on the patience of a saint, but a knock came on the interior door of the flat. My mother opened it. It was Laddu.

'Come in,' my mother said. 'We were just about to make tea. Where is Sharmin?'

Laddu indicated by a gesture that he hardly knew or cared. 'I have been making repairs to the back wall,' he said.

'I didn't notice,' my father said sardonically. 'When were you doing that?'

'Oh, this week,' Laddu said, not sitting down.

'I didn't know anything was wrong with the wall,' my father said, in his most clipped and abrupt voice. 'What seemed to be the problem?'

'Structural weakness,' Laddu said. It was not the first time he had cited this important principle. The structural weakness of bookcases, of paintwork, of stairs, even of the red Tajik carpet in their salon had been cited in exactly this way in the past year. 'It was rather a bigger job than I had anticipated.'

'I see,' my father said.

'If we divide the costs of it on an equal basis,' Laddu said, in his most reasonable way, 'then that will mean you pay me – let me see – one hundred – no, two hundred and thirty – forty-seven taka. It was the outlay on equipment, you see,' Laddu went on, seeing something in his brother-in-law's eye. 'Everything is so much more expensive, these days.'

'Well, let's go and have a look at the job,' my father said. 'I want to make sure it's been done well, before I pay for – pay for *half* of it.'

'It's been done well,' Laddu said. My mother came into the salon with a tray of tea, samosas and sweet things. 'No, thank you, Shiri, I can't stay at all. If you could just give me some money towards the repair – if you don't have it all, that's quite all right. I can wait until tomorrow for the remainder. The trouble is the cost of materials and tools, it's quite shocking.'

'Well, let's go and look at what you've done,' my father said. 'I don't know why you didn't mention that you were about to undertake structural work. It might not have been at all convenient.'

'Convenient?' Laddu said. 'It needed to be done. Listen,

242

Mahmood. You are living in my father's house. Do you understand? It's my father's house. You're living here because I said it
was all right, on my father's agreement. Now you need to pay
for it. It's my family's house, and it's time for you to pay when
I need – when I need to make some small repairs. Do you understand?'

No one ever shouted at my father. Perhaps, in all Nana's family,
only Laddu had inherited his capacity for shouting. Unlike Nana,
who shouted, as far as anyone knew, only twice in his life, Laddu
not only had the capacity to shout but indulged it often. Sometimes an argument would begin downstairs, and would continue
upstairs, Laddu having abandoned Sharmin to come to start
another one with his sister and brother-in-law.

'Yes, I understand very well,' my mother said. 'It is not just
your father's house. It is my father's house as well. Mahmood
will go and look at the work you have done on the wall when
he has a moment.'

3.

There was nobody in the house but Bubbly and Pultoo. Bubbly
was inside; Pultoo was painting a picture in the half-lit glass-
sided porch to the side. It was a task from the art school. He
was painting a portrait and had chosen this unusual place to
paint in because the light was filtered, diffused and full of
shadows. For years, Pultoo had known that shadows were not
black, but took on the colour of the object they fell on, a notch
or two down. He had known that since he was eleven, eight
years ago. It had come with the force of a revelation. He
wondered who had first noticed that fact. Since then, the
painting of shadows had been an especial treat for him. It was
true that shadows clarified the structures of an object – a still-
life under candle-light, painted in the near dark, became a

matter of highlights and glints, possible to place exactly on the paper and then conjure up the whole ensemble. His friend Alam sat in the twilight shadows of the porch, his face tense and worried. Pultoo worked in watercolours, steadily, scrupulously, with the minimum of underdrawing to guide his brush. It was going to be good: Pultoo could see that he had caught the likeness.

'What are you doing here?' Bubbly said, coming out. 'Everyone will trip over you. Don't you have a room to paint in on the other side of the house?'

'I wanted to paint this here,' Pultoo said. 'Now be a good girl and leave us in peace.'

'Why do you want to paint here?' Bubbly said. 'There's nothing here but a plain wall. That is boring to paint.'

'The light falls through the glass in an interesting way,' Alam said. He was a friend of Pultoo's from school, not artistic at all, and was now studying something practical at Dacca University. It was strange that Pultoo had been such friends with him at school, and Bubbly did not know that they had remained friends. His family were the owners of a tea plantation near Srimongol, only now coming back into business, but formerly very extensive, and not artistic at all. When he spoke, his voice was deep and memorable for so slight a person, but some inner fire had broken out unpredictably on his surface, resulting in a thick moustache and huge hands, nose, ears and feet.

'Did my brother say that?' Bubbly said.

'Why?' Pultoo said. 'Why shouldn't Alam say it first?'

'It sounds like the sort of thing you would say,' Bubbly said. 'I could make this much more interesting and attractive to paint. For instance, I could bring a table, and place a flower in a vase – just one flower, it wouldn't be a whole arrangement. That would be so much nicer than a blank brick wall, wouldn't it?'

Pultoo ignored his younger sister. His brush dipped, raised, applied; he dipped it in the cloudy water, knocked it on the side, continued.

'You've moved,' he observed to Alam. 'Try not to move your position.'

'Sorry,' Alam said. 'Was it more like that?'

'In any case,' Bubbly said, 'you've got to move soon, because people are going to start coming round. I don't want them having to tread all around you. I told you my friends were going to come round this afternoon. Can't you start again in the other room, out of the way?'

'Who is coming round?' Pultoo said. 'I'm sorry, I missed that.'

'Oh, just the old gang,' Bubbly said. 'Pinky and Milly, you know.'

'Pinky Chowdhury?' Alam said. 'I know her brother awfully well. How is he? He was talking of travelling, the little brother, the last time I saw him, but that must be six months ago.'

'Oh, yes,' Bubbly said. 'He had a divine time in Bombay. He said he really never wished to return. But he did return,' she finished lamely.

'Don't say you know my sister's friends,' Pultoo said.

'Of course I do,' Alam said. 'Everyone knows them.'

Pultoo made a hmphing sort of noise. Bubbly's friends were a trial to the family. Apart from Boro-mama, almost all of Nana and Nani's children were intellectual in some way: they sang, or they wrote poetry, or took an interest in music or the Bengali crafts. When they were old enough, they took up distinguished professions, like the law or medicine, or became academics. Their friends had come round, one after the other, and discussed political freedoms, and poetry, and Bengali film around the dinner table or on the couch. It had been so since Boro-mama had left home and taken his badmash friends with him. The family had hatched out like chicks from an egg, and Nana found them congenial company, and most of their friends too.

Bubbly was different. Even when she was small, her friends had been what Nana dismissively referred to as 'silly little girls'. He did not like to see small girls sitting about for hours dressing each other up and talking about love, he said; there was a fearful row when Bubbly, aged nine, was found to have borrowed her mother's scent and sprayed it all over herself and her friends in the course of some game of femininity. His objection, really, was to the fact that he did not know the parents of the children whom Bubbly made friends with. His other children, mostly, had played well with Khandekar's children, the doctor's children, the children of Sufiya Kamal the poet, of painters and scientists and lawyers. Those were the sorts of people that Nana knew; their children came plainly, sensibly dressed, had nice manners, and Nana liked to see them. Bubbly's friends came from people Nana did not know, and whose world was quite unfamiliar to him. Some of them kept shops, or factories, or import-export. Their children arrived like large glittering insects, in pink and diamanté; they wore party dresses on all occasions; they were called Polly and Rita Chatterji, Anita and Jolly and Molly and Milly, and they called each other Sweetie, and enquired about the source of each other's hairbands, all afternoon long. Nana was almost indignant when he saw them arriving, and morosely quoted Michael Dutta in their hearing. Bubbly wept and begged to be allowed to dress in such a way; she was refused, but found ways to ornament herself through judicious use of pocket money. It was a challenge to Nana and his family.

The parents of his other children's friends would draw up, come in, pass the time of day, make themselves agreeable. Sometimes, when the time came for Bubbly's friends to be collected, a car would draw up outside, and a rude hooting of the horn would indicate that it was time to go. Nobody would step out; the child would merely say, 'Oh, I must dash,' and head off, without saying goodbye properly to her hosts.

There had been the occasional unexpected friend before. Pultoo's friend Alam was one of those – he was not somebody who showed much interest in poetry or law or politics. He would often begin an observation by saying, 'My father always says . . .' followed by some trite and reactionary observation from the world of tea, hardly applicable to real circumstances at all. 'What I detest about that boy,' Nana said, 'is that he is quite incapable of listening to anyone else's experience, however interesting. Something more interesting always happened to his family, and he rushes to share it with us.'

Nobody could understand why Pultoo was friends with him. But he came, and his presence, over the years, was tolerated because the rest of Pultoo's friends were so different, so much more normal. Bubbly's friends were all very much the same: they were silly, and adorned, and rich, and not as charmingly well mannered as they thought they were. 'I think they are rather fun,' Nani would say, after Nana had finished quoting Nazrul on the subject. She was an expert at that favourite Bengali occupation, making the best of it.

Bubbly sidled out of the house and stood behind Pultoo for a minute or two. She observed Alam, and then the painting. Then she bent down and put her face almost against the painting, imitating in a ridiculous way the manner of connoisseurs. 'I see,' she said, in the imitation of a deep voice. 'But you've made his nose too big.'

'He has a big nose,' Pultoo said judiciously.

'Not as big as that,' Bubbly said. 'People will look at that and say that they don't see how he could reasonably have a nose as big as that one.'

'Well, the shading will moderate it a little,' Pultoo said. 'I have to give a sense of it, though – I want it to look big.'

'I don't think you should talk about me as if I am not here,' Alam said. 'My aunt once had her portrait painted. She has it hanging in her drawing room. Of course, that was by a famous artist, when she was travelling in Paris. She always says—'

'The fact of the matter is,' Pultoo said, 'once you sit down in front of a painter, and have your appearance rendered by brush and pencil, you become no more than an arrangement of planes and volume. Light and shade falling on a surface. I don't think of it even as a nose. It is just a geometrical problem.'

'Well, it is not a geometrical problem to me,' Alam said. 'It is what I use to smell things with.'

'That was surprisingly witty,' Bubbly said. 'I like your friend. He can stay, if he likes.'

'You should see the portrait of my aunt,' Alam said to Bubbly. 'It really is a remarkable painting. She visited every painter in Paris before she decided on which one to commission. You see, the fact is . . .'

But then it was that the gate was pushed open, and through it came Pinky Chowdhury, or someone similar, her sister Sonia, or perhaps just a friend, and two or three others, Milly, Mishti, Tina, coming to the door chattering like birds, and Bubbly spread her arms wide in greeting, and Alam stood up, too, smiling, as if he had anything to do with it. The portrait session was over for the day.

4.

Around this time, the tension started to surface between Boro-mama's family downstairs in Rankin Street, and our family upstairs in the same house.

'Sunchita,' my mother said, 'you are keeping us waiting now. What is it?'

'I don't know what book to take,' my sister said. 'I just can't decide.'

'It really doesn't matter,' my mother said. 'We are only going to Nana's for the afternoon. I don't know why you want to take a book at all.'

'But I have almost finished my book,' Sunchita said, not paying any attention. 'I am going to finish it in half an hour, and then I won't have anything else to read. But I can't start another book before I've finished this one. I am just going to have to take both books.'

'Sunchita,' my father said, tapping his umbrella on the parquet, 'you are going to take one book, and one book only. It doesn't matter which one. Now. Have you decided?'

'I can't decide,' Sunchita said. 'Why can't I take both?'

'Because I say you can't,' my mother said. 'You can take one book, or neither. You're keeping us waiting now, and you're keeping Rustum waiting downstairs.'

The rest of us – my elder sister, my brother and I – were sitting on the bench in the hallway, clean and scrubbed, in our best visiting clothes. It was only Sunchita who, every week, indulged in this indecisiveness, and it was always over a book. The thought of finishing a book and having no other to hand was terrible to her.

Downstairs, there was the sound of the red Vauxhall starting up. 'You see?' my father said. 'Rustum is losing his patience now. He is running his engine to show what a hurry he is in.'

My father said this to hurry Sunchita up, but he was not serious. Five minutes later, however, when we finally got to the gate, Rustum and the red Vauxhall were nowhere to be seen. The boy downstairs, when asked, said in a puzzled way that Advocate-sahib's car had come, indeed it had, lent by Advocate-sahib, and had taken master and mistress to visit friends in Azimpur. Boro-mama had seen an opportunity, and for his own purposes had swiped the car that Nana had sent to fetch us. We had to go in a pair of rickshaws, to Nana's astonishment when we arrived.

On that occasion, nobody said anything to Boro-mama. The breach could almost have been designed to make anyone complaining about it sound small-minded. After all, why should not Boro-mama use his father's car as much as my parents, for whom it had been despatched? The same might be true of a peculiar incident in which their cook was found to have borrowed six wooden spoons from the upstairs family without asking. Who complains about the loss of a wooden spoon or six? It was beneath the dignity even of our cook to complain about the inconvenience.

'Madam,' Majeda said, coming in the next day, 'there is no

water in the house to bathe the children. Is there a problem with the pipes?'

My mother did not know, but went downstairs to discover. The water in the house flowed from a large underground tank that supplied both our house and Mr Khan's house next door. Downstairs, she found Mr Khan already talking to Laddu; his water, too, had dried up without warning or reason. Her brother was saying that he could not understand it, but my mother went with their gardener to the pump that controlled the flow of water, and discovered that there was plenty of water in the tank, but that somebody had closed off the flow. There was no reason for anyone to do this. It must have been Laddu or Sharmin, both of whom denied knowing anything about it. It was a puzzle to them, as well. My mother returned upstairs in a temper.

Such small inconveniences arrived almost every day. 'You see,' my father said, 'your brother simply wants to make us think that it is at his behest that we live here at all. One of these days he will go too far. I'd like to see the look on his face when he realizes that we're not there any longer to keep him in funds.'

'He asked me for ten taka yesterday for replacement lightbulbs,' my mother said.

'Lightbulbs for downstairs, I expect,' my father said.

My father did not work at home, in the chambers, every day. Quite often he went to court. I used to like to go with him. The atmosphere of the courthouse was special to me; a grand white building, in broad, flat grounds. Often you would see old men congregating there, reading newspapers leaning against a tree, talking with energy. Inside, as you walked through the cloisters, the rooms of the court officials were open; dusty, brown, dim-lit rooms, high-piled with papers, all tied with ribbon, and between, the small, beetling men, their heads down between their shoulders, noting one thing after another. Around each doorway, a penumbra of red spattering as paan-chewers had cleaned their mouths before entering the inner rooms. I liked to go there. It was like nowhere else.

When my father came home one day from appearing in court, he found to his surprise that the house was covered with a web of bamboo scaffolding. Boro-mama was outside, inspecting the structure from the front gate of the house. 'What is this?' my father said. 'What is happening?'

'Structural repairs,' Boro-mama said, gazing upwards with his hand shading his eyes from the sun. 'It's necessary, I'm afraid.'

Upstairs, my mother was almost hysterical. Two workmen had gained access to the house and had walked in without a by-your-leave. All day, they had been erecting scaffolding, and had finished only half an hour before. My mother had sent all four of us to a back room with Majeda. She had not been able to extract from the workmen any kind of description of the work they were supposed to be carrying out, and when Laddu appeared after lunch, he flatly insisted that he had told her, months before, that the work was going to commence, and when it was going to commence, and why it was necessary. My mother had gone upstairs in a rage. She had gone to the salon, pulled a pillow over her head, and waited for it to come to a conclusion.

'That's enough,' my father said. 'We can't allow that. Have you given Laddu any money for the work yet?' My mother had not. 'Good. We're leaving tonight.'

5.

A feud is an ineffective way of removing the hated one from your life. The face and behaviour present themselves ceaselessly. It would be nice to say that the months during which my mother and father saw nothing of the family were peaceful ones. They removed themselves not just from Boro-mama and his family, and his attempts to get them to supplement his family existence. My father blamed Nana for insisting that we live in his old house – for trying to place us under an obligation, as he put it. So he

251

would not visit Nana, or allow my mother to see her sisters, or allow his children to play with their cousins. All the stubbornness of my father came out on this occasion.

His law practice was a successful one. As long as I can remember, there were waiting rooms full of clients – country men, grizzled old disgruntlements filling the antechamber with smoke, men hobbling off, fumbling for wads of notes, knotted up deep in the waistbands of their lungis. There was always a clerk explaining to the waiting clients that Advocate-sahib was very busy this morning, and that he would only ask for a small amount of patience. There was always Majeda, impressing on us children that we must play quietly, and not disturb Papa. Perhaps, at first, some of this business had come to my father through Nana, who liked to help out his family – he valued the obligations that such help imposed. But that had been a long time ago. An obligation only remains so if it may be taken back by the giver. After some time it becomes a possession of the recipient. And if Nana had once passed on some of these clients to Father's early practice, he could not have taken them back now. Those old country families – merchants, landlords, entrepreneurs, income-tax lawyers, politicians, some merely respectable, some so very grand that, a century before, one would have called them zamindars, and some with backgrounds and history best not examined too closely – they all valued my father's skill and discipline. I daresay Nana made them feel somewhat shy, as if they were begging for favours, and my father would take years to become as grand as that.

Father had every reason to think he was making his own way in the world. Any obligation he had once possessed had slid away. Long before, he had refused to live with Nana when they had returned from Barisal, when Boro-mama had run away. He preferred to find somewhere to live that was his own. Only the strange circumstances after the end of the war could have persuaded him to live in a house owned by Nana. He would always find an excuse to bring the arrangement to an end. Boro-mama's behaviour was a useful excuse of this sort.

252

For the next months, though we removed ourselves from the lives of our aunts, and cousins, and grandparents, they were always present in our own. Father was easily capable of saying, following on from nothing at all, 'Mary has always been under the thumb,' or, on a Sunday night, 'I wonder what idiocies they are all sharing at this exact moment,' or 'I hope Bubbly is getting enough to eat – I would hate to think that the circumstances were affecting her dinners,' or there would be a quarter of an hour of examination and re-examination of Boro-mama's character and the history of his bad behaviour. When he was not talking about our relations in this way, I believe that he was often thinking about them. I think Boro-mama's face and name were the first that came to him on waking in the morning, and the last that kept him from sleep at night. My very early childhood is paced out by my father, going back and forth in the sitting room; is lit by the lamp going on in the small hours in the office as my father, sleepless and resentful, goes to his books to blot out the faces he will not see, the faces he cannot get rid of.

The drawing room and office were in a new house. After our precipitate departure with nothing more than suitcases in a brace of taxis, we were taken in for six weeks by a family friend – a bemused, cheerful old lawyer with a big empty house in Dhanmondi. He could easily spare us three rooms while Mother and Father looked for somewhere more permanent. I believe he was something of an old gossip – he was in the process of winding down his practice in his sixties, and when lawyers lose the professional occasion of talking, an amateur habit tends to rise up in its place. He was forever dropping in to hear the latest about Boro-mama, encouraging denunciations and the dragging up of ancient resentments. 'But what really rankles . . .' my father would say, and his friend, his legs up in the planter's chair opposite, would nod and shake his head, his big eyes begging for more. His name was Tunu; we were encouraged to call him Tunu-chacha, but it seemed immensely clever and hilarious to call him Nunu-chacha instead. That means 'Penis-uncle', which was what my sisters and I called the old gossip when we were alone. Nunuchacha! I could laugh even now.

I believe that he would have been perfectly happy if we had stayed for months. It was one of the most exciting things that had ever happened to him, I believe, the old tittle-tattler. But after six weeks, a new house had been found, and we moved in. Workmen visited the house in Rankin Street and emptied the upper storey, delivering it all to the new home. My father swore that he would never go near the old house again.

From time to time, by chance, one of my parents happened to encounter one of the family, and the meeting was awkward, brief and evasive. They moved in the same circles, and we could not avoid being at Sufiya's, for instance, at the same time. My father would pass a greeting with whichever one of his wife's sisters it happened to be, before thanking his hostess and leaving without too much delay. The family accepted this; my mother did not enjoy it at all. And friends of the family did not really understand.

It was during the wedding season, almost between parties, that my mother met Pultoo's friend Alam. She was leaving, or arriving, and he was arriving, or leaving. At first she could not place him, but he greeted her, and there was something familiar about him.

'Such a busy day,' she said.

'Irrational, for everyone to marry all at once,' he said. 'My mother says that once, ten years ago, she went to eleven weddings in the same day . . .'

Then, of course, my mother remembered him. 'How is my brother?' she said. 'Did he ever finish the portrait he was making of you?'

'Oh, yes,' Alam said. 'Why? When was the last time you saw him?'

'Not so recently,' she said. 'We moved out of the house in Rankin Street, you know.'

'Yes, I remember hearing something about that,' Alam said. 'These things happen, I dare say.'

254

My mother did not really want to be discussing the matter with a worldly boy she hardly knew, but Alam continued.

'There was a dispute in my family, over some land in Srimongol, and two of my uncles, people say they hardly spoke to each other for years on end. It must have been twenty or thirty years ago. So sad for everyone when that happens. But the curious thing was that, after a year or two, neither brother could recall what on earth had been the initial cause of the disagreement. It was something to do with who said what to whom, and who had the better right to some land, which was really of no importance, but the argument continued for years, with them not speaking to each other, and so on. It was really very peculiar.'

'I see,' my mother said. 'I must be going.'

Perhaps she was going into a wedding, but she turned round and left, taking a cycle-rickshaw all the way home. She could not bear the thought that such people – mere boys called Alam, hangers-on, the son of nothing but plantation owners who had never read a book or admired a painting in their lives, the sort of people who cared only for how much per pound this year's tea would fetch – that such people were not only discussing relations between her husband and her family, but thought nothing of talking to her face about it. And comparing it to squabbles over commerce. My mother had agreed not to visit, or spend time with, her sisters and brothers, but this did not seem to have removed them from her thoughts. She thought hard about them all the way home, and for a long time after that.

6.

Over the next few months, Boro-mama in some way changed physically. Afterwards, everyone said that it was for the lack of anything to do, or anything to pass the time. Since what had occupied Laddu's time had been dreaming up money-making enterprises that his brother-in-law upstairs would fund, no one really regretted this. Boro-mama's family was supposed to stay downstairs in Rankin Street, but with time they spread upstairs, colonizing first a couple of rooms so that the girls could have a room each, then a sitting room for Laddu himself.

Laddu spent all his time in his sitting room upstairs, and in some way this changed him physically. How, exactly? I do not know. He could not have grown fat; I do not think he grew thinner, or lost his hair, or aged prematurely, or took on a spiritual air with long solitary contemplation. The exact nature of Boro-mama's physical change is a mystery to me, though everyone insists on it. Perhaps, like many men in the middle of the 1970s, he decided to make a sharp reversal in the direction of his haircut, losing four inches from all over his head.

It is one of those mysteries that arise in the telling of a family story. 'You see,' an aunt will say, 'when I next saw him, I hardly recognized him, he had changed so much . . .'

'Changed how?' I will say. Because of course when I see my sisters and brother, they seem just the same people I always knew, hardly changed since we were children together, although now they are nearly fifty. How could a brother change so much that his sister could hardly recognize him?

'I don't know how he had changed,' my aunt will say. 'He had changed, that is all. Changed so much I didn't know who he was.' Aunts are not keen observers, and all they knew was that in the next year and a half, Boro-mama's alteration was undisputed. They all agreed on it.

Certainly, when the gate of our new house opened, a year and a half after we had moved into it, my mother saw the visitor but did not immediately identify the shape as her elder brother's. There were many visitors to the house, mostly clients of my father's, and she assumed that it was one of those. It was unexpected that with him was a small boy, but sometimes clients did bring their children, for whatever reason, and they were made to sit quietly in the smoke-filled waiting room while their fathers talked business. Shibli, too, had changed in outward appearance: he was a fifth larger than the last time any of us had seen him, living with Nana and Nani. It was not to be expected that my mother would identify him from an upper room, either.

The office clerk let them in. He had never seen his employer's brother-in-law, and naturally showed them to the waiting room. Boro-mama always thought everyone knew exactly who he was – he was the eldest son, after all – and, since he had not told the office clerk who he wanted to visit and for what reason, a moment of confusion followed. Something of the story must have filtered through to the office workers and the domestic servants, because with a little doubt in his eye, the office clerk asked Boro-mama to wait with Shibli, not in the waiting room but in the hallway, while he went to see if my mother was in. 'I know she's in,' Boro-mama said. 'I saw her shadow in the windows on to the balcony, upstairs.' The office clerk asked him to wait, and went to see my mother.

I was sitting with her, being read to, though my sister Sunchita was paying more attention to the story than I was, curled up in my mother's lap, following the text as my mother's finger travelled over it.

My mother broke off when she heard what the office clerk had to say. 'My brother? Here?' She set the book down and stood up, brushing my sister to one side; Sunchita took the book from her, and started to read herself, not interested in this interruption.

Our manners were not as formal as my grandparents', and my mother expected that Laddu would have come through with the office clerk. So when the office clerk said, 'Shall I ask him to come through?' she was nervous, her intentions all shattered and unclear.

'Yes – no, wait, one moment. Give me a pen,' she said, and on the blank back of the Dacca Book Fair postcard that lay on the table by the sofa, she quickly wrote in blue ink with the clerk's fountain pen, 'My brother is here – please come as soon as you can. Two minutes will be enough.' She fanned it to dry it, and folded it in three. There was no other paper to hand. 'Give this to Advocate-sahib,' she said. 'And ask my brother to come through.'

'Is it Boro-mama or Choto-mama?' I said. I knew the difference between Big-uncle and Little-uncle; my sisters had told me all about them. The one who painted, the clever, nice one, and the frightening one with the awful son called Shibli, who lived with Nana. But a year and a half is a long time in early childhood, and though my sisters remembered them, to me they were like characters in my sister Sunchita's story-books, ogres and dwarfs and beautiful princesses, lying just out of reach, at the end of a quest still not undertaken.

'It's Big-uncle,' my mother said. 'And I think that must be Shibli with him – you remember Shibli, your cousin . . . Come in, brother!' she said, as he came into the room. 'How are you? You're looking . . .' And she trailed off because, again, there was that change in his appearance, and whether it was an improvement or just one of those alterations that time and decisions bring, she could not say. 'Well, I would hardly have known him,' she said in later years. But why? Was his faced puffed out with mumps? Had he dyed his hair blond with peroxide? Had he arrived wearing glasses for the first time, or concealed his face behind a monkey-mask? I do not think any of these.

'Yes,' Laddu said, not ungraciously. 'Everyone says that. How are you, Shiri?'

'Sunchita, Saadi,' my mother said. 'Say hello to your uncle, and to your cousin Shibli.'

But that was too much for us: we took one look at Shibli and Boro-mama, and went entwined into safety, burying our faces in each other's shoulders so as not to look at the strangers, to make them disappear with our not-seeing. Shibli, on his part, did exactly the same thing, burying his face in his father's legs, clutching him as the safest adult in the room. We were all merely visitors to each other.

'Where are your manners, Shibli?' Boro-mama said. 'Really, I am quite ashamed. He is only a little bit shy – in a moment he will be perfectly friendly, but sometimes he doesn't like to meet new people.'

'Sunchita and Saadi are just the same,' my mother said, delighted to have found something to talk about so readily. 'I think it must be some fear of being abandoned they have in their little heads.'

'And goodness knows why,' Boro-mama said. 'No one could live more secure lives than they do, surely.'

My mother might have retorted that Shibli had, in fact, been taken from his parents to live with his grandparents without consultation, and that perhaps he did not think he lived a very secure life at all. This fate of Shibli's, in later years, seemed terribly glamorous to us, his cousins, but when we were very young, who knows? It might have been terrifying, and the reason why we shrank into each other when visitors came. If our unknown uncle could give away his youngest child to Nana and Nani, then there seemed no reason why our parents might not decide on a whim to give us away to any visiting person – to one of the rather smelly men who clustered in the smoke-filled vestibule down-stairs, to one of the grand old ladies who came to drink tea and eat sandesh and rosogollai. Or even to Boro-mama now that he had turned up, to make up for the son he had given away. Perhaps we thought some or all of this, and so we tried to hide when attention was brought to us.

The office clerk came back into the room, and handed my mother the postcard on which she had sent my father a message. She unfolded it in her lap. At the bottom, in thick HB pencil, he had angrily written, 'No. Under no circumstances,' and his initials. Then he had evidently had a second thought, and written, 'Send for me when your brother has gone,' and initialled again.

'I am very sorry,' my mother said. 'But Mahmood is caught up with an important client – he won't be able to extricate himself this afternoon, he says, with regrets. Could you,' she called to the office clerk, now leaving the room, 'could you ask the kitchen to send up some tea?'

259

The office clerk agreed, with rather bad grace.

'I see your little Saadi has grown a lot,' Boro-mama said.

'Yes, indeed,' my mother said. 'He is really too heavy to lift, now.'

'Well, he was always too heavy to lift,' Boro-mama said, laughing heartily. 'Does he still like his food as much as he always did?'

'Sunchita is the great reader in the family,' my mother said. 'She reads so well for her age! She is always asking me to read to her, and then I can't read quickly enough for her, and she complains, and takes the book away, and before I know it, she is in a corner, reading some quite difficult book by herself. She is so far ahead of all the other children at her school. Her teacher does not know what to do with her. Papa would be so proud.'

'Good, good,' Boro-mama said. Sunchita, who had been emerging somewhat, now buried her face in a cushion. But she liked being praised in this way, I knew she did: I could tell from the set of her shoulders.

There was a stiff pause.

'What does Shibli most enjoy doing?' my mother asked. 'Don't be shy, Shibli. Tell me – what are your favourite things?'

'Oh, he likes to play in the garden, to run about, to jump, that sort of thing,' Boro-mama said impatiently. 'All little boys like to do that, don't they?'

My mother nodded. Fortunately, at this point, the tea arrived, and for five minutes they could talk about whether the children could have a very milky tea, really just milk in a cup, whether it was strong enough for Boro-mama, whether he would have a pakora or a spoonful of chaat or a piece of the special cake, made only that morning in the kitchen, a speciality of Majeda's, the children's ayah.

'Had you heard that Mira is marrying?' Boro-mama finally said, when the demands of tea had been established and finished with.

'Oh, how wonderful!' my mother said. 'I am so happy. When? Tell me everything.'

Boro-mama was not her ideal choice of person within the family to tell her about her younger sister's marriage – anyone else would have been better. But he was here, and he told her.

'He is a young lecturer at the university – in physics. They think very highly of him down there, in everything he does. He studied abroad for two years, in Britain. They tell me what he studied, but you don't expect me to understand what it is he has set his mind to. My wife understands it, or some of it, or so she says. Anyway, he seems a solid sort of young man and Mira is very happy. It is really a love-match. Mira would have come herself, but she particularly asked me to come.'

'Yes, I understand,' my mother said, overcome with embarrassment.

'I know there have been difficulties between us in the past,' Boro-mama said, 'but I think we should try to set these things on one side.'

'Well . . .' my mother began. She was thinking of what my father would say, if he were there in the room. She did not think that 'difficulties' was the word for his rage with Boro-mama. In her hand she clutched the postcard with its angry scribble from my father. He was refusing to see his brother-in-law at all. It did not seem likely that he would try to set these difficulties on one side.

'Mira is getting married on the twenty-sixth of this month,' Boro-mama said. 'Papa has sent me to ask you and Mahmood to come to her wedding, even if just for half an hour. It would make her so happy. Papa thinks you should come.'

'Well, that is very good of Mira to think of us,' my mother said. 'I will have to speak to my husband, of course, and I will let Father know.'

They talked a little more – about the troubles in the country, about the famine, about the neighbours in Rankin Street, and then, before they knew it, it was time for Boro-mama and Shibli to go. 'Say goodbye to your cousins, Shibli,' Boro-mama said, but the boy clung on, and would not be detached. 'Say goodbye,' he said, now becoming a little irritated, and he pulled Shibli loose, and pushed him firmly against us. There was nothing of an embrace or the regard of fond cousins in that nearness; it was just Shibli's howling face, pushed up against our own, then pulled impatiently away. My mother smiled weakly, her hands one in the other, saying goodbye in an ineffectual, benevolent, unspecific manner.

7.

'Laddu has changed so much,' my mother said. My father had heard the gate shut behind the visitors, and had not waited for my mother to send a note. He had come out immediately, abandoning his client. 'I would hardly have known him.'

'Changed in what way?' my father said.

'Well . . .' my mother said. 'It is quite hard to put your finger on it.'

My father made a remark to the effect that it was not very likely that Boro-mama had changed in any important, useful or significant way, then said that it was surely time the children were having their tea. We had had our tea, but my father's intentions were clear, and Majeda came to carry us away.

'Mira-aunty is getting married,' Sunchita informed her.

'Oh, how lovely,' Majeda said.

'On the twenty-sixth, Boro-mama said. I do hope that I am allowed to have a salwaar kameez. When Fatima's sister got married, in the village, she wore a beautiful salwaar kameez, all in purple, and it shone like the sun.'

'Who is Fatima, child?'

'Fatima!' my sister said. 'In my book. You were reading it to me only last week. She travelled all the way to the village, and

262

her sister cried for joy when she saw her, because she thought that she had been lost for ever in the jungle, eaten up by wild animals, and then a wise woman, her didi ma, saved her and gave her the beautiful new clothes and came with her to the village on the very day and at the very hour that her poor sister was getting married, and her sister cried and cried when she saw her, in her beautiful new salwaar kameez, in purple, remember. Don't you remember? I want a salwaar kameez just like that for Mira-aunty's wedding.'

'Do you think anyone is going to cry for joy when they see you?' I said scornfully.

'Saadi, don't be rude to your sister,' Majeda said. 'No little gentleman is rude to his sister – remember what Papa told you?'

'In any case,' Sunchita said, not caring one bit what I had said, 'they will cry when they see me, I'm sure of it. They don't know what has happened to us. You don't remember them, but I remember them all. There was Boro-mama and Choto-mama, there was Era-aunty, and Mary-aunty, and Dahlia-aunty, and Nadira-aunty—'

'I remember them all,' I said. 'You aren't the only one who can remember them. I remember them all, too. And if they cry when they see you, they will cry when they see me, too. They will cry so much, crying and crying and crying, they'll never be able to stop.'

'No one is going to cry,' Majeda said. 'Don't wish for people to cry. There is enough crying in the world.'

And that was true to a point, because we did not, after all, go to Mira's wedding. It was said among the servants to be a shame for the children's sake, because children always love a wedding. I do not know what Mira and her new husband thought, or the other aunts and uncles, or Nana and Nani. But the day of Mira-aunty's wedding, my mother stayed in her room, and I know that she cried almost all day long. For her, on that occasion, there was not enough weeping in the world.

8.

My brother and my sister Sushmita talked, too.

'Other people have aunts and uncles,' Sushmita said, 'but we only have parents.'

'We have aunts and uncles,' Zahid said sensibly. 'It is just that we never see them. But one day we will see them.'

'Where are you going to put my article?' Sushmita said. 'Is it going to be on the cover of the magazine?'

At this time, Zahid at his school was the editor of the school magazine. He was very involved with it: he instructed people what they should write. For the rest of us, it was clear that Zahid's magazine would be full of nothing but articles about how things were made, how a steam engine worked, how you could make a simple radio, the invention of the steam engine by James Watt. The teachers at the school liked and admired Zahid's magazine, much of which he wrote himself, and all of it he rewrote to his own taste. But he did not write it to please the teachers. He wrote it because he thought that was what everyone should be interested in, the most interesting subjects in the world.

'I have almost finished my article,' Sushmita said. 'But I want to know where you are going to put it in your magazine.'

'That depends,' Zahid said dismissively. Under some pressure from my mother, he had asked Sushmita to write an article for his magazine. Sushmita did not go to the same school as Zahid; she went to a girls' school, as he went to a boys' school. He had been told by my mother that it would be interesting for his readers to discover what it was like at a girls' school, and that he should ask Sushmita to write such an article. She had spent a week writing the article: 'A Day in the Life of a School for Girls'. She was proud of it; she had been reading parts out to all of us. Zahid puffed and sighed when he heard any of it. He could not think that it would be of general interest.

'My article will be dynamite,' Sushmita said. 'It is quite an ordinary story, but the implications are tremendous.'

'How can the implications be tremendous?' Zahid said, bursting into a rage. 'You are talking nonsense.'

'The education of women is a subject that everyone should be concerned with,' Sushmita said. 'Even your reading public. They will have daughters one day, too. They should know what the education of women in this country is like.'

'I am sure it is nothing but silliness,' Zahid said. 'I will tell you what I think of your article when it is finished. I make no promises.'

'You promised to print it,' Sushmita said.

'I will print it if it meets our required standard,' Zahid said.

9.

My parents did not go to Mira's wedding, but nobody went to the next wedding in the family. One morning, Nana came down to breakfast; he hurriedly ate a roti, drank some hot tea, and was out of the house. More slowly, the rest of the family came down, dawdled about the breakfast table, went about their day calmly. Some went to work; some stayed inside and read, or worked at their household tasks; Nani was supervising the cleaning of the silver, an annual task she always rather enjoyed. Some of the others, the younger ones, went to school or college for the day. Among the ones who should have been going to college was Bubbly, but she was not seen by anyone during the day. Because of the long-drawn-out nature of the family's breakfast, which could go on for hours as one or another came down and asked for tea, nobody expected to see anyone else at any particular time. It was really only the servants who knew that Bubbly had not been seen all day.

When she did not appear in the evening as dinner was served,

Nana asked where she was. Nobody knew. 'Have you seen her today?' Nana asked, but not even Pultoo had – he had the least to do.

'Sir, please,' Nana's houseboy said, stepping forward. Nana looked at him with surprise: they were not supposed to listen to conversations within the family. But he went on, and explained that Bubbly had left the house the previous night. She had not, in fact, slept at home. Where had she gone? He did not know. Nani rose to her feet, the tablecloth crushed between her two hands. The hubbub in the little room was immense. Nana asked Nadira to go up to Bubbly's room, and she returned saying that all Bubbly's best clothes were gone, and a suitcase, and so was Bubbly's favourite possession, the porcelain figurine of a ballerina she had had since she was eight, glimpsed in an advertisement in a girls' magazine, obtained after begging for it from all her sisters. She would not go anywhere for good without her china ballerina, everyone knew. In Nadira's hand was an envelope, addressed in Bubbly's loose, dramatic hand to her mother.

Of course Bubbly had run away to marry Pultoo's friend Alam. She knew, she said, that her father would never give consent for her to marry Alam. They were very much in love. He was from a very good family. Bubbly did not want to live with people whose idea of entertainment was to sit and listen to old poems and songs. She wanted to live in a place where there was a television in every room, washing-machines and other labour-saving devices, and no one talking about politics. She hoped that her family would come to like Alam, since he was her choice of husband, and in the meantime she hoped that her family, if she met them, would refrain from making the kind of remarks about Alam and his family that she had had to put up with silently for years. She was sorry, but there it was.

She was the second of Nana's children to marry by eloping. They forgave her and him, and the remarks about Alam and his family stopped abruptly. People made their living in all sorts of different ways, after all, Nana remarked, and Nani would chime in that it would be a dull world if we were all the same. Word was passed to Bubbly through Alam's plantation-owning parents that there was no reason for Bubbly and Alam to hide themselves away. No word came for two weeks, and then a stiff little note with only formal expressions of warmth, saying that the plantation owners were delighted to welcome little Bubbly into their family. The marriage had taken place two weeks before.

Pultoo took it hardest – he could not understand why he had had no idea what had been happening between his closest sister Bubbly and his friend Alam. But Nana kept reflecting about the wedding: how had he offended them? What did his children think about him that they could marry in such a sly James-Bond, secret-service manner? Of course he would have wanted to be there. He would not have cared if his daughter had wanted to marry a street-sweeper, if she truly loved him. It was perfectly acceptable to be in trade, to make your living by thinking of nothing but taka-per-pound, and currency fluctuations, and the future value of tea. A lot of people did so. It was true that they were not necessarily the most interesting people in the world, but that was only a personal opinion, after all. Some people might enjoy the company of tea-merchants, night after night in the remote hills as darkness fell and there was nothing to do until bedtime except eat, and play cards, and talk about the tea crop, and not a book in the house. It was easy to imagine some people enjoying that sort of thing. What, really, had he done to offend them?

Nana had long ago determined that he would never require a child of his to marry anybody in particular. (That was one of the things that was held against him by his friends and contemporaries when two of his children eloped with unsuitable people.) All his children in the end married out of love, or as a consequence of their own decisions. But on the whole, most of them, unlike Bubbly, did marry somebody whom they must have known their father would approve of. When they finally returned, Bubbly was bold and forward, Alam was cringing and embarrassed, as if suppressing a snigger, but Nana seemed painfully anxious to please, showing his new son-in-law to a chair, asking him what he preferred to eat, insisting that Rustum should drive them home – Alam's parents' house, where they were living for the time being, was only a half hour's walk away but Nana insisted. He could not understand, as he began to say, where he had gone wrong.

10.

So that was why, not very long afterwards, an old man appeared at the gate of our new house. He was shown in, and ascended with a ceremonious, pompous manner. He allowed his arm to be taken as he was guided into the salon where my mother sat. She shooed my sisters away, and the door into the world of adults was closed against them. Nobody knew who he was.

'You were early back from court today,' my mother said to my father, as he came down from changing in the evening.

'Yes, the case collapsed,' my father said. 'I knew it would. There was no case to answer. It was all perfect nonsense.'

'That was the land case?' my mother said.

'Yes. You see . . .' my father said, and went on to explain the ins and outs of the case, his hands working in the air, though it had amounted to nothing in the end.

When he had finished, and was in a thoroughly good mood, my mother said, tentatively, 'Lutfur-chacha was here today.'

'Who?' my father said.

'Lutfur-uncle,' mother said. 'My uncle, your uncle. From Jhen-aidah.'

'Little-uncle Lutfur!' father said. 'It has been years since we saw him – he came to visit once, when we were in Barisal, didn't he? I had quite forgotten about Lutfur-uncle.'

(This was not surprising. There were many uncles in the country, some my father's relations, some my mother's, some both, and some not really the uncle of either of them, but just nominated as members of the immense crowd of uncles. I have no idea, really, whether Lutfur-uncle was any relation by blood to any of us. He would have been my great-uncle, as always afterwards he was described, but in fact it is quite possible that my father once acted for him in a long-running court case, or something of that nature.)

'He was sorry not to see you,' Mother said.

'What was he doing in Dacca? Is he visiting?'

'Yes, he has been here for a month. Unfortunately, he goes back to the country tomorrow, or he would have liked to see you. Apparently,' my mother pressed on dauntlessly, 'Nadira is marrying soon.'

'Nadira-sister?' my father said. 'Every month, another of your sisters marries. How did Lutfur-uncle hear about that?'

'In fact,' my mother said, 'Papa particularly asked if he would come to see us to let us know. Papa, and Nadira, they both particularly asked if we could come to the wedding.'

'No,' my father said. 'Under no circumstances.' His face darkened; he got up to leave. My mother would have done better to leave the discussion until after my father had eaten his dinner. He would still have said no; he would still have left the room to immure himself in his study; but he would have done so with better grace.

'For Nadira, though . . .' my mother said.

'It doesn't matter who is marrying,' my father said. 'There must be an apology before anything can change. I said that before, and nothing has changed.'

'You haven't even asked who Nadira is marrying,' my mother said, her voice slightly rising. But my father left the room, and went to sit in his chambers, to go on working.

Great-uncle Lutfur was the first visitor. Afterwards, my mother wondered whether he was chosen by Grandfather as being the most insignificant member of the family to begin the campaign. Nana was cunning, and my father had the sort of rudimentary, lawyerly cunning that never imagines anyone else could operate on the same level of tactical planning. He saw himself as a fox in a coop of hens, never imagining that behind the blithe open gaze of those hens there might be teeth, and a thorough knowledge of vulpine habits. Nana knew where Father was vulnerable, and he proceeded to run rings round him.

Two days later Mary and Era came, to offer the same invitation. The doors to the salon were closed again, but this time there was nothing but huge laughter from behind them. Mother had not seen any of her sisters for two years, and there was plenty to talk over. Mary and Era, too, must have been delighted to be liberated from Nana's edict forbidding anyone to say anything rude about Bubbly's new husband Alam. That must have been the main topic of conversation, too, when Pultoo visited, also offering an invitation to Nadira's wedding. Pultoo had actually been to Srimongol to stay with Bubbly and Alam at their new house amid the tea-gardens – I had seen photographs, and they were very like the pictures of English houses among hedges I so enjoyed in my sisters' book *The Radiant Way*, the English textbook. Pultoo was able to be very amusing on the subject of Bubbly's new family. Alam had been Pultoo's friend in the first place, but he knew exactly what the family were like. The grandmother's lamentable attempts to explain not just how the family had come to Bangladesh but the history of events that had led up to their removal was brought out to delight his eldest sister. 'No – wait – it was Gandhi-ji who was killed, and the English princess, she stayed, and she married a maharajah, and they say, in the end, the Englishman, he renounced the world. Oh dear, am I confusing matters? Alam, tell me, have I remembered things correctly?' My mother laughed and laughed; it seemed she had almost forgotten how to.

For some reason, both of these visits took place on days when my father was in court, and he came home to find my mother glowing, and happy, and free of any sense of resentment, her sisters or brother having just left. Still Father said no to the invitation. After all, it was only his wife's younger sibling. Perhaps the campaign – the diplomatic *démarche* – planned by Nana moved into a graver stage in the next days, when a motor-rickshaw pulled up outside, and out stepped Nani herself, and Nadira in a beautiful silver-edged periwinkle sari. 'You've made your new home lovely,' Nani said. I remember that, because my mother, resigned to a sequence of visits with the same purpose, had made more elaborate preparations for the reception of guests in the afternoon. Those elaborate preparations for the reception of guests included putting me in my best clean shirt and red shorts, and my sister Sunchita in a pretty pink dress and ankle socks, and telling us that we were to sit up nicely, and not under any circumstances take more than one slice of cake. How children dressed in the 1970s on best occasions! I mostly remember how lovely Nadira looked; I was still quite small, though, I hope, well behaved. But afterwards, my father still said no.

And that seemed to be that. Boro-mama would not be despatched. If my father said no when the bride and her mother came, what more could be done? My sisters and I were terribly upset. We had never been to a wedding. Sunchita longed to be a bridesmaid, about which she had read in novels. I had just heard about the food to be had. We begged and pulled and whined at my mother. But she said, 'Your father says that we may not go. So that is the end of it.' She walked away. I knew there was more she wanted to say.

Of course there was something else Nana could do in his campaign. But nobody even imagined that he would do it. It was on a Saturday afternoon, some time after three, when the red Vauxhall pulled up outside the house. 'It's Nana,' Sushmita called out – she was at the front of the house. And there he was: Rustum opened the door for him, and he got out of the car, dressed at his most irresistibly natty, his black shoes shining, a white handkerchief pressed and folded into a square in the top pocket of his jacket. Nana was barely known to pay calls on anyone, least of all his own family. They came to him, even after they were married and had families of their own. It was a standing joke to his children that, after a brief initial tour of inspection, he hardly knew where they lived. It was simply extraordinary that he should pay a visit, on his own, to our house. He had chosen a time when my father was at home – Nana knew, of course, the opening hours of the Bar library. And my father came to the gate, opening it himself, and welcomed Nana into the house.

He stayed for half an hour, and afterwards, both my mother and father saw him out, walking him to the car and waving him off. It had been the friendliest visit imaginable. Just as he was about to get into the car, my mother said, 'And Nadira, where is she going to live, after the marriage?'

Nana looked surprised. 'In Sheffield,' he said, and seeing that the name meant little to my mother and father, he clarified. 'In England. Her husband has a job, teaching in England. They are going to leave immediately after the wedding.'

He got into the car, and Rustum drove him away. We all waved until they had gone quite out of sight. My mother turned to my father and said, 'I've made my mind up. You don't have to go. But I am going to Nadira's wedding with the children. Enough,' she said, 'is enough.'

My father's eyes filled with admiration. He knew my mother had her limits, and he knew her strengths. 'Yes,' he said. 'I think you're right.'

'It doesn't matter if you go or not,' she said. 'But it's my duty to go, and to take the children.'

My father leant on the heavy iron gate; he pushed it shut. He wiped his hands on the sides of his cavalry twill trousers, and pushed the bolt to. 'Yes,' he said. 'Let's go.'

12: Nadira's Wedding

1.

At the gates of the house, the beggars sat. They were so thin. Repeatedly, they raised one forearm to their faces, their mouths only half filled with teeth, their lips opening and shutting, saying something to the street. But there was nobody in the street. There was nobody but more beggars, clustering outside the gates of the Dhanmondi houses. We children had been forbidden, for many months now, to play in the streets, or to walk through them, even with our ayahs or each other. It was rumoured that children had been stolen away for ransom demands, that ordinary people had been set upon and robbed by the starving, that people had been crushed to death in riots in Gulistan. There was no food in Bangladesh, and we were going to a wedding feast. Some people blamed Sheikh Mujib, the president of the country. Others blamed farmers, for hoarding food in anticipation of profits to come. I can remember the famine in Bangladesh, and the look of the people dying on the streets. I can remember it remotely, through the pane of glass in the rear of the red Vauxhall. That is how I viewed it.

As the gates of Nana's house were opened, the beggars on the pavements struggled to rise. Some of them were strong enough to do so; others made an effort; some more simply lay there, their hands outstretched, splayed open waiting for alms, just as they had been for many days. Some of those last were unmoving. I looked at what might be out there. But the gates were opened, and quickly closed again behind the red Vauxhall. Inside, the engagement day was about to begin.

2.

As my mother got out of the car, her sisters came, all at once, to embrace her. 'Oh – this is so nice,' she said, smothered by them in their beautiful saris, the pink, the green, the blue.

'And Mahmood,' Mary said, coming round the car to greet my father. His head was held high.

'And Mahmood – and the children, too,' Era was saying. 'How grown-up the girls look.'

Sunchita was in a pretty red-and-white polka-dotted dress, Sushmita in a proper sari, pink and silver, like a beautiful fancy cake. Though my father had put on a suit and tie, I had been allowed to wear a Panjabi shirt and pyjama trousers.

'How nice,' my mother kept saying. 'How nice . . .' as if the people about her had returned from the dead, and not just been kept from her for two years by my father's obstinacy. As she repeated her words, she reached out and touched her sisters' faces, one after the other, and they touched her in the same way. 'But where is Nadira?'

'You must come and see,' Mira said. 'You couldn't manage to see me on my wedding day, so you just have to accept we are going to make the most of you today.'

In a bustle of apologies and regrets and hush-nows and more apologies, my mother was swept off by her sisters. I followed the women, as small boys may, tagging along with my sisters into the bridal chamber, strolling along with my hands in my pockets, thrust under my long shirt.

Nadira had met her husband Iqtiar in the following way. Like her, he was a singer. He was a small man, very tidy in appearance, with deep black eyes and a humorous expression. They had met first of all at the famous music school, Chhayanat. It had undergone a popular revival after independence. He was an academic by profession, but was, like her, an enthusiastic performer, too. On the first day of the new year in 1973, the Pahela Boishak festival, Nadira and Iqtiar had met for the first time at the concert that Chhayanat had organized. 'It is a true love match,' Era said – she liked a romance in her family. But they had done everything properly, and Iqtiar had obtained the permission of Nadira's family and of his own. It was not like the elopement of Bubbly or of Boro-mama.

In the bedroom, Nadira sat on a chair, her body canted nervously forwards. She was dressed dramatically, her sari red and deep blue, ornamented in gold, her hair up like a film star's. I remembered how wonderful she could look, knowing she would look wonderful in the future but never so wonderful as she did today at her wedding. 'What is that child doing here?' she said, referring to me. But I knew she did not mean it, and I went to embrace her. Her face was hedged about with gold, powdered and perfumed; she looked lovely, smelt like a goddess after a bath in rose and geranium petal oil, but, because of the complicated jewellery, it was like trying to kiss someone through a barbed-wire fence. I was first, but then she raised herself and put her arms around my mother.

'And Mahmood is here, too,' my mother said. But Nadira was exclaiming with excitement over my sisters' appearance. She did not seem to hear that.

3.

Downstairs, in the first sitting room, the old men were sitting. Lutfur-chacha, Khandekar-nana, Nana's friend the doctor, and others; Iqtiar, Nadira's husband, was not there, just his brothers and an uncle. He and his brothers had come shortly before with gifts: a sari set for Nadira, boxes of sweets, carried shoulder high, box after box, and even gifts of paan. (My great-grand-mother would not have approved of that, I am sure, and it still seems to me rather a private thing, not something to give as a present. You don't know how people like their paan to be.) Then Iqtiar had departed in the proper way. In the first sitting room, they were talking about the mahr, the sum of money with which the groom buys the bride. Nobody had thought about it.

'Well, I expect Nadira will want something,' Iqtiar's brother said, a little baffled. 'I really don't know what it should be.'

'When I married my wife . . .' Khandekar-nana said, but then he remembered it had been a long time ago, in Calcutta, in a different currency. 'What do young people do nowadays?'

'Oh, it depends,' the doctor said. 'Some people like to make a big fuss. But I don't think it's at all necessary.'

'But,' one of Iqtiar's brothers said, 'it is important not to insult your bride with a small sum of money.'

'No one wants to be insulted,' another brother said. 'No one wants to insult anyone, I mean. Iqtiar told me that he just wants to do whatever Nadira expects. Surely someone can go and ask her what she is expecting.'

It seemed as if everyone was about to agree that that would be a very good idea. But then Lutfur-chacha got hold of what Iqtiar's brother had just said. 'I don't think her father would approve of that at all,' he said. 'There is a right and a wrong way to do everything. I never heard of a groom asking his bride what she wanted and then carrying out her orders. That is beginning the marriage on exactly the wrong foot, a husband asking a wife what he should do with his own money. Her father would be very cross if he heard what had been done there.'

'It is true,' the doctor said thoughtfully, 'that if her father wanted things to be done in a certain way, then he would prob-ably have let everyone know how things were to be done. Is it likely that he would let everybody proceed in the dark in a matter like this, if he thought it was at all proper to do anything differently?'

(Both Nana and Iqtiar's father had stayed away from this important discussion, just as they were supposed to. Some of those in the room had never had to come to a decision about a family matter without being instructed by Nana. They could have done with my father, but he was outside, embarrassedly talking to the gardeners as the many children outside raced about the flowerbeds.)

'I still don't see why we can't ask Nadira,' somebody said. 'I don't believe she's expecting anything at all. She would have mentioned it.'

'But you have to pay the mahr,' Lutfur-chacha said, apparently deeply shocked.

'Indeed you do,' Khandekar-nana said gravely. So there seemed no further discussion to be had.

4.

On the veranda, watching the children run about in the garden, was Pultoo in his first moustache. About him were Iqtiar, Alam, his friends Kajol and Kanay. Pultoo's sister, Alam's wife Bubbly, perched sociably on the edge of an armchair, plump and happy. At the edge of the group was my father. All he had said to any other guest since arriving had been 'Is Laddu here?' But his brother-in-law was not there. Nobody knew if he was intending to come.

'There is nothing that anyone can do,' Pultoo was saying. 'Well, not nothing. We can open the gates, and we can go out and give those people rice. How many?'

'Two hundred,' Kajol said. 'Maybe three hundred. How many guests come to a wedding? You could ask them all to forgo the

277

food they would have eaten, and simply take it out on to the streets instead, to give it to those people outside the gates.'

'So three hundred people eat today,' Pultoo said. 'But how many people are there beyond those three hundred people? How do we feed them?'

'And if you go on giving away your food,' Alam said, 'then soon you join the ranks of the hungry, too. Until you decide to stop giving away your food. My father, in Srimongol, the other day some people came to his door. And they said—'

'But if everyone did that,' Kanaq said, 'there would be food enough for everyone. It would be shared out equally, and everyone would have a little bit, but nobody would have too much, and nobody would starve.'

'I have heard that idea somewhere before,' Bubbly said dismissively. 'It is all the fault of the government. There is plenty of food. It is just a question of getting it to the right people.'

'The Friend of Bengal is doing his best,' Pultoo said plaintively. 'I believe the factors are against him.'

They talked a little about Sheikh Mujib, their voices below a certain level. It was hard to think that the Sheikh Mujib whom the full streets and empty markets cursed was the same one that they had known, been with in the same room. There was no point in going out handing out bowls of rice and dal, they agreed – or, rather, there was a point, and all of them did it. A group of old ladies came to Nani every day, sometimes holding their huge-eyed grandchildren by the hand; they were country women, come to Dacca in the hope of food, walking a hundred miles or more. Nani fed them every day. You saw them sitting in a corner of the garden, moulding the rice with their fingers, eating in silence. Others, very like them, you saw waiting around the dustbins at the back of the house. You could not feed everyone, Nani said. The house took on its duties, and it tried to tell those it could not help directly about the food-distribution centres on the university campus. You could not feed everyone, Nana accepted, when Nani raised the question with him, and the wedding of Nadira had to take its proper form.

'The truth of the matter is,' Kajol said to Kanaq, 'that if the farmers in the country stopped hoarding, there would be no famine.' He spoke in a low voice, so that Alam and Bubbly would not hear. They had been known to defend country farmers; to say that they had a right to make a living, to feed themselves and their families.

'Everyone knows that,' Kanaq said, in the same voice. 'The fact is, they think there will be a proper shortage soon, and when that happens, they will make an enormous fortune. If Mujib would just requisition the land of the property owners, there would be no famine any more.'

And then they went on to talk about mounting a concert of Tagore's songs to raise funds for the famine victims. My father listened, his arms crossed, saying nothing.

5.

In Nadira's room, they were talking about absent friends.

'If only Shafi could be here,' Mary-aunty said. 'He would have enjoyed it so much.'

'Oh, I know,' Era-aunty said. 'He would have loved it.'

Shafi was not my own uncle, but an uncle nevertheless. He was my cousin Rubi's uncle. When Rubi came, she and I would play a game we had invented in the garden. It was called churui vati, or picnic, and we ate pretend food and pretended to serve each other. She was very proud of her uncle Shafi, and often told stories about his bravery, and boasted of having an uncle in uniform, as I did not. He was the only man in the whole of my immense extended family who had been in the military. One day he had come to visit Nana, to talk about something very serious, with Nana, Papa and Mama, and Rubi's mother and father, who were related to him and to me in ways I never quite worked out. Halwa and chanachur were produced for them to eat with the tea. I had seen that Shafi was shaking, nervous and afraid; he could hardly talk at all. I had heard of him before, and wondered why he was not wearing his military uniform. Then he went, and I never saw him again. And after a few days, my cousin Rubi told me that he had disappeared. For weeks, Rubi would cry. I did not know why the army had killed Rubi's uncle Shafi. Afterwards, Rubi would not play the game of picnic we so often played together.

'I wish Shafi could have been here,' Mira-aunty said to my mother, and my mother agreed.

There must have been some sense that discussion had been going on downstairs about the bride's purchase-price, the mahr. But now Lutfur-nana, an old man, appeared at the door with an apologetic air. His Panjabi was creased about his hips where he had sat for so long; he looked like a puppet that had been placed for too long in the toy trunk. I was sitting on Nadira's lap, my arms held firmly to my sides in case I should wriggle on her sari, or turn and play with her jewellery. I remembered that Lutfur-nana was the old man who had come first of all to persuade my mother to come to Mira's wedding. But he seemed to have been forgiven.

'It must be time to go down to dinner,' Nadira murmured. 'Is everyone here now?'

'We have been talking,' Lutfur-nana said, 'about the mahr. And we all agree—'

'I really don't mind,' Nadira said. 'Really, just do whatever my husband thinks best. I know you will all decide for the best, whatever it is. It is honestly no business of mine. I don't want to know about the money – it seems so unrefined to take an interest. If my husband gives me one taka, then I will be quite satisfied with that. Everything is perfectly all right. Now. Saadi. Off you go. Get off. It must be time for dinner now.'

So Lutfur-nana was dismissed, and Nadira had her one taka. At least, I don't know any different, at this distance in time. And everyone went down to eat the traditional mutton biriani.

6.

Nadira's husband Iqtiar's family lived only three or four streets away. It was quite close enough, a month later, two days before the wedding, for his family to come in procession on foot to Nana's house. It was for the bride's turmeric day.

The gates of their house were opened, and out came his brothers, his father, his uncles, some small boys, nephews. In their hands were sweets, shining presents, wrapped and ribboned; somewhere among them were turmeric paste and henna to decorate the bride. At the head of the procession, four small boys were carrying two enormous fish, two rui; perhaps ten pounds each. Iqtiar that morning had been to Sadarghat and had found these great shining animals, caught overnight in the river. All morning his brothers had been at work, and the fish were decorated now, one dressed as a bridegroom, the other in a ruffled paper sari as a bride. In blue pastel chalk on the rim of each silver dish, someone had written 'Iqtiar' and 'Nadira'. Behind, there was mishti doi in terracotta pots in the hands of the uncles, and, in the arms of his youngest brother, held tenderly like the phantom of a dancer, Nadira's wedding sari. She had chosen it, and told Iqtiar what she was going to wear, and where he should find it, and squared the merchant, and made absolutely sure by asking Iqtiar to describe it in as much detail as he possibly could. Still, he had fetched it, and paid for it. It was his responsibility, and now his brother was bringing it to Nadira on the bride's turmeric day.

The procession, some fifteen-strong, walked in a stately, suppressed, self-conscious way. It was unusual for people to take a walk on the streets of Dacca so richly dressed, these days. The small boys tried not to show what they felt.

('What is the turmeric day?' the man to whom I am telling this story asks.

'Well, you know turmeric?'

'Yes, I know turmeric,' he says. 'It is a yellow spice, very difficult to get out of clothes.'

'Well, the turmeric day is a day devoted to turmeric. They make a paste out of it; they put it on the bride.'

'Who puts it on the bride?'

'Well, her friends do. The henna decorates her hands and feet, complicated abstract designs, while she sits on a small platform.'

'Why is it called a turmeric day, and not a henna day?' he asks, but I am going to ignore that question.

'She is coloured yellow all over. With turmeric. That is what I am talking about. It makes her skin lovely and soft. Do you want to know any more?' I say to the man who is asking these questions.

'No,' he says, 'that is quite clear, thank you.')

In orange, like monks, they walked, their expressions directed forward and almost upwards. Around them, the city amassed with its hands outstretched for alms. In those circumstances, it took a certain power to continue at the same pace, to go on as if no one to your left, no one to your right, no one with veins stretched tight under skin and over bones is asking for food. But the relations of the bridegroom walked forward, not speeding up or slowing down. They were allowed to proceed.

But in Nana's house the men had been at work. The whole house was transformed. Pultoo had directed the arrangements. On the stairs, small lamps were painted and hanging at every step; Zahid, my brother, had been set to work by Pultoo, and Kajol and Kanaq, and the house was lit with two hundred small lamps. As you walked up the stairs, the heat to left and right was as a fire in winter, and sometimes, as one went out somewhere, there was a fierce sudden smell in the room of extinguished flame, as of hot carbon, and Rustum would go to refill the lamp with oil and relight it. The floor was painted with henna in patterns; the stage upon which Nadira already sat was richly ornamented. She was sitting on it, her arms smeared with the yellow paste with its metallic smell. Every surface was laden with lamps and candles;

every single member of my family had been put to work. The table had been set on the veranda, and thirty places laid at it. Even I had been entrusted with a task – I had had to lay the unlit lamps up the staircase. The house of a Dacca lawyer, normally so orderly and restrained, had been transformed into a world of flame, lights and fantasy, and at its centre was Nadira, her sultry eyes lowered, waiting for her lover to arrive. He would not come: first would come his brothers and his uncles and his cousins, glowing in orange and bearing gifts. But later he would come. The whole house had taken on the rich smell of meat and birds, of fish, of biriani, of spice, and of the turmeric paste masking my aunt, transforming her. I stood back, clutching my mother's hand. The metal gates to my grandfather's house were booming with the beat of fists. Inside, the wedding feast was entering its second phase.

7.

And then later, after the dinner – after all of it – when I should really have been sent to bed, all those men, the brothers and cousins and uncles and friends of Iqtiar leapt up from the table, at some signal which no one saw, and with sudden wet fists of colour – of raw reds, of pinks and yellows, of blues and purples, of orange and greens and mauves, all of dry powder and water dripping from the fists – with all of that, they leapt up and flung the dyes and pastes of blinding colour in each other's faces, at the clothes of the children, of the bride's family, of everyone at the table on the veranda. The garden was dark, and itching with cicadas, and the veranda hung with nets, and the air was, in a second, full of colour. I had never seen anything like that. In an instant, Nana's garden was a storm of pigment, and everyone was laughing or rushing inside, or joining in and throwing back what dyes and shades and pigment they could.

In a minute I was soaked in a red dye; it was in my mouth with the taste of iron, and everyone about me – my sisters, Zahid, Pultoo, even Dahlia – was joining in. Everyone's clothes were ruined. Nana, all at once, was there among us. He had not been there before. He called out for peace. 'And where is she?' he said, as the clouds of colour subsided and everyone gave way to choking. But she had gone. No one had seen her go. It was as if Nadira had known exactly what was about to happen, and slipped away before Iqtiar's forces could orchestrate her ruin.

Still, at the turmeric day, there was no sign of Boro-mama. It was as if he had been instructed not to come at all.

8.

It could not be helped. After the month of preliminaries, of going round to each other's houses in procession for feasting and gift-giving and gossiping, the day on which Nadira and Iqtiar were to be married had arrived.

Nadira and her sisters were waiting for the car to take them to the hotel.

'They were beautiful cards Pultoo made,' Dahlia said. 'How many did you send out, in the end?'

'I thought he would send out cards with a lady without her clothes on,' Bubbly said. 'But they were nice. He is clever and talented, Little-brother. Everyone in Srimongol said how clever and talented he was.'

'I think we sent out well over a hundred,' Nadira said. 'How do I look? Is my makeup smudged?'

'Oh, Nadira,' Mary said. She was anxiously waiting at the window, but now turned and came to her sister; she placed one hand where she could, on the elbow, in unsmudging reassurance. 'I remember the day you were born. And here you are, getting married.'

'The monsoon broke, and then the next day Nadira was born. A monsoon baby is the best,' Era said.

'No, you're wrong,' Mary said. 'You aren't remembering properly. Nadira was born and the monsoon broke the next day. Everyone was sitting about, fanning themselves, cursing the heat, waiting for the rains to come, and then there was Nadira instead. When it rained the next day, everybody said it would be good for the baby in its first days. It is so easy to make those kinds of confusion.'

'Sister,' Era said, 'I remember perfectly. I remember the doctor coming through the gate in Rankin Street with his bag, and struggling with his bag and an umbrella at the same time. You must remember that.'

'No, sister,' Mary said. 'The important detail—'

'The important detail is the doctor, struggling with his umbrella, and the rains beginning. Shiri, don't you remember?'

My mother spread her hands wide, smiling. 'When you say the circumstances, Era, it sounds as if that is how it happened. But then Mary has a story, which sounds to me as if that is the real story. I was there, I know that. And I know that some years the rains break before Nadira's birthday, and sometimes after; and I remember being at home in Rankin Street, and it raining so hard outside, and there was a baby in the house, crying so loud. But it could have been Mira, or it could have been Nadira. I think you will have to ask Big-brother.'

'Where is Big-brother?' Dahlia said. 'He is coming, isn't he? And Sharmin?'

'Yes, yes,' Nadira said. 'Don't fret. Everyone is coming. Do I look—'

'Stop asking that, all the time,' my mother said. 'You look perfect. Don't play with your hair and don't keep touching your face in that nervous way, and everything will be just perfect.'

'You will come and visit me?' Nadira said. 'When we go to live in England? In Sheffield?'

'We will do our very best,' Dahlia said. 'It is such a long way. And it won't be for ever that you go.'

'Please, try to come,' Nadira said. 'I want you to come, all of you.'

'Do you remember when Shiri went to Barisal?' Mary said. 'After she got married? I don't know why, but none of us ever went to see her. It was just such a long way to go, and at the end of it, there was just Barisal. Did we come to visit you, Shiri?'

'Well,' my mother said, 'I think Mira was planning to come and visit, but then, as things turned out, I came home in any case. I don't remember why Mira wanted to come and visit. I don't think anyone asked her to. But she wrote a letter saying she was hoping to come and stay, and then, of course, Mahmood became very concerned, and wondered whether we had enough furniture to entertain a guest. It was a strange thing to wonder, because when we moved into that house in Barisal there was nothing but furniture in it – the rooms just filled up with furniture from all the neighbours that none of them wanted. It took us weeks to clear it away and find somewhere else to store it. And then Mira's letter arrived and Mahmood became concerned that he would have to go and find a bed and a chair and a table and all those things that guests seem to need.'

'And then I didn't come after all,' Mira said.

'No, that's so,' my mother said. 'It wasn't your fault, truly, though. I think you would have come if I hadn't come home again. I don't know why you wanted to come. I kept saying in my letters how beastly Barisal was. I'm sure it wasn't really. I'm sure if you went back there it would be just a place like any other. But you know how things were.'

'We thought you were just being polite,' Era said. 'I thought you were saying those things about Barisal because you thought, if you pretended it was lovely, we would all feel that we had no excuse for not coming to visit. We thought you were putting us off as visitors.'

'But Mira wanted to come anyway,' my mother said sensibly.

'Please come to Sheffield,' Nadira said, her eyes big and frightened. 'I don't know what I would do if I thought I wasn't going to—'

'Nadira, don't you start crying,' Mira said. 'If you start crying, we are just going to start all over again.'

'I'm not going to cry,' Nadira said. 'And there is the first car. I think it's the first car, isn't it?'

9.

Pultoo had organized all the children, and half a dozen cousins, to stand at the door of the hotel where Iqtiar and Nadira were to marry. The hotel reception halls were hung with garlands, and decorated under Pultoo's direction: banners, flowers, lamps, bowls of water with water-lilies floating in them; he had even cleverly veiled some of the lights with coloured cellophane to warm up the light in the room. At the door, his nieces and nephews and cousins and cousins' children were leaping up and down with excitement. The rest of Nadira's family had gone inside, and it was only for Pultoo and his gang of merry pranksters to carry out the last act of Pultoo's meticulous plot. In each hand, all of the gang held a shoe. They were Iqtiar's shoes, and Pultoo had stolen every last one of them.

The night before, one of Iqtiar's brothers had let Pultoo into their house after everyone had gone to bed. The same brother, who had been told all about the prank, had managed to remove not just Iqtiar's wedding shoes, but every pair of shoes Iqtiar owned from the bridegroom's room. Pultoo had brought a sack, and the seven pairs of shoes had gone into it before he had fled. Behind him, Iqtiar's brother was covering his mouth and trying not to laugh.

Now, all fourteen shoes were in the hands of Pultoo's gang. 'Remember,' Pultoo said to us. 'He doesn't get them back – not a single shoe – without paying us the ransom money. Do you understand, Saadi?'

'Yes, yes,' I said. 'I understand, Choto-mama. He doesn't get his old shoe back from me.'

Choto-mama had asked me the question because I was the smallest of the conspirators, and the one most likely to forget what I was supposed to do and hand the shoe over if Iqtiar-uncle asked politely. But Choto-mama underestimated me. I was going to hang on for dear life.

And then, on the other side of the glass doors of the hotel, the cars of Iqtiar and his family drew up. His father and uncles, his cousins, sisters, brothers – including the brother who had been Pultoo's co-conspirator – came into the hotel, laughing. We could see why: every one of them was wearing shoes, except for Iqtiar, coming in last. He was barefoot, and looking very serious.

'You see,' Iqtiar's brother explained later, 'Iqtiar knew that Pultoo was going to steal his wedding shoes. He told us two days before. He said that he didn't care – that if Pultoo stole the wedding shoes, he was going to wear his best shoes anyway. He did not reckon on two things. The first was that one of the culprits was in the room, and in his own family. Namely, me. The second was that the pranksters had set their hearts on stealing not just the wedding shoes he had bought for the express purpose. We were planning to steal all his shoes, altogether.

'Well, when he woke, and started getting dressed, it did not take him long to understand that all his shoes were gone. So he said to me, "Who takes the same size in shoes as I do, bhai?" And I had to admit that I did. So he said, "Give me your shoes, bhai." "I am not giving you these shoes," I said. "I am wearing these shoes, to your wedding, you fool." "Well, give me your best shoes," he said. "I have sent them away to be cleaned," I said. "Well, your second-best shoes," he said. "The sole is detached, and the heel has come off," I said. "Then your third-best shoes," he said. "Alas," I said. "Those too have been stolen by the pranksters. They must have mistaken my third-best shoes

288

for your best pair." "Then give me your fourth-best shoes,' he said, in a fit of rage. "My fourth-best shoes?" I said. "Your fourth-best shoes," he said. "I have lent my fourth-best shoes to Grandmother," I said. "She finds them very comfortable." "Is there nobody else in this family who can lend me a pair of shoes?" Iqtiar-brother then shouted out. But answer came there none.'

I had been nominated by the gang to negotiate a price for the return of Iqtiar's shoes. I was the youngest, and that was my task. I was pushed to the front. In my hand, I was gripping one of the wedding shoes. Pultoo had thoroughly briefed me in what I was to say.

'You must pay me off!' I shouted. 'Iqtiar-mama! I have your shoes. You must pay me before I give them to you. Do you understand?'

'I understand, Saadi,' Iqtiar said, in his bare feet. Behind him, his brothers and uncles gathered, giggling. Iqtiar was keeping a straight face. But I knew he was not cross. I knew he was expecting exactly this exchange. 'How much do you want for my shoes?'

Pultoo had told me what to ask. 'I want a thousand taka!' I said. 'Not one taka less. One thousand taka.'

'Oh, that is nonsense,' Pultoo said. 'For one thousand taka I can buy two hundred shoes, better than those old things. I will give you twenty taka, and that is my final offer.'

'No! No! No!' I shouted. Behind me, my brother and sisters, my aunts and cousins, all Nadira's relatives, were laughing and pointing.

'I knew you shouldn't have thrown paint over Saadi,' Pultoo called. 'He is going to drive a hard bargain.'

'Twenty taka!'

'No!' I shouted.

'Thirty!'

'No!'

'Forty!'

'No, no, no, no, no!'

'He's good, this little one,' someone murmured behind me.

'Fifty!' Iqtiar said, with an air of finality.

'No!' I said. 'No, no, no, no, no. One thousand taka, or nothing!'

'Come on, Saadi,' Pultoo said, poking me in the back. In fact, he had agreed that I would refuse to take any money until Iqtiar reached fifty taka, and then I would give way and take the money. That would be mine. In the event, I was quite delirious with the excitement of standing firm in the negotiation. I saw no reason to stop at fifty. It did not occur to me that the whole business had been squared with Iqtiar.

'Very well then,' Iqtiar said. He folded his arms. He glowered down at me. He turned to his supporters, bewailing this tiny monster. 'What can I do?' he said. 'How can a man negotiate with a monster, a terror, a pocket financial genius, a merchant-king three feet tall? How is it possible? Very well then,' Iqtiar-uncle said. 'Sixty.'

From behind, Pultoo or somebody else gave me a firm shake about the head. That was good enough. Iqtiar handed over the sixty taka to me as everyone cheered and applauded and laughed. As the money went into my palm, the left shoe was taken away from me, and the right from Shibli, and Iqtiar slipped them on his bare feet. Around us, in the foyer of the hotel, people who were not invited, passers-by, complete strangers, applauded. The whole hotel glittered with light and flowers, flame and mirrors. Proceeding into the hall where the marriage was to take place, I felt at the centre of the marvellous event. It was time for Iqtiar to get married.

10.

The Kazi was inside; he was somebody that Nana knew. In a beautiful black sherwani and cap, he sat and waited patiently, smiling. I knew he had published books about religion; it was an honour, Mother had said, that he was conducting Nadira's wedding for her, and I should take care not to misbehave in front of him. He had seen the chaos of the shoe-theft before, many times, and he smiled as both sides came laughing into the room to take their places. There were two assistants with him. One was carrying a marriage register, for official purposes; the other, the Mulavi, had nothing with him. He carried what he needed in his head.

There were some official transactions to be got through. The Kazi went to Nadira, and asked her what she thought; he went to Iqtiar, now flushed but shod, and asked him the same. But you know what a wedding is like. You have seen how the veil is draped over the pair of them, a mirror before them; you know how the groom looks in the mirror and says what he feels on first seeing his bride; you know that he usually says that it is as if he has seen the moon. The Mulavi stood, and he said what he had to say: 'Enter the garden, you and your wives,' he said, his tone ringing out in the room, 'in beauty and rejoicing.' You could not help seeing how very thin the Mulavi was. His eyes were enormous in his face.

11.

Nana rose when he saw my father at the reception, and came towards him. For the first time since Nadira's wedding had begun, they embraced. Nana had chosen his moment: he wanted to embrace my father in front of everybody. The reception was held at Iqtiar's family house. They were English teachers, and their house was in the English colony in Dacca. Behind high walls, the events in the street that we had seen on driving from the wedding to the reception retreated a little bit.

'Look,' Mrs Khandekar said, to one of her friends. 'Look, my old friend is making it up with his son-in-law.'

'Making it up?' she said. 'How?'

'They fell out. There was a terrible falling-out, not between those two, but between brothers-in-law. Or so I believe. They were dividing a house between them, and some people are not made to divide a single house. It was terrible at the time, and I don't believe they have spoken for two years.'

'But it was not those two who fell out, was it?' the friend said. 'If he fell out with his brother-in-law, shouldn't he make it up with that brother-in-law?'

'I don't know that that will happen,' Mrs Khandekar said. 'But there we are.'

On a dais at the far end of the room, music began. It was a small group; players on harmonium, tabla and sitar. They sat cross-legged against fat red cushions, concentrating on their work. I did not recognize what they were playing – it was a wedding song, I now assume, so I would not have heard it before. But I recognized them. Two out of the three of them were Nadira's music teachers. There was the tall one and the short one; they were the ones Nana's family treated with such respect, standing up and saying farewell when they left for the day. On the dais, Altaf and Amit practised their art; the tabla pattered like rain, in gusts and spurts; the harmonium gave its thoughtful song; and the sitar reflectively punctuated the sound, like drops of water in a still pond. I ran up to the dais, knowing who they were, expecting that they would greet me. But they continued to play on the dais, which was draped in blue velvet. Only the harmonium player raised his face and looked at me. He smiled – he nearly smiled.

Nana was leading my father and mother up to the top table. 'Look, look,' Mrs Khandekar said. She always enjoyed a dramatic scene, and Nana making a place of special dignity for my mother and father was satisfying all her longings in this respect. But then there was a flurry of attention from the other end of the room, and people could be seen to be backing away, to be making room, to be standing if they had been sitting, and reversing if they had been standing. Nana abandoned my mother and father where they were. Who was it? Some dignitary, some judge, some painter, some poet, some film-maker, some professor, some politician? Something was drawing Nana away from the scene, but what it was nobody could tell through the crush. Somewhere in there, somebody was sparing time from his office, his fame, his celebrity, congratulating Nadira and Iqtiar, finding a kind word for Pultoo, shaking the hands of his colleagues and acquaintances. Nana hurried over, knowing his obligations.

'You will always remember today, won't you?' an old woman said to me. I could tell she was trying to be good with children. But I was more interested in the food, which was now arriving. Bowls of rice, of meat in a rich sauce, of whole fish beautifully decorated and roasted, plates of pickles, more meat, and then the vegetables: potol piled high, okra, potato and cauliflower dishes, yellow like a meadow flower, biriani, stews, curries, plates of dry grilled meat, everything you could imagine. My mother and father were seated at the best table – I could see that my mother was flushed with embarrassment and pleasure. My father, upright, was embarrassed and pleased in a different way. And it now seemed as if the drama of the scene had hardly begun. Nana's obeisance before his daughter and son-in-law, the interruption of the arriving dignitary, those had merely been prefatory to the large drama of reconciliation playing itself out at Nadira's wedding. Then, all of a sudden, there was Boro-mama, coming towards them. Mother and Father had not seen him. 'Look,' I said to Sunchita, but she had already seen him, and was saying the same thing to Sushmita.

'Look . . .'

Boro-mama took a dish of rice from one waiter, and made a gesture to another, bearing a dish of meat, to stand by him. He came to stand behind my mother and father, and I could see him saying something, quite gently. I found my hand being taken, and I looked up. It was Sharmin-aunty, wearing a vivid silver sari. On the top table, Father looked about in surprise; but on his face was an expression of pleasure and relief. Boro-mama did something very beautiful: he served my father rice, just as a waiter would, and then my mother. He handed the bowl of rice back to the waiter, and then served them both, first my father, then my mother, with the meat. He had the air of someone so unconscious of his stance, so natural in his gesture, that I did not realize almost everyone in the room was watching what he was doing. My father stood up and embraced Boro-mama. He was not an embracing man, my father, but he knew when an embrace was called for. And then I knew that everyone in the room had been watching, because the near-silence that had fallen was now broken, and everyone started talking again.

12.

Nadira-aunty and her new husband left Dacca two days later. I had never been to Dacca airport before. Perhaps I was so excited at the prospect of going there that I did not fully understand that I would never see Nadira-aunty again. This time I would get to see an aeroplane up close.

I did not know how far Sheffield was from Dacca. I knew only that it was near London, which I had seen in pictures in Nana's album. I had also seen pictures of England in a school book, from which my sisters learnt English. It was called *The Radiant Way*, and its heroes, Sushmita had told me, pointing to the pictures, were Jack and Matt, boys in ties and shorts.

I had heard stories about planes from my friend Rashid. He had an uncle named Younus, who lived and worked in Dubai. Neither Rashid nor I knew where Dubai was, nor had we seen any photograph. But many presents had come for Rashid from Dubai, carried on aeroplanes. Two-in-one tape recorders, walkie-talkie phones, tiger-faced kombol, golden tablecloths and dried dates: all these had come from Dubai, carried by Rashid's Younus-mama on an aeroplane. One day, Rashid came to my house with a toy gun. He owned up that he did not care for it and its terrible noise. He much preferred the wooden pistol he had, like mine.

Another time, Rashid's Younus-mama presented his family with a large jar of water. Rashid told me it was holy water, from Mecca. I was awestruck, and afterwards asked my mother what holy water was.

She said, 'Rubbish. Who said it was holy water?'

'Rashid,' I said.

'Well,' she said, 'if Rashid gives you any, don't drink it.'

Rashid was a boy who liked to boast, and he also showed me chocolates that had been handed out on the aeroplane to his uncle, and a pen bearing a picture of the plane. Rashid said it was the same plane that he himself had seen. Though nobody, Rashid said, could go near the plane, he had gone near it, gone with his father.

'How could they let you near the plane?' I asked.

Not only did Rashid have an uncle who travelled to Dubai, he also had a relation who worked at Dacca airport – a military official. 'He took us,' Rashid said airily.

I was eaten up with envy and longing. I wanted to see if it was the same plane that was depicted on the pen. I longed to see the plane. But mostly I longed to possess the pen with a picture of the plane on it.

'Can I come to see the planes with you?' I had said.

'My father says you need to have a big man to be allowed to go in,' Rashid said. 'Do you have an uncle in the military, by any chance?'

He knew the answer. 'No,' I said.

'I don't think you can go,' Rashid said. 'I believe you need a big man as an uncle to be allowed to go inside, to go close to the plane.'

'Acha,' I said, agreeing coldly. I did not want to discuss this any longer. I was sad, and ashamed to be sad, that I did not have any uncle who was in the military.

But now I was going to see the planes, without the help of any big man as my uncle. I was going to see them because

Nadira-aunty was going away. We went to Nana's house, and there, upstairs, Nadira was finishing her packing. There were three big brown leather suitcases.

I knew that Nadira had bought many new clothes. She was wearing a new dark blue sari – my favourite colour for her to wear – and I reached out and touched the hem. 'You like this colour on me, Saadi?' she said. 'You like this navy blue?'

I nodded. I did not know why the colour was called 'navy blue'. But Nadira always looked at her most beautiful when she wore this colour. I did not understand why. When I wore shorts of dark blue, I did not like the way it made my legs look very dark. I preferred to wear white or grey shorts, or sometimes even red. But that was my personal preference.

Nadira was placing books in the suitcase to take with her. I recognized a collection of songs by Tagore. I had seen it many times on top of the harmonium. In it was a song I loved, a song called 'We Are All Kings'; it was the only song that Nadira-aunty ever let me sing with her.

'Are you taking the harmonium?' I asked Nadira.

'No,' she said. 'It is too heavy.'

'Iqtiar-mama says he is going to buy a new one for you, Nadira,' my mother said, referring to Nadira's new husband. 'I heard him say so last night.'

'Oh, I know,' Nadira said. 'He is so sweet. But all the same . . .'

'You can't help wanting to take your own harmonium,' Nani said. 'I understand.'

And that meant a lot to Nani, since the harmonium had been given to Nadira as a present by Nana, quite out of the blue, on her sixteenth birthday.

'Well,' Nadira said, 'what is done is done. I can't take everything, and Iqtiar is going to buy me a new harmonium when we get to Sheffield. It won't be the same, but the harmoniums in England might be good in their own way.'

'And perhaps someone will be going to England, before too long,' Nani said. 'If they do, they can bring something with them.'

'Oh, Ma,' Nadira said. 'If they come . . .'

'I don't know who is coming,' Nani said.

'And perhaps no one will come,' my mother sensibly said. 'Don't take that for granted.'

'But if they do,' Nadira said, 'they could bring my notebooks, they could bring my music – they could even bring my harmonium. Who is going to England?'

'Well, it could be Omar-uncle,' my mother said. (Omar was a remote uncle; he, too, was studying in England, and flitting to and fro like a bat; he had friends studying in England; their wives, too, came and went. It could be anyone who had a spare suitcase for everything Nadira could not take with her.) But then I had a bright idea.

'Pumpkin-aunty,' I said, 'can I keep your notebooks safe?'

'Don't call me "Pumpkin",' Nadira said. 'It is not polite. I know I am fatter than I was a month ago. It is not my fault. There was just so much to eat in the last month. People would be offended if you didn't eat.'

'Pumpkin-aunty,' I said again.

'Shiri, curb your child,' Nadira said, but I pressed on.

'I'll keep your notebooks,' I said. 'I will keep them safe with my exercise books. They would never be lost there. I promise I won't lose them.'

Nadira was not cross with me for calling her 'Pumpkin'. She rubbed the back of her hand against my cheek; she would not pinch it as some grown-ups did. She gave me the most beautiful smile, and said, 'Are you sure, Little-pumpkin?'

'I promise,' I said.

'Then here you are,' Nadira said. 'They are yours. I trust you.'

The next day, we returned from the airport to our own house. By now Nadira would be in mid-air, with her clever, handsome husband. She would be above the clouds, high in the sky. This time tomorrow she would be in a completely different country, and she would be walking through it, cold and wet, but glowing in her beautiful navy blue sari. I could see her, as if in the illustrations to my English book. I went to my room, and to the shelf where my mother had placed all Nadira's notebooks. Into them she had copied her favourite songs. The first in the book was 'Amra Sobai Raja'. I smiled and held that notebook with one hand. I loved that song, 'We Are All Kings'. I started humming it. 'Amra Sobai Raja'.

13: What Happened to Them All?

1.

What happened to them?

After Nana died, the house in Dhanmondi was divided among his children. There was a lawsuit, which I am not going to go into. Boro-mama threw himself at the legal questions with all the energy he was capable of. It went on for some years, creating a good deal of bad blood. At the end of it, the house and its plot were divided between three Boro-mama, Choto-mama and my mother. (The aunts were satisfied to take possession of some other property in the north of Dacca and in the countryside that my grandfather had been amassing over the years.) Boro-mama took over most of the land that went with the Dhanmondi house, and moved his family into the servants' house in the garden. He did not enjoy it for very long. As often happens at the end of very long lawsuits, he died, quite suddenly, a month after its conclusion. His wife and children quickly sold the land to developers, as most of Dhanmondi was doing in the 1990s. Choto-mama and my mother divided the house, deprived of most of its land, between them, and did not sell it. Nowadays, half the house is lived in by my brother, his wife and children; the other half is Pultoo's – he has a painting academy where my grandfather's law library used to be. The last time I was in Dacca, the mothers of the district kept coming in with their shy and delighted children, each of them with a paintbox and a portfolio, and the sun shone through the leaves of the tamarind and mango trees, still just as they were in the front garden.

The end Sheikh Mujib came to is known to everyone. They were not so very far from us, so we heard the noise of his end, too. You will find in the history books the reason why some people were so very angry with him. I just remember being woken up, very early on an August morning, by the noise of demolition, the crackle, once more, of fire and gunshot. It was very close indeed. By then everybody knew what to do when this happened. My mother got us up and bustled us, still clutching our coverlets, into the salon, away from the road, far from any public windows. My father telephoned a friend, a government official who lived nearby – it was only six in the morning, but people in those days slept on their nerves, and woke quickly at the sound of gunfire. The friend said only this: 'It's happened.'

Somewhere around five in the morning, a tank was driven through the front wall of Sheikh Mujib's house. Military officers entered the house. Sheikh Mujib did not live with much security. He had gone on walking to Sufiya's all through his presidency. He must have had guns in the house, but that was all. All his family were there, apart from two daughters. One of those was Sheikh Hasina, the daughter who had so amused my mother with her meanness over a few sacks of chilli: she was in Germany. Sheikh Mujib's sons and their wives and children, his wife and other family members were roused immediately. We know that the wives took their children to Sheikh Mujib's wife's bedroom as fast as they could. Perhaps they thought that there might be safety there. Or perhaps they wanted to die together. The soldiers shot them all. An adult son of Sheikh Mujib's fled into his bathroom, where the killers found him, breaking down the door and shooting into the room, smashing the glass on the wall. Sheikh Mujib went to meet his murderers on the stairs. He was a very simple man, and said, 'What do you want?' to them. They are said to have spoken a brief arraignment, although this information only comes from them, years later, in the cause of their own propaganda and defence. They may, in reality, have shot straight away, killing Sheikh Mujib on the stairs of his own house. For many years, he had been known by his honorific title of Bangobandhu, a title awarded him by the students in the late 1960s: a Friend of Bengal. Nobody survived.

The house was not demolished afterwards, but simply shut up and abandoned. In later years, it was reopened as a museum, just as it had been left on that August morning when my father's friend said, 'It's happened,' to him over the telephone. Sheikh Mujib's bedroom toiletries are exactly where they were, showing that his preferred brand of talcum was Johnson's baby powder, and that, like most sophisticated men in the world at that particular time, his habitual cologne was the beautiful oriental scent, Old Spice. These remain on his dressing-table; also undisturbed are the shattered mirror in his son's bathroom, his blood on the stairs, preserved by Perspex sheets, and, dried on to the ceiling of his wife's bedroom, fragments of the brains of his daughters-in-law and grandchildren. You may visit the museum where the Friend of Bengal lived and died in Dhanmondi six days a week, between ten a.m. and five p.m.

'He was a very simple man,' Sufiya's daughter Sultana will tell you. 'Once, when I was very young, and of no purpose or use to anyone, I was very late for my class at the university, and Sheikh Mujib's big black sedan drew up as I was hurrying along. He was not yet president of the country, but still, everyone in the country knew who he was. He popped his head out of the window and said, "Can I give you a lift?" Just as the daughter of his old friend, you understand. Well, I demurred, and he insisted, and so I got in, wondering how it would look when I was dropped off for my class at the university by Sheikh Mujib – you know how these things worry you when you are young. But he chatted away quite happily, about Hasina his daughter, who was in my class, of course, and asking how we all were, and before I knew it, we were at the courthouse. He apologized greatly, very simply, very sincerely, but he said he would have to get out before me. His driver would take me wherever I wanted to go, but he had to get out here, at the courthouse. "You see," he said, "they want to send me to jail again." You know, at this time, he was always being sent off to jail by the Pakistanis. "And I really must be on time to be prosecuted. If I am late, they are only going to send me to jail again for contempt of court, the scoundrels." That is what he said. So he got out at the courthouse, and I had the very great embarrassment of drawing up at the university in this great black car, and everyone thinking it was my family's car. I believe that Sheikh Mujib was as embarrassed by this splendour as I was. He had a nice sense of humour. He may have wanted me to know just how embarrassing it was to be driven about in this way.'

Sheikh Mujib himself was buried in his village, but the twenty members of his family and household who were killed on that August morning are buried together, in a line of sad, noble hummocks, in the cemetery in Dacca – Dhaka, the city is now called. The men who killed them afterwards became Members of Parliament, ministers, ambassadors; only many years later, three and a half decades, were they brought to trial for their crimes. The victims for whose death they were tried, and go on being tried, included the eight-year-old Sheikh Russell, who died pleading to be sent abroad to his sister in Germany, and two unborn children.

I went to see Sufiya in her beautiful house when she was very old. The house was just as it had been: people still came to visit her, to drink tea, to interest her in radical causes. Sometimes, she said, the people who came to see her did so out of mindless curiosity, and some of them even stole a book as a memento from the bookshelf on the terrace. 'Everyone thinks I am a rich woman and can afford to replace anything,' she complained mildly. 'But I am not. And in any case, books are like people. You cannot replace them. I wish people would understand that.' She had survived the announcement of her death on Calcutta radio by decades. By her extreme old age, the house she lived in was no longer surrounded by other houses: her neighbours had sold their land to developers, and all about her blocks of luxury flats had risen. In Dhanmondi, her house remained, its garden in the perpetual near darkness imposed on it by high-rises; Sheikh Mujib's house remained, turned into a museum; and my grandfather's house remained, just as it was. There were not many others. I felt this was a bond between me and Sufiya, and I went to see her to ask her to speak at a rally for the Burmese politician Aung San Suu Kyi. She received me very courteously; she gave me a cup of tea with sandesh and samosas; she said she would write a letter in support, but she was, alas, too old to leave the house to give a speech at the rally, as I asked. She did write a letter, a beautiful one, which the leader of the student movement read out at the rally, and that was the last time I saw her.

She died, full of honours, of nothing worse than old age; the state gave her a funeral, and many tens of thousands of people came. The offer was made to lay her in the field in front of the parliament building, that lovely grey fort by an American architect, begun by the Pakistanis, finished by the Bangladeshis. But she said she would prefer to be in the ordinary cemetery with everyone else. She liked other people, and I think she would have felt lonely in the field of honour with nobody but a president or two to keep her company. I have been told that almost her last words, in the hospice where she died, were 'Has Tulsi eaten properly?'

Tulsi was the nurse who had been assigned to look after her in her last days.

2.

Many years later, I married a writer, who has listened to the story as I have told it to him. One of his books was translated into Romanian, and he was required to travel to that country, with the strange white palace, the largest in the world, at its useless centre. While he was there, he told me, he had dinner with his Romanian publisher and the publisher's wife. The publisher's wife was, it seemed, a well-known journalist in Romania, and many years before, she had been sent by the Romanian Bureau of Overseas Journalism to cover the conflict in East Pakistan. She had not thought – she said, lighting another cigarette over a half-full plate in the restaurant – she had not thought that she would be covering the birth of a new nation. She had not known that new nations were born in such a way. She had imagined, she said, that she would be covering the repression of a revolt, and the resumption of ordinary life under the previous political masters.

(I guess that she started telling this story because my husband explained who I was, and where I came from, and what stories about me he could remember, and dull things like that. He spared my feelings. He did not tell me so.)

But there, one day, was a new nation. No one knew what had

happened to its new leader: Sheikh Mujib – the man whom Nana, and Khandekar, and Sultana had known and been neighbours to – was in prison in Pakistan, and would not be released for months. There did not seem much hope for the new country, if there was a new country. But the Pakistanis had left in mud and blood and smoke, leaving nothing much but informers behind them in their borrowed houses.

The publisher's wife had left her hotel and walked towards the centre of Dacca, to see what there was to be seen. She had needed, after all, a story to write. There was nothing. Nobody was about at all. People had not heard. (This is what she said, though I have seen the newspaper of the first day of the new country many times since, and I think she was not quite correct in her memory.) They would, she assumed, come out of their houses in time. They preferred not to be the first one on the street. The first one on the street was, in fact, the Romanian publisher's wife, who had no fear, and who trod the tank-torn highway with interest, listening for signs of life.

There was no sound, she said. A silence, which is unusual in Dacca; there were fewer cars and lorries in Dacca in 1971, but there were some, and there would always be the noises of the street. It was so quiet that she could hear the birds singing. She had no idea there were birds left alive to sing in the centre of Dacca. She had been walking for nearly ten minutes in this silent city when a sound drew her attention from a nearby quarter, a street or two into the warren. For one second she thought it must be the noise of a machine-gun, far off, but it was close and quiet and mechanical. She identified it: it was the sound of a sewing-machine, hard at work.

She made her way into the back-streets, and after a couple of turns, there was a tailor, sitting under the awning of his shop, his Panjabi shirt flapping as he worked the pedals of his old British sewing-machine. He smiled enormously, nodding as he fed what he was working under the needle. 'I could not imagine what it was,' the Romanian publisher's wife said, retelling the story. 'Then

I saw – it was a flag. It was the flag you saw at demonstrations, but here it was, the flag of the new country, and he was making it as best he could. It is hard, you know, to cut out a circle accurately, but he had done quite a good job of making a red circle, and he had sewn it properly on his green flag, his green rectangle, you know, a little to the right of centre. He explained it all to me, as if I had never heard it before – the red was the blood shed in the struggle for independence, and the green . . . ah, I forget what the green was for. He finished it. I asked him what he was going to do now, and do you know what he said? He said, "I'm going to make another one." He spoke quite good English, and I complimented him on it. His father had made suits in Calcutta, for Englishmen. But that day he was only going to make flags, until he ran out of the cloth he had dyed himself. So I asked him if I could buy one, on this special day, and he sold it to me for, I think, two dollars.' She had folded up the flag, and taken it home to Romania, and had kept it ever since.

Two years after that, her journalistic privileges of travel were revoked, and for twenty years, she never again left her country, and had never been back to mine. That was what my husband's Romanian publisher told him, and I think she believed it, having told it many times, though the streets of Dacca were certainly not empty on the morning of independence, but crowded with celebrants, letting off firecrackers. Still, that was the story as she told it, and the story she liked to tell, so I have told it too, however untruthfully.

This has been the story of my early life. I have tried not to invent anything, and to tell everything as I was told it. I have tried to be as good a storyteller as my mother was. In later years, my mother's girlhood acquaintance Sheikh Hasina came to be prime minister of the country. She was Sheikh Mujib's daughter. My mother would sometimes say, 'Was it Hasina who liked that dish that Sharmin used to cook – you remember, the way she steamed rui with ginger and lemon? Do you remember? I know we used to cook it when we were all living in Papa's house, all through that summer. Don't you remember? It was so simple, but very good. We never tired of it, remember? And afterwards I'm sure that Hasina came to dinner once at somebody's house, and they'd had Sharmin's rui recipe, and so they asked us for the recipe to cook for Hasina, and Hasina liked it so much we gave the recipe to her as well, and she said she would always cook rui like that in future. I'm almost sure. I can't think who it was who was having Hasina round for dinner. Could it have been Kamal? I really can't think. Of course, Hasina has always been peculiar about food. I remember, when we were both girls, I went round to their house with Sultana, and she was in a fury. It was for no reason at all. You see, she had ordered up thirteen sacks of chillis from the country. Was it thirteen sacks? I'm almost sure it was. But what would Hasina be doing with thirteen sacks of chillis? And when the sacks had arrived, the very morning that Sultana and I were visiting her, she had gone to the kitchen to count them, and there were only eleven. A whole two sacks had gone missing on the way. Imagine. You see . . .'

And my father would tuck his napkin into his collar in his dry way. He would cough reprovingly at this point in the story, and smile at my mother to show that he was not serious. He would say, 'Not Hasina and her sacks of chillis again. We must have heard this story so many times.'

London-Geneva-Dhaka
January 2011

Author's Note

This is a novel of the formation of Bangladesh. Until 1971, it formed an eastern province of Pakistan, divided from the western part by geography, language, and culture. It broke from the western side in a savagely violent war of independence. In December 1971, after the deaths of uncounted innocent victims in the civil war, a new country was declared: Bangla Desh, the Home of the Bengalis.

Scenes from Early Life is the story of one upper-middle-class Bengali family, a novel which is told in the form of a memoir. The narrator speaks in the voice of Zaved Mahmood, the author's husband, who was born in late 1970 shortly before the outbreak of the war of independence.

Acknowledgements

A word about names. All Bengalis have a proper, formal name which they often acquire when they first go to school, or on another early encounter with officialdom. These are not much used in this story. Then most of them have a pet name, used by family and close friends – this is the way in which most of the characters are referred to here. Bengalis are much more ready than Europeans to refer to their relations by the degree of the relationship. Here, the ones most commonly used are *mama* and *mami*, meaning (maternal) uncle and aunt, *nana* and *nani*, meaning (maternal) grandparents, *bhai*, brother, and *appa*, sister. Where necessary, these are qualified by *boro*, meaning big, or *choto*, meaning small. Hence the narrator's two maternal uncles are referred to as Boro-mama, Big-uncle, or Laddu, and the younger as Choto-mama, Small-uncle, or Pultoo. That is what their family tends to call them, although neither is a formal name that would be entered on a government form.

Mujibur Rahman, the first president of Bangladesh, was much more frequently referred to as Sheikh Mujib, which is the name I have preferred to use, but also by the splendid honorific Bangobandhu, the Friend of Bengal, a name you will still hear on Bangladeshi lips. I have reserved this for very elevated circumstances, although for many Bangladeshis it seems quite ordinary.

This is not a history of the struggle for Bangladesh's independence, but the rendering of a family's passionately held memories. It does not pretend to be an account of the millions who died in the war and the famines that followed. These are the emphases of my husband's memories, and they may coincide with others' or flatly contradict them. But in any case, this is not the full story, which could never be told.

I would like to thank the many friends and family in Bangladesh who welcomed me into their houses and shared their memories of this time. Sultana and Sayeeda Kamal invited me into the beautiful house of their mother, Begum Sufiya Kamal, and shared memories of her and of Zainul Abedin, showing me many treasures. The house in Dhanmondi still stands, alone where all its neighbours have been replaced by high-rises, and I would like to thank its current occupants, Syed Hasan Mahmud (Choto-mama) and my brother-in-law Zahid for their welcome. Also miraculously preserved in a fast-developing city is the house in Rankin Street, along with its neighbour; Mr A. R. Khan welcomed us in, and shared his vivid memories of the time of Zaved's childhood. I would also like to thank the Hossain family, especially Sara Hossain and David Bergman, Mr Helal of the Bangladeshi Parliament, for sparing time from his crowded schedule to show me around Louis Kahn's wonderful building, Farah Ghuznavi for her hospitality at her family's enchanted *rajbari*, and many other friends in Bangladesh and elsewhere. Particular thanks go to my poet brother-in-law Jahir Hasan for generously finding me translations of several important and near-unobtainable classics from the mainstream of the Bengali literary arts, including Shahidullah Kaiser's *Sangshaptak*, the work of one of the intellectuals targeted and murdered by Pakistani forces in the course of the genocide. A deep debt of literary gratitude is acknowledged in the last sentence of the novel.

As is clear, this account, with its gaps and wilfully ahistorical emphases, has not been shaped by systematic research. But among the books I found most useful and helpful in complementing my vivid interlocutors were Jahanara Imam's diary of her 1971 experiences, the harrowing and passionate *Of Blood and Fire*, and Archer K. Blood's outsider's account, *The Cruel Birth of Bangladesh* (both the University Press, Dhaka).